The Sowers

The Sowers

Henry Seton Merriman

WILDSIDE PRESS
Doylestown, Pennsylvania

1895

The Sowers

A publication of

WILDSIDE PRESS

P.O. Box 301
Holicong, PA 18928–0301

www.wildsidepress.com

Chapter I

A WAIF ON THE STEPPE

"In this country charity covers no sins!"

The speaker finished his remark with a short laugh. He was a big, stout man; his name was Karl Steinmetz, and it is a name well known in the Government of Tver to this day. He spoke jerkily, as stout men do when they ride, and when he had laughed his good-natured, half-cynical laugh, he closed his lips beneath a huge gray mustache. So far as one could judge from the action of a square and deeply indented chin, his mouth was expressive at that time — and possibly at all times — of a humorous resignation. No reply was vouchsafed to him, and Karl Steinmetz bumped along on his little Cossack horse, which was stretched out at a gallop.

Evening was drawing on. It was late in October, and a cold wind was driving from the northwest across a plain which for sheer dismalness of aspect may give points to Sahara and beat that abode of mental depression without an effort. So far as the eye could reach there was no habitation to break the line of horizon. A few stunted fir trees, standing in a position of permanent deprecation, with their backs turned, as it were, to the north, stood sparsely on the plain. The grass did not look good to eat, though the Cossack horses would no doubt have liked to try it. The road seemed to have been drawn by some Titan engineer with a ruler from horizon to horizon.

Away to the south there was a forest of the same stunted pines, where a few charcoal-burners and resin-tappers eked out a forlorn and obscure existence. There are a score of such settlements, such gloomy forests, dotted over this plain of Tver, which covers an area of nearly two hundred square miles. The remainder of it is pasture, where miserable cattle and a few horses, many sheep and countless pigs, seek their food pessimistically from God.

Steinmetz looked round over this cheerless prospect with a twinkle of amused resignation in his blue eyes, as if this creation were a little practical joke, which he, Karl Steinmetz, appreciated at its proper worth. The whole scene was suggestive of immense distance, of countless miles in all directions — a suggestion not conveyed by any scene in England, by few in Europe. In our crowded island we have no conception of a thousand miles. How can we? Few of us have traveled five hundred at a stretch. The land through which these men were riding is the home of great distances — Russia. They rode, moreover, as if they knew it — as if they had ridden for days and were aware of more days in front of them.

The companion of Karl Steinmetz looked like an Englishman. He was young and fair and quiet. He looked like a youthful athlete from Oxford or Cambridge — a simpleminded person who had jumped higher or run quicker than anybody else without conceit, taking himself, like St. Paul, as he found himself and giving the credit elsewhere. And one finds that, after all, in this world of deceit, we are most of us that which we look like. You, madam, look thirty-five to a day, although your figure is still youthful, your hair untouched by gray, your face unseamed by care. You may look in your mirror and note these accidents with satisfaction; you may feel young and indulge in the pastimes of youth without effort. But you are thirty-five. We know it. We who look at you can see it for ourselves, and, if you could only be brought to believe it, we think no worse of you on that account.

The man who rode beside Karl Steinmetz with gloomy eyes and a vague suggestion of flight in his whole demeanor was, like reader and writer, exactly what he seemed. He was the product of an English public school and university. He was, moreover, a modern product of those seats of athletic exercise. He had little education and highly developed muscles — that is to say, he was no scholar but essentially a gentleman — a good enough education in its way, and long may Britons seek it!

This young man's name was Paul Howard Alexis, and Fortune had made him a Russian prince. If, however, anyone, even Steinmetz, called him prince, he blushed and became confused. This terrible title had brooded over him while at Eton and Cambridge. But no one had found him out; he remained Paul Howard Alexis so far as England and his friends were concerned. In Russia, however, he was known (by name only, for he avoided Slavonic society) as Prince Pavlo Alexis. This plain was his; half the Government of Tver was his; the great Volga rolled through his possessions; sixty miles behind him a grim stone castle bore his name, and a tract of land as vast as Yorkshire was peopled by humble-minded persons who cringed at the mention of his Excellency.

All this because thirty years earlier a certain Princess Natásha Alexis had fallen in love with plain Mr. Howard of the British Embassy in St. Petersburg. With Slavonic enthusiasm (for the Russian is the most romantic race on earth) she informed Mr. Howard of the fact, and duly married him. Both these persons were now dead, and Paul Howard Alexis owed it to his mother's influence in high regions that the responsibilities of princedom were his. At the time when this title was accorded to him he had no say in the matter. Indeed, he had little say in any matters except meals, which he still took in liquid form. Certain it is, however, that he failed to appreciate his honors as soon as he grew up to a proper comprehension of them.

Equally certain is it that he entirely failed to recognize the enviability of his position as he rode across the plains of Tver toward the yellow Volga by the side of Karl Steinmetz.

"This is great nonsense," he said suddenly. "I feel like a Nihilist or some theatrical person of that sort. I do not think it can be necessary, Steinmetz."

"Not necessary," answered Steinmetz in thick guttural tones, "but prudent."

This man spoke with the soft consonants of a German.

"Prudent, my dear prince."

"Oh, drop that!"

"When we sight the Volga I will drop it with pleasure. Good

Heavens! I wish I were a prince. I should have it marked on my linen, and sit up in bed to read it on my nightshirt."

"No, you wouldn't, Steinmetz," answered Alexis, with a vexed laugh. "You would hate it just as much as I do, especially if it meant running away from the best bear-shooting in Europe."

Steinmetz shrugged his shoulders.

"Then you should not have been charitable — charity, I tell you, Alexis, covers no sins in this country."

"Who made me charitable? Besides, no decent-minded fellow could be anything else here. Who told me of the League of Charity, I should like to know? Who put me into it? Who aroused my pity for these poor beggars? Who but a stout German cynic called Steinmetz?"

"Stout, yes — cynic, if you will — German, no!"

The words were jerked out of him by the galloping horse.

"Then what are you?"

Steinmetz looked straight in front of him, with a meditation in his quiet eyes which made a dreamy man of him.

"That depends."

Alexis laughed.

"Yes, I know. In Germany you are a German, in Russia a Slav, in Poland a Pole, and in England anything the moment suggests."

"Exactly so. But to return to you. You must trust to me in this matter. I know this country. I know what this League of Charity was. It was a bigger thing than any dream of. It was a power in Russia — the greatest of all — above Nihilism — above the Emperor himself. Ach Gott! It was a wonderful organization, spreading over this country like sunlight over a field. It would have made men of our poor peasants. It was God's work. If there is a God — bien entendu — which some young men deny, because God fails to recognize their importance, I imagine. And now it is all done. It is crumbled up by the scurrilous treachery of some miscreant. Ach! I should like to have him out here on the plain. I would choke him. For money, too! The devil — it must have been the devil — to sell that secret to the Government!"

"I can't see what the Government wanted it for," growled Alexis moodily.

"No, but I can. It is not the Emperor; he is a gentleman, although he has the misfortune to wear the purple. No, it is those about him. They want to stop education; they want to crush the peasant. They are afraid of being found out; they live in their grand houses, and support their grand names on the money they crush out of the starving peasant."

"So do I, so far as that goes."

"Of course you do! And I am your steward — your crusher. We do not deny it, we boast of it, but we exchange a wink with the angels — eh?"

Alexis rode on in silence for a few moments. He sat his horse as English foxhunters do — not prettily — and the little animal with erect head and scraggy neck was evidently worried by the unusual grip on his ribs. For Russians sit back, with a short stirrup and a loose seat, when they are traveling. One must not form one's idea of Russian horsemanship from the erect carriage affected in the Newski Prospect.

"I wish," he said abruptly, "that I had never attempted to do any good; doing good to mankind doesn't pay. Here I am running away from my own home as if I were afraid of the police! The position is impossible."

Steinmetz shook his shaggy head.

"No. No position is impossible in this country — except the Czar's — if one only keeps cool. For men such as you and I any position is quite easy. But these Russians are too romantic — too exaltés — they give way to a morbid love of martyrdom: they think they can do no good to mankind unless they are uncomfortable."

Alexis turned in his saddle and looked keenly into his companion's face.

"Do you know," he said, "I believe you founded the Charity League?"

Steinmetz laughed in his easy, stout way.

"It founded itself," he said; "the angels founded it in heaven. I hope a committee of them will attend to the eternal misery of the dog who betrayed it."

"I trust they will, but in the meantime I stick to my opinion that it is unnecessary for me to leave the country. What have I done? I do not belong to the League; it is composed entirely of Russian nobles; I don't admit that I am a Russian noble."

"But," persisted Steinmetz quietly, "you subscribe to the League. Four hundred thousand rubles — they do not grow at the roadside."

"But the rubles have not my name on them."

"That may be, but we all — *they all* — know where they are likely to come from. My dear Paul, you cannot keep up the farce any longer. You are not an English gentleman who comes across here for sporting purposes; you do not live in the old Castle of Osterno three months in the year because you have a taste for mediaeval fortresses. You are a Russian prince, and your estates are the happiest, the most enlightened in the empire. That alone is suspicious. You collect your rents yourself. You have no German agents — no German vampires about you. There are a thousand things suspicious about Prince Pavlo Alexis if those that be in high places only come to think about it. They have not come to think about it — thanks to our care and to your English independence. But that is only another reason why we should redouble our care. You must not be in Russia when the Charity League is picked to pieces. There will be trouble — half the nobility in Russia will be in it. There will be confiscations and degradations: there will be imprisonment and Siberia for some. You are better out of it, for you are not an Englishman; you have not even a Foreign Office passport. Your passport is your patent of nobility, and that is Russian. No, you are better out of it."

"And you — what about you?" asked Paul, with a little laugh — the laugh that one brave man gives when he sees another do a plucky thing.

"I! Oh, I am all right! I am nobody; I am hated of all the peasants because I am your steward and so hard — so cruel. That is my certificate of harmlessness with those that are about the Emperor."

Paul made no answer. He was not of an argumentative mind, being a large man, and consequently inclined to the sins of omission rather than to the active form of doing wrong. He had an enormous faith in Karl Steinmetz, and, indeed, no man knew Russia better than this cosmopolitan adventurer. Steinmetz it was who pricked forward with all speed, wearing his hardy little horse to a drooping semblance of its former self. Steinmetz it was who had recommended quitting the traveling carriage and taking to the saddle, although his own bulk led him to prefer the slower and more comfortable method of covering space. It would almost seem that he doubted his own ascendancy over his companion and master, which semblance was further increased by a subtle ring of anxiety in his voice while he argued. It is possible that Karl Steinmetz suspected the late Princess Natásha of having transmitted to her son a small hereditary portion of that Slavonic exaltation and recklessness of consequence which he deplored.

"Then you turn back at Tver?" enquired Paul, at length breaking a long silence.

"Yes; I must not leave Osterno just now. Perhaps later, when the winter has come, I will follow. Russia is quiet during the winter, very quiet. Ha, ha!"

He shrugged his shoulders and shivered. But the shiver was interrupted. He raised himself in his saddle and peered forward into the gathering darkness.

"What is that," he asked sharply, "on the road in front?"

Paul had already seen it.

"It looks like a horse," he answered — "a strayed horse, for it has no rider."

They were going west, and what little daylight there was lived on the western horizon. The form of the horse, cut out in black relief against the sky, was weird and ghostlike. It was standing by the side of the road, apparently grazing. As they approached it, its outlines became more defined.

"It has a saddle," said Steinmetz at length. "What have we here?"

The beast was evidently famishing, for, as they came near, it never ceased its occupation of dragging the wizened tufts of grass up, root and all.

"What have we here?" repeated Steinmetz.

And the two men clapped spurs to their tired horses.

The solitary waif had a rider, but he was not in the saddle. One foot was caught in the stirrup, and as the horse moved on from tuft to tuft it dragged its dead master along the ground.

Chapter II

BY THE VOLGA

"This is going to be unpleasant," muttered Steinmetz, as he cumbrously left the saddle. "That man is dead — has been dead some days; he's stiff. And the horse has been dragging him face downward. God in heaven! this will be unpleasant."

Paul had leaped to the ground, and was already loosening the dead man's foot from the stirrup. He did it with a certain sort of skill, despite the stiffness of the heavy riding-boot, as if he had walked a hospital in his time. Very quickly Steinmetz came to his assistance, tenderly lifting the dead man and laying him on his back.

"Ach!" he exclaimed; "we are unfortunate to meet a thing like this."

There was no need of Paul Alexis' medical skill to tell that this man was dead; a child would have known it. Before searching the pockets Steinmetz took out his own handkerchief and laid it over a face which had become unrecognizable. The horse was standing over them. It bent its head and sniffed wonderingly at that which had once been its master. There was a singular, scared look in its eyes.

Steinmetz pushed aside the enquiring muzzle.

"If you could speak, my friend," he said, "we might want you. As it is, you had better continue your meal."

Paul was unbuttoning the dead man's clothes. He inserted his hand within the rough shirt.

"This man," he said, "was starving. He probably fainted from sheer exhaustion and rolled out of the saddle. It is hunger that killed him."

"With his pocket full of money," added Steinmetz, withdrawing his hand from the dead man's pocket and displaying a bundle of notes and some silver.

There was nothing in any of the other pockets — no paper, no clue of any sort to the man's identity.

The two finders of this silent tragedy stood up and looked around them. It was almost dark. They were ten miles from a habitation. It does not sound much; but a traveler would be hard put to place ten miles between himself and a habitation in the whole of the British Islands. This, added to a lack of road or path which is unknown to us in England, made ten miles of some importance.

Steinmetz had pushed his fur cap to the back of his head, which he was scratching pensively. He had a habit of scratching his forehead with one finger, which denoted thought.

"Now, what are we to do?" he muttered. "Can't bury the poor chap and say nothing about it. I wonder where his passport is? We have here a tragedy."

He turned to the horse, which was grazing hurriedly.

"My friend of the four legs," he said, "it is a thousand pities that you are dumb."

Paul was still examining the dead man with that callousness which denotes one who, for love or convenience, has become a doctor. He was a doctor — an amateur. He was a Caius man.

Steinmetz looked down at him with a little laugh. He noticed the tenderness of the touch, the deft fingering which had something of respect in it. Paul Alexis was visibly one of those men who take mankind seriously, and have that in their hearts which for want of a better word we call sympathy.

"Mind you do not catch some infectious disease," said Steinmetz gruffly. "I should not care to handle any stray moujik one finds dead about the roadside; unless, of course, you think there is more money about him. It would be a pity to leave that for the police."

Paul did not answer. He was examining the limp, dirty hands of the dead man. The fingers were covered with soil, the nails were broken. He had evidently clutched at the earth and at every tuft of grass, after his fall from the saddle.

"Look here, at these hands," said Paul suddenly. "This is an Englishman. You never see fingers this shape in Russia."

Steinmetz stooped down. He held out his own square-tipped fingers in comparison. Paul rubbed the dead hand with his sleeve as if it were a piece of statuary.

"Look here," he continued, "the dirt rubs off and leaves the hand quite a gentlemanly color. This" — he paused and lifted Steinmetz's handkerchief, dropping it again hurriedly over the mutilated face — "this thing was once a gentleman."

"It certainly has seen better days," admitted Steinmetz, with a grim humor which was sometimes his. "Come, let us drag him beneath that pine tree and ride on to Tver. We shall do no good, my dear Alexis, wasting our time over the possible antecedents of a gentleman who, for reasons of his own, is silent on the subject."

Paul rose from the ground. His movements were those of a strong and supple man, one whose muscles had never had time to grow stiff. He was an active man, who never hurried. Standing thus upright he was very tall — nearly a giant. Only in St. Petersburg, of all the cities of the world, could he expect to pass unnoticed — the city of tall men and plain women. He rubbed his two hands together in a singularly professional manner which sat amiss on him.

"What do you propose doing?" he asked. "You know the laws of this country better than I do."

Steinmetz scratched his forehead with his forefinger.

"Our theatrical friends the police," he said, "are going to enjoy this. Suppose we prop him up sitting against that tree — no one will run away with him — and lead his horse into Tver. I will give notice to the police, but I will not do so until you are in the Petersburg train. I will, of course, give the ispravnik to understand that your princely mind could not be bothered by such details as this — that you have proceeded on your journey."

"I do not like leaving the poor beggar alone all night," said Paul. "There may be wolves — the crows in the early morning."

"Bah! that is because you are so soft-hearted. My dear fellow, what business is it of ours if the universal laws of nature are illustrated upon this unpleasant object? We all live on each other. The wolves and the crows have the last word. Tant mieux for the wolves and the crows! Come, let us carry him to that tree."

The moon was just rising over the line of the horizon. All around them the steppe lay in grim and lifeless silence. In such a scene, where life seemed rare and precious, death gained in its power of inspiring fear. It is different in crowded cities, where an excess of human life seems to vouch for the continuity of the race, where, in a teeming population, one life more or less seems of little value. The rosy hue of sunset was fading to a clear green, and in the midst of a cloudless sky, Jupiter — very near the earth at that time — shone intense, and brilliant like a lamp. It was an evening such as only Russia and the great North lands ever see, where the sunset is almost in the north and the sunrise holds it by the hand. Over the whole scene there hung a clear, transparent night, green and shimmering, which would never be darker than an English twilight.

The two living men carried the nameless, unrecognizable dead to a resting-place beneath a stunted pine a few paces removed from the road. They laid him decently at full length, crossing his soil-begrimed hands over his breast, tying the handkerchief down over his face.

Then they turned and left him, alone in that luminous night. A waif that had fallen by the great highway without a word, without a sign. A half-run race — a story cut off in the middle; for he was a young man still; his hair, all dusty, draggled, and bloodstained, had no streak of gray; his hands were smooth and youthful. There was a vague suspicion of sensual softness about his body, as if this might have been a man who loved comfort and ease, who had always chosen the primrose path, had never learned the salutary lesson of self-denial. The incipient stoutness of limb contrasted strangely with the drawn meagerness of his body, which was contracted by want of food. Paul Alexis was right. This man had died of starvation, within ten miles of the great Volga, within nine miles of the outskirts of Tver, a city second to Moscow, and once her rival. Therefore it could only be that he had purposely avoided the dwellings of men; that he was a fugitive of some sort or another. Paul's theory that this was an Englishman had not been received with enthusiasm by Steinmetz; but that philosopher had stooped to inspect the narrow, tell-tale fingers. Steinmetz, be it noted, had an infinite capacity for holding his tongue.

They mounted their horses and rode away without looking back. But they did not speak, as if each were deep in his own thoughts. Material had indeed been afforded them, for who could tell who this featureless man might be? They were left in a state of hopeless curiosity, as who, having picked up a page with "Finis" written upon it, falls to wondering what the story may have been.

Steinmetz had thrown the bridle of the straying horse over his arm, and the animal trotted obediently by the side of the fidgety little Cossacks.

"That was bad luck," exclaimed the elder man at length, "d———d bad luck! In this country the less you find, the less you see, the less you understand, the simpler is your existence. Those Nihilists, with their mysterious ways and their reprehensible love of explosives, have made honest men's lives a burden to them."

"Their motives were originally good," put in Paul.

"That is possible; but a good motive is no excuse for a bad means. They wanted to get along too quickly. They are pig-headed, exalted, unpractical to a man. I do not mention the women, because when women meddle in politics they make fools of themselves, even in England. These Nihilists would have been all very well if they had been content to sow for posterity. But they wanted to see the fruits of their labors in one generation. Education does not grow like that. It requires a couple of generations to germinate. It has to be manured by the brains of fools before it is of any use. In England it has reached this stage; here in Russia the sowing has only begun. Now, we were doing some good. The Charity League was the thing. It began by training their starved bodies to be ready for the education when it came. And very little of it would have come in our time. If you educate a hungry man, you set a devil loose upon the world. Fill their stomachs before you feed their brains, or you will give them mental indigestion; and a man with mental indigestion raises hell or cuts his own throat."

"That is just what I want to do — fill their stomachs. I don't care about the rest. I'm not responsible for the progress of the world or the good of humanity," said Paul.

He rode on in silence; then he burst out again in the curt phraseology of a man whose feeling is stronger than he cares to admit.

"I've got no grand ideas about the human race," he said. "A very little contents me. A little piece of Tver, a few thousand peasants, are good enough for me. It seems rather hard that a fellow can't give away of his surplus money in charity if he is such a fool as to want to."

Steinmetz was riding stubbornly along. Suddenly he gave a little chuckle — a guttural sound expressive of a somewhat Germanic satisfaction.

"I don't see how they can stop us," he said. "The League, of course, is done; it will crumble away in sheer panic. But here, in Tver, they cannot stop us."

He clapped his great hand on his thigh with more glee than one would have expected him to feel; for this man posed as a cynic — a despiser of men, a scoffer at charity.

"They'll find it very difficult to stop me," muttered Paul Alexis.

It was now dark — as dark as ever it would be. Steinmetz peered through the gloom toward him with a little laugh — half tolerance, half admiration.

The country was here a little more broken. Long, low hills, like vast waves, rose and fell beneath the horses' feet. Ages ago the Volga may have been here, and, slowly narrowing, must have left these hills in deposit. From the crest of an incline the horsemen looked down over a vast rolling table-land, and far ahead of them a great white streak bounded the horizon.

"The Volga!" said Steinmetz. "We are almost there. And there, to the right, is the Tversha. It is like a great catapult. Gott! what a wonderful night! No wonder these Russians are romantic. What a night for a pipe and a long chair! This horse of mine is tired. He shakes me most abominably."

"Like to change?" enquired Paul curtly.

"No; it would make no difference. You are as heavy as I,

although I am wider! Ah! there are the lights of Tver."

Ahead of them a few lights twinkled feebly, sometimes visible and then hidden again as they rode over the rolling hillocks. One plain ever suggests another, but the resemblance between the steppes of Tver and the great Sahara is at times startling. There is in both that roll as of the sea — the great roll that heaves unceasingly round the Capes of Good Hope and Horn. Looked at casually, Tver and Sahara's plains are level, and it is only in crossing them that one realizes the gentle up and down beneath the horses' feet.

Soon Steinmetz raised his head and sniffed in a loud Teutonic manner. It was the reek of water; for great rivers, like the ocean, have their smell. And the Volga is a revelation. Men travel far to see a city, but few seem curious about a river. Every river has, nevertheless, its individuality, its great silent interest. Every river has, moreover, its influence, which extends to the people who pass their lives within sight of its waters. Thus the Guadalquivir is rapid, mysterious, untrammeled — breaking frequently from its boundary. And it runs through Andalusia. The Nile — the river of ages — runs clear, untroubled through the centuries, between banks untouched by man. The Rhine — romantic, cultivated, artificial, with a rough subcurrent and a muddy bed — through Germany. The Seine and the Thames — shallow — shallow — shallow. And we — who live upon their banks!

The Volga — immense, stupendous, a great power, an influence two thousand four hundred miles long. Some have seen the Danube, and think they have seen a great river. So they have; but the Russian giant is seven hundred miles longer. A vast yellow stream, moving on to the distant sea — slow, gentle, inexorable, overwhelming.

All great things in nature have the power of crushing the human intellect. Russians are thus crushed by the vastness of their country, of their rivers. Man is but a small thing in a great country, and those who live by Nile, or Guadalquivir, or Volga seem to hold their lives on condition. They exist from day to day by the tolerance of their river.

Steinmetz and Paul paused for a moment on the wooden floating bridge and looked at the great river. All who cross that bridge, or the railway bridge higher up the stream, must do the same. They pause and draw a deep breath, as if in the presence of something supernatural.

They rode on without speaking through the squalid town — the whilom rival and the victim of brilliant Moscow. They rode straight to the station, where they dined in, by the way, one of the best railway refreshment rooms in the world. At one o'clock the night express from Moscow to St. Petersburg, with its huge American locomotive, rumbled into the station. Paul secured a chair in the long saloon car, and then returned to the platform. The train waited twenty minutes for refreshments, and he still had much to say to Steinmetz; for one of these men owned a principality and the other governed it. They walked up and down the long platform, smoking endless cigarettes, talking gravely.

Steinmetz stood on the platform and watched the train pass slowly away into the night. Then he went toward a lamp, and taking a pocket-handkerchief from his pocket, examined each corner of it in succession. It was a small pocket-handkerchief of fine cambric. In one corner were the initials S.S.B., worked neatly in white — such embroidery as is done in St. Petersburg.

"Ach!" exclaimed Steinmetz shortly; "something told me that that was he."

He turned the little piece of cambric over and over, examining it slowly, with a heavy Germanic cunning. He had taken this handkerchief from the body of the nameless rider who was now lying alone on the steppe twelve miles away.

Steinmetz returned to the large refreshment room, and ordered the waiter to bring him a glass of Benedictine, which he drank slowly and thoughtfully.

Then he went toward the large black stove which stands in the railway restaurant at Tver. He opened the door with the point of his boot. The wood was roaring and crackling within. He threw the handkerchief in and closed the door.

"It is as well, mon prince," he muttered, "that I found this, and not you."

Chapter III

DIPLOMATIC

"*A*ll that there is of the most brilliant and least truthful in Europe," M. Claude de Chauxville had said to a lady earlier in the evening, apropos of the great gathering at the French Embassy, and the mot had gone the round of the room.

In society a little mot will go a long way. M. le Baron de Chauxville was, moreover, a manufacturer of mots. By calling he was attaché to the French Embassy in London; by profession he was an epigrammatist. That is to say, he was a sort of social revolver. He went off if one touched him conversationally, and like others among us, he frequently missed fire.

Of course, he had but little real respect for the truth. If one wishes to be epigrammatic, one must relinquish the hope of being either agreeable or veracious. M. de Chauxville did not really intend to convey the idea that any of the persons assembled in the great guest chambers of the French Embassy that evening were anything but what they seemed.

He could not surely imagine that Lady Mealhead — the beautiful spouse of the seventh Earl Mealhead — was anything but what she seemed: namely, a great lady. Of course, M. de Chauxville knew that Lady Mealhead had once been the darling of the music halls, and that a thousand hearts had vociferously gone out to her from sixpenny and even threepenny galleries when she answered to the name of Tiny Smalltoes. But then M. de Chauxville knew as well as you

and I — Lady Mealhead no doubt had told him — that she
was the daughter of a clergyman, and had chosen the stage
in preference to the school-room as a means of supporting
her aged mother. Whether M. de Chauxville believed this or
not, it is not for us to enquire. He certainly looked as if he
believed it when Lady Mealhead told him — and his expressive
Gallic eyes waxed tender at the mention of her mother, the
relict of the late clergyman, whose name had somehow been
overlooked by Crockford. A Frenchman loves his mother —
in the abstract.

Nor could M. de Chauxville take exception at young Cyril
Squyrt, the poet. Cyril looked like a poet. He wore his hair
over his collar at the back, and below the collar-bone in front.
And, moreover, he was a poet — one of those who write for
ages yet unborn. Besides, his poems could be bought (of the
publisher only; the railway bookstall men did not understand
them) beautifully bound; really beautifully bound in white
kid, with green ribbon — a very thin volume and very thin
poetry. Meddlesome persons have been known to state that
Cyril Squyrt's father kept a prosperous hot-sausage-and-
mashed-potato shop in Leeds. But one must not always believe all that one hears.

It appears that beneath the turf, or on it, all men are equal,
so no one could object to the presence of Billy Bale, the man,
by Gad! who could give you the straight tip on any race, and
looked like it. We all know Bale's livery stable, the same being
Billy's father; but no matter. Billy wears the best cut riding-
breeches in the Park, and, let me tell you, there are many folk
in society with a smaller recommendation than that.

Now, it is not our business to go round the rooms of the
French Embassy picking holes in the earthly robes of society's
elect. Suffice it to say that everyone was there. Miss Kate
Whyte, of course, who had made a place in society and held
it by the indecency of her language. Lady Mealhead said she
couldn't stand Kitty Whyte at any price. We are sorry to use
such a word as indecency in connection with a young person
of the gentler sex, but facts must sometimes be recognized.
And it is a bare fact that society tolerated, nay, encouraged,
Kitty Whyte, because society never knew, and always wanted
to know, what she would say next. She sailed so near to the

unsteady breeze of decorum that the safer-going craft hung breathlessly in her wake in the hope of an upset.

Everyone, in fact, was there. All those who have had greatness thrust upon them, and the others, those who thrust themselves upon the great — those, in a word, who reach such as are above them by doing that which should be beneath them. Lord Mealhead, by the way, was not there. He never is anywhere where the respectable writer and his highborn reader are to be found. It is discreet not to enquire where Lord Mealhead is, especially of Lady Mealhead, who has severed more completely her connection with the past. His lordship is, perchance, of a sentimental humor, and loves to wander in those pasteboard groves where first he met his Tiny — and very natural, too.

There was music and the refreshments. It was, in fact, a reception. Gaul's most lively sons bowed before Albion's fairest daughters, and displayed that fund of verve and esprit which they rightly pride themselves upon possessing, and which, of course, leave mere Englishmen so far behind in the paths of love and chivalry.

When not thus actively engaged they whispered together in corners and nudged each other, exchanging muttered comments, in which the word charmante came conveniently to the fore. Thus, the lightsome son of republican Gaul in society.

It is, however, high time to explain the reason of our own presence — of our own reception by France's courteous representative. We are here to meet Mrs. Sydney Bamborough, and, moreover, to confine our attention to the persons more or less implicated in the present history.

Mrs. Sydney Bamborough was undoubtedly the belle of the evening. She had only to look in one of the many mirrors to make sure of that fact. And if she wanted further assurance a hundred men in the room would have been ready to swear to it. This lady had recently dawned on London society — a young widow. She rarely mentioned her husband; it was understood to be a painful subject. He had been attached to several embassies, she said; he had a brilliant career before him, and suddenly he had died abroad. And then she gave a little sigh and a bright smile, which, being interpreted, meant

"Let us change the subject."

There was never any doubt about Mrs. Sydney Bamborough. She was aristocratic to the tips of her dainty white fingers — composed, gentle, and quite sure of herself. Quite the grand lady, as Lady Mealhead said. But Mrs. Sydney Bamborough did not know Lady Mealhead, which may have accounted for the titled woman's little sniff of interrogation. As a matter of fact, Etta Sydney Bamborough came from excellent ancestry, and could claim an uncle here, a cousin there, and a number of distant relatives everywhere, should it be worth the while.

It was safe to presume that she was rich from the manner in which she dressed, the number of servants and horses she kept, the general air of wealth which pervaded her existence. That she was beautiful anyone could see for himself — not in the shop windows, among the presumably self-selected types of English beauty, but in the proper place — namely, in her own and other aristocratic drawing rooms.

She was talking to a tall, fair Frenchman — in perfect French — and was herself nearly as tall as he. Bright brown hair waved prettily back from a white forehead, clever, dark gray eyes and a lovely complexion — one of those complexions which, from a purity of conscience or a steadiness of nerve, never change. Cheeks of a faint pink, an expressive, mobile mouth, a neck of dazzling white. Such was Mrs. Sydney Bamborough, in the prime of her youth.

"And you maintain that it is five years since we met," she was saying to the tall Frenchman.

"Have I not counted every day?" he replied.

"I do not know," she answered, with a little laugh, that little laugh which tells wise men where flattery may be shot like so much conversational rubbish. Some women are fathomless pits, the rubbish never seems to fill them. "I do not know, but I should not think so."

"Well, madam, it is so. Witness these gray hairs. Ah! those were happy days in St. Petersburg."

Mrs. Sydney Bamborough smiled — a pleasant society smile, not too pronounced and just sufficient to suggest pearly teeth. At the mention of St. Petersburg she glanced round to see that they were not overheard. She gave a little shiver.

"Don't speak of Russia!" she pleaded. "I hate to hear it mentioned. I was so happy. It is painful to remember."

Even while she spoke the expression of her face changed to one of gay delight. She nodded and smiled toward a tall man who was evidently looking for her, and took no notice of the Frenchman's apologies.

"Who *is* that?" asked the young man. "I see him everywhere lately."

"A mere English gentleman, Mr. Paul Howard Alexis," replied the lady.

The Frenchman raised his eyebrows. He knew better. This was no plain English gentleman. He bowed and took his leave. M. de Chauxville of the French Embassy was watching every movement, every change of expression, from across the room.

In evening dress the man whom we last saw on the platform of the railway station at Tver did not look so unmistakably English. It was more evident that he had inherited certain characteristics from his Russian mother — notably, his great height, a physical advantage enjoyed by many aristocratic Russian families. His hair was fair and inclined to curl, and there the foreign suggestion suddenly ceased. His face had the quiet concentration, the unobtrusive self-absorption which one sees more strongly marked in English faces than in any others. His manner of moving through the well-dressed crowd somewhat belied the tan of his skin. Here was an out-of-door, athletic youth, who knew how to move in drawing rooms — a big man who did not look much too large for his surroundings. It was evident that he did not know many people, and also that he was indifferent to his loss. He had come to see Mrs. Sydney Bamborough, and that lady was not insensible to the fact.

To prove this she diverged from the path of veracity, as is the way of some women.

"I did not expect to see you here," she said.

"You told me you were coming," he answered simply. The inference would have been enough for some women, but not for Etta Sydney Bamborough.

"Well, is that a reason why you should attend a diplomatic

soirée, and force yourself to bow and smirk to a number of white-handed little dandies whom you despise?"

"The best reason," he answered quietly, with an honesty which somehow touched her as nothing else had touched this beautiful woman since she had become aware of her beauty.

"Then you think it worth the bowing and the smirking?" she asked, looking past him with innocent eyes. She made an imperceptible little movement toward him as if she expected him to whisper. She was of that school. But he was not. His was not the sort of mind to conceive any thought that required whispering. Some persons in fact went so far as to say that he was hopelessly dull, that he had no subtlety of thought, no brightness, no conversation. These persons were no doubt ladies upon whom he had failed to lavish the exceedingly small change of compliment.

"It is worth that and more," he replied, with his ready smile. "After all, bowing and smirking come very easily. One soon gets accustomed to it."

"One has to," she replied with a little sigh. "Especially if one is a woman, which little mishap comes to some of us, you know. I wonder if you could find me a chair."

She was standing with her back to a small sofa capable of holding three, but calculated to accommodate two. She did not of course see it. In fact she looked everywhere but toward it, raising her perfectly gloved fingers tentatively for his arm.

"I am tired of standing," she added.

He turned and indicated the sofa, toward which she immediately advanced. As she sat down he noted vaguely that she was exquisitely dressed, certainly one of the best dressed women in the room. Her costume was daring without being startling, being merely black and white largely, boldly contrasted. He felt indefinitely proud of the dress. Some instinct in the man's simple, strong mind told him that it was good for women to be beautiful, but his ignorance of the sex being profound he had no desire to analyze the beauty. He had no mental reservation with regard to her. Indeed it would have been hard to find fault with Etta Sydney Bamborough, looking upon her merely as a beautiful woman, exquisitely dressed. In a cynical age this man was without cynicism. He did not dream of reflecting that the lovely hair owed half its beauty to the clever handling of a maid, that the perfect dress had been the all-absorbing topic of many of its wearer's leisure hours. He was, in fact, young for his years, and what is youth but a happy ignorance? It is only when we know too much that Gravity marks us for her own.

Mrs. Sydney Bamborough looked up at him with a certain admiration. This man was like a mountain breeze to one who has breathed nothing but the faded air of drawing rooms.

She drew in her train with a pretty curve of her gloved wrist.

"You look as if you did not know what it was to be tired; but perhaps you will sit down. I can make room."

He accepted with alacrity.

"And now," she said, "let me hear where you have been. I have only had time to shake hands with you the last twice that we have met! You said you had been away."

"Yes; I have been to Russia."

Her face was steadily beautiful, composed and ready.

"Ah! How interesting! I have been in Petersburg. I love Russia." While she spoke she was actually looking across the room toward the tall Frenchman, her late companion.

"Do you?" answered Paul eagerly. His face lighted up after the manner of those countenances that belong to men of one idea. "I am very much interested in Russia."

"Do you know Petersburg?" she asked rather hurriedly. "I mean — society there?"

"No. I know one or two people in Moscow."

She nodded, suppressing a quick little sigh which might have been one of relief had her face been less pleasant and smiling.

"Who?" she asked indifferently. She was interested in the lace of her pocket-handkerchief, of which the scent faintly reached him. He was a simple person, and the faint odor gave him a distinct pleasure — a suggested intimacy.

He mentioned several well-known Muscovite names, and she broke into a sudden laugh.

"How terrible they sound," she said gaily, "even to me, and I have been to Petersburg. But you speak Russian, Mr. Alexis?"

"Yes," he answered. "And you?"

She shook her head and gave a little sigh.

"I? Oh, no. I am not at all clever, I am afraid."

Chapter IV

DON QUIXOTE

*P*aul had been five months in England when he met Mrs. Sydney Bamborough. Since his hurried departure from Tver a winter had come and gone, leaving its mark as winters do. It left a very distinct mark on Russia. It was a famine winter. From the snow-ridden plains that lie to the north of Moscow, Karl Steinmetz had written piteous descriptions of an existence which seemed hardly worth the living. But each letter had terminated with a prayer, remarkably near to a command, that he, Paul Howard Alexis, should remain in England. So Paul stayed in London, where he indulged to the full a sadly mistaken hobby. This man had, as we have seen, that which is called a crank, or a loose screw, according to the fancy of the speaker. He had conceived the absurd idea of benefiting his fellow-beings, and of turning into that mistaken channel the surplus wealth that was his. This, moreover, if it please you, without so much as forming himself into a society.

This is an age of societies, and, far from concealing from the left hand the good which the right may be doing, we publish abroad our charities on all hands. We publish in a stout volume our names and donations. We even go so far as to cultivate an artificial charity by meat and drink and speeches withal. When we have eaten and drunk, the plate is handed round, and from the fullness of our heart we give abundantly. We are cunning even in our well-doing. We do not pass round the plate until the decanters have led the way. And thus we degrade that quality of the human heart which is the best of all.

But Paul Howard Alexis had the good fortune to be rich out of England, and that roaring lion of modern days, organized charity, passed him by. He was thus left to evolve from his own mind a mistaken sense of his duty toward his neighbor. That there were thousands of well-meaning persons in black and other coats ready to prove to him that revenues gathered from Russia should be spent in the East End or the East Indies, goes without saying. There are always well-meaning persons among us ready to direct the charity of others. We have all met those virtuous persons who do good by proxy. But Paul had not. He had never come face to face with the charity broker — the man who stands between the needy and the giver, giving nothing himself, and living on his brokerage, sitting in a comfortable chair, with his feet on a Turkey carpet in his office on a main thoroughfare. Paul had met none of these, and the only organized charity of which he was cognizant was the great Russian Charity League, betrayed six months earlier to a government which has ever turned its face against education and enlightenment. In this he had taken no active part, but he had given largely of his great wealth. That his name had figured on the list of families sold for a vast sum of money to the authorities of the Ministry of the Interior seemed all too sure. But he had had no intimation that he was looked upon with small favor. The more active members of the League had been less fortunate, and more than one nobleman had been banished to his estates.

Although the sum actually paid for the papers of the Charity League was known, the recipient of the blood money had never been discovered. It was a large sum, for the government had been quick to recognize the necessity of nipping this movement in the bud. Education is a dangerous matter to deal with; England is beginning to find this out for herself. For on the heels of education socialism ever treads. When at last education makes a foothold in Russia, that foothold will be on the very step of the autocratic throne. The Charity League had, as Steinmetz put it, the primary object of prepar-

ing the peasant for education, and thereafter placing education within his reach. Such proceedings were naturally held
by those in high places to be only second to Nihilism.

All this, and more which shall transpire in the course of
this narration, was known to Paul. In face of the fact that his
name was prominently before the Russian Ministry of the
Interior, he proceeded all through the winter to ship road-
making tools, agricultural implements, seeds, and food.

"The prince," said Steinmetz to those who were interested
in the matter, "is mad. He thinks that a Russian principality
is to be worked on the same system as an English estate."

He would laugh and shrug his shoulders, and then he
would sit down and send a list of further requirements to
Paul Howard Alexis, Esquire, in London.

Paul had met Mrs. Sydney Bamborough on one or two
occasions, and had been interested in her. From the first he
had come under the influence of her beauty. But she was then
a married woman. He met her again toward the end of the
terrible winter to which reference has been made, and found
that a mere acquaintanceship had in the meantime developed
into friendship. He could not have told when and where the
great social barrier had been surmounted and left behind. He
only knew in an indefinite way that some such change had
taken place, as all such changes do, not in intercourse, but in
the intervals of absence. It is a singular fact that we do not
make our friends when they are near. The seed of friendship
and love alike is soon sown, and the best is that which
germinates in absence.

That friendship had rapidly developed into something else
Paul became aware early in the season; and, as we have seen
from his conversation, Mrs. Sydney Bamborough, innocent
and guileless as she was, might with all modesty have divined
the state of his feelings had she been less overshadowed by
her widow's weeds.

She apparently had no such suspicion, for she asked Paul
in all good faith to call the next day and tell her all about
Russia — "dear Russia."

"My cousin Maggie," she added, "is staying with me. She
is a dear girl. I am sure you will like her."

Paul accepted with alacrity, but reserved to himself the

option of hating Mrs. Sydney Bamborough's cousin Maggie, merely because that young lady existed and happened to be staying in Upper Brook Street.

At five o'clock the next afternoon he presented himself at the house of mourning, and completely filled up its small entrance-hall.

He was shown into the drawing room, where he discovered Miss Margaret Delafield in the act of dragging her hat off in front of the mirror over the mantelpiece. He heard a suppressed exclamation of amused horror, and found himself shaking hands with Mrs. Sydney Bamborough.

The lady mentioned Paul's name and her cousin's relationship in that casual manner which constitutes an introduction in these degenerate days. Miss Delafield bowed, laughed, and moved toward the door. She left the room, and behind her an impression of breeziness and health, of English girlhood and a certain bright cheerfulness which acts as a filter in social muddy waters.

"It is very good of you to come — I was moping," said Mrs. Sydney Bamborough. She was, as a matter of fact, resting before the work of the evening. This lady thoroughly understood the art of being beautiful.

Paul did not answer at once. He was looking at a large photograph which stood in a frame on the mantelpiece — the photograph of a handsome man of twenty-eight or thirty, small-featured, fair, and shifty looking.

"Who is that?" he asked abruptly.

"Do you not know? My husband."

Paul muttered an apology, but he did not turn away from the photograph.

"Oh, never mind," said Mrs. Sydney Bamborough, in reply to his regret that he had stumbled upon a painful subject. "I never —"

She paused.

"No," she went on, "I won't say that."

But, so far as conveying what she meant was concerned, she might just as well have uttered the words.

"I do not want a sympathy which is unmerited," she said gravely.

He turned and looked at her, sitting in a graceful attitude, the incarnation of a most refined and nineteenth-century misfortune. She raised her eyes to his for a moment — a sort of photographic instantaneous shutter, exposing for the hundredth part of a second the sensitive plate of her heart. Then she suppressed a sigh — badly.

"I was married horribly young," she said, "before I knew what I was doing. But even if I had known I do not suppose I should have had the strength of mind to resist my father and mother."

"They forced you into it?"

"Yes," said Mrs. Bamborough. And it is possible that a respectable and harmless pair of corpses turned in their respective coffins somewhere in the neighborhood of Norwood.

"I hope there is a special hell reserved for parents who ruin their daughters' lives to suit their own ambition," said Paul, with a sudden concentrated heat which rather startled his hearer.

This man was full of surprises for Etta Sydney Bamborough. It was like playing with fire — a form of amusement which will be popular as long as feminine curiosity shall last.

"You are rather shocking," she said lightly. "But it is all over now, so we need not dig up old grievances. Only I want you to understand that that photograph represents a part of my life which was only painful — nothing else."

Paul, standing in front of her, looked down thoughtfully at the beautiful upturned face. His hands were clasped behind him, his firm mouth set sternly beneath the great fair mustache. In Russia the men have good eyes — blue, fierce, intelligent. Such eyes had the son of the Princess Alexis. There was something in Etta Bamborough that stirred up within him a quality which men are slowly losing — namely, chivalry. Steinmetz held that this man was quixotic, and what Steinmetz said was usually worth some small attention. Whatever faults that poor knight of La Mancha who has been the laughingstock of the world these many centuries — whatever faults or foolishness may have been his, he was at all events a gentleman.

Paul's instinct was to pity this woman for the past that had been hers; his desire was to help her and protect her, to watch over her and fight her battles for her. It was what is called Love. But there is no word in any spoken language that covers so wide a field. Every day and all day we call many things love which are not love. The real thing is as rare as genius, but we usually fail to recognize its rarity. We misuse the word, for we fail to draw the necessary distinctions. We fail to recognize the plain and simple truth that many of us are not able to love — just as there are many who are not able to play the piano or to sing. We raise up our voices and make a sound, but it is not singing. We marry and we give in marriage, but it is not loving. Love is like a color — say, blue. There are a thousand shades of blue, and the outer shades are at last not blue at all, but green or purple. So in love there are a thousand shades, and very, very few of them are worthy of the name.

That which Paul Howard Alexis felt at this time for Etta was merely the chivalrous instinct that teaches men their primary duty toward women — namely, to protect and respect them. But out of this instinct grows the better thing — Love.

There are some women whose desire it is to be all things to all men instead of everything to one. This was the stumbling-block in the way of Etta Bamborough. It was her instinct to please all at any price, and her obedience to such instinct was often unconscious. She hardly knew perhaps that she was trading upon a sense of chivalry rare in these days, but had she known she could not have traded with a keener comprehension of the commerce.

"I should like to forget the past altogether," she said. "But it is hard for women to get rid of the past. It is rather terrible to feel that one will be associated all one's life with a person for whom no one had any respect. He was not honorable or —"

She paused; for the intuition of some women is marvelous. A slight change of countenance had told her that charity, especially toward the dead, is a commendable quality.

"The world," she went on rather hurriedly, "never makes allowances — does it? He was easily led, I suppose. And people said things of him that were not true. Did you ever hear of him in Russia — of the things they said of him?"

She waited for the answer with suppressed eagerness — a good woman defending the memory of her dead husband —

a fair lioness protecting her cub.

"No; I never hear Russian gossip. I know no one in St. Petersburg, and few in Moscow."

She gave a little sigh of relief.

"Then perhaps poor Sydney's delinquencies have been forgotten," she said. "In six months everything is forgotten now. He has only been dead six months, you know. He died in Russia."

All the while she was watching his face. She had moved in a circle where everything is known — where men have faces of iron and nerves of steel to conceal what they know. She could hardly believe that Paul Alexis knew so little as he pretended.

"So I heard a month ago," he said.

In a flash of thought Etta remembered that it was only within the last four weeks that this admirer had betrayed his admiration. Could this be that phenomenon of the three-volume novel, an honorable man? She looked at him with curiosity — without, it is to be feared, much respect.

"And now," she said cheerfully, "let us change the subject. I have inflicted enough of myself and my affairs upon you for one day. Tell me about yourself. Why were you in Russia last summer?"

"I am half a Russian," he answered. "My mother was Russian, and I have estates there."

Her surprise was a triumph of art.

"Oh! You are not Prince Pavlo Alexis?" she exclaimed.

"Yes, I am."

She rose and swept him a deep courtesy, to the full advantage of her beautiful figure.

"My respects — mon prince," she said; and then, quick as lightning, for she had seen displeasure on his face, she broke into a merry laugh.

"No, I won't call you that; for I know you hate it. I have heard of your prejudices, and if it is of the slightest interest to you, I think I rather admire them."

It is to be presumed that Mrs. Sydney Bamborough's memory was short. For it was a matter of common knowledge in the diplomatic circles in which she moved that Mr. Paul Howard Alexis of Piccadilly House, London, and Prince

Pavlo Alexis of the province of Tver, were one and the same man.

Having, however, fully established this fact, from the evidence of her own ears, she conversed very pleasantly and innocently upon matters, Russian and English, until other visitors arrived and Paul withdrew.

Chapter V

THE BARON

*A*mong the visitors whom Paul left behind him in the little drawing room in Brook Street was the Baron Claude de Chauxville, Baron of Chauxville and Chauxville le Duc, in the Province of Seine-et-Marne, France, attaché to the French Embassy to the Court of St. James; before men a rising diplomatist, before God a scoundrel. This gentleman remained when the other visitors had left, and Miss Maggie Delafield, seeing his intention of prolonging a visit of which she had already had sufficient, made an inadequate excuse and left the room.

Miss Delafield, being a healthy-minded young English person of that simplicity which is no simplicity at all, but merely simple-heartedness, had her own ideas of what a man should be, and M. de Chauxville had the misfortune to fall short of those ideas. He was too epigrammatic for her, and beneath the brilliancy of his epigram she felt at times the presence of something dark and nauseous. Her mental attitude toward him was contemptuous and perfectly polite.

With the reputation of possessing a dangerous fascination —
one of those reputations which can only emanate from the
man himself — M. de Chauxville neither fascinated nor
intimidated Miss Delafield. He therefore disliked her intensely. His vanity was colossal, and when a Frenchman is
vain he is childishly so.

M. de Chauxville watched the door close behind Miss
Delafield with a queer smile. Then he turned suddenly on his
heels and faced Mrs. Sydney Bamborough.

"Your cousin," he said, "is a typical Englishwoman — she
only conceals her love."

"For you?" enquired Mrs. Sydney Bamborough.

The baron shrugged his shoulders.

"Possibly. One can never tell. She conceals it very well if it
exists. However, I am indifferent. The virtue of the violet is
its own reward, perhaps, for the rose always wins."

He crossed the room toward Mrs. Sydney Bamborough,
who was standing near the mantelpiece. Her left hand was
hanging idly by her side. He took the white fingers and
gallantly raised them to his lips, but before they had reached
that fount of truth and wisdom she jerked her hand away.

M. de Chauxville laughed — the quiet, assured laugh of a
man who has read in books that he who is bold enough can
win any woman, and believes it. He was of those men who
treat and speak of women as a class — creatures to be dealt
with successfully according to generality and maxim. It is a
singular thing, by the way, that men as a whole continue to
disbelieve in a woman's negative — singular, that is, when one
reflects that the majority of men have had at least one negative
which has remained a negative, so far as they were concerned,
all the woman's life.

"I am aware," said M. de Chauxville, "that the rose has
thorns. One reason why the violet is hors de concours."

Etta smiled — almost relenting. She was never quite safe
against her own vanity. Happy the woman who is, and rare.

"I suspect that the violet is innocent of any desire to enter
into competition," said Etta.

"Knowing," suggested De Chauxville, "that although the
race is not always to the swift, it is usually so. Please do not
stand. It suggests that you are waiting for me to go or for

some one else to come."

"Neither."

"Then prove it by taking this chair. Thus. Near the fire, for it is quite an English spring. A footstool. Is it permitted to admire your slippers — what there is of them? Now you look comfortable."

He attended to her wants, divined them, and perhaps created them with a perfect grace and much too intimate a knowledge. As a carpet knight he was faultless. And Etta thought of Paul, who could do none of these things — or would do none of them — Paul, who never made her feel like a doll.

"Will you not sit down?" she said, indicating a chair, which he did not take. He selected one nearer to her.

"I can think of nothing more desirable."

"Than what?" she asked. Her vanity was like a hungry fish. It rose to everything.

"A chair in this room."

"A modest desire," she said. "Is that really all you want in this world?"

"No," he answered, looking at her.

She gave a little laugh and moved rather hurriedly.

"I was going to suggest that you could have both at certain fixed periods — whenever — I am out."

"I am glad you did not suggest it."

"Why?" she asked sharply.

"Because I should have had to go into explanations. I did not say all."

Mrs. Bamborough was looking into the fire, only half listening to him. There was something in the nature of a duel between these two. Each thought more of the next stroke than of the present party.

"Do you ever say all, M. de Chauxville?" she asked.

The baron laughed. Perhaps he was vain of the reputation that was his, for this man was held to be a finished diplomatist. A finished diplomatist, be it known, is one who is a dangerous foe and an unreliable friend.

"Perhaps — now that I reflect upon it," continued the clever woman, disliking the clever man's silence, "the person who said all would be intolerable."

"There are some things which go without it," said De Chauxville.

"Ah?" looking lazily back at him over her shoulder.

"Yes."

He was cautious, for he was fighting on a field which women may rightly claim for their own. He really loved Etta. He was trying to gauge the meaning of a little change in her tone toward him — a change so subtle that few men could have detected it. But Claude de Chauxville — accomplished steersman through the shoals of human nature, especially through those very pronounced shoals who call themselves women of the world — Claude de Chauxville knew the value of the slightest change of manner, should that change manifest itself more than once.

The ring of indifference, or something dangerously near it, in Etta's voice had first been noticeable the previous evening, and the attaché knew it. It had been in her voice whenever she spoke to him then. It was there now.

"Some things," he continued, in a voice she had never heard before, for this man was innately artificial, "which a woman usually knows before they are told to her."

"What sort of things, M. le Baron?"

He gave a little laugh. It was so strange a thing to him to be sincere that he felt awkward and abashed. He was surprised at his own sincerity.

"That I love you — hum. You have known it long?"

The face which he could not see was not quite the face of a good woman. Etta was smiling.

"No — o," she almost whispered.

"I think you must have known it," he corrected suavely. "Will you do me the honor of becoming my wife?"

It was very correctly done, Claude de Chauxville had regained control over himself. He was able to think about the riches which were evidently hers. But through the thought he loved the woman.

The lady lowered the feather screen which she was holding between her face and the fire. Regardless of the imminent danger in which she was placing her complexion, she studied the glowing cinders for some moments, weighing something or some persons in her mind.

"No, my friend," she answered in French, at length.

The baron's face was drawn and white. Beneath his trim black mustache there was a momentary gleam of sharp white teeth as he bit his lip.

He came nearer to her, leaning one hand on the back of her chair, looking down. He could only see the beautifully dressed hair, the clean-cut profile. She continued to look into the fire, conscious of the hand close to her shoulder.

"No, my friend," she repeated. "We know each other too well for that. It would never do."

"But when I tell you that I love you," he said quietly, with his voice well in control.

"I did not know that the word was in your vocabulary — you, a diplomat."

"And a man — you put the word there — Etta."

The hand-screen was raised for a moment in objection — presumably to the Christian name of which he had made use.

He waited; passivity was one of his strong points. It had frightened men before this.

Then, with a graceful movement, she swung suddenly round in her chair, looking up at him. She broke into a merry laugh.

"I believe you are actually in earnest!" she cried.

He looked quietly down into her face without moving a muscle in response to her change of humor.

"Very clever," he said.

"What?" she asked, still smiling.

"The attitude, the voice, everything. You have known all along that I am in earnest, you have known it for the last six months. You have seen me often enough when I was — well, not in earnest, to know the difference."

Etta rose quickly. It was some lightninglike woman's instinct that made her do so. Standing, she was taller than M. de Chauxville.

"Do not let us be tragic," she said coldly. "You have asked me to marry you; why, I don't know. The reason will probably transpire later. I appreciate the honor, but I beg to decline it. Et voilà tout. All is said."

He spread out apologetic hands.

"All is not said," he corrected, with a dangerous suavity. "I acknowledge the claim enjoyed by your sex to the last word. In this matter, however, I am inclined to deny it to the individual."

Etta Sydney Bamborough smiled. She leaned against the mantelpiece, with her chin resting on her curved fingers. The attitude was eminently calculated to show to full advantage a faultless figure. She evidently had no desire to cheapen that which she would deny. She shrugged her shoulders and waited.

De Chauxville was vain, but he was clever enough to conceal his vanity. He was hurt, but he was man enough to hide it. Under the passivity which was his by nature and practice, he had learned to think very quickly. But now he was at a disadvantage. He was unnerved by his love for Etta — by the sight of Etta before him daringly, audaciously beautiful — by the thought that she might never be his.

"It is not only that I love you," he said, "that I have a certain position to offer you. These I beg you to take at their poor value. But there are other circumstances known to both of us which are more worthy of your attention — circumstances which may dispose you to reconsider your determination."

"Nothing will do that," she replied; "not any circumstance."

Etta was speaking to De Chauxville and thinking of Paul Alexis.

"I should like to know since when you have discovered that you never could under any circumstances marry me," pursued M. de Chauxville. "Not that it matters, since it is too late. I am not going to allow you to draw back now. You have gone too far. All this winter you have allowed me to pay you conspicuous and marked attentions. You have conveyed to me and to the world at large the impression that I had merely to speak in order to obtain your hand."

"I doubt," said Etta, "whether the world at large is so deeply interested in the matter as you appear to imagine. I am sorry that I have gone too far, but I reserve to myself the right of retracing my footsteps wherever and whenever I please. I am sorry I conveyed to you or to anyone else the impression that you had only to speak in order to obtain my hand, and I can only conclude that your overweening vanity has led you into a mistake which I will be generous enough to hold my tongue about."

The diplomatist was for a moment taken aback.

"Mais —" he exclaimed, with indignant arms outspread; and even in his own language he could find nothing to add to the expressive monosyllable.

"I think you had better go," said Etta quietly. She went toward the fireplace and rang the bell.

M. de Chauxville took up his hat and gloves.

"Of course," he said coldly, his voice shaking with suppressed rage, "there is some reason for this. There is, I presume, some one else — some one has been interfering. No one interferes with me with impunity. I shall make it my business to find out who is this —"

He did not finish: for the door was thrown open by the butler, who announced:

"Mr. Alexis."

Paul came into the room with a bow toward De Chauxville, who was going out, and whom he knew slightly.

"I came back," he said, "to ask what evening next week you are free. I have a box for the 'Huguenots.'"

Paul did not stay. The thing was arranged in a few moments, and as he left the drawing room he heard the wheels of De Chauxville's carriage.

Etta stood for a moment when the door had closed behind the two men, looking at the portière which had hidden them from sight, as if following them in thought. Then she gave a little laugh — a queer laugh that might have had no heart in it, or too much for the ordinary purposes of life. She shrugged her shoulders and took up a magazine, with which she returned to the chair placed for her before the fire by Claude de Chauxville.

In a few minutes Maggie came into the room. She was carrying a bundle of flannel.

"The weakest thing I ever did," she said cheerfully, "was to join Lady Crewel's working guild. Two flannel petticoats for the young by Thursday morning. I chose the young because the petticoats are so ludicrously small."

"If you never do anything weaker than that," said Etta,

looking into the fire, "you will not come to much harm."

"Perhaps not; what have you been doing — something weaker?"

"Yes. I have been quarreling with M. de Chauxville."

Maggie held up a petticoat by the selvage (which a male writer takes to be the lower hem), and looked at her cousin through the orifice intended for the waist of the young.

"If one could manage it without lowering one's dignity," she said, "I think that that is the best thing one could possibly do with M. de Chauxville."

Etta had taken up the magazine again. She was pretending to read it.

"Yes; but he knows too much — about everybody," she said.

Chapter VI

THE TALLEYRAND CLUB

*I*t has been said of the Talleyrand Club that the only qualifications required for admittance to its membership are a frock-coat and a glib tongue. To explain the whereabouts of the Talleyrand Club were only a work of supererogation. Many hansom cabmen know it. Hansom cabmen know more than they are credited with.

The Talleyrand, as its name implies, is a diplomatic club, but ambassadors and ministers enter not its portals. They send their juniors. Some of these latter are in the habit of stating that London is the hub of Europe and the Talleyrand smoking-room its grease-box. Certain is it that such men as

Claude de Chauxville, as Karl Steinmetz, and a hundred others who are or have been political scene-shifters, are to be found in the Talleyrand rooms.

It is a quiet club, with many members and sparse accommodation. Its rooms are never crowded, because half of its members are afraid of meeting the other half. It has swinging glass doors to its every apartment, the lower portion of the glass being opaque, while the upper moiety affords a peephole. Thus, if you are sitting in one of the deep, comfortable chairs to be found in all these small rooms, you will be aware from time to time of eyes and a bald head above the ground glass. If you are nobody, eyes and bald head will prove to be the property of a gentleman who does not know you, or knows you and pretends that he does not. If you are somebody, your solitude will depend upon your reputation.

There are quite a number of bald heads in the Talleyrand Club — bald heads surmounting youthful, innocent faces. The innocence of these gentlemen is quite remarkable. Like a certain celestial, they are "childlike and bland"; they ask guileless questions; they make blameless mistakes in respect to facts, and require correction, which they receive meekly. They know absolutely nothing, and their thirst for information is as insatiable as it is unobtrusive.

The atmosphere is vivacious with the light sound of many foreign tongues; it bristles with the ephemeral importance of cheap titles. One never knows whether one's neighbor is an ornament to the Almanac de Gotha, or a disgrace to a degenerate colony of refugees.

Some are plain Messieurs, Señores, or Herren. Bluff foreigners with upright hair and melancholy eyes, who put up philosophically with a cheaper brand of cigar than their souls love. Among the latter may be classed Karl Steinmetz — the bluffest of the bluff — innocent even of his own innocence.

Karl Steinmetz in due course reached England, and in natural sequence the smoking-room — room B on the left as you go in — of the Talleyrand.

He was there one evening after an excellent dinner taken with humorous resignation, smoking the largest cigar the waiter could supply, when Claude de Chauxville happened to have nothing better or nothing worse to do.

De Chauxville looked through the glass door for some seconds. Then he twisted his waxed mustache and lounged in. Steinmetz was alone in the room, and De Chauxville was evidently – almost obviously – unaware of his presence. He went to the table and proceeded to search in vain for a newspaper that interested him. He raised his eyes casually and met the quiet gaze of Karl Steinmetz.

"Ah!" he exclaimed.

"Yes," said Steinmetz.

"You – in London?"

Steinmetz nodded gravely.

"Yes," he repeated.

"One never knows where one has you," Claude de Chauxville went on, seating himself in a deep armchair, newspaper in hand. "You are a bird of passage."

"A little heavy on the wing – now," said Steinmetz.

He laid his newspaper down on his stout knees and looked at De Chauxville over his gold eye-glasses. He did not attempt to conceal the fact that he was wondering what this man wanted with him. The baron seemed to be wondering what object Steinmetz had in view in getting stout. He suspected some motive in the obesity.

"Ah!" he said deprecatingly. "That is nothing. Time leaves its mark upon all of us. It was not yesterday that we were in Petersburg together."

"No," answered Steinmetz. "It was before the German Empire – many years ago."

De Chauxville counted back with his slim fingers on the table – delightfully innocent.

"Yes," he said, "the years seem to fly in coveys. Do you ever see any of our friends of that time – you who are in Russia?"

"Who were our friends of that time?" parried Steinmetz, polishing his glasses with a silk handkerchief. "My memory is a broken reed – you remember?"

For a moment Claude de Chauxville met the full, quiet, gray eyes.

"Yes," he said significantly, "I remember. Well – for instance, Prince Dawoff?"

"Dead. I never see him – thank Heaven!"

"The princess?"

"I never see; she keeps a gambling house in Paris."

"And little Andrea?"

"Never sees me. Married to a wholesale undertaker, who has buried her past."

"En gros?"

"Et en détail."

"The Count Lanovitch," pursued De Chauxville, "where is he?"

"Banished for his connection with the Charity League."

"Catrina?"

"Catrina is living in the province of Tver — we are neighbors — she and her mother, the countess."

De Chauxville nodded. None of the details really interested him. His indifference was obvious.

"Ah! the Countess Lanovitch," he said reflectively, "she was a foolish woman."

"And is."

M. de Chauxville laughed. This clumsy German ex-diplomat amused him immensely. Many people amuse us who are themselves amused in their sleeve.

"And — er — the Sydney Bamboroughs," said the Frenchman, as if the name had almost left his memory.

Karl Steinmetz lazily stretched out his arm and took up the *Morning Post.* He unfolded the sheet slowly, and having found what he sought, he read aloud:

"'His Excellency the Romanian Ambassador gave a select dinner-party at 4 Craven Gardens, yesterday. Among the guests were the Baron de Chauxville, Feneer Pasha, Lord and Lady Standover, Mrs. Sydney Bamborough, and others.'"

Steinmetz threw the paper down and leant back in his chair.

"So, my dear friend," he said, "it is probable that you know more about the Sydney Bamboroughs than I do."

If Claude de Chauxville was disconcerted he certainly did not show it. His was a face eminently calculated to conceal whatever thought or feeling might be passing through his mind. Of an even white complexion — verging on pastiness — he was handsome in a certain statuesque way. His features were always composed and dignified; his hair, thin and straight, was never out of order, but ever smooth and sleek upon his high, narrow brow. His eyes had that dullness which is characteristic of many Frenchmen, and may perhaps be attributed to the habitual enjoyment of too rich a cuisine and too many cigarettes.

De Chauxville waved aside the small contretemps with easy nonchalance.

"Not necessarily," he said, in cold, even tones. "Mrs. Sydney Bamborough does not habitually take into her confidence all who happen to dine at the same table as herself. Your confidential woman is usually a liar."

Steinmetz was filling his pipe; this man had the evil habit of smoking a wooden pipe after a cigar.

"My very dear De Chauxville," he said, without lookup, "your epigrams are lost on me. I know most of them. I have heard them before. If you have anything to tell me about Mrs. Sydney Bamborough, for Heaven's sake tell it to me quite plainly. I like plain dishes and unvarnished stories. I am a German, you know; that is to say, a person with a dull palate and a thick head."

De Chauxville laughed again in an unemotional way.

"You alter little," he said. "Your plainness of speech takes me back to Petersburg. Yes, I admit that Mrs. Sydney Bamborough rather interested me. But I assume too much; that is no reason why she should interest you."

"She does not, my good friend, but you do. I am all attention."

"Do you know anything of her?" asked De Chauxville perfunctorily, not as a man who expects an answer or intends to believe that which he may be about to hear.

"Nothing."

"You are likely to know more?"

Karl Steinmetz shrugged his heavy shoulders, and shook his head doubtfully.

"I am not a lady's man," he added gruffly; "the good God has not shaped me that way. I am too d———d fat. Has Mrs. Sydney Bamborough fallen in love with me? Has some imprudent person shown her my photograph? I hope not. Heaven forbid!"

He puffed steadily at his pipe, and glanced quickly at De Chauxville through the smoke.

"No," answered the Frenchman quite gravely. Frenchmen, by the way, do not admit that one may be too middle-aged, or too stout, for love. "But she is au mieux with the prince."

"Which prince?"

"Pavlo."

The Frenchman snapped out the word, watching the other's benevolent countenance. Steinmetz continued to smoke placidly and contentedly.

"My master," he said at length. "I suppose that some day he will marry."

De Chauxville shrugged his shoulders. He touched the button of the electric bell, and when the servant appeared, ordered coffee. He selected a cigarette from a silver case with considerable care, and having lighted it smoked for some moments in silence. The servant brought the coffee, which he drank thoughtfully. Steinmetz was leaning back in his deep chair, with his legs crossed. He was gazing into the fire, which burned brightly, although it was nearly May. The habits of the Talleyrand Club are almost continental. The rooms are always too warm. The silence was that of two men knowing each other well.

"And why not Mrs. Sydney Bamborough?" asked Steinmetz suddenly.

"Why not, indeed?" replied De Chauxville. "It is no affair of mine. A wise man reduces his affairs to a minimum, and his interest in the affairs of his neighbor to less. But I thought it would interest you."

"Thanks."

The tone of the big man in the armchair was not dry. Karl Steinmetz knew better than to indulge in that pastime. Dryness is apt to parch the fount of expansiveness.

De Chauxville's attention was apparently caught by an illustration in a weekly paper lying open on the table near to him. Your shifty man likes something to look at. He did not speak for some moments. Then he threw the paper aside.

"Who was Sydney Bamborough, at any rate?" he asked, with a careless assumption of a slanginess which is affected by society in its decadent periods.

"So far as I remember," answered Steinmetz, "he was something in the Diplomatic Service."

"Yes, but what?"

"My dear friend, you had better ask his widow when next you sit beside her at dinner."

"How do you know that I sat beside her at dinner?"

"I did not know it," replied Steinmetz, with a quiet smile which left De Chauxville in doubt as to whether he was very stupid or exceedingly clever.

"She seems to be very well off," said the Frenchman.

"I am glad, as she is going to marry my master."

De Chauxville laughed almost awkwardly, and for a fraction of a second he changed countenance under Steinmetz's quiet eyes.

"One can never know whom a woman intends to marry," said he carelessly, "even if they can themselves, which I doubt. But I do not understand how it is that she is so much better off, or appears to be, since the death of her husband."

"Ah, she is much better off, or appears to be, since the death of her husband," said the stout man, in his slow Germanic way.

"Yes."

De Chauxville rose, stretched himself and yawned. Men are not always, be it understood, on their best behavior at their club.

"Good-night," he said shortly.

"Good-night, my very dear friend."

After the Frenchman had left, Karl Steinmetz remained quite motionless and expressionless in his chair, until such time as he concluded that De Chauxville was tired of watching him through the glass door. Then he slowly sat forward in his chair and looked back over his shoulder.

"Our friend," he muttered, "is afraid that Paul is going to marry this woman. Now, I wonder why?"

These two had met before in a past which has little or nothing to do with the present narrative. They had disliked each other with a completeness partly bred of racial hatred, partly the outcome of diverse interests. But of late years they had drifted apart. There was no reason why the friendship, such as it was, should not have lapsed into a mere bowing acquaintance. For these men were foreigners, understanding fully the value of the bow as an interchange of masculine courtesy. Englishmen bow badly.

Steinmetz knew that the Frenchman had recognized him before entering the room. It was to be presumed that he had deliberately chosen to cross the threshold, knowing that a recognition was inevitable. Karl Steinmetz went farther. He suspected that De Chauxville had come to the Talleyrand Club, having heard that he was in England, with the purpose in view of seeking him out and warning him against Mrs. Sydney Bamborough.

"It would appear," murmured the stout philosopher, "that we are about to work together for the first time. But if there is one thing that I dislike more than the enmity of Claude de Chauxville it is his friendship."

Chapter VII

OLD HANDS

*K*arl Steinmetz lifted his pen from the paper before him and scratched his forehead with his forefinger.

"Now, I wonder," he said aloud, "how many bushels there are in a ton. Ach! how am I to find out? These English weights and measures, this English money, when there is a metrical system!"

He sat and hardly looked up when the clock struck seven. It was a quiet room this in which he sat, the library of Paul's London house. The noise of Piccadilly reached his ears as a faint roar, not entirely unpleasant, but sociable and full of life. Accustomed as he was to the great silence of Russia, where sound seems lost in space, the hum of a crowded humanity was a pleasant change to this philosopher, who loved his kind while fully recognizing its little weaknesses.

While he sat there still wondering how many bushels of seed made a ton, Paul Alexis came into the room. The younger man was in evening dress. He looked at the clock rather eagerly.

"Will you dine here?" he asked, and Steinmetz wheeled around in his chair. "I am going out to dinner," he explained further.

"Ah!" said the elder man.

"I am going to Mrs. Sydney Bamborough's."

Steinmetz bowed his head gravely. He said nothing. He was not looking at Paul, but at the pattern of the carpet. There was a short silence. Then Paul said, with entire simplicity:

"I shall probably ask her to marry me."

"And she will probably say yes."

"I am not so sure about that," said Paul, with a laugh. For this man was without conceit. He had gradually been forced to admit that there are among men persons whose natural inclination is toward evil, persons who value not the truth, nor hold by honesty. But he was guileless enough to believe that women are not so. He actually believed that women are truthful and open and honorable. He believes it still, which is somewhat startling. There are a few such dullards yet. "I do not see why she should," he went on gravely. He was standing by the empty fireplace, a manly, upright figure; one who was not very clever, not brilliant at all, somewhat slow in his speech, but sure, deadly sure, in the honesty of his purpose.

Karl Steinmetz looked at him and smiled openly, with the quaint air of resignation that was his.

"You have never seen her, eh?" enquired Paul.

Steinmetz paused, then he told a lie, a good one, well told, deliberately.

"No."

"We are going to the opera, Box F2. If you come in I shall have pleasure in introducing you. The sooner you know each other the better. I am sure you will approve."

"I think you ought to marry money."

"Why?"

Steinmetz laughed.

"Oh," he answered, "because everybody does who can. There is Catrina Lanovitch, an estate as big as yours, adjoining yours. A great Russian family, a good girl who — is willing."

Paul laughed, a good wholesome laugh.

"You are inclined to exaggerate my manifold and obvious qualifications," he said. "Catrina is a very nice girl, but I do not think she would marry me even if I asked her."

"Which you do not intend to do."

"Certainly not."

"Then you will make an enemy of her," said Steinmetz quietly. "It may be inconvenient, but that cannot be helped. A woman scorned — you know. Shakespeare or the Bible, I always mix them up. No, Paul; Catrina Lanovitch is a dangerous enemy. She has been making love to you these last four years, and you would have seen it if you had not been a fool! I am afraid, my good Paul, you are a fool, God bless you for it!"

"I think you are wrong," said Paul rather curtly; "not about me being a fool, but about Catrina Lanovitch. If you are right, however, it only makes me dislike her instead of being perfectly indifferent to her."

His honest face flushed up finely, and he turned away to look at the clock again.

"I hate your way of talking about women, Steinmetz," he said. "You're a cynical old beast, you know."

"Heaven forbid, my dear prince! I admire all women — they are so clever, so innocent, so pure-minded. Do not your English novels prove it, your English stage, your newspapers, so high-toned? Who supports the novelist, the playwright, the actor, who but your English ladies?"

"Better than being cooks — like your German ladies," retorted Paul stoutly. "If you *are* German this evening. Better than being cooks."

"I doubt it! I very much doubt it, my friend. At what time shall I present myself at Box F2 this evening?"

"About nine — as soon as you like."

Paul looked at the clock. The pointers lagged horribly. He knew that the carriage was certain to be at the door, waiting in the quiet street with its great restless horses, its two perfectly trained men, its gleaming lamps and shining harness. But he would not allow himself the luxury of being the first arrival. Paul had himself well in hand. At last it was time to go.

"See you later," he said.

"Thank you — yes," replied Steinmetz, without looking up.

So Paul Howard Alexis sallied forth to seek the hand of the lady of his choice, and as he left his own door that lady was receiving Claude de Chauxville in her drawing room. The two had not met for some weeks — not indeed since Etta had told the Frenchman that she could not marry him. Her invitation to dine, couched in the usual friendly words, had been the first move in that game commonly called "bluff." Claude de Chauxville's acceptance of the same had been the second move. And these two persons, who were not afraid of each other, shook hands with a pleasant smile of greeting, while Paul hurried toward them through the busy streets.

"Am I forgiven — that I am invited to dinner?" asked De Chauxville imperturbably, when the servant had left them alone.

Etta was one of those women who are conscious of their dress. Some may protest that a lady moving in such circles would not be so. But in all circles women are only women, and in every class of life we meet such as Etta Bamborough. Women who, while they talk, glance down and rearrange a flower or a piece of lace. It is a mere habit, seemingly small and unimportant; but it marks the woman and sets her apart.

Etta was standing on the hearthrug, beautifully dressed — too beautifully dressed, it is possible, to sit down. Her maid had a moment earlier confessed that she could do no more, and Etta had come down stairs a vision of luxury, of womanly loveliness. Nevertheless, there appeared to be something amiss. She was so occupied with a flower at her shoulder that she did not answer at once.

"Forgiven for what?" she asked at length, in that preoccupied tone of voice which tells wise men that only questions of dress will be considered.

De Chauxville shrugged his shoulders in his graceful Gallic way.

"Mon Dieu!" he exclaimed. "For a crime which requires

no excuse, and no explanation other than a mirror."

She looked up at him innocently.

"A mirror?"

"Yours. Have you forgiven me for falling in love with you? It is, I am told, a crime that women sometimes condone."

"It was no crime," she said. She had heard the wheels of Paul's carriage. "It was a misfortune. Please let us forget that it ever happened."

De Chauxville twirled his neat mustache, looking keenly at her the while.

"You forget," he said. "But I — will remember."

She did not answer, but turned with a smile to greet Paul.

"I think you know each other," she said gracefully when she had shaken hands, and the two men bowed. They were foreigners, be it understood. There were three languages in which they could understand each other with equal ease.

"Where *is* Maggie?" exclaimed Mrs. Bamborough. "She is always late."

"When I am here," reflected De Chauxville. But he did not say it.

Miss Delafield kept them waiting a few minutes, and during that time Etta Sydney Bamborough gave a very fine display of prowess with the double-stringed bow. When a man attempts to handle this delicate weapon, he usually makes, if one may put it thus crudely, an ass of himself. He generally succeeds in snapping one and probably both of the strings, injuring himself most certainly in the process.

Not so, however, this clever lady. She had a smile and an epigram for Claude de Chauxville, a grave air of sympathetic interest in more serious affairs for Paul Alexis. She was bright and amusing, guileless and very worldly wise in the same breath — simple for Paul and a match for De Chauxville, within the space of three seconds. Withal she was a beautiful woman beautifully dressed. A thousand times too wise to scorn her womanhood, as learned fools are prone to do in print and on platform in these wordy days, but wielding the strongest power on earth, to wit, that same womanhood, with daring and with skill. A learned woman is not of much account in the world. A clever woman moves as much of it as lies in her neighborhood — that is to say, as much as she cares to rule. For women love power, but they do not care to wield it at a distance.

Paul was asked to take Mrs. Sydney Bamborough down to dinner by the lady herself.

"Mon ami," she said in a quiet aside to De Chauxville, before making her request, "it is the first time the prince dines here."

She spoke in French. Maggie and Paul were talking together at the other end of the room. De Chauxville bowed in silence.

At dinner the conversation was necessarily general, and, as such, is not worth reporting. No general conversation, one finds, is of much value when set down in black and white. It is not even grammatical nowadays. To be more correct, let us note that the talk lay between Etta and M. de Chauxville, who had a famous supply of epigrams and bright nothings delivered in such a way that they really sounded like wisdom. Etta was equal to him, sometimes capping his sharp wit, sometimes contenting herself with silvery laughter. Maggie Delafield was rather distraite, as De Chauxville noted. The girl's dislike for him was an iron that entered the quick of his vanity anew every time he saw her. There was no petulance in the aversion, such as he had perceived with other maidens who were only resenting a passing negligence or seeking to pique his curiosity. This was a steady and, if you will, unmaidenly aversion, which Maggie conscientiously attempted to conceal.

Paul, it is to be feared, was what hostesses call heavy in hand. He laughed where he saw something to laugh at, but not elsewhere, which in some circles is considered morose and in bad form. He joined readily enough in the conversation, but originated nothing. Those topics which occupied his mind did not present themselves as suitable to this occasion. His devotion to Etta was quite obvious, and he was simple enough not to care that it should be so.

Maggie was by turns quite silent and very talkative. When Paul and Etta were speaking together she never looked at them, but fixedly at her own plate, at a decanter, or a salt-cellar. When she spoke she addressed her remarks — valueless enough in themselves — exclusively to the man she disliked, Claude de Chauxville.

There was something amiss in the pretty little room. There were shadows seated around that pretty little table à quatre, beside the guests in their pretty dresses and their black coats; silent cold shadows, who ate nothing, while they chilled the dainty food and took the sweetness from the succulent dishes. These shadows had crept in unawares, a silent partie carrée, to take their phantom places at the table, and only Etta seemed able to jostle hers aside and talk it down. She took the whole burden of the conversation upon her pretty shoulders, and bore it through the little banquet with unerring skill and unflinching good humor. In the midst of her merriest laughter, the clever gray eyes would flit from one man's face to the other. Paul had been brought here to ask her to marry him. Claude de Chauxville had been invited that he might be tacitly presented to his successful rival. Maggie was there because she was a woman and made the necessary fourth. Puppets all, and two of them knew it. And some of us know it all our lives. We are living, moving puppets. We let ourselves be dragged here and pushed there, the victim of one who happens to have more energy of mind, a greater steadfastness of purpose, a keener grasp of the situation called life. We smirk and smile, and lose the game because we have begun by being anvils, and are afraid of trying to be hammers.

But Etta Sydney Bamborough had to deal with metal of a harder grain than the majority of us. Claude de Chauxville was for the moment forced to assume the humble rôle of anvil because he had no choice. Maggie Delafield was passive for the time being, because that which would make her active was no more than a tiny seedling in her heart. The girl bid fair to be one of those women who develop late, who ripen slowly, like the best fruit.

During the drive to the opera house the two women in Etta's snug little brougham were silent. Etta had her thoughts to occupy her. She was at the crucial point of a difficult game. She could not afford to allow even a friend to see so much as the corners of the cards she held.

In the luxurious box it was easily enough arranged — Etta and Paul together in front, De Chauxville and Maggie at the other corner of the box.

"I have asked my friend Karl Steinmetz to come in during

the evening," said Paul to Etta when they were seated. "He is anxious to make your acquaintance. He is my — prime minister over in Russia."

Etta smiled graciously.

"It is kind of him," she answered, "to be anxious to make my acquaintance."

She was apparently listening to the music; in reality she was hurrying back mentally over half a dozen years. She had never had much to do with the stout German philosopher, but she knew enough of him to scorn the faint hope that he might have forgotten her name and her individuality. Etta Bamborough had never been disconcerted in her life yet; this incident came very near to bringing about the catastrophe.

"At what time," she asked, "is he coming in?"

"About half-past nine."

Etta had a watch on a bracelet on her arm. Such women always know the time.

It was a race, and Etta won it. She had only half an hour. De Chauxville was there, and Maggie with her quiet, honest eyes. But the widow of Sydney Bamborough made Paul ask her to be his wife, and she promised to give him his answer later. She did it despite a thousand difficulties and more than one danger — accomplished it with, as the sporting people say, plenty to spare — before the door behind them was opened by the attendant, and Karl Steinmetz, burly, humorously imperturbable and impenetrable, stood smiling gravely on the situation.

He saw Claude de Chauxville, and before the Frenchman had turned round the expression on Steinmetz's large and placid countenance had changed from the self-consciousness usually preceding an introduction to one of a dim recognition.

"I have had the pleasure of meeting madame somewhere before, I think. In St. Petersburg, was it not?"

Etta, composed and smiling, said that it was so, and introduced him to Maggie. De Chauxville took the opportunity of leaving that young lady's side, and placing himself near enough to Paul and Etta to completely frustrate any further attempts at confidential conversation.

For a moment Steinmetz and Paul were left standing together.

"I have had a telegram," said Steinmetz in Russian. "We must go back to Tver. There is cholera again. When can you come?"

Beneath his heavy mustache Paul bit his lip.

"In three days," he answered.

"True? You will come with me?" enquired Steinmetz, under cover of the clashing music.

"Of course."

Steinmetz looked at him curiously. He glanced toward Etta, but he said nothing.

Chapter VIII

SAFE!

*T*he season wore on to its perihelion – a period, the scientific books advise us, of the highest clang and crash of speed and whirl, of the greatest brilliancy and deepest glow of a planet's existence. The business of life, the pursuit of pleasure, and the scientific demolition of our common enemy, Time, received all the care which such matters require.

Débutantes bloomed and were duly culled by aged connoisseurs of such wares, or by youthful aspirants with the means to pay the piper in the form of a handsome settlement. The usual number of young persons of the gentler sex entered the lists of life, with the mistaken notion that it is love that makes the world go round, to ride away from the joust wiser and sadder women.

There was the same round of conventional pleasures which the reader and his humble servant have mixed in deeply or dilettante, according to his taste or capacity for such giddy work. There was withal the usual heart-burning, heart-barter-ing, heart — anything you will but breaking. For we have not breaking hearts among us today. Providence, it would seem, has run short of the commodity, and deals out only a few among a number of persons.

Amid the whirl of rout, and ball, and picnic, race-meeting, polo-match, and what-not, Paul Howard Alexis stalked mis-understood, distrusted; an object of ridicule to some, of pity to others, of impatience to all. A man, if it please you, with a purpose — a purpose at the latter end of the nineteenth century, when most of us, having decided that there is no future, take it upon ourselves to despise the present.

Paul soon discovered that he was found out — at no time a pleasant condition of things, except, indeed, when callers are about. That which Eton and Cambridge had failed to lay their fingers upon, every matchmaking mother had found out for herself in a week. That the discovery had been carefully kept in each maternal breast, it is needless to relate. Ces dames are not confidential upon such matters between themselves. When they have scented their game they stalk him, and if possible bag him in a feline solitude which has no fears for stout, ambitious hearts. The fear is that some other prowling mother of an eligible maiden may hit upon the same scent.

Paul was invited to quiet dinners and a little music, to quiet dinners without the music, to a very little music and no dinner whatever. The number of ladies who had a seat in a box thrown upon their hands at the last minute — a seat next to Angelina in her new pink, or Blanche in her sweet poult de soie — the number of these ladies one can only say was singular, because politeness forbids one to suggest that it was suspicious. Soft cheeks became rosy at his approach — partly, perhaps, because soft and dainty toes in satin slippers were trodden upon with maternal emphasis at that moment. Soft eyes looked love into eyes that, alas! only returned preoccu-pation. There was always room on an engagement card for Paul's name. There was always space in the smallest drawing room for Paul's person, vast though the latter was. There was

— fond mothers conveyed it to him subtly after supper and champagne — an aching void in more than one maiden heart which was his exact fit.

But Paul was at once too simple and too clever for matron and maid alike. Too simple, because he failed to understand the inner meaning of many pleasant things that the guileless fair one said to him. Too clever, because he met the subtle matron with the only arm she feared, a perfect honesty. And when at last he obtained his answer from the coy and hesitating Etta, there was no gossip in London who could put forward a just cause or impediment.

Etta gave him the answer one evening at the house of a mutual friend, where a multitude of guests had assembled ostensibly to hear certain celebrated singers, apparently to whisper recriminations on their entertainer's champagne. It was a dull business — except, indeed, for Paul Howard Alexis. As for the lady — the only lady his honest, simple world contained — who shall say? Inwardly she may have been in trembling, coy alarm, in breathless, blushing hesitation. Outwardly she was, however, exceedingly composed and self-possessed. She had been as careful as ever of her toilet — as hard to please; as — dare we say snappish with her maids? The beautiful hair had no one of its aureate threads out of place. The pink of her shell-like cheek was steady, unruffled, fair to behold. Her whole demeanor was admirable in its well-bred repose. Did she love him? Was it in her power to love any man? Not the humble chronicler — not any man, perhaps, and but few women — can essay an answer. Suffice it that she accepted him. In exchange for the title he could give her, the position he could assure to her, the wealth he was ready to lavish upon her, and, lastly, let us mention, in the effete, old-fashioned way, the love he bore her — in exchange for these she gave him her hand.

Thus Etta Sydney Bamborough was enabled to throw down her cards at last and win the game she had played so skillfully. The widow of an obscure little Foreign Office clerk, she might have been a baroness, but she put the smaller honor aside and aspired to a prince. Behind the gay smile there must have been a quick and resourceful brain, daring to scheme, intrepid in execution. Within the fair breast there must have been a heart resolute, indomitable, devoid of weak scruple. Mark the last. It is the scruple that keeps the reader and his humble servant from being greater men than they are.

"Yes," says Etta, allowing Paul to take her perfectly gloved hand in his great, steady grasp; "yes, I have my answer ready."

They were alone in the plashy solitude of an inner conservatory, between the songs of the great singers. She was half afraid of this strong man, for he had strange ways with him — not uncouth, but unusual and somewhat surprising in a finnicking, emotionless generation.

"And what is it?" whispers Paul eagerly. Ah! what fools men are — what fools they always will be!

Etta gave a little nod, looking shamefacedly down at the pattern of her lace fan.

"Is that it?" he asked breathlessly.

The nod was repeated, and Paul Howard Alexis was thereby made the happiest man in England. She half expected him to take her in his arms, despite the temporary nature of their solitude. Perhaps she half wished it; for behind her business-like and exceedingly practical appreciation of his wealth there lurked a very feminine curiosity and interest in his feelings — a curiosity somewhat whetted by the manifold differences that existed between him and the society lovers with whom she had hitherto played the pretty game.

But Paul contented himself with raising the gloved fingers to his lips, restrained by a feeling of respect for her which she would not have understood and probably did not merit.

"But," she said with a sudden smile, "I take no responsibility. I am not very sure that it will be a success. I can only try to make you happy — goodness knows if I shall succeed!"

"You have only to be yourself to do that," he answered, with loverlike promptness and a blindness which is the special privilege of those happy fools.

She gave a strange little smile.

"But how do I know that our lives will harmonize in the least? I know nothing of your daily existence; where you live — where you want to live."

"I should like to live mostly in Russia," he answered honestly.

Her expression did not change. It merely fixed itself as one sees the face of a watching cat fix itself, when the longed for mouse shows a whisker.

"Ah!" she said lightly, confident in her own power; "that will arrange itself later."

"I am glad I am rich," said Paul simply, "because I shall be able to give you all you want. There are many little things that add to a woman's comfort; I shall find them out and see that you have them."

"Are you so very rich, Paul?" she asked, with an innocent wonder. "But I don't think it matters; do you? I do not think that riches have much to do with happiness."

"No," he answered. He was not a person with many theories upon life or happiness or such matters — which, by the way, are in no way affected by theories. By taking thought we cannot add a cubit to the height of our happiness. We can only undermine its base by too searching an analysis of that upon which it is built.

So Paul replied "No," and took pleasure in looking at her, as any lover must needs have done.

"Except, of course," she said, "that one may do good with great riches."

She gave a little sigh, as if deploring the misfortune that hitherto her own small means had fallen short of the happy point at which one may begin doing good.

"Are you so very rich, Paul?" she repeated, as if she was rather afraid of those riches and mistrusted them.

"Oh, I suppose so. Horribly rich!"

She had withdrawn her hand. She gave it to him again, with a pretty movement usually understood to indicate bashfulness.

"It can't be helped," she said. "We" — she dwelt upon the word ever so slightly — "we can perhaps do a little good with it."

Then suddenly he blurted out all his wishes on this point — his quixotic aims, the foolish imaginings of a too chivalrous soul. She listened, prettily eager, sweetly compassionate of the sorrows of the peasantry whom he made the object of his simple pity. Her gray eyes contracted with horror when he told her of the misery with which he was too familiar. Her pretty lips quivered when he told her of little children born only to starve because their mothers were starving. She laid her gloved fingers gently on his when he recounted tales of strong men — good fathers in their simple, barbarous way — who were well content that the children should die rather than be saved to pass a miserable existence, without joy, without hope.

She lifted her eyes with admiration to his face when he told her what he hoped to do, what he dreamed of accomplishing. She even made a few eager, heartfelt suggestions, fitly coming from a woman — touched with a woman's tenderness, lightened by a woman's sympathy and knowledge.

It was in its way a tragedy, the picture we are called to look upon — these newly made lovers, not talking of themselves, as is the time-honored habit of such. Surrounded by every luxury, both highborn, refined, and wealthy; both educated, both intelligent. He, simple-minded, earnest, quite absorbed in his happiness, because that happiness seemed to fall in so easily with the busier, and, as some might say, the nobler side of his ambition. She, failing to understand his aspirations, thinking only of his wealth.

"But," she said at length, "shall you — we — be allowed to do all this? I thought that such schemes were not encouraged in Russia. It is such a pity to pauperize the people."

"You cannot pauperize a man who has absolutely nothing," replied Paul. "Of course, we shall have difficulties; but, together, I think we shall be able to overcome them."

Etta smiled sympathetically, and the smile finished up, as it were, with a gleam very like amusement. She had been vouchsafed for a moment a vision of herself in some squalid Russian village, in a hideous Russian-made tweed dress, dispensing the necessaries of life to a people only little raised above the beasts of the field. The vision made her smile, as well it might. In Petersburg life might be tolerable for a little in the height of the season — for a few weeks of the brilliant Northern winter — but in no other part of Russia could she dream of dwelling.

They sat and talked of their future as lovers will, knowing as little of it as any of us, building up castles in the air, such edifices as we have all constructed, destined, no doubt, to the same rapid collapse as some of us have quailed under. Paul, with lamentable honesty, talked almost as much of his stupid peasants as of his beautiful companion, which pleased her not too well. Etta, with a strange persistence, brought the conversation ever back and back to the house in London, the house in Petersburg, the great grim castle in the Government of Tver, and the princely rent-roll. And once on the subject of Tver, Paul could scarce be brought to leave it.

"I am going back there," he said at length.

"When?" she asked, with a composure which did infinite credit to her modest reserve. Her love was jealously guarded. It lay too deep to be disturbed by the thought that her lover would leave her soon.

"Tomorrow," was his answer.

She did not speak at once. Should she try the extent of her power over him? Never was lover so chivalrous, so respectful, so sincere. Should she gauge the height of her supremacy? If it proved less powerful than she suspected, she would at all events be credited with a very natural aversion to parting from him.

"Paul," she said, "you cannot do that. Not so soon. I cannot let you go."

He flushed up to the eyes suddenly, like a girl. There was a little pause, and the color slowly left his face. Somehow that pause frightened Etta.

"I am afraid I must go," he said gravely at length.

"Must — a prince?"

"It is on that account," he replied.

"Then I am to conclude that you are more devoted to your peasants than to — me?"

He assured her to the contrary. She tried once again, but nothing could move him from his decision. Etta was perhaps a small-minded person, and as such failed to attach due importance to this proof that her power over him was limited. It ceased, in fact, to exist as soon as it touched that strong sense of duty which is to be found in many men and in remarkably few women.

It almost seemed as if the abrupt departure of her lover was in some sense a relief to Etta Sydney Bamborough. For, while he, loverlike, was grave and earnest during the small remainder of the evening, she continued to be sprightly and gay. The last he saw of her was her smiling face at the window as her carriage drove away.

Arrived at the little house in Upper Brook Street, Maggie and Etta went into the drawing room, where biscuits and wine were set out. Their maids came and took their cloaks away, leaving them alone.

"Paul and I are engaged," said Etta suddenly. She was picking the withered flowers from her dress and throwing them carelessly on the table.

Maggie was standing with her back to her, with her two hands on the mantelpiece. She was about to turn round when she caught sight of her own face in the mirror, and that which she saw there made her change her intention.

"I am not surprised," she said, in an even voice, standing like a statue. "I congratulate you. I think he is — nice."

"You also think he is too good for me," said Etta, with a little laugh. There was something in that laugh — a ring of wounded vanity, the wounded vanity of a bad woman who is in the presence of her superior.

"No!" answered Maggie slowly, tracing the veins of the marble across the mantelpiece. "No — o, not that."

Etta looked up at her. It was rather singular that she did not ask what Maggie did think. Perhaps she was afraid of a certain British honesty which characterized the girl's thought and speech. Instead she rose and indulged in a yawn which may have been counterfeit, but it was a good counterfeit.

"Will you have a biscuit?" she said.

"No, thanks."

"Then shall we go to bed?"

"Yes."

Chapter IX

THE PRINCE

*T*he village of Osterno, lying, or rather scrambling, along
the banks of the river Oster, is at no time an exhilarating
spot. It is a large village, numbering over nine hundred souls,
as the board affixed to its first house testifieth in incomprehensible Russian figures.

A "soul," be it known, is a different object in the land of
the Czars to that vague protoplasm about which our young
persons think such mighty thoughts, our old men write such
famous big books. A soul is namely a man — in Russia the
women have not yet begun to seek their rights and lose their
privileges. A man is therefore a "soul" in Russia, and as such
enjoys the doubtful privilege of contributing to the land-tax
and to every other tax. In compensation for the first-named
impost he is apportioned his share of the common land of
the village, and by the cultivation of this ekes out an existence
which would be valueless if he were a teetotaler. It is melancholy to have to record this fact in the pages of a respectable
volume like the present; but facts — as the orator who deals
in fiction is ever ready to announce — facts cannot be ignored.
And any man who has lived in Russia, has dabbled in Russian
humanity, and noted the singular unattractiveness of Russian
life — any such man can scarcely deny the fact that if one
deprives the moujik of his privilege of getting gloriously and
frequently intoxicated, one takes away from that same moujik

the one happiness of his existence.

That the Russian peasant is by nature one of the cheeriest, the noisiest, and lightest-hearted of men is only another proof of the Creator's power; for this dimly lighted "soul" has nothing to cheer him on his forlorn way but the memory of the last indulgence in strong drink and the hope of more to come. He is harassed by a ruthless tax-collector; he is shut off from the world by enormous distances over impracticable roads. When the famine comes, and come it assuredly will, the moujik has no alternative but to stay where he is and starve. Since Alexander II. of philanthropic memory made the Russian serf a free man, the blessings of freedom have been found to resolve themselves chiefly into a perfect liberty to die of starvation, of cold, or of dire disease. When he was a serf this man was of some small value to some one; now he is of no consequence to anyone whatsoever except himself, and, with considerable intelligence, he sets but small store upon his own existence. Freedom, in fact, came to him before he was ready for it; and, hampered as he has been by petty departmental tyranny, governmental neglect, and a natural stupidity, he has made very small progress toward a mental independence. All that he has learnt to do is to hate his tyrants. When famine urges him, he goes blindly, helplessly, dumbly, and tries to take by force that which is denied by force.

With us in England the poor man raises up his voice and cries aloud when he wants something. He always wants something — never work, by the way — and therefore his voice pervades the atmosphere. He has his evening newspaper, which is dear at the moderate sum of a halfpenny. He has his professional organizers, and his Trafalgar Square. He even has his members of Parliament. He does no work, and he does not starve. In his generation the poor man thinks himself wise. In Russia, however, things are managed differently. The poor man is under the heel of the rich. Some day there will be in Russia a Terror, but not yet. Some day the moujik will erect unto himself a rough sort of a guillotine, but not in our day. Perhaps some of us who are young men now may dimly read in our dotage of a great upheaval beside which the Terror of France will be tame and uneventful. Who can tell? When

a country begins to grow, its mental development is often
startlingly rapid.

But we have to do with Russia of today, and the village of
Osterno in the Government of Tver. Not a "famine" Government, mind you! For these are the Volga Provinces — Samara,
Pensa, Voronish, Vintka, and a dozen others. No! Tver the
civilized, the prosperous, the manufacturing center.

Osterno is built of wood. Should it once fairly catch alight
in a high wind, all that will be left of this town will be a few
charred timbers and some dazed human beings. The inhabi-
tants know their own danger, and endeavor to meet it in their
fatalistic manner. Each village has its fire organization. Each
"soul" has his appointed place, his appointed duty, and his
special contribution — be it bucket or rope or ladder — to
bring to the conflagration. But no one ever dreams of being
sober and vigilant at the right time, so the organization, like
many larger such, is a broken reed.

The street, bounded on either side by low wooden houses,
is, singularly enough, well paved. This, the traveler is told, by
the tyrant Prince Pavlo, who made the road because he did
not like driving over ruts and through puddles — the usual
Russian rural thoroughfare. Not because Prince Pavlo wanted
to give the peasants work, not because he wanted to save them
from starvation — not at all, although, in the gratification of
his own whim, he happened to render those trifling services;
but merely because he was a great "bárin" — a prince who
could have anything he desired. Had not the other bárin —
Steinmetz by name — superintended the work? Steinmetz the
hated, the loathed, the tool of the tyrant whom they never
see. Ask the "starost" — the mayor of the village. He knows
the bárins, and hates them.

Michael Roon, the starosta or elder of Osterno, president
of the Mir, or village council, principal shopkeeper, mayor
and only intelligent soul of the nine hundred, probably had
Tartar blood in his veins. To this strain may be attributed the
narrow Tartar face, the keen black eyes, the short, spare figure
which many remember to this day, although Michael Roon
has been dead these many years.

Removed far above the majority of his fellow-villagers in
intelligence and energy, this man administered the law of his

own will to his colleagues on the village council.

It was late in the autumn, one evening remembered by many for its death-roll, that the starosta was standing at the door of his small shop. He was apparently idle. He never sold vodka, and the majority of the villagers were in one of the three thriving "kabaks" which drove a famous trade in strong drink and weak tea. It was a very hot evening. The sun had set in a pink haze which was now turning to an unhealthy gray, and spreading over the face of the western sky like the shadow of death across the human countenance.

The starosta shook his head forebodingly. It was cholera weather. Cholera had come to Osterno. Had come, the starosta thought, to stay. It had settled down in Osterno, and nothing but the winter frosts would kill it, when hunger-typhus would undoubtedly succeed it.

Therefore the starosta shook his head at the sunset, and forgot to regret the badness of the times from a commercial point of view. He had done all he could. He had notified to the Zemstvo the condition of his village. He had made the usual appeal for help, which had been forwarded in the usual way to Tver, where it had apparently been received with the usual philosophic silence.

But Michael Roon had also telegraphed to Karl Steinmetz, and since the dispatch of this message had the starosta dropped into the habit of standing at his doorway in the evening, with his hands clasped behind his back and his beady black eyes bent westward along the prince's high-road.

On the particular evening with which we have to do the beady eyes looked not in vain; for presently, far along the road, appeared a black speck like an insect crawling over the face of a map.

"Ah!" said the starosta. "Ah! he never fails."

Presently a neighbor dropped in to buy some of the dried leaf which the starosta, honest tradesman, called tea. He found the purveyor of Cathay's produce at the door.

"Ah!" he said, in a voice thick with vodka. "You see something on the road?"

"Yes."

"A cart?"

"No, a carriage. It moves too quickly."

A strange expression came over the peasant's face, at no time a pleasing physiognomy. The bloodshot eyes flared up suddenly like a smoldering flame in brown paper. The unsteady, drink-sodden lips twitched. The man threw up his shaggy head, upon which hair and beard mingled in unkempt confusion. He glared along the road with eyes and face aglow with a sullen, beastlike hatred.

"A carriage! Then it is for the castle."

"Possibly," answered the starosta.

"The prince — curse him, curse his mother's soul, curse his wife's offspring!"

"Yes," said the starosta quietly. "Yes, curse him and all his works. What is it you want, little father — tea?"

He turned into the shop and served his customer, duly inscribing the debt among others in a rough, cheap book.

The word soon spread that a carriage was coming along the road from Tver. All the villagers came to the doors of their dilapidated wooden huts. Even the kabaks were emptied for a time. As the vehicle approached it became apparent that the horses were going at a great pace; not only was the loose horse galloping, but also the pair in the shafts. The carriage was an open one, an ordinary North Russian traveling carriage, not unlike the vehicle we call the victoria, set on high wheels.

Beside the driver on the box sat another servant. In the open carriage sat one man only, Karl Steinmetz.

As he passed through the village a murmur of many voices followed him, not quite drowned by the rattle of his wheels, the clatter of the horses' feet. The murmur was a curse. Karl Steinmetz heard it distinctly. It made him smile with a queer expression beneath his great gray mustache.

The starosta, standing in his door-way, saw the smile. He raised his voice with his neighbors and cursed. As Steinmetz passed him he gave a little jerk of the head toward the castle. The jerk of the head might have been due to an inequality of the road, but it might also convey an appointment. The keen, haggard face of Michael Roon showed no sign of mutual understanding. And the carriage rattled on through the stricken village.

Two hours later, when it was quite dark, a closed carriage,

with two bright lamps flaring into the night, passed through the village toward the castle at a gallop.

"It is the prince," the peasants said, crouching in their low door-ways. "It is the prince. We know his bells — they are of silver — and we shall starve during the winter. Curse him — curse him!"

They raised their heads and listened to the galloping feet with the patient, dumb despair which is the curse of the Slavonic race. Some of them crept to their doors, and, looking up, saw that the castle windows were ablaze with light. If Paul Howard Alexis was a plain English gentleman in London, he was also a great prince in his country, keeping up a princely state, enjoying the gilded solitude that belongs to the high-born. His English education had educed a strict sense of discipline, and as in England, and, indeed, all through his life, so in Russia did he attempt to do his duty.

The carriage rattled up to the brilliantly lighted door, which stood open, and within, on either side of the broad entrance-hall, the servants stood to welcome their master. A strange, picturesque, motley crew: the majordomo, in his black coat, and beside him the other house-servants — tall, upright fellows, in their bright livery. Beyond them the stable-men and keepers, a little army, in red cloth tunics, with wide trousers tucked into high boots, all holding their fur caps in their hands, standing stiffly at attention, clean, honest, and not too intelligent.

The castle of Osterno is built on the lines of many Russian country seats, and not a few palaces in Moscow. The Royal Palace in the Kremlin is an example. A broad entrance-hall, at the back of which a staircase as broad stretches up to a gallery, around which the dwelling-rooms are situated. At the head of the staircase, directly facing the entrance-hall, high folding doors disclose the drawing room, which is almost a throne room. All gorgeous, lofty, spacious, as only Russian houses are. Truly this northern empire, this great white land, is a country in which it is good to be an emperor, a prince, a noble, but not a poor man.

Paul passed through the ranks of his retainers, himself a head taller than the tallest footman, a few inches broader than the sturdiest keeper. He acknowledged the low bows by a quick nod, and passed up the staircase. Steinmetz — in evening dress, wearing the insignia of one or two orders which he had won in the more active days of his earlier diplomatic life — was waiting for him at the head of the stairs.

The two men bowed gravely to each other. Steinmetz threw open the door of the great room and stood aside. The prince passed on, and the German followed him, each playing his part gravely, as men in high places are called to do. When the door was closed behind them and they were alone, there was no relaxation, no smile of covert derision. These men knew the Russian character thoroughly. There is, be it known, no more impressionable man on the face of God's earth. Paul and Steinmetz had played their parts so long that these came to be natural to them as soon as they passed the Volga. We are all so in a minor degree. In each house, to each of our friends, we are unconsciously different in some particular. One man holds us in awe, and we unconsciously instill that feeling. Another considers us a buffoon, and, lo! we are exceedingly funny.

Paul and Steinmetz knew that the people around them in Osterno were somewhat like the dumb and driven beast. These peasants required overawing by a careful display of pomp — an unrelaxed dignity. The line of demarcation between the noble and the peasant is so marked in the land of the Czar that it is difficult for Englishmen to realize or believe it. It is like the line that is drawn between us and our dogs. If we suppose it possible that dogs could be taught to act and think for themselves; if we take such a development as practicable, and consider the possibilities of social upheaval lying behind such an education, we can in a minute degree realize the problem which Prince Pavlo Alexis and all his fellow-nobles will be called upon to solve within the lifetime of men already born.

Chapter X

THE MOSCOW DOCTOR

"Colossal!" exclaimed Steinmetz, beneath his breath. With a little trick of the tongue he transferred his cigar from the right-hand to the left-hand corner of his mouth. "Colossal — l!" he repeated.

For a moment Paul looked up from the papers spread out on the table before him — looked with the preoccupied air of a man who is adding up something in his mind. Then he returned to his occupation. He had been at this work for four hours without a break. It was nearly one o'clock in the morning. Since dinner Karl Steinmetz had consumed no less than five cigars, while he had not spoken five words. These two men, locked in a small room in the middle of the castle of Osterno — a room with no window, but which gained its light from the clear heaven by a shaft and a skylight on the roof — locked in thus they had been engaged in the addition of an enormous mass of figures. Each sheet had been carefully annotated and added by Steinmetz, and as each was finished he handed it to his companion.

"Is that fool never coming?" asked Paul, with an impatient glance at the clock.

"Our very dear friend the starosta," replied Steinmetz, "is no slave to time. He is late."

The room had the appearance of an office. There were two safes — square chests such as we learn to associate with the name of Griffiths in this country. There was a huge writing-table — a double table — at which Paul and Steinmetz were seated. There were sundry stationery cases and an almanac or so suspended on the walls, which were oaken panels. A large white stove — common to all Russian rooms — stood against the wall. The room had no less than three doors, with a handle on no one of them. Each door opened with a key, like a cupboard.

Steinmetz had apparently finished his work. He was sitting back in his chair, contemplating his companion with a little smile. It apparently tickled some obtuse Teutonic sense of humor to see this prince doing work which is usually assigned to clerks — working out statistics and abstruse calculations as to how much food is required to keep body and soul together.

The silence of the room was almost oppressive. A Russian village after nightfall is the quietest human habitation on earth. For the moujik — the native of a country which will some day supply the universe with petroleum — cannot afford to light up his humble abode, and therefore sits in darkness. Had the village of Osterno possessed the liveliness of a Spanish hamlet, the sound of voices and laughter could not have reached the castle perched high up on the rock above.

But Osterno was asleep: the castle servants had long gone to rest, and the great silence of Russia wrapped its wings over all. "When, therefore, the clear, coughing bark of a wolf was heard, both occupants of the little room looked up. The sound was repeated, and Steinmetz slowly rose from his seat.

"I can quite believe that our friend is able to call a wolf or a lynx to him," he said. "He does it uncannily well."

"I have seen him do so," said Paul, without looking up. "But it is a common enough accomplishment among the keepers."

Steinmetz had left the room before he finished speaking. One of the doors of this little room communicated with a large apartment used as a secretary's office, and through this by a small staircase with a side entrance to the castle. By this side entrance the stewards of the different outlying estates were conducted to the presence of the resident secretary — a German selected and overawed by Karl Steinmetz — a mere calculating machine of a man, with whom we have no affairs to transact.

Before many minutes had elapsed Steinmetz came back, closely followed by the starosta, whose black eyes twinkled and gleamed in the sudden light of the lamp. He dropped on his knees when he saw Paul — suddenly, abjectly, like an animal, in his dumb attitude of deprecation.

With a jerk of his head Paul bade him rise, which the man did, standing back against the paneled wall, placing as great a distance between himself and the prince as the size of the room would allow.

"Well," said Paul curtly, almost roughly, "I hear you are in trouble in the village."

"The cholera has come, Excellency."

"Many deaths?"

"Today — eleven."

Paul looked up sharply.

"And the doctor?"

"He has not come yet, Excellency. I sent for him — a fortnight ago. The cholera is at Oseff, at Dolja, at Kalisheffa. It is everywhere. He has forty thousand souls under his care. He has to obey the Zemstvo, to go where they tell him. He takes no notice of me."

"Yes," interrupted Paul, "I know. And the people themselves, do they attempt to understand it — to follow out my instructions?"

The starosta spread out his thin hands in deprecation. He cringed a little as he stood. He had Jewish blood in his veins, which, while it raised him above his fellows in Osterno, carried with it the usual tendency to cringe. It is in the blood; it is part of what the people who stood without Pilate's palace took upon themselves and upon their children.

"Your Excellency," he said, "knows what they are. It is slow. They make no progress. For them one disease is as another. 'Bog dal e Bog vzial,' they say. 'God gave and God took!'"

He paused, his black eyes flashing from one face to the other.

"Only the Moscow doctor, Excellency," he said significantly, "can manage them."

Paul shrugged his shoulders. He rose from his seat, glancing at Steinmetz, who was looking on in silence, with his queer, mocking smile.

"I will go with you now," he said. "It is late enough already."

The starosta bowed very low, but he said nothing.

Paul went to a cupboard and took from it an old fur coat, dragged at the seams, stained about the cuffs a dull brown — doctors know the color. Such stains have hanged a man before now, for they are the marks of blood. Paul put on this coat. He took a long, soft silken scarf such as Russians wear in winter, and wrapped it round his throat, quite concealing the lower part of his face. He crammed a fur cap down over his ears.

"Come," he said.

Karl Steinmetz accompanied them down stairs, carrying a lamp in one hand. He closed the door behind them, but did not lock it. Then he went upstairs again to the quiet little room, where he sat down in a deep chair. He looked at the open door of the cupboard from which Paul Alexis had taken his simple disguise, with a large, tolerant humor.

"El Señor Don Quixote de la Mancha," he said sleepily.

It is said that to a doctor nothing is shocking and nothing is disgusting. But doctors are, after all, only men of stomach like the rest of us, and it is to be presumed that what nauseates one will nauseate the other. When the starosta unceremoniously threw open the door of the miserable cabin belonging to Vasilli Tula, Paul gave a little gasp. The foul air pouring out of the noisome den was such that it seemed impossible that human lungs could assimilate it. This Vasilli Tula was a notorious drunkard, a discontent, a braggart. The Nihilist propaganda had in the early days of that mistaken mission reached him and unsettled his discontented mind. Misfortune seemed to pursue him. In higher grades of life than his there are men who, like Tula, make a profession of misfortune.

Paul stumbled down two steps. The cottage was dark. The starosta had apparently trodden on a chicken, which screamed shrilly and fluttered about in the dark with that complete abandon which belongs to chickens, sheep, and some women.

"Have you no light?" cried the starosta.

Paul retreated to the top step, where he had a short-lived struggle with a well-grown calf which had been living in the room with the family, and evinced a very creditable desire for fresh air.

"Yes, yes, we have a little petroleum," said a voice. "But we have no matches."

The starosta struck a light.

"I have brought the Moscow doctor to see you."

"The Moscow doctor!" cried several voices. "Sbogom — sbogom! God be with you!"

In the dim light the whole of the floor seemed to get up and shake itself. There were at least seven persons sleeping in the hut. Two of them did not get up. One was dead. The other was dying of cholera.

A heavily built man reached down from the top of the brick stove a cheap tin paraffin lamp, which he handed to the starosta. By the light of this Paul came again into the hut. The floor was filthy, as may be imagined, for beasts and human beings lived here together.

The man — Vasilli Tula — threw himself down on his knees, clawing at Paul's coat with great unwashed hands, whining out a tale of sorrow and misfortune. In a moment they were all on their knees, clinging to him, crying to him for help: Tula himself, a wild-looking Slav of fifty or thereabouts; his wife, haggard, emaciated, horrible to look upon, for she was toothless and almost blind; two women and a loutish boy of sixteen.

Paul pushed his way, not unkindly, toward the corner where the two motionless forms lay half concealed by a mass of ragged sheepskin.

"Here," he said, "this woman is dead. Take her out. When will you learn to be clean? This boy may live — with care. Bring the light closer, little mother. So, it is well. He will live. Come, don't sit crying. Take all these rags out and burn them. All of you go out. It is a fine night. You are better in the cart-shed than here. Here, you, Tula, go round with the starosta to his store. He will give you clean blankets."

They obeyed him blindly. Tula and one of the young women (his daughters) dragged the dead body, which was that of a very old woman, out into the night. The starosta had

retired to the door-way when the lamp was lighted, his courage having failed him. The air was foul with the reek of smoke
and filth and infection.

"Come, Vasilli Tula," the village elder said, with suspicious
eagerness. "Come with me, I will give you what the good
doctor says. Though you owe me money, and you never try
to pay me."

But Tula was kissing and mumbling over the hem of Paul's
coat. Paul took no notice of him.

"We are starving, Excellency," the man was saying. "I can
get no work. I had to sell my horse in the winter, and I cannot
plough my little piece of land. The Government will not help
us. The Prince — curse him! — does nothing for us. He lives
in Petersburg, where he spends all his money, and has food
and wine more than he wants. The Count Stépan Lanovitch
used to assist us — God be with him! But he has been sent to
Siberia because he helped the peasants. He was like you; he
was a great bárin, a great noble, and yet he helped the
peasants."

Paul turned round sharply and shook the man off.

"Go," he said, "with the starosta and get what I tell you. A
great, strong fellow like you has no business on his knees to
any man! I will not help you unless you help yourself. You
are a lazy good-for-nothing. Get out!"

He pushed him out of the hut, and kicked after him a few
rags of clothing which were lying about on the floor, all filthy
and slimy.

"Good God!" muttered he under his breath, in English,
"that a place like this should exist beneath the very walls of
Osterno!"

From hut to hut he went all through that night on his
mission of mercy — without enthusiasm, without high-flown
notions respecting mankind, but with the simple sense of
duty that was his. These people were his things — his dumb
and driven beasts. In his heart there may have existed a grudge
against the Almighty for placing him in a position which was
not only intensely disagreeable, but also somewhat ridiculous. For he did not dare to tell his friends of these things.
He had spoken of them to no man except Karl Steinmetz,
who was in a sense his dependent. English public school and

university had instilled into him the intensely British feeling of shame respecting good works. He could take chaff as well as any man, for he was grave by habit, and a grave man receives the most chaff most good-humoredly. But he had a nervous dread of being found out. He had made a sort of religion of suppressing the fact that he was a prince; the holy of holies of this cult was the fact that he was a prince who sought to do good to his neighbor — a prince in whom one might repose trust.

This was not the first time by any number that he had gone down into his own village insisting in a rough-and-ready way on cleanliness and purity.

"The Moscow doctor" — the peasants would say in the kabak over their vodka and their tea — "the Moscow doctor comes in and kicks our beds out of the door. He comes in and throws our furniture into the street But afterward he gives us new beds and new furniture."

It was a joke that always obtained in the kabak. It flavored the vodka, and with that fiery poison served to raise a laugh.

The Moscow doctor was looked upon in Osterno and in many neighboring villages as second only to God. In fact, many of the peasants placed him before their Creator. They were stupid, vodka-soddened, hapless men. The Moscow doctor they could see for themselves. He came in, a very tangible thing of flesh and blood, built on a large and manly scale; he took them by the shoulders and bundled them out of their own houses, kicking their bedding after them. He scolded them, he rated them and abused them. He brought them food and medicine. He understood the diseases which from time to time swept over their villages. No cold was too intense for him to brave should they be in distress. He asked no money, and he gave none. But they lived on his charity, and they were wise enough to know it.

What wonder if these poor wretches loved the man whom they could see and hear above the God who manifested himself to them in no way! The orthodox priests of their villages had no money to spend on their parishioners. On the contrary, they asked for money to keep the churches in repair. What wonder, then, if these poor ignorant, helpless peasants would listen to no priest; for the priest could not explain to them why it was that God sent a four-month-long winter which cut them off from the rest of the world behind impassable barriers of snow; that God sent them droughts in the summer so that there was no crop of rye; that God scourged them with dread and horrible disease!

It is almost impossible for us to realize, in these days of a lamentably cheap press and a cheaper literature, the mental condition of men and women who have no education, no newspaper, no news of the world, no communication with the universe. To them the mystery of the Moscow doctor was as incomprehensible as to us is the Deity. They were so near to the animals that Paul could not succeed in teaching them that disease and death followed on the heels of dirt and neglect. They were too ignorant to reason, too low down the animal scale to comprehend things which some of the dumb animals undoubtedly recognize.

Paul Alexis, half Russian, half English, understood these people very thoroughly. He took advantage of their ignorance, their simplicity, their unfathomable superstition. He governed as no other could have ruled them, by fear and kindness at once. He mastered them by his vitality, the wholesome strength of his nature, his infinite superiority. He avoided the terrible mistake of the Nihilists by treating them as children to whom education must be given little by little instead of throwing down before them a mass of dangerous knowledge which their minds, unaccustomed to such strong food, are incapable of digesting.

A British coldness of blood damped as it were the Russian quixotism which would desire to see result follow upon action — to see the world make quicker progress than its Creator has decreed. With very unsatisfactory material Paul was setting in motion a great rock which will roll down into the ages unconnected with his name, clearing a path through a very thick forest of ignorance and tyranny.

Chapter XI

CATRINA

*T*he man who carries a deceit, however innocent, with him through life is apt to be somewhat handicapped in that unfair competition. He is like a ship at sea with a "sprung" main-mast. A side breeze may arise at any moment which throws him all aback and upon his beam-ends. He runs illegitimate risks, which are things much given to dragging at a man's mind, handicapping his thoughts.

Paul suffered in this way. It was a distinct burthen to him to play a double part, although each was innocent enough in itself. At school, and later on at the 'Varsity, he had consistently and steadily suppressed a truth from friend and foe alike — namely, that he was in his own country a prince. No great crime on the face of it; but a constant suppression of a very small truth is as burdensome as any suggestion of false-hood. It makes one afraid of contemptible foes, and doubtful of the value of one's own friendship.

Paul was a simple-minded man. He was not afraid of the Russian Government. Indeed, he cultivated a fine contempt for that august body. But he was distinctly afraid of being found out, for that discovery could only mean an incontinent cessation of the good work which rendered his life happy.

The fear of being deprived of this interest in existence should certainly have been lessened, if not quite allayed, by the fact that a greater interest had been brought into his life in the pleasant form of a prospective wife. When he was in London with Etta Sydney Bamborough he did not, however, forget Osterno. He only longed for the time when he could take Etta freely into his confidence and engage her interest in the object of his ambition — namely, to make the huge Osterno estate into that lump of leaven which might in time leaven the whole of the empire.

That a man is capable of sustaining two absorbing interests at once is a matter of everyday illustration. Are we not surrounded by men who do their work well in life, and love their wives well at home, without allowing the one to interfere with the other? That women are capable of the same seems exceedingly probable. But we are a race of sheep who run after each other, guided for the moment by a catchword which will not bear investigation, or an erroneous deduction set in alliterative verse which clings to the mind and sways it. Thus we all think that woman's whole existence is, and is only capable of, love, because a poet, in the trickiness of his trade, once said so.

Now, Paul held a different opinion. He thought that Etta could manage to love him well, as she said she did, and yet take an interest in that which was in reality the object of his life. He intended to take the earliest opportunity of telling her all about the work he was endeavoring to carry out at Osterno, and the knowledge that he was withholding something from her was a constant burden to an upright and honest nature.

"I think," he said one morning to Steinmetz, "that I will write and tell Mrs. Sydney Bamborough all about this place."

"I should not do that," replied Steinmetz with a leisurely promptitude.

They were alone in a great smoking-room of which the walls were hung all round with hunting trophies. Paul was smoking a post-prandial cigar. Steinmetz reflected gravely over a pipe. They were both reading Russian newspapers — periodicals chiefly remarkable for that which they leave unsaid.

"Why not?" asked Paul.

"On principle. Never tell a woman that which is not interesting enough to magnify into a secret."

Paul turned over his newspaper. He began reading again. Then, suddenly, he looked up.

"We are engaged to be married," he observed pointedly.

Steinmetz took his pipe from his lips slowly and imperturbably. He was a man to whom it was no satisfaction to impart news. He either knew it before or did not take much interest in the matter.

"That makes it worse," he said. "A woman only conceals what is bad about her husband. If she knows anything that is likely to make other women think that their husbands are inferior, she will tell it."

Paul laughed.

"But this is not good," he argued. "We have kept it so confoundedly quiet that I am beginning to feel as if it is a crime."

Steinmetz uncrossed his legs, crossed them again, and then spoke after mature reflection:

"As I understand the law of libel, a man is punished, not for telling a lie, but for telling either the truth or a lie with malicious intent. I imagine the Almighty will take the intent into consideration, if human justice finds it expedient to do so!"

Paul shrugged his shoulders. Argument was not his strong point, and, like most men who cannot argue, he was almost impervious to the arguments of others. He recognized the necessity for secrecy — the absolute need of a thousand little secretive precautions and disguises which were intensely disagreeable to him. But he also grumbled at them freely, and whenever he made such objection Karl Steinmetz grew uneasy, as if the question which he disposed of with facile philosophy or humorous resignation had behind it a possibility and an importance of which he was fully aware. It was on these rare occasions that he might have conveyed to a keen observer the impression that he was playing a very dangerous game with a smiling countenance.

"All that we do," pursued Steinmetz, "is to bow to a lamentable necessity for deceit. I have bowed to it all my life. It has been my trade, perhaps. It is not our fault that we are placed in charge of four or five thousand human beings who are no more capable of helping themselves than are sheep. It is not our fault that the forefathers of these sheep cut down the forests and omitted to plant more, so that the flocks with whom we have to deal have no fuel. It is not our fault that a most terrific winter annually renders the land unproductive for four months. It is not our fault that the government to which we are forced to bow — the Czar whose name lifts our hats from our heads — it is not our fault that progress and education are taboo, and that all who endeavor to forward the cause of humanity are promptly put away in a safe place where they are at liberty to forward their own salvation and nothing else. Nothing is our fault, mein lieber, in this country. We have to make the best of adverse circumstances. We are not breaking any human law, and in doing nothing we should be breaking a divine command."

Paul flicked the ash off his cigar. He had heard all this before. Karl Steinmetz's words were usually more remarkable for solid thoughtfulness than for brilliancy of conception or any great novelty of expression.

"Oh!" said Paul quietly, "I am not going to leave off. You need not fear that. Only I shall have to tell my wife. Surely a woman could help us in a thousand ways. There is such a lot that only a woman understands."

"Yes!" grunted Steinmetz; "and only the right sort of woman."

Paul looked up sharply.

"You must leave that to me," he said.

"My very dear friend, I leave everything to you."

Paul smiled.

There was no positive proof that this was not strictly true. There was no saying that Karl Steinmetz did not leave everything to everybody. But wise people thought differently.

"You don't know Etta," he said, half shyly. "She is full of sympathy and pity for these people."

Steinmetz bowed gravely.

"I have no doubt of it."

"And yet you say that she must not be told."

"Certainly not. A secret is considerably strained if it be divided between two people. Stretching it to three will probably break it. You can tell her when you are married. Does she consent to live in Osterno?"

"Oh, yes. I think so."

"Um — m!"

"What did you say?"

"Um — m," repeated Steinmetz, and the conversation somewhat naturally showed signs of collapse.

At this moment the door was opened, and a servant in bright livery, with powdered wig, silk stockings, and a countenance which might have been of wood, brought in a letter on a silver tray.

Paul took the square envelope and turned it over, displaying as he did so a coronet in black and gold on the corner, like a stamp.

Karl Steinmetz saw the coronet. He never took his quiet, unobtrusive glance from Paul's face while he opened the letter and read it.

"A fresh difficulty," said Paul, throwing the note across to his companion.

Steinmetz looked grave while he unfolded the thick stationery.

"Dear Paul [the letter ran]:

"I hear you are at Osterno and that the Moscow doctor is in your country. We are in great distress at Thors — cholera, I fear. The fame of your doctor has spread to my people, and they are clamoring for him. Can you bring or send him over? You know your room here is always in readiness. Come soon with the great doctor, and also Herr Steinmetz. In doing so you will give more than pleasure to your old friend,

"CATRINA LANOVITCH.

"P.S. Mother is afraid to go out of doors for fear of infection. She thinks she has a little cold."

Steinmetz folded the letter very carefully, pressing the seam of it reflectively with his stout forefinger and thumb.

"I always think of the lie first," he said. "It's my nature or my misfortune. We can easily write and say that the Moscow doctor has left."

He paused, scratching his brow pensively with his curved forefinger. It is to be feared that he was seeking not so much the truth as the most convenient perversion of the same.

"But then," he went on, "by doing that we leave these poor devils to die in their — styes. Catrina cannot manage them. They are worse than our people."

"Whatever is the best lie to tell," burst in Paul — "as we seem to live in an atmosphere of them — I must go to Thors; that is quite certain."

"There is no must in the case," put in Steinmetz quietly, as a parenthesis. "No man is compelled to throw himself in the way of infection. But I know you will go, whatever I say."

"I suppose I shall," admitted Paul.

"And Catrina will find you out at once."

"Why?"

Steinmetz drew in his feet. He leant forward and knocked his pipe on one of the logs that lay ready to light in the great open fireplace.

"Because she loves you," he said shortly. "There is no coming the Moscow doctor over her, mien lieber."

Paul laughed rather awkwardly. He was one of the few men — daily growing fewer — who hold that a woman's love is not a thing to be tossed lightly about in conversation.

"Then —" he began, speaking rather quickly, as if afraid that Steinmetz was going to say more. "If," he amended, "you think she will find out, she must not see me, that is all."

Steinmetz reflected again. He was unusually grave over this matter. One would scarcely have taken this stout German for a person of any sentiment whatever. Nevertheless he would have liked Paul to marry Catrina Lanovitch in preference to Etta Sydney Bamborough, merely because he thought that the former loved him, while he felt sure that the latter did not. So much for the sentimental point of view — a starting-point, by the way, which usually makes all the difference in a man's life. For a man needs to be loved as much as a woman needs it. From the practical point of view, Karl Steinmetz knew too much about Etta to place entire reliance on the goodness of her motives. He keenly suspected that she was marrying Paul for his money — for the position he could give her in the world.

"We must be careful," he said. "We must place clearly before ourselves the risks that we are running before we come to any decision. For you the risk is simply that of unofficial banishment. They can hardly send you to Siberia because you are half an Englishman; and that impertinent country has a habit of getting up and shouting when her sons are interfered with. But they can easily make Russia impossible for you. They can do you more harm than you think. They can do these poor devils of peasants of yours more harm than we can comfortably contemplate. As for me," he paused and shrugged his great shoulders, "it means Siberia. Already I am a suspect — a persona non grata."

"I do not see how we can refuse to help Catrina," said Paul, in a voice which Steinmetz seemed to know, for he suddenly gave in.

"As you will," he said.

He sat up, and, drawing a small table toward him, took up a pen reflectively. Paul watched him in silence.

When the letter was finished, Steinmetz read it aloud:

"My Dear Catrina:
    "The Moscow doctor and your obedient servant will be (D.V.) in Thors by seven o'clock tonight. We propose spending about an hour in the village, if you will kindly advise the starosta to be ready for us. As our time is limited, and we are much needed in Osterno, we shall have to deprive ourselves of the pleasure of calling at the castle. The prince sends kind remembrances, and proposes riding over to Thors to avail himself of your proffered hospitality in a day or two. With salutations to the countess,

"Your old friend,
"Karl Steinmetz."

Steinmetz waited with the letter in his hand for Paul's approval. "You see," he explained, "you are notoriously indifferent to the welfare of the peasants. It would be unnatural if you suddenly displayed so much interest as to induce you to go to Thors on a mission of charity."

Paul nodded. "All right," he said. "Yes, I see; though I confess I sometimes forget what the deuce I *am* supposed to be."

Steinmetz laughed pleasantly as he folded the letter. He rose and went to the door.

"I will send it off," he said. He paused on the threshold and looked back gravely. "Do not forget," he added, "that Catrina Lanovitch loves you."

Chapter XII

AT THORS

*B*elow the windows of a long, low, stone house, in its architecture remarkably like a fortified farm — below these deep-embrasured windows the river Oster mumbled softly. One of the windows was wide open, and with the voice of the water a wonderful music rolled out to mingle and lose itself in the hum of the pine-woods.

The room was a small one; beneath the artistic wall-paper one detected the outline of square-hewn stones. There were women's things lying about; there were flowers in a bowl on a low, strong table. There were a few good engravings on the wall; deep-curtained windows, low chairs, a sofa, a fan. But it was not a womanly room. The music filling it, vibrating back from the grim stone walls, was not womanly music. It was more than manly. It was not earthly, but almost divine. It happened to be Grieg, with the halting beat of a disabled, perhaps a broken, heart in it, as that master's music usually has.

The girl was alone in the room. The presence of anyone would have silenced something that was throbbing at the back of the chords. Quite suddenly she stopped. She knew how to play the quaint last notes. She knew something that no master had ever taught her.

She swung round on the stool and faced the light. It was afternoon — an autumn afternoon in Russia — and the pink light made the very best of a face which was not beautiful at all, never could be beautiful — a face about which even the owner, a woman, could have no possible illusion. It was broad and powerful, with eyes too far apart, forehead too broad and low, jaw too heavy, mouth too determined. The eyes were almond-shaped, and slightly sloping downward and inward — deep, passionate blue eyes set in a Mongolian head. It was the face of a woman who could, morally speaking, make mincemeat of nine young men out of ten. But she could not have made one out of the number love her. For it has been decreed that women shall win love — except in some happy exceptions — by beauty only. The same unwritten law has it that a man's appearance does not matter — a law much appreciated by some of us, and duly canonized by not a few.

The girl was evidently listening. She glanced at a little golden clock on the mantelpiece, and then at the open window. She rose — she was short, and somewhat broadly built — and went to the window.

"He will be back," she said to herself, "in a few minutes now."

She raised her hand to her forehead, and pressed back her hair with a little movement of impatience, expressive, perhaps, of a great suspense. She stood idly drumming on the windowsill for a few moments; then, with a quick little sigh, she went back to the piano. As she moved she gave a jerk of the head from time to time, as schoolgirls who have too much hair are wont to do. The reason of this nervous movement was a wondrous plait of gold reaching far below her waist. Catrina Lanovitch almost worshipped her own hair. She knew without any doubt that not one woman in ten thousand could rival her in this feminine glory — knew it as indubitably as she knew that she was plain. The latter fact she faced with an unflinching, cold conviction which was not feminine at all. She did not say that she was hideous, for the sake of hearing a contradiction or a series of saving clauses. She never spoke of it to anyone. She had grown up with it, and as it was beyond doubt, so was it outside discussion. All her femininity seemed to be concentrated, all her vanity centered, on her hair. It was her one pride, perhaps her one hope. Women have been loved for their voices. Catrina's voice was musical enough, but it was deep and strong. It was passionate, tender if she wished, fascinating; but it was not lovable. If the voice may win love, why not the hair?

Catrina despised all men but one — that one she worshipped. She lived night and day with one great desire, beside which heaven and hell were mere words. Neither the hope of the one nor the fear of the other in any way touched or affected her desire. She wanted to make Paul Alexis love her; and, womanlike, she clung to the one womanly charm that was hers — the wonderful golden hair. Pathetic, aye, pathetic — with a grin behind the pathos, as there ever is.

She sat down at the piano, and her strong, small hands tore the heart out of each wire. There are some people who get farther into a piano than others, making the wires speak as with a voice. Catrina Lanovitch had this trick. She only played a Russian people-song — a simple lay such as one may hear issuing from the door of any kabak on a summer evening. But she infused a true Russian soul into it — the soul that is cursed with a fatal power of dumb and patient endurance. She did not sway from side to side as do some people who lose themselves in the intoxication of music. But she sat quite upright, her sturdy, square shoulders motionless. Her strange eyes were fixed with the stillness of distant contemplation.

Suddenly she stopped and leaped to her feet. She did not go to the window, but stood listening beside the piano. The beat of a horse's hoofs on the narrow road was distinctly audible, hollow and sodden as is the sound of a wooden road. It came nearer and nearer, and a certain unsteadiness indicated that the horse was tired.

"I thought he might have come," she whispered, and she sat down breathlessly.

When the servant came into the room a few minutes later Catrina was at the piano.

"A letter, mademoiselle," said the maid.

"Lay it on the table," answered Catrina, without looking round. She was playing the closing bars of a nocturne.

She rose slowly, turned, and seized the letter as a starving man seizes food. There was something almost wolflike in her eyes.

"Steinmetz," she exclaimed, reading the address. "Steinmetz. Oh! why won't he write to me?"

She tore open the letter, read it, and stood holding it in her hand, looking out over the trackless pine-woods with absorbed, speculative eyes. The sun had just set. The farthest ridge of pine trees stood out like the teeth of a saw in black relief on the rosy sky. Catrina Lanovitch watched the rosiness fade into pearly gray.

"Madame the Countess awaits mademoiselle for tea," said the maid's voice suddenly, in the gloom of the door-way.

"I will come."

The village of Thors — twenty miles farther down the river Oster, twenty miles nearer to the junction of that river with the Volga — was little more than a hamlet in the days of which we write. Some day, perhaps, the three hundred souls of Thors may increase and multiply — some day when Russia is attacked by the railway fever. For Thors is on the Chorno-Ziom — the belt of black and fertile soil that runs right across the vast empire.

Karl Steinmetz, a dogged watcher of the Wandering Jew — the deathless scoffer at our Lord's agony, who shall never die, who shall leave cholera in his track wherever he may wander — Karl Steinmetz knew that the Oster was in itself a Wandering Jew. This river meandered through the lonesome country, bearing cholera germs within its waters. Whenever Osterno had cholera it sent it down the river to Thors, and so on to the Volga.

Thors lay groaning under the scourge, and the Countess Lanovitch shut herself within her stone walls, shivering with fear, begging her daughter to return to Petersburg.

It was nearly dark when Karl Steinmetz and the Moscow doctor rode into the little village, to find the starosta, a simple Russian farmer, awaiting them outside the kabak.

Steinmetz knew the man, and immediately took command of the situation with that unquestioned sense of authority which in Russia places the bárin on much the same footing as that taken by the Anglo-Indian in our eastern empire.

"Now, starosta," he said, "we have only an hour to spend in Thors. This is the Moscow doctor. If you listen to what he tells you, you will soon have no sickness in the village. The worst houses first — and quickly. You need not be afraid, but if you do not care to come in, you may stay outside."

As they walked down the straggling village-street the Moscow doctor told the starosta in no measured terms, as was his wont, wherein lay the heart of the sickness. Here, as in Osterno, dirt and neglect were at the base of all the trouble. Here, as in the larger village, the houses were more like the abode of four-footed beasts than the dwellings of human beings.

The starosta prudently remained outside the first house to which he introduced the visitors. Paul went fearlessly in, while Steinmetz stood in the door-way, holding open the door.

As he was standing there he perceived a flickering light approaching him. The light was evidently that of an ordinary hand-lantern, and from the swinging motion it was easy to divine that it was being carried by some one who was walking quickly.

"Who is this?" asked Steinmetz.

"It is likely to be the Countess Catrina, Excellency."

Steinmetz glanced back into the cottage, which was dark save for the light of a single petroleum lamp. Paul's huge form could be dimly distinguished bending over a heap of humanity and foul clothing in a corner.

"Does she visit the cottages?" asked Steinmetz sharply.

"She does, God be with her! She has no fear. She is an angel. Without her we should all be dead."

"She won't visit this, if I can help it," muttered Steinmetz.

The light flickered along the road toward them. In the course of a few minutes it fell on the stricken cottage, on the starosta standing in the road, on Steinmetz in the door-way.

"Herr Steinmetz, is that you?" asked a voice, deep and musical, in the darkness.

"Zum Befehl," answered Steinmetz, without moving.

Catrina came up to him. She was clad in a long dark cloak, a dark hat, and wore no gloves. She brought with her a clean aromatic odor of disinfectants. She carried the lantern herself, while behind her walked a man-servant in livery, with a large basket in either hand.

"It is good of you," she said, "to come to us in our need — also to persuade the good doctor to come with you."

"It is not much that we can do," answered Steinmetz, taking the small outstretched hand within his large soft grasp; "but that little you may always count upon."

"I know," she said gravely.

She looked up at him, expecting him to step aside and allow her to pass into the cottage; but Steinmetz stood quite still, looking down at her with his pleasant smile.

"And how is it with you?" he asked, speaking in German, as they always did together.

She shrugged her shoulders.

"Oh!" she answered indifferently, "I am well, of course. I always am. I have the strength of a horse. Of course I have been troubled about these poor people. It has been terrible. They are worse than children. I cannot quite understand why God afflicts them so. They have never done any harm. They are not like the Jews. It seems unjust. I have been very busy, in my small way. My mother, you know, does not take much interest in things that are not clean."

"Madame the Countess reads French novels and the fictional productions of some modern English ladies," suggested Steinmetz quietly.

"Yes; but she objects to honest dirt," said Catrina coldly. "May I go in?"

Steinmetz did not move.

"I think not. This Moscow man is eccentric. He likes to do good sub rosa. He prefers to be alone."

Catrina tried to look into the cottage; but Karl Steinmetz, as we know, was fat, and filled up the whole door-way.

"I should like to thank him for coming to us, or, at least, to offer him hospitality. I suppose one cannot pay him."

"No; one cannot pay him," answered Steinmetz gravely.

There was a little pause. From the interior of the cottage came the murmured gratitude of the peasants, broken at times by a wail of agony — the wail of a man. It is not a pleasant sound to hear. Catrina heard it, and it twisted her plain, strong face in a sudden spasm of sympathy.

Again she made an impatient little movement.

"Let me go in," she urged. "I may be able to help."

Steinmetz shook his head.

"Better not!" he said. "Besides, your life is too precious to these poor people to run unnecessary risks."

She gave a strange, bitter laugh.

"And what about you?" she said. "And Paul?"

"You never hear of Paul going into any of the cottages," snapped Steinmetz sharply. "For me it is different. You have never heard that of Paul."

"No," she answered slowly; "and it is quite right. His life — it is different for him. How — how is Paul?"

"He is well, thank you."

Steinmetz glanced down at her. She was looking across the plains beyond the boundless pine forests that lay between Thors and the Volga.

"Quite well," he went on, kindly enough. "He hopes to ride over and pay his respects to the countess tomorrow or the next day."

And the keen, kind eyes saw what they expected in the flickering light of the lamp.

At this moment Steinmetz was pushed aside from within, and a hulking young man staggered out into the road, propelled from behind with considerable vigor. After him came a shower of clothes and bedding.

"Pah!" exclaimed Steinmetz, spluttering. "Himmel! What filth! Be careful, Catrina!"

But Catrina had slipped past him. In an instant he had caught her by the wrist.

"Come back!" he cried. "You must not go in there!"

She was just over the threshold.

"You have some reason for keeping me out," she returned, wriggling in his strong grasp. "I will — I will!"

With a twist she wrenched herself free and went into the dimly lighted room.

Almost immediately she gave a mocking laugh.

"Paul!" she said.

Chapter XIII

UNMASKED

*F*or a moment there was silence in the hovel, broken only by the wail of the dying man in the corner. Paul and Catrina faced each other — she white and suddenly breathless, he half frowning. But he did not meet her eyes.

"Paul," she said again, with a lingering touch on the name. The sound of her voice, a rough sort of tenderness in her angry tone, made Steinmetz smile in his grim way, as a man may smile when in pain.

"Paul, what did you do this for? Why are you here? Oh, why are you in this wretched place?"

"Because you sent for me," he answered quietly. "Come, let us go out. I have finished here. That man will die. There is nothing more to be done for him. You must not stay in here."

She gave a short laugh as she followed him. He had to stoop low to pass through the door-way. Then he turned and held out his hand, for fear she should trip over the high threshold. She nodded her thanks, but refused the proffered assistance.

Steinmetz lingered behind to give some last instructions, leaving Paul and Catrina to walk on down the narrow street alone. The moon was just rising — a great yellow moon such as only Russia knows — the land of the silver night.

"How long have you been doing this?" asked Catrina

suddenly. She did not look toward him, but straight in front of her.

"For some years now," he replied simply.

He lingered. He was waiting for Steinmetz, who always rose to such emergencies, who understood secrets and how to secure them when they seemed already lost. He did not quite understand what was to be done with Catrina — how she was to be silenced. She had found him out with such startling rapidity that he felt disposed to admit her right to dictate her own terms. On a straight road this man was fearless and quick, but he had no taste or capacity for crooked ways.

Catrina walked on in silence. She was not looking at the matter from his point of view at all.

"Of course," she said at length, "of course, Paul, I admire you for it immensely. It is just like you to go and do the thing quietly and say nothing about it; but — oh, you must go away from here. I — I — it is too horrible to think of your running such risks. Rather let them all die like flies than that. You mustn't do it. You mustn't."

She spoke in English hurriedly, with a little break in her voice which he did not understand.

"With ordinary precautions the risk is very small," he said practically.

"Yes. But do you take ordinary precautions? Are you sure you are all right now?"

She stopped. They were quite alone in the one silent street of the stricken village. She looked up into his face. Her hands were running over the breast of the tattered coat he wore. It was lamentably obvious, even to him, that she loved him. In her anxiety she either did not know what she was doing, or she did not care whether he knew or not. She merely gave sway to the maternal instinct which is in the love of all women. She felt his hands; she reached up and touched his face.

"Are you sure — are you sure you have not taken it?" she whispered.

He walked on, almost roughly.

"Oh, yes; quite," he said.

"I will not allow you to go into anymore houses in Thors. I cannot — I will not! Oh, Paul, you don't know. If you do,

I will tell them all who you are, and — and the Government will stop you."

"What would be the good of that?" said Paul awkwardly. "Your father cared for his peasants, and was content to run risks for them. I suppose you care about them, too, as you go into their houses."

"Yes; but —"

She paused, gave a strange little reckless laugh, and was silent. Heaven forbid that we should say that she wanted him to know that she loved him. Chivalry bids us believe that women guard the secret of their love inviolate from the world. But what was Catrina to do? Men are in the habit of forgetting that plain women are women at all. Surely some of them may be excused for reminding us at times that they also are capable of loving — that they also desire to be loved. Happy is the man who loves and is loved of a plain woman; for she will take her own lack of beauty into consideration, and give him more than most beautiful women have it in their power to give.

"Of course," Catrina went on, with a sudden anger which surprised herself, "I cannot stop you from doing this at Osterno, though I think it is wicked; but I can prevent you from doing it here, and I certainly shall!"

Paul shrugged his shoulders.

"As you like," he said. "I thought you cared more about the peasants."

"I do not care a jot about the peasants," she answered passionately, "as compared — It is you I am thinking about, not them. I think you are selfish, and cruel to your friends."

"My friends have never shown that they are consumed with anxiety on my account."

"That is mere prevarication. Leave that to Herr Steinmetz and such men, whose business it is; you don't do it well. Your friends may feel a lot that they do not show."

She spoke the words shortly and sharply. Surreptitious good is so rare, that when it is found out it very naturally gets mixed up with secret evil, and the perpetrator of the hidden good deed feels guilty of a crime. Paul was in this lamentable position, which he proceeded to further aggravate by seeking to excuse himself.

"I did it after mature consideration. I tried paying another man, but he shirked his work and showed the white feather; so Steinmetz and I concluded that there was nothing to be done but do our dirty work ourselves."

"Which, being translated, means that you do it."

"Pardon me. Steinmetz does his share."

Catrina Lanovitch was essentially a woman, despite her somewhat masculine frame. She settled Karl Steinmetz's account with a sniff of contempt.

"And that is why you have been so fond of Osterno the last two years?" she asked innocently.

"Yes," he answered, falling into the trap.

Catrina winced. One does not wince the less because the pain is expected. The girl had the Slav instinct of self-martyrdom, which makes Russians so very different from the pleasure-loving nations of Europe.

"Only that?" she enquired.

Paul glanced down at her.

"Yes," he answered quietly.

They walked on in silence for a few moments. Paul seemed tacitly to have given up the idea of visiting anymore of the stricken cottages. They were going toward the long old house, which was called the castle more by courtesy than by right.

"How long are you going to stay in Osterno?" asked Catrina at length.

"About a fortnight; I cannot stay longer. I am going to be married."

Catrina stopped dead. She stood for a moment looking at the ground with a sort of wonder in her eyes, not pleasant to see. It was the look of one who, having fallen from a great height, is not quite sure whether it means death or not. Then she walked on.

"I congratulate you," she said. "I only hope she will make you happy. She is — beautiful, I suppose?"

"Yes," answered Paul simply.

The girl nodded her head.

"What is her name?"

"Etta Sydney Bamborough."

Catrina had evidently never heard the name before. It conveyed nothing to her. Womanlike, she went back to her first question.

"What is she like?"

Paul hesitated.

"Tall, I suppose?" suggested the stunted woman at his side.

"Yes."

"And graceful?"

"Yes."

"Has she — pretty hair?" asked Catrina.

"I think so — yes."

"You are not observant," said the girl in a singularly even and emotionless voice. "Perhaps you never noticed."

"Not particularly," answered Paul.

The girl raised her face. There was a painful smile twisting her lips. The moonlight fell upon her; the deep shadows beneath the eyes made her face wear a grin. Some have seen such a grin on the face of a drowning man — a sight not to be forgotten.

"Where does she live?" asked Catrina. She was unaware of the thought of murder that was in her own heart. Nevertheless, the desire — indefinite, shapeless — was there to kill this woman, who was tall and beautiful, whom Paul Alexis loved.

It must be remembered in extenuation that Catrina Lanovitch had lived nearly all her life in the province of Tver. She was not modern at all. Deprived of the advantages of our enlightened society press, without the benefit of our decadent fictional literature, she had lamentably narrow views of life. She was without that deep philosophy which teaches you, mademoiselle, who read this guileless tale, that nothing matters very much; that love is but a passing amusement, the plaything of an hour; that if Tom is faithless, Dick is equally amusing; while Harry's taste in gloves and compliments is worthy of some consideration. That these things be true — that at all events the modern young lady thinks them true — is a matter of no doubt whatever. Has not the modern lady novelist told us so? And is not the modern lady novelist notable for her close observation of human nature, her impartial judgment of human motives, her sublime truth of delineation when she sits down to describe the thing she calls a man? By a close study of the refined feminine literature of the day the modern young lady acquires not only the knowledge of some startling social delinquencies — retailed, not as if they were quite the exception, but as if they were quite the correct thing — but also she will learn that she is human. She will realize how utterly absurd it is to attempt to be anything else. If persons in books, she will reflect, are not high-minded or pure-minded, or even clean-minded, it is useless for an ordinary person out of a book to attempt to be any of these.

This is the lesson of some new writers, and Catrina Lanovitch had, fortunately enough, lacked the opportunity of learning it.

She only knew that she loved Paul, and that what she wanted was Paul's love to go with her all through her life. She was not self-analytical, nor subtle, nor given to thinking about her own thoughts. Perhaps she was old-fashioned enough to be romantic. If this be so, we must bear with her romance, remembering that, at all events, romance serves to elevate, while realism tends undoubtedly toward deterioration.

Catrina hated Etta Sydney Bamborough with a simple half-barbaric hatred because she had gained the love of Paul Alexis. Etta had taken away from her the only man whom Catrina could ever love all through her life. The girl was simple enough, unsophisticated enough, never to dream of compromise. She never for a moment entertained the cheap, consolatory thought that in time she would get over it; she would marry somebody else, and make that compromise which is responsible for more misery in this world than ever is vice. In her great solitude, growing to womanhood as she had in the vast forest of Tver, she had learned nearly all that she knew from the best teacher, Nature; and she held the strange, effete theory that it is wicked for a woman to marry a man she does not love, or to marry at all for any reason except love. St. Paul and a few others held like theories, but nous avons changé tout cela.

"Where does she live?" asked Catrina.

"In London."

They walked on in silence for a few moments. They were walking slowly, and they presently heard the footsteps of Karl Steinmetz and the servant close behind them.

"I wonder," said Catrina, half to herself, "whether she loves you?"

It was a question, but not one that a man can answer. Paul said nothing, but walked gravely on by the side of this woman, who knew that even if Etta Sydney Bamborough should try she could never love him as she herself did.

When Karl Steinmetz joined them they were silent.

"I suppose," he said in English, "that we may rely upon the discretion of the Fraülein Catrina?"

"Yes," answered the girl; "you may, so far as Osterno is concerned. But I would rather that you did not visit our people here. It is too dangerous in several ways."

"Ah!" murmured Steinmetz, respectfully acquiescent. He was looking straight in front of him, with an expression of countenance which was almost dense. "Then we must bow to your decision," he went on, turning toward the tall man striding along at his side.

"Yes," said Paul simply.

Steinmetz smiled grimly to himself. It was one of his half-cynical theories that women hold the casting vote in all earthly matters, and when an illustration such as this came to prove the correctness of his deductions, he only smiled. He was not by nature a cynic — only by the force of circumstances.

"Will you come to the castle?" asked the girl at length, and Steinmetz by a gesture deferred the decision to Paul.

"I think not tonight, thanks," said the latter. "We will take you as far as the gate."

Catrina made no comment. When the tall gate-way was reached she stopped, and they all became aware of the sound of horses' feet behind them.

"What is this?" asked Catrina.

"Only the starosta bringing our horses," replied Steinmetz. "He has discovered nothing."

Catrina nodded and held out her hand.

"Good-night," she said, rather coldly. "Your secret is safe with me."

"Set a thief to catch a thief," reflected Steinmetz. He said nothing, however, when he shook hands.

They mounted their horses and rode back the way they had come. For half an hour no one spoke. Then Paul broke the silence. He only said one word:

"D———n."

"Yes," returned Steinmetz quietly. "Charity is a dangerous plaything."

Chapter XIV

A WIRE-PULLER

*T*he Palace of Industry — where, with a fine sense of the fitness of the name, the Parisians amuse themselves — was in a blaze of electric light and fashion. The occasion was the Concours Hippique, an ultra-equine fête, where the lovers of the friend of man, and such persons as are fitted by an ungenerous fate with limbs suitable to horsy clothes, meet and bow. In France, as in a neighboring land (less sunny), horsiness is the last refuge of the diminutive. It is your small man who is ever the horsiest in his outward appearance, just as it is your very plain young person who is keenest at the Sunday-school class.

When a Frenchman is horsy he never runs the risk of being mistaken for a groom or a jockey, as do his turfy compeers in England. His costume is so exaggeratedly suggestive of the stable and the horse as to leave no doubt whatever that he is an amateur of the most pronounced type. His collar is so white and stiff and portentous as to make it impossible for him to tighten up his own girths. His breeches are so breechy about the knees as to render an ascent to the saddle a feat which it is not prudent to attempt without assistance. His gloves are so large and seamy as to make it extremely difficult to grasp the bridle, and quite impossible to buckle a strap. Your French horseman is, in fact, rather like a knight of old, inasmuch as his attendants are required to set him on his horse with his face turned in the right direction, his bridle in his left hand, his whip in his right, and, it is to be supposed, his heart in his mouth. When he is once up there, however, the gallant son of Gaul can teach even some of us, my fox-hunting masters, the way to sit a horse!

We have, however, little to do with such matters here, except in so far as they affect the persons connected with this record. The Concours Hippique, be it therefore known, was at its height. Great deeds of horsemanship had been successfully accomplished. The fair had smiled beneath penciled eyebrows upon the brave in uniform and breeches. At the time when we join the fashionable throng, the fair are smiling their brightest. It is, in fact, an interval for refreshment.

A crowd of well-dressed men jostled each other good-naturedly around a long table, where insolent waiters served tepid coffee, and sandwiches that had been cut by the hand of a knave. In the background a number of ladies nodded encouragement to their cavaliers in the intervals of scrutinizing each other's dresses. Many penciled eyebrows were raised in derision of too little style displayed by some innocent rival, or brought down in disapproval of too much of the same vague quality displayed by one less innocent.

In the midst of these, as in his element, moved the Baron Claude de Chauxville, smiling his courteous, ready smile, which his enemies called a grin. He took up less room than the majority of the men around him; he succeeded in passing through narrower places, and jostled fewer people. In a word, he proved to his own satisfaction, and to the discomfiture of many a younger man, his proficiency in the gentle art of getting on in the world.

Not far from him stood a stout gentleman of middle age, with a heavy fair mustache brushed upward on either side. This man had an air of distinction which was notable even in this assembly; for there were many distinguished people present, and a Frenchman of note plays his part better than do we dull, self-conscious islanders. This man looked like a general, so upright was he, so keen his glance, so independent the carriage of his head.

He stood with his hands behind his back, looking gravely on at the social festivity. He bowed and raised his hat to many, but he entered into conversation with none.

"Ce Vassili," he heard more than once whispered, "c'est un homme dangereux."

And he smiled all the more pleasantly.

Now, if a very keen observer had taken the trouble to ignore the throng and watch two persons only, that observer might have discovered the fact that Claude de Chauxville was slowly and purposely making his way toward the man called Vassili.

De Chauxville knew and was known of many. He had but recently arrived from London. He found himself called upon to shake hands à l'anglais with this one and that, giving all and sundry his impressions of the perfidious Albion with a verve and neatness truly French. He went from one to the other with perfect grace and savoir-faire, and each change of position brought him nearer to the middle-aged man with upturned mustache, upon whom his movements were by no means lost.

Finally De Chauxville bumped against the object of his quest – possibly, indeed, the object of his presence at the Concours Hippique. He turned with a ready apology.

"Ah!" he exclaimed; "the very man I was desiring to see."

The individual known as "ce Vassili" – a term of mingled contempt and distrust – bowed very low. He was a plain commoner, while his interlocutor was a baron. The knowledge of this was subtly conveyed in his bow.

"How can I serve M. le Baron?" he enquired in a voice which was naturally loud and strong, but had been reduced by careful training to a tone inaudible at the distance of a few paces.

"By following me to the Café Tantale in ten minutes," answered De Chauxville, passing on to greet a lady who was bowing to him with the labored grace of a Parisienne.

Vassili merely bowed and stood upright again. There was something in his attitude of quiet attention, of unobtrusive scrutiny and retiring intelligence, vaguely suggestive of the police – something which his friends refrained from mentioning to him; for this Vassili was a dignified man, of like susceptibilities with ourselves, and justly proud of the fact that he belonged to the Corps Diplomatique. What position he occupied in that select corporation he never vouchsafed to define. But it was known that he enjoyed considerable emoluments, while he was never called upon to represent his country or his emperor in any official capacity. He was attached, he said, to the Russian Embassy. His enemies called him a spy; but the world never puts a charitable construction on that of which it only has a partial knowledge.

In ten minutes Claude de Chauxville left the Concours Hippique. In the Champs Elysées he turned to the left, up toward the Bois du Boulogne; turned to the left again, and took one of the smaller paths that lead to one or other of the sequestered and somewhat select cafés on the south side of the Champs Elysées.

At the Café Tantale — not in the garden, for it was winter, but in the inner room — he found the man called Vassili consuming a pensive and solitary glass of liqueur.

De Chauxville sat down, stated his requirements to the waiter in a single word, and offered his companion a cigarette, which Vassili accepted with the consciousness that it came from a coroneted case.

"I am rather thinking of visiting Russia," said the Frenchman.

"Again," added Vassili, in his quiet voice.

De Chauxville looked up sharply, smiled, and waved the word away with a gesture of the fingers that held a cigarette.

"If you will — again."

"On private affairs?" enquired Vassili, not so much, it would appear, from curiosity as from habit. He put the question with the assurance of one who has a right to know.

De Chauxville nodded acquiescence through the tobacco smoke.

"The bane of public men — private affairs," he said epigrammatically.

But the attaché to the Russian Embassy was either too dense or too clever to be moved to a sympathetic smile by a cheap epigram.

"And M. le Baron wants a passport?" he said, lapsing into

the useful third person, which makes the French language so much more fitted to social and diplomatic purposes than is our rough northern tongue.

"And more," answered De Chauxville. "I want what you hate parting with — information."

The man called Vassili leaned back in his chair with a little smile. It was an odd little smile, which fell over his features like a mask and completely hid his thoughts. It was apparent that Claude de Chauxville's tricks of speech and manner fell here on barren ground. The Frenchman's epigrams, his method of conveying his meaning in a non-committing and impersonal generality, failed to impress this hearer. The difference between a Frenchman and a Russian is that the former is amenable to every outward influence — the outer thing penetrates. The Russian, on the contrary, is a man who works his thoughts, as it were, from internal generation to external action. The action, moreover, is demonstrative, which makes the Russian different from other northern nations of an older civilization and a completer self-control.

"Then," said Vassili, "if I understand M. le Baron aright, it is a question of private and personal affairs that suggests this journey to — Russia?"

"Precisely."

"In no sense a mission?" suggested the other, sipping his liqueur thoughtfully.

"In no sense a mission. I give you a proof. I have been granted six months' leave of absence, as you probably know."

"Precisely so, mo' cher Baron." Vassili had a habit of applying to everyone the endearing epithet, which lost a consonant somewhere in his mustache. "When a military officer is granted a six months' leave, it is exactly then that we watch him."

De Chauxville shrugged his shoulders in deprecation, possibly with contempt for any system of watching.

"May one call it an affaire de coeur?" asked Vassili, with his grim smile.

"Certainly. Are not all private affairs such, one way or the other?"

"And you want a passport?"

"Yes — a special one."

"I will see what I can do."

"Thank you."

Vassili emptied his glass, drew in his feet, and glanced at the clock.

"But that is not all I want," said De Chauxville.

"So I perceive."

"I want you to tell me what you know of Prince Pavlo Alexis."

"Of Tver?"

"Of Tver. What you know from your point of view, you understand, my dear Vassili. Nothing political, nothing incriminating, nothing official. I only want a few social details."

Again the odd smile fell over the dignified face.

"In case," said Vassili, rather slowly, "I should only impart to you stale news and valueless details with which you are already acquainted, I must ask you to tell me first what you know — from your point of view."

"Certainly," answered De Chauxville, with engaging frankness. "The man I know slightly is the sort of thing that Eton and Oxford turn out by the dozen. Well dressed, athletic, silent, a thorough gentleman — et voilà tout."

The face of Vassili expressed something remarkably like disbelief.

"Ye — es," he said slowly.

"And you?" suggested De Chauxville.

"You leave too much to my imagination," said Vassili. "You relate mere facts — have you no suppositions, no questions in your mind about the man?"

"I want to know what his purpose in life may be. There is a purpose — one sees it in his face. I want also to know what he does with his spare time; he must have much to dispose of in England."

Vassili nodded, and suddenly launched into detail.

"Prince Pavlo Alexis," he said, "is a young man who takes a full and daring advantage of his peculiar position. He defies many laws in a quiet, persistent way which impresses the smaller authorities and to a certain extent paralyzes them. He was in the Charity League — deeply implicated. He had a narrow escape. He was pulled through by the cleverest man in Russia."

"Karl Steinmetz?"

"Yes," answered Vassili behind the rigid smile; "Karl Steinmetz."

"And that," said De Chauxville, watching the face of his companion, "is all you can tell me?"

"To be quite frank with you," replied the man who had never been quite frank in his life, "that is all I want to tell you."

De Chauxville lighted a cigarette, with exaggerated interest in the match.

"Paul is a friend of mine," he said calmly. "I may be staying at Osterno with him."

The rigid smile never relaxed.

"Not with Karl Steinmetz on the premises," said Vassili imperturbably.

"The astute Mr. Steinmetz may be removed to some other sphere of usefulness. There is a new spoke in his Teutonic wheel."

"Ah!"

"Prince Paul is about to marry — the widow of Sydney Bamborough."

"Sydney Bamborough," repeated Vassili musingly, with a perfect expression of innocence on his well-cut face. "I have heard that name before."

De Chauxville laughed quietly, as if in appreciation of a pretty trick which he knew as well as its performer.

"She is a friend of mine."

The attaché, as he was pleased to call himself, to the Russian Embassy, leant his arms on the table, bending forward and bringing his large, fleshy face within a few inches of De Chauxville's keen countenance.

"That makes all the difference," he said.

"I thought it would," answered De Chauxville, meeting the steady gaze firmly.

Chapter XV
IN A WINTER CITY

St. Petersburg under snow is the most picturesque city in the world. The town is at its best when a high wind has come from the north to blow all the snow from the cupola of St. Isaac's, leaving that golden dome, in all its brilliancy, to gleam and flash over the whitened sepulcher of a city.

In winter the Neva is a broad, silent thoroughfare between the Vassili Ostrow and the Admiralty Gardens. In the winter the pestilential rattle of the cobble-stones in the side streets is at last silent, and the merry music of sleigh-bells takes its place. In the winter the depressing damp of this northern Venice is crystallized and harmless.

On the English Quay a tall, narrow house stands looking glumly across the river. It is a suspected house, and watched; for here dwelt Stépan Lanovitch, secretary and organizer of the Charity League.

Although the outward appearance of the house is uninviting, the interior is warm and dainty. The odor of delicate hothouse plants is in the slightly enervating atmosphere of the apartments. It is a Russian fancy to fill the dwelling-rooms with delicate, forced foliage and bloom. In no country of the world are flowers so worshipped, is money so freely spent in floral decoration. There is something in the sight, and more especially in the scent of hothouse plants, that appeals to the complex siftings of three races which constitute a modern

Russian.

We, in the modest self-depreciation which is a national characteristic, are in the habit of thinking, and sometimes saying, that we have all the good points of the Angle and the Saxon rolled satisfactorily into one Anglo-Saxon whole. We are of the opinion that mixed races are the best, and we leave it to be understood that ours is the only satisfactory combination. Most of us ignore the fact that there are others at all, and very few indeed recognize the fact that the Russian of today is essentially a modern outcome of a triple racial alliance of which the best component is the Tartar.

The modern Russian is an interesting study, because he has the remnant of barbaric tastes, with ultra-civilized facilities for gratifying the same. The best part of him comes from the East, the worst from Paris.

The Countess Lanovitch belonged to the school existing in Petersburg and Moscow in the early years of the century — the school that did not speak Russian but only French, that chose to class the peasants with the beasts of the field, that apparently expected the deluge to follow soon.

Her drawing room, looking out on to the Neva, was characteristic of herself. Camellias held the floral honors in vase and pot. The French novel ruled supreme on the side-table. The room was too hot, the chairs were too soft, the moral atmosphere too lax. One could tell that this was the dwelling-room of a lazy, self-indulgent, and probably ignorant woman.

The countess herself in nowise contradicted this conclusion. She was seated on a very low chair, exposing a slippered foot to the flame of a wood fire. She held a magazine in her hand, and yawned as she turned its pages. She was not so stout in person as her loose and somewhat highly colored cheeks would imply. Her eyes were dull and sleepy. The woman was an incarnate yawn.

She looked up, turning lazily in her chair, to note the darkening of the air without the double windows.

"Ah!" she said aloud to herself in French, "when will it be teatime?"

As she spoke the words, the bells of a sleigh suddenly stopped with a rattle beneath the window.

Immediately the countess rose and went to the mirror over the mantelpiece. She arranged without enthusiasm her straggling hair, and put straight a lace cap which was chronically crooked. She looked at her reflection pessimistically, as well she might. It was the puffy red face of a middle-aged woman given to petty self-indulgence.

"While she was engaged in this discouraging pastime the door was opened, and a maid came in with the air of one who has gained a trifling advantage by the simple method of peeping.

"It is M. Steinmetz, Mme. la Comtesse."

"Ah! Do I look horrible, Célestine? I have been asleep."

Célestine was French, and laughed with all the charm of that tactful nation.

"How can Mme. la Comtesse ask such a thing? Madame might be thirty-five!"

It is to be supposed that the staff of angelic recorders have a separate set of ledgers for French people, with special discounts attaching to pleasant lies.

Madame shook her head — and believed.

"M. Steinmetz is even now taking off his furs in the hall," said Célestine, retiring toward the door.

"It is well. We shall want tea."

Steinmetz came into the room with an exaggerated bow and a twinkle in his melancholy eyes.

"Figure to yourself, my dear Steinmetz," said the countess vivaciously. "Catrina has gone out — on a day like this! Mon Dieu! How gray, how melancholy!"

"Without, yes! But here, how different!" replied Steinmetz in French.

The countess cackled and pointed to a chair.

"Ah! you always flatter. What news have you, bad character?"

Steinmetz smiled pensively, not so much suggesting the desire to impart as the intention to withhold that which the lady called news.

"I came for yours, countess. You are always amusing — as well as beautiful," he added, with his mouth well controlled beneath the heavy mustache.

The countess shook her head playfully, which had the

effect of tilting her cap to one side.

"I! Oh, I have nothing to tell you. I am a nun. What can one do — what can one hear in Petersburg? Now in Paris it is different. But Catrina is so firm. Have you ever noticed that, Steinmetz? Catrina's firmness, I mean. She wills a thing, and her will is like a rock. The thing has to be done. It does itself. It comes to pass. Some people are so. Now I, my clear Steinmetz, only desire peace and quiet. So I give in. I gave in to poor Stépan. And now he is exiled. Perhaps if I had been firm — if I had forbidden all this nonsense about charity — it would have been different. And Stépan would have been quietly at home instead of in Tomsk, is it, or Tobolsk? I always forget which. Well, Catrina says we must live in Petersburg this winter, and — nous voilà!"

Steinmetz shrugged his shoulders with a commiserating smile. He took the countess's troubles indifferently, as do the rest of us when our neighbor's burden does not drag upon our own shoulders. It suited him that Catrina should be in Petersburg, and it is to be feared that the feelings of the Countess Lanovitch had no weight as against the convenience of Karl Steinmetz.

"Ah, well!" he said, "you must console yourself with the thought that Petersburg is the brighter for some of us. Who is this — another visitor?"

The door was thrown open, and Claude de Chauxville walked into the room with the easy grace which was his.

"Mme. la Comtesse," he said, bowing over her hand.

Then he stood upright, and the two men smiled grimly at each other. Steinmetz had thought that De Chauxville was in London. The Frenchman counted on the other's duties to retain him in Osterno.

"Pleasure!" said De Chauxville, shaking hands.

"It is mine," answered Steinmetz.

The countess looked from one to the other with a smile on her foolish face.

"Ah!" she exclaimed; "how pleasant it is to meet old friends! It is like by-gone times."

At this moment the door opened again and Catrina came in. In her rich furs she looked almost pretty.

She shook hands eagerly with Steinmetz; her deep eyes

searched his face with a singular, breathless scrutiny.

"Where are you from?" she asked quickly.

"London."

"Catrina," broke in the countess, "you do not remember M. de Chauxville! He nursed you when you were a child."

Catrina turned and bowed to De Chauxville.

"I should have remembered you," he said, "if we had met accidentally. After all, childhood is but a miniature — is it not so?"

"Perhaps," answered Catrina; "and when the miniature develops it loses the delicacy which was its chief charm."

She turned again to Steinmetz, as if desirous of continuing her conversation with him.

"M. de Chauxville, you surely have news?" broke in the countess's cackling voice. "I have begged M. Steinmetz in vain. He says he has none; but is one to believe so notorious a bad character?"

"Madame, it is wise to believe only that which is convenient. But Steinmetz, I promise you, is the soul of honor. What sort of news do you crave for? Political, which is dangerous; social, which is scandalous; or court news, which is invariably false?"

"Let us have scandal, then."

"Ah! I must refer you to the soul of honor."

"Who," answered Steinmetz, "in that official capacity is necessarily deaf, and in a private capacity is naturally dull."

He was looking very hard at De Chauxville, as if he was attempting to make him understand something which he could not say aloud. De Chauxville, from carelessness or natural perversity, chose to ignore the persistent eyes.

"Surely the news is from London," he said lightly; "we have nothing from Paris."

He glanced at Steinmetz, who was frowning.

"I can hardly tell you stale news that comes from London via Paris, can I?" he continued.

Steinmetz was tapping impatiently on the floor with his broad boot.

"About whom — about whom?" cried the countess, clapping her soft hands together.

"Well, about Prince Paul," said De Chauxville, looking at

Steinmetz with airy defiance.

Steinmetz moved a little. He placed himself in front of Catrina, who had suddenly lost color. She could only see his broad back. The others in the room could not see her at all. She was rather small, and Steinmetz hid her as behind a screen.

"Ah!" he said to the countess, "his marriage! But Madame the Countess assuredly knows of that."

"How could she?" put in De Chauxville.

"The countess knew that Prince Paul was going to be married," explained Karl Steinmetz very slowly, as if he wished to give some one time. "With such a man as he, 'going to be' is not very far from being."

"Then it is an accomplished fact?" said the countess sharply.

"Yesterday," answered Steinmetz.

"And you were not there!" exclaimed Countess Lanovitch, with uplifted hands.

"Since I was here," answered Steinmetz.

The countess launched into a disquisition on the heinousness of marrying any but a compatriot. The tone of her voice was sharp, and the volume of her words almost amounted to invective. As Steinmetz was obviously not listening, the lady imparted her views to the Baron de Chauxville.

Steinmetz waited for some time, then he turned slowly toward Catrina without actually looking at her.

"It is dangerous," he said, "to stay in this warm room with your furs."

"Yes," she answered, rather faintly; "I will go and take them off."

Steinmetz held the door open for her, but he did not look at her.

Chapter XVI

THE THIN END

"*B*ut I confess I cannot understand why I should not be called the Princess Alexis — there is nothing to be ashamed of in the title. I presume you have a right to it?"

Etta looked up from her occupation of fixing a bracelet, with a little glance of enquiry toward her husband.

They had been married a month. The honeymoon — a short one — had been passed in the house of a friend, indeed a relation of Etta's own, a Scotch peer who was not above lending a shooting-lodge in Scotland on the tacit understanding that there should be some quid pro quo in the future.

In answer Paul merely smiled, affectionately tolerant of her bright sharpness of manner. Your bright woman in society is apt to be keen at home. What is called vivacity abroad may easily degenerate into snappiness by the hearth.

"I think it is rather ridiculous being called plain Mrs. Howard-Alexis," added Etta, with a pout.

They were going to a ball — the first since their marriage. They had just dined, and Paul had followed his wife into the drawing room. He took a simple-minded delight in her beauty, which was of the description that is at its best in a gorgeous setting. He stood looking at her, noting her grace, her pretty, studied movements. There were, he reflected, few women more beautiful — none, in his own estimation, fit to compare with her.

She had hitherto been sweetness itself to him, enlivening his lonely existence, shining suddenly upon his self-contained nature with a brilliancy that made him feel dull and tongue-tied.

Already, however, he was beginning to discover certain small differences, not so much of opinion as of thought, between Etta and himself. She attached an importance to social function, to social opinion, to social duties, which he in no wise understood. Invitations were showered upon them. A man who is a prince and prefers to drop the title need not seek popularity in London. The very respectable reader probably knows as well as his humble servant, the writer, that in London there is always a social circle just a little lower than one's own which opens its doors with noble, disinterested hospitality, and is prepared to lick the blacking from any famous foot.

These invitations Etta accepted eagerly. Some women hold it little short of a crime to refuse an invitation, and go through life regretting that there is only one evening to each day. To Paul these calls were nothing new. His secretary had hitherto drawn a handsome salary for doing little more than refuse such.

It was in Etta's nature to be somewhat carried away by glitter. A great ballroom, brilliant illumination, music, flowers, and diamonds had an effect upon her which she enjoyed in anticipation. Her eyes gleamed brightly on reading the mere card of invitation. Some dull and self-contained men are only to be roused by the clatter and whirl of a battlefield, and this stirs them into brilliancy, changing them to new men. Etta, always brilliant, always bright, exceeded herself on her battlefield — a great social function.

Since their marriage she had never been so beautiful, her eyes had never been so sparkling, her color so brilliant as at this moment when she asked her husband to let her use her title. Hers was the beauty that blooms not for one man alone, but for the multitude; that feeds not on the love of one, but on the admiration of many. The murmur of the man in the street who turned and stared into her carriage was more than the devotion of her husband.

"A foreign title," answered Paul, "is nothing in England. I soon found that out at Eton and at Trinity. It was impossible there. I dropped it, and I have never taken it up again."

"Yes, you old stupid, and you have never taken the place you are entitled to, in consequence."

"What place? May I button that?"

"Thanks."

She held out her arm while he, with fingers much too large for such dainty work, buttoned her glove.

"The place in society," she answered.

"Oh; does that matter? I never thought of it."

"Of course it matters," answered the lady, with an astonished little laugh. (It is wonderful what an importance we attach to that which has been dearly won.) "Of course it matters," answered Etta; "more than — well, more than anything."

"But the position that depends upon a foreign title cannot be of much value," said the pupil of Karl Steinmetz.

Etta shook her pretty head reflectively.

"Of course," she answered, "money makes a position of its own, and everybody knows that you are a prince; but it would be nicer, with the servants and everybody, to be a princess."

"I am afraid I cannot do it," said Paul.

"Then there is some reason for it," answered his wife, looking at him sharply.

"Yes, there is."

"Ah!"

"The reason is the responsibility that attaches to the very title you wish to wear."

The lady smiled, a little scornfully perhaps.

"Oh! Your grubby old peasants, I suppose," she said.

"Yes. You remember, Etta, what I told you before we were married — about the people, I mean?"

"Oh, yes!" answered Etta, glancing at the clock and hiding a little yawn behind her fan.

"I did not tell you all," went on Paul, "partly because it was inexpedient, partly because I feared it might bore you. I only told you that I was vaguely interested in the peasants, and thought it would be a good thing if they could be gradually educated into a greater self-respect, a greater regard for cleanliness and that sort of thing."

"Yes, dear, I remember," answered Etta, listlessly contemplating her gloved hands.

"Well, I have not contented myself with thinking this during the last two or three years. I have tried to put it into practice. Steinmetz and I have lived at Osterno six months of the year on purpose to organize matters on the estate. I was deeply implicated in the — Charity League —"

Etta dropped her fan with a clatter into the fender.

"Oh! I hope it is not broken," she gasped, with a singular breathlessness.

"I do not think so," replied Paul, picking up the fan and returning it to her. "Why, you look quite white! What does it matter if it is broken? You have others."

"Yes, but —" Etta paused, opening the fan and examining the sticks so closely that her face was hidden by the feathers. "Yes, but I like this one. What is the Charity League, dear?"

"It was a large organization gotten up by the hereditary nobles of Russia to educate the people and better their circumstances by discriminate charity. Of course it had to be kept secret, as the bureaucracy is against any attempt to civilize the people — against education or the dissemination of news. The thing was organized. We were just getting to work when some one stole the papers of the League from the house of Count Stépan Lanovitch and sold them to the Government. The whole thing was broken up; Lanovitch and others were exiled, I bolted home, and Steinmetz faced the storm alone in Osterno. He was too clever for them, and nothing was brought home to us. But you will understand that it is necessary for us to avoid any notoriety, to live as quietly and privately as possible."

"Yes, of course; but —"

"But what?"

"You can never go back to Russia," said Etta slowly, feeling her ground, as it were.

"Oh, yes, I can. I was just coming to that. I want to go back this winter. There is so much to be done. And I want you to come with me."

"No, Paul. No, no! I couldn't do that!" cried Etta, with a ring of horror in her voice, strangely out of keeping with her peaceful and luxurious surroundings.

"Why not?" asked the man who had never known fear.

"Oh, I should be afraid. I couldn't. I hate Russia!"

"But you don't know it."

"No," answered Etta, turning away and busying herself with her long silken train. "No, of course not. Only Petersburg, I mean. But I have heard what it is. So cold and dismal and miserable. I feel the cold so horribly. I wanted to go to the Riviera this winter. I really think, Paul, you are asking me too much."

"I am only asking a proof that you care for me."

Etta gave a little laugh — a nervous laugh with no mirth in it.

"A proof! But that is so bourgeois and unnecessary. Haven't you proof enough, since I am your wife?"

Paul looked at her without any sign of yielding. His attitude, his whole being, was expressive of that immovability of purpose which had hitherto been concealed from her by his quiet manner. Steinmetz knew of the mental barrier within this Anglo-Russian soul, against which prayer and argument were alike unavailing. The German had run against it once or twice in the course of their joint labors, and had invariably given way at once.

Etta looked at him. The color was coming back to her face in patches. There was something unsteady in her eyes — something suggesting that for the first time in her life she was daunted by a man. It was not Paul's speech, but his silence that alarmed her. She felt that trivial arguments, small feminine reasons, were without weight.

"Now that you are married," she said, "I do not think you have any right to risk your life and your position for a fad."

"I have done it with impunity for the last two or three years," he answered. "With ordinary precautions the risk is small. I have begun the thing now; I must go on with it."

"But the country is not safe for us — for you."

"Oh, yes, it is," answered Paul. "As safe as ever it has been."

Etta paused. She turned round and looked into the fire. He could not see her face.

"Then the Ch — Charity League is forgotten?" she said.

"No," answered her husband quietly. "It will not be forgotten until we have found out who sold us to the Government."

Etta's lips moved in a singular way. She drew them in and held them with her teeth. For a moment her beautiful face wore a hunted expression of fear.

"What will you gain by that?" she asked evenly.

"I? Oh, nothing. I do not care one way or the other. But there are some people who want the man — very much."

Etta drew in a long, deep breath.

"I will go to Osterno with you, if you like," she said. "Only — only I must have Maggie with me."

"Yes, if you like," answered Paul, in some surprise.

The clock struck ten, and Etta's eyes recovered their brightness. Womanlike, she lived for the present. The responsibility of the future is essentially a man's affair. The present contained a ball, and it was only in the future that Osterno and Russia had to be faced. Let us also give Etta Alexis her due. She was almost fearless. It is permissible to the bravest to be startled. She was now quite collected. The even, delicate color had returned to her face.

"Maggie is such a splendid companion," she said lightly. "She is so easy to please. I think she would come if you asked her, Paul."

"If you want her, I shall ask her, of course; but it may hinder us a little. I thought you might be able to help us — with the women, you know."

There was a queer little smile on Etta's face — a smile, one might have thought, of contempt.

"Yes, of course," she said. "It is so nice to be able to do good with one's money."

Paul looked at her in his slow, grave way, but he said nothing. He knew that his wife was cleverer and brighter than himself. He was simple enough to think that this superiority of intellect might be devoted to the good of the peasants of Osterno.

"It is not a bad place," he said — "a very fine castle, one of the finest in Europe. Before I came away I gave orders for your rooms to be done up. I should like everything to be nice for you."

"I know you would, dear," she answered, glancing at the clock. (The carriage was ordered for a quarter-past ten.) "But

I suppose," she went on, "that, socially speaking, we shall be rather isolated. Our neighbors are few and far between."

"The nearest," said Paul quietly, "are the Lanovitches."

"*Who?*"

"The Lanovitches. Do you know them?"

"Of course not," answered Etta sharply. "But I seem to know the name. Were there any in St. Petersburg?"

"The same people," answered Paul; "Count Stépan Lanovitch."

Etta was looking at her husband with her bright smile. It was a little too bright, perhaps. Her eyes had a gleam in them. She was conscious of being beautifully dressed, conscious of her own matchless beauty, almost dauntless, like a very strong man armed.

"Well, I think I am a model wife," she said: "to give in meekly to your tyranny; to go and bury myself in the heart of Russia in the middle of winter — By the way, we must buy some furs; that will be rather exciting. But you must not expect me to be very intimate with your Russian friends. I am not quite sure that I like Russians" — she went toward him, laying her two hands gently on his broad breast and looking up at him — "not quite sure — especially Russian princes who bully their wives. You may kiss me, however, but be very careful. Now I must go and finish dressing. We shall be late as it is."

She gathered together her fan and gloves, for she had petulantly dragged off a pair which did not fit.

"And you will ask Maggie to come with us?" she said.

He held open the door for her to pass out, gravely polite even to his wife — this old-fashioned man.

"Yes," he answered; "but why do you want me to ask her?"

"Because I want her to come."

Chapter XVII

CHARITY

*I*n these democratic days a very democratic theory has exploded. Not so very long ago we believed, or made semblance of belief, that it is useless to put a high price upon a ticket with the object of securing that selectness for which the highborn crave. "If they want to come," Lady Champignon (wife of Alderman Champignon) would say, "they do not mind paying the extra half-guinea."

But Lady Champignon was wrong. It is not that the self-made man cannot or will not pay two guineas for a ball-ticket. It is merely that, in his commercial way, he thinks that he will not have his money's worth, and therefore prefers keeping his two guineas to spend on something more tangible — say food. The nouveau riche never quite purges his mind of the instinct commercial, and it therefore goes against the grain to pay heavily for a form of entertainment which his soul had not the opportunity of learning to love in its youth. The aristocrat, on the other hand, has usually been brought up to the cultivation of enjoyment, and he therefore spends with perfect equanimity more on his pleasure than the bourgeois mind can countenance.

The ball to which Paul and Etta were going was managed by some titled ladies who knew their business well. The price of the tickets was fabulous. The lady patronesses of the great Charity Ball were tactful and unabashed. They drew the necessary line (never more necessary than it is today) with a firm hand.

The success of the ball was therefore a foregone conclusion. In French fiction there is invariably a murmur of applause when the heroine enters a room full of people, which fact serves, at all events, to show the breeding and social status of persons with whom French novelists are in the habit of associating. There was therefore no applause when Paul and Etta made their appearance, but that lady had, nevertheless, the satisfaction of perceiving glances, not only of admiration, but of interest and even of disapproval, among her own sex. Her dress she knew to be perfect, and when she perceived the craning pale face of the inevitable lady-journalist, peering between the balusters of a gallery, she thoughtfully took up a prominent position immediately beneath that gallery, and slowly turned round like a beautifully garnished joint before the fire of cheap publicity.

To Paul this ball was much like others. There were a number of the friends of his youth — tall, clean-featured, clean-limbed men, with a tendency toward length and spareness — who greeted him almost affectionately. Some of them introduced him to their wives and sisters, which ladies duly set him down as nice but dull — a form of faint praise which failed to damn. There were a number of ladies to whom it was necessary for him to bow in acknowledgment of past favors which had missed their mark. From the gallery the washed-out female journalists poked out their eager faces — for they were women still, and liked to look upon a man when he was strong.

And all the while Karl Steinmetz was storming in his guttural English at the door, upbraiding hired waiters for their stupidity in accepting two literal facts literally. The one fact was that they were forbidden to admit anyone without a ticket; the second fact being that tickets were not to be obtained at the price of either one or the other of the two great motives of man — Love or Money.

Steinmetz was Teutonic and imposing, with the ribbon of a great Order on his breast. He mentioned the names of several ladies who might have been, but were not, of the committee. Finally, however, he mentioned the historic name of one whose husband had braved more than one Russian emperor successfully for England.

"Yes, me lord, her ladyship's here," answered the man.

Steinmetz wrote on a card, "In memory of '56, let me in," and sent in the missive.

A few minutes later a stout, smiling lady came toward him with outstretched hand.

"What mischief are you about?" she enquired, "you stormy petrel! This is no place for your deep-laid machinations. We are here to enjoy ourselves and found a hospital. Come in, however. I am delighted to see you. You used to be a famous dancer — well, some little time ago."

"Yes, my dear countess, let us say some little time ago. Ach, those were days! those were days! You do not mind the liberty I have taken?"

"I am glad you took it. But your card gave me a little tug at the heart. It brought back so much. And still plain Karl Steinmetz — after all. We used to think much of you in the old days. Who would have thought that all the honors would have slipped past you?"

Steinmetz shrugged his shoulders with a heart-whole laugh.

"Ah, what matter? Who cares, so long as my old friends remember me? Who would have thought, my dear madam, that the map of Europe would have been painted the colors it is today? It was a kaleidoscope — the clatter of many stools, and I fell down between them all. Still plain Karl Steinmetz — still very much at your service. Shall I send my check for five guineas to you?"

"Yes, do; I am secretary. Always businesslike; a wonderful man you are still."

"And you, my dear countess, a wonderful lady. Always gay, always courageous. I have heard and sympathized. I have heard of many blows and wounds that you have received in the battle we began — well, some little time ago."

"Ah, don't mention them! They hurt nonetheless because we cover them with a smile, eh? I dare say you know. You have been in the thick of the fight yourself. But you did not come here to chat with me, though your manner might lead one to think so. I will not keep you."

"I came to see Prince Pavlo," answered Steinmetz. "I must thank you for enabling me to do so. I may not see you again this evening. My best thanks, my very dear lady."

He bowed, and with his half-humorous, half-melancholy smile, left her.

The first face he recognized was a pretty one. Miss Maggie Delafield was just turning away from a partner who was taking his congé, when she looked across the room and saw Steinmetz. He had only met her once, barely exchanging six words with her, and her frank, friendly bow was rather a surprise to him. She came toward him, holding out her hand with an open friendliness which this young lady was in the habit of bestowing upon men and women impartially — upon persons of either sex who happened to meet with her approval. She did not know what made her incline to like this man, neither did she seek to know. In a quiet, British way Miss Delafield was a creature of impulse. Her likes and dislikes were a matter of instinct, and, much as one respects the doctrine of charity, it is a question whether an instinctive dislike should be quashed by an exaggerated sense of neighborly duty. Steinmetz she liked, and there was an end to it.

"I was afraid you did not recognize me," she said.

"My life has not so many pleasures that I can afford to forget one of them," replied Steinmetz, in his somewhat old-fashioned courtesy. "But an old — buffer, shall I say? — hardly expects to be taken much notice of by young ladies at a ball."

"It is not ten minutes since Paul assured me that you were the best dancer that Vienna ever produced," said the girl, looking at him with bright, honest eyes.

Karl Steinmetz looked down at her, for he was a tall man when Paul Alexis was not near. His quiet gray eyes were almost affectionate. There was a sudden sympathy between these two, and sudden sympathies are the best.

"Will you give an old man a trial?" he asked. "They will laugh at you."

She handed him her program.

"Let them laugh!" she said.

He took the next dance, which happened to be vacant on her card. Almost immediately the music began, and they glided off together. Maggie began with the feeling that she was dancing with her own father, but this wore off before they had made much progress through the crowd, and gave way to the sensation that she had for partner the best dancer she had ever met, gray-haired, stout, and middle-aged.

"I wanted to speak to you," she said.

"Ah!" Steinmetz answered. He was steering with infinite skill. In that room full of dancers no one touched Maggie's elbow or the swing of her dress, and she, who knew what such things meant, smiled as she noted it.

"I have been asked to go and stay at Osterno," she said. "Shall I go?"

"By whom?"

"By Paul."

"Then go," said Steinmetz, making one of the few mistakes of his life.

"You think so — you want me to go?"

"Ach! you must not put it like that. How well you dance — colossal! But it does not affect me — your going, fraülein."

"Since you will be there?"

"Does that make a difference, my dear young lady?"

"Of course it does."

"I wonder why."

"So do I," answered Maggie frankly. "I wonder why. I have been wondering why, ever since Paul asked me. If you had not been going I should have said 'No' at once."

Karl Steinmetz laughed quietly.

"What do I represent?" he asked.

"Safety," she replied at once.

She gave a queer little laugh and went on dancing.

"And Paul?" he said, after a little while.

"Strength," replied Maggie promptly.

He looked down at her — a momentary glance of wonder. He was like a woman, inasmuch as he judged a person by a flicker of the eyelids — a glance, a silence — in preference to judging by the spoken word.

"Then with us both to take care of you, may we hope that you will brave the perils of Osterno? Ah — the music is stopping."

"If I may assure my mother that there are no perils."

Something took place beneath the gray mustache — a smile or a pursing up of the lips in doubt.

"Ah, I cannot go so far as that. You may assure Lady Delafield that I will protect you as I would my own daughter. If — well, if the good God in heaven had not had other uses for me I should have had a daughter of your age. Ach! the music has stopped. The music always does stop, Miss Delafield; that is the worst of it. Thank you for dancing with an old buffer."

He took her back to her chaperon, bowed in his old-world way to both ladies, and left them.

"If I can help it, my very dear young friend," he said to himself as he crossed the room, looking for Paul, "you will not go to Osterno."

He found Paul talking to two men.

"You here!" said Paul, in surprise.

"Yes," answered Steinmetz, shaking hands. "I gave Lady Fontain five guineas to let me in, and now I want a couple of chairs and a quiet corner, if the money includes such."

"Come up into the gallery," replied Paul.

A certain listlessness which had been his a moment before vanished when Paul recognized his friend. He led the way up the narrow stairs. In the gallery they found a few people — couples seeking, like themselves, a rare solitude.

"What news?" asked Paul, sitting down.

"Bad!" replied Steinmetz. "We have had the misfortune to make a dangerous enemy — Claude de Chauxville."

"Claude de Chauxville," repeated Paul.

"Yes. He wanted to marry your wife — for her money."

Paul leaned forward and dragged at his great fair mustache. He was not a subtle man, analyzing his own thoughts. Had he been, he might have wondered why he was not more jealous in respect to Etta.

"Or," went on Steinmetz, "it may have been — the other thing. It is a singular thing that many men incapable of a lifelong love, can conceive a lifelong hatred based on that love. Claude de Chauxville has hated me all his life; for very good reasons, no doubt. You are now included in his antipathy because you married madame."

"I dare say," replied Paul carelessly. "But I am not afraid of Claude de Chauxville, or any other man."

"I am," said Steinmetz. "He is up to some mischief. I was

calling on the Countess Lanovitch in Petersburg when in walked Claude de Chauxville. He was constrained at the sight of my stout person, and showed it, which was a mistake. Now, what is he doing in Petersburg? He has not been there for ten years, at least. He has no friends there. He revived a minute acquaintance with the Countess Lanovitch, who is a fool of the very first water. Before I came away I heard from Catrina that he had wheedled an invitation to Thors out of the old lady. Why, my friend, why?"

Paul reflected, with a frown.

"We do not want him out there," he said.

"No; and if he goes there you must remain in England this winter."

Paul looked up sharply.

"I do not want to do that. It is all arranged," he said. "Etta was very much against going at first, but I persuaded her to do so. It would be a mistake not to go now."

Looking at him gravely, Steinmetz muttered, "I advise you not to go."

Paul shrugged his shoulders.

"I am sorry," he said. "It is too late now. Besides, I have invited Miss Delafield, and she has practically accepted."

"Does that matter?" asked Steinmetz quietly.

"Yes. I do not want her to think that I am a changeable sort of person."

Steinmetz rose, and standing with his two hands on the marble rail he looked down into the room below. The music of a waltz was just beginning, and some of the more enthusiastic spirits had already begun dancing, moving in and out among the uniforms and gay dresses.

"Well," he said resignedly; "it is as you will. There is a certain pleasure in outwitting De Chauxville. He is so d———d clever!"

Chapter XVIII
IN THE CHAMPS ÉLYSÉES

"Y ou must accept," Steinmetz repeated to Paul. "There is no help for it. We cannot afford to offend Vassili, of all people in the world."

They were standing together in the saloon of a suite of rooms assigned for the time to Paul and his party in the Hôtel Bristol in Paris. Steinmetz, who held an open letter in his hand, looked out of the window across the quiet Place Vendôme. A north wind was blowing with true Parisian keenness, driving before it a fine snow, which adhered bleakly to the northern face of a column which is chiefly remarkable for the facility with which it falls and rises again.

Steinmetz looked at the letter with a queer smile. He held it out from him as if he distrusted the very stationery.

"So friendly," he exclaimed; "so very friendly! 'Ce bon Steinmetz' he calls me. 'Ce bon Steinmetz' — confound his cheek! He hopes that his dear prince will waive ceremony and bring his charming princess to dine quite en famille at his little pied à terre in the Champs Élysées. He guarantees that only his sister, the marquise, will be present, and he hopes that 'Ce bon Steinmetz,' will accompany you, and also the young lady, the cousin of the princess."

Steinmetz threw the letter down on the table, left it there for a moment, and then, picking it up, he crossed the room and threw it into the fire.

"Which means," he explained, "that M. Vassili knows we are here, and unless we dine with him we shall be subjected to annoyance and delay on the frontier by a stupid — a singularly and suspiciously stupid — minor official. If we refuse, Vassili will conclude that we are afraid of him. Therefore we must accept. Especially as Vassili has his weak points. He loves a lord, 'Ce Vassili.' If you accept on some of that stationery I ordered for you with a colossal gold coronet, that will already be of some effect. A chain is as strong as its weakest link. M. Vassili's weakest link will be touched by your gorgeous note-paper. If ce cher prince and la charmante princesse are gracious to him, Vassili is already robbed of half his danger."

Paul laughed. It was his habit either to laugh or to grumble at Karl Steinmetz's somewhat subtle precautions. The word "danger" invariably made him laugh, with a ring in his voice which seemed to betoken enjoyment.

"Of course," he said, "I leave these matters to you. Let us show Vassili, at all events, that we are not afraid of him."

"Then sit down and accept."

That which M. Vassili was pleased to call his little dog-hole in the Champs Élysées was, in fact, a gorgeous house in the tawdry style of modern Paris — resplendent in gray iron railings, and high gateposts surmounted by green cactus plants cunningly devised in cast iron.

The heavy front door was thrown open by a lackey, and others bowed in the halls as if by machinery. Two maids pounced upon the ladies with the self-assurance of their kind and country, and led the way upstairs, while the men removed fur coats in the hall. It was all very princely and gorgeous and Parisian.

Vassili and his sister the marquise — a stout lady in ruby velvet and amethysts, who invariably caused Maggie Delafield's mouth to twitch whenever she opened her own during the evening — received the guests in the drawing room. They were standing on the white fur hearthrug side by side, when the doors were dramatically thrown open, and the servant rolled the names unctuously over his tongue.

Steinmetz, who was behind, saw everything. He saw Vassili's masklike face contract with stupefaction when he set eyes on Etta. He saw the self-contained Russian give a little gasp, and mutter an exclamation before he collected himself sufficiently to bow and conceal his face. But he could not see Etta's face for a moment or two — until the formal greetings were over. When he did see it, he noted that it was as white as marble.

"Aha! Ce bon Steinmetz!" cried Vassili, with less formality, holding out his hand with frank and boyish good humor.

"Aha! Ce cher Vassili!" returned Steinmetz, taking the hand.

"It is good of you, M. le Prince, and you, madame, to honor us in our small house," said the marquise in a guttural voice such as one might expect from within ruby velvet and amethysts. Thereafter she subsided into silence and obscurity so far as the evening was concerned and the present historian is interested.

"So," said Vassili, with a comprehensive bow to all his guests — "so you are bound for Russia. But I envy you — I envy you. You know Russia, Mme. la Princesse?"

Etta met his veiled gaze calmly.

"A little," she replied.

There was no sign of recognition in his eyes now, nor pallor on her face.

"A beautiful country, but the rest of Europe does not believe it. And the estate of the prince is one of the vastest, if not the most beautiful. It is a sporting estate, is it not, prince?"

"Essentially so," replied Paul. "Bears, wolves, deer, besides, of course, black game, capercailzie, ptarmigan — everything one could desire."

"Speaking as a sportsman," suggested Vassili gravely.

"Speaking as a sportsman."

"Of course —" Vassili paused, and with a little gesture of the hand included Steinmetz in the conversation. It may have been that he preferred to have him talking than watching. "Of course, like all great Russian landholders, you have your troubles with the people, though you are not, strictly speaking, within the famine district."

"Not quite; we are not starving, but we are hungry," said Steinmetz bluntly.

Vassili laughed, and shook a gold eye-glass chidingly.

"Ah, my friend, your old pernicious habit of calling a spade a spade! It is unfortunate that they should hunger a little, but what will you? They must learn to be provident, to work harder and drink less. With such people experience is the only taskmaster possible. It is useless talking to them. It is dangerous to pauperize them. Besides, the accounts that one reads in the newspapers are manifestly absurd and exaggerated. You must not, mademoiselle," he said, turning courteously to Maggie, "you must not believe all you are told about Russia."

"I do not," replied Maggie, with an honest smile which completely baffled M. Vassili. He had not had much to do with people who smiled honestly.

"Vrai!" he said, with grave emphasis; "I am not joking. It is a matter of the strictest fact that fiction has for the moment fixed its fancy upon my country — just as it has upon the East End of your London. Mon Dieu! what a lot of harm fiction with a purpose can do!"

"But we do not take our facts from fiction in England," said Maggie.

"Nor," put in Steinmetz, with his blandest smile, "do we allow fiction to affect our facts."

Vassili glanced at Steinmetz sideways.

"Here is dinner," he said. "Mme. la Princesse, may I have the honor?"

The table was gorgeously decorated; the wine was perfect; the dishes Parisian. Everything was brilliant, and Etta's spirits rose. Such little things affect the spirits of such little-minded women. It requires a certain mental reserve from which to extract cheerfulness over a chop and a pint of beer withal, served on a doubtful cloth. But some of us find it easy enough to be witty and brilliant over good wine and a perfectly appointed table.

"It is exile; it is nothing short of exile," protested Vassili, who led the conversation. "Much as I admire my own country, as a country, I do not pretend to regret a fate that keeps me resident in Paris. For men it is different, but for madame, and for you, mademoiselle — ach!" He shrugged his shoulders and looked up to the ceiling in mute appeal to the gods above it. "Beauty, brilliancy, wit — they are all lost in Russia."

He bowed to the princess, who was looking, and to Maggie, who was not.

"What would Paris say if it knew what it was losing?" he added in a lower tone to Etta, who smiled, well pleased. She was not always able to distinguish between impertinence and flattery. And indeed they are so closely allied that the distinction is subtle.

Steinmetz, on the left hand of the marquise, addressed one or two remarks to that lady, who replied with her mouth full. He soon discovered that that which was before her interested her more than anything around, and during the banquet he contented himself by uttering an exclamation of delight at a particular flavor which the lady was kind enough to point out to him with an eloquent and emphatic fork from time to time.

Vassili noted this with some disgust. He would have preferred that Karl Steinmetz were greedy or more conversational.

"But," the host added aloud, "ladies are so good. Perhaps you are interested in the peasants?"

Etta looked at Steinmetz, who gave an imperceptible nod.

"Yes," she answered, "I am."

Vassili followed her glance, and found Steinmetz eating with grave appreciation of the fare provided.

"Ah!" he said in an expectant tone; "then you will no doubt pass much of your time in endeavoring to alleviate their troubles — their self-inflicted troubles, with all deference to ce cher prince."

"Why with deference to me?" asked Paul, looking up quietly, with something in his steady gaze that made Maggie glance anxiously at Steinmetz.

"Well, I understand that you hold different opinions," said the Russian.

"Not at all," answered Paul. "I admit that the peasants have themselves to blame — just as a dog has himself to blame when he is caught in a trap."

"Is the case analogous? Let me recommend those olives — I have them from Barcelona by a courier."

"Quite," answered Paul; "and it is the obvious duty of those who know better to teach the dog to avoid the places where the traps are set. Thanks, the olives are excellent."

"Ah!" said Vassili, turning courteously to Maggie, "I some-times thank my star that I am not a landholder — only a poor bureaucrat. It is so difficult to comprehend these questions, mademoiselle. But of all men in or out of Russia it is possible our dear prince knows best of what he is talking."

"Oh, no!" disclaimed Paul, with that gravity at which some were ready to laugh. "I only judge in a small way from, a small experience."

"Ah! you are too modest. You know the peasants thor-oughly, you understand them, you love them — so, at least, I have been told. Is it not so, Mme. la Princesse?"

Karl Steinmetz was frowning over an olive.

"I really do not know," said Etta, who had glanced across the table.

"I assure you, madame, it is so. I am always hearing good of you, prince."

"From whom?" asked Paul.

Vassili shrugged his peculiarly square shoulders.

"Ah! From all and sundry."

"I did not know the prince had so many enemies," said Steinmetz bluntly, whereat the marquise laughed suddenly, and apparently approached within bowing distance of apo-plexy.

In such wise the conversation went on during the dinner, which was a long one. Continually, repeatedly, Vassili ap-proached the subject of Osterno and the daily life in that sequestered country. But those who knew were silent, and it was obvious that Etta and Maggie were ignorant of the life to which they were going.

From time to time Vassili raised his dull, yellow eyes to the servants, who d'ailleurs were doing their work perfectly, and invariably the master's glance fell to the glasses again. These the servants never left in peace — constantly replenishing, constantly watching with that assiduity which makes men thirsty against their will by reason of the repeated reminder.

But tongues wagged no more freely for the choice vintages poured upon them. Paul had a grave, strong head and that self-control against which alcohol may ply itself in vain. Karl Steinmetz had taken his degree at Heidelberg. He was a seasoned vessel, having passed that way before.

Etta was bright enough — amusing, light, and gay — so long as it was a question of mere social gossip; but whenever Vassili spoke of the country to which he expressed so deep a devotion, she, seeming to take her cue from her husband and his agent, fell to pleasant, non-committing silence.

It was only after dinner, in the drawing room, while musicians discoursed Offenbach and Rossini from behind a screen of fern and flower, that Vassili found an opportunity of addressing himself directly to Etta. In part she desired this opportunity, with a breathless apprehension behind her bright society smile. Without her assistance he never would have had it.

"It is most kind of you," he said in French, which language had been spoken all the evening in courtesy to the marquise, who was now asleep — "it is most kind of you to condescend to visit my poor house, princess. Believe me, I feel the honor deeply. When you first came into the room — you may have observed it — I was quite taken aback. I — I have read in books of beauty capable of taking away a man's breath. You must excuse me — I am a plain-spoken man. I never met it until this evening."

Etta excused him readily enough. She could forgive plenty of plain-speaking of this description. Had she not been inordinately vain, this woman, like many, would have been extraordinarily clever. She laughed, with little sidelong glances.

"I only hope that you will honor Paris on your way home to England," went on Vassili, who had a wonderful knack of judging men and women, especially shallow ones. "Now, when may that be? When may we hope to see you again? How long will you be in Russia, and —"

"Ce Vassili is the best English scholar I know!" broke in Steinmetz, who had approached somewhat quietly. "But he will not talk, princess — he is so shy."

Paul was approaching also. It was eleven o'clock, he said, and travelers who had to make an early start would do well to get home to bed.

When the tall doors had been closed behind the departing guests, Vassili walked slowly to the fireplace. He posted himself on the bear-skin hearthrug, his perfectly shod feet well apart — a fine dignified figure of a man, of erect and military carriage; a very mask of a face — soulless, colorless, emotionless ever.

He stood biting at his thumb-nail, looking at the door through which Etta Alexis had just passed in all the glory of her beauty, wealth, and position.

"The woman," he said slowly, "who sold me the Charity League papers — and she thinks I do not recognize her!"

Chapter XIX

ON THE NEVA

*K*arl Steinmetz had apparently been transacting business on the Vassili Ostrov, which the traveled reader doubtless knows as the northern bank of the Neva, a part of Petersburg — an island, as the name tells us, where business is transacted; where steamers land their cargoes and riverside loafers impede the traffic.

What the business of Karl Steinmetz may have been is not of moment or interest; moreover, it was essentially the affair of a man capable of holding his own and his tongue against the world.

He was recrossing the river, not by the bridge, which requires a doffed hat by reason of its shrine, but by one of the numerous roads cut across the ice from bank to bank. He duly reached the southern shore, ascending to the Admiralty Gardens by a flight of sanded steps. Here he lighted a cigar, and, tucking his hands deep into the pockets of his fur coat, he proceeded to walk slowly through the bare and deserted public garden.

A girl had crossed the river in front of him at a smart pace. She now slackened her speed so much as to allow him to pass her. Karl Steinmetz noticed the action. He noticed most things — this dull German. Presently she passed him again. She dropped her umbrella, and before picking it up described a circle with it — a maneuver remarkably like a signal. Then she turned abruptly and looked into his face, displaying a pleasing little round physiognomy with a smiling mouth and exaggeratedly grave eyes. It was a face of all too common a type in these days of cheap educational literature — the face of a womanly woman engaged in unwomanly work.

Then she came back.

Steinmetz raised his hat in his most fatherly way.

"My dear young lady," he said in Russian, "if my personal appearance has made so profound an impression as my vanity prompts me to believe, would it not be decorous of you to conceal your feelings beneath a maiden modesty? If, on the other hand, the signals you have been making to me are of profound political importance, let me assure you that I am no Nihilist."

"Then," said the girl, beginning to walk by his side, "what are you?"

"What you see — a stout middle-aged man in easy circumstances, happily placed in social obscurity. Which means that I have few enemies and fewer friends."

The girl looked as if she would like to laugh, had such exercise been in keeping with a professional etiquette.

"Your name is Karl Steinmetz," she said gravely.

"That is the name by which I am known to a large staff of creditors," replied he.

"If you will go to No. 4, Passage Kazan, at the back of the cathedral, second-floor back room on the left at the top of the stairs, and go straight into the room, you will find a friend who wishes to see you," she said, as one repeating a lesson by rote.

"And who are you, my dear young lady!"

"I — I am no one. I am only a paid agent."

"Ah!"

They walked on in silence a few paces. The bells of St. Isaac's Church suddenly burst out into a wild carillon, as is their way, effectually preventing further conversation for a few moments.

"Will you go?" asked the girl, when the sound had broken off as suddenly as it had commenced.

"Probably. I am curious and not nervous — except of damp sheets. My anonymous friend does not expect me to stay all night, I presume. Did he — or is it a she, my fatal beauty? — did *it* not name an hour?"

"Between now and seven o'clock."

"Thank you."

"God be with you!" said the girl, suddenly wheeling round and walking away.

Without looking after her Steinmetz walked on, gradually increasing his pace. In a few minutes he reached the large house standing within iron gates at the upper end of the English quay, the house of Prince Pavlo Howard Alexis.

He found Paul alone in his study. In a few words he explained the situation.

"What do you think it means?" asked the prince.

"Heaven only knows!"

"And you will go?"

"Of course," replied Steinmetz. "I love a mystery, especially in Petersburg. It sounds so like a romance written in the Kennington Road by a lady who has never been nearer to Russia than Margate."

"I had better go with you," said Paul.

"Gott! No!" exclaimed Steinmetz; "I must go alone. I will take Parks to drive the sleigh, if I may, though. Parks is a steady man, who loves a rough-and-tumble. A typical British coachman — the brave Parks!"

"Back in time for dinner?" asked Paul.

"I hope so. I have had such mysterious appointments thrust upon me before. It is probably a friend who wants a hundred-ruble note until next Monday."

The cathedral clock struck six as Karl Steinmetz turned out of the Nevski Prospekt into the large square before the sacred edifice. He soon found the Kazan Passage — a very nest of toyshops — and, following the directions given, he mounted a narrow staircase. He knocked at the door on the left hand at the top of the stairs.

"Come in!" said a voice which caused him to start.

He pushed open the door. The room was a small one, brilliantly lighted by a paraffin lamp. At the table sat an old man with broad benevolent face, high forehead, thin hair, and that smile which savors of the milk of human kindness, and in England suggests Nonconformity.

"You!" ejaculated Steinmetz. "Stépan!"

"Yes. Come in and close the door."

He laid aside his pen, extended his hand, and, rising, kissed Karl Steinmetz on both cheeks after the manner of Russians.

"Yes, my dear Karl. It seems that the good God has still a little work for Stépan Lanovitch to do. I got away quite easily, in the usual way, through a paid Evasion Agency. I have been forwarded from pillar to post like a prize fowl, and reached Petersburg last night. I have not long to stay. I am going south. I may be able to do some good yet. I hear that Paul is working wonders in Tver."

"What about money?" asked Steinmetz, who was always practical.

"Catrina sent it, the dear child! That is one of the conditions made by the Agency — a hard one. I am to see no relations. My wife — well, bon Dieu! it does not matter much. She is occupied in keeping herself warm, no doubt. But Catrina! that is a different matter. Tell me — how is she? That is the first thing I want to know."

"She is well," answered Steinmetz. "I saw her yesterday."

"And happy?" The broad-faced man looked into Steinmetz's face with considerable keenness.

"Yes."

It was a moment for mental reservations. One wonders whether such are taken account of in heaven.

"And Paul?" asked the Count Stépan Lanovitch at once. "Tell me about him."

"He is married," answered Steinmetz.

The Count Lanovitch was looking at the lamp. He continued to look at it as if interested in the mechanism of the burner. Then he turned his eyes to the face of his companion.

"I wonder, my friend," he said slowly, "how much you

know?"

"Nothing," answered Steinmetz.

The count looked at him enquiringly, heaved a sharp sigh, and abandoned the subject.

"Well," he said, "let us get to business. I have much to ask and to tell you. I want you to see Catrina and to tell her that I am safe and well, but she must not attempt to see me or correspond with me for some years yet. Of course you heard no account of my trial. I was convicted, on the evidence of paid witnesses, of inciting to rebellion. It was easy enough, of course. I shall live either in the south or in Austria. It is better for you to be in ignorance."

Steinmetz nodded his head curtly.

"I do not want to know," he said.

"Will you please ask Catrina to send me money through the usual channel? No more than she has been sending. It will suffice for my small wants. Perhaps some day we may meet in Switzerland or in America. Tell the dear child that. Tell her I pray the good God to allow that meeting. As for Russia, her day has not come yet. It will not come in our time, my dear friend. We are only the sowers. So much for the future. Now about the past. I have not been idle. I know who stole the papers of the Charity League and sold them. I know who bought them and paid for them."

Steinmetz closed the door. He came back to the table. He was not smiling now — quite the contrary.

"Tell me," he said. "I want to know that badly."

The Count Lanovitch looked up with a peculiar soft smile — acquired in prison. There is no mistaking it.

"Oh, I bear no ill will," he said.

"I do," answered Steinmetz bluntly. "Who stole the papers from Thors?"

"Sydney Bamborough."

"Good God in heaven! Is that true?"

"Yes, my friend."

Steinmetz passed his broad hand over his forehead as if dazed.

"And who sold them?" he asked.

"His wife."

Count Lanovitch was looking at the burner of the lamp.

There was a peculiar crushed look about the man, as if he had reached the end of his life, and was lying like a ship, hopelessly disabled in smooth water, where nothing could affect him more.

Steinmetz scratched his forehead with one finger, reflectively.

"Vassili bought them," he said; "I can guess that."

"You guess right," returned Lanovitch quietly.

Steinmetz sat down. He looked round as if wondering whether the room was very hot. Then with a large handkerchief he wiped his brow.

"You have surprised me," he admitted. "There are complications. I shall sit up all night with your news, my dear Stépan. Have you details? Wonderful — wonderful! Of course there is a God in heaven. How can people doubt it — eh?"

"Yes," said Stépan Lanovitch quietly. "There is a God in heaven, and at present he is angry with Russia. Yes, I have details. Sydney Bamborough came to stay at Thors. Of course he knew all about the Charity League — you remember that. It appears that his wife was waiting for him and the papers at Tver. He took them from my room, but he did not get them all. Had he got them all you would not be sitting there, my friend. The general scheme he got — the list of committee names, the local agents, the foreign agents. But the complete list of the League he failed to find. He secured the list of subscribers, but learned nothing from it because the sums were identified by a numeral only, the clue to the numbers being the complete list, which I burned when I missed the other papers."

Steinmetz nodded curtly.

"That was wise," he said. "You are a clever man, Stépan, but too good for this world and its rascals. Go on."

"It would appear that Bamborough rode to Tver with the papers, which he handed to his wife. She took them to Paris while he intended to come back to Thors. He had a certain cheap cunning and unbounded impertinence. But — as you know, perhaps — he disappeared."

"Yes," said Steinmetz, scratching his forehead with one finger. "Yes — he disappeared."

Karl Steinmetz had one great factor of success in this world

— an infinite capacity for holding his cards.

"One more item," said the count, in his businesslike, calm way. "Vassili paid that woman seven thousand pounds for the papers."

"And probably charged his masters ten," added Steinmetz.

"And now you must go!"

The count rose and looked at his watch — a cheap American article, with a loud tick. He held it out with his queer washed-out smile, and Steinmetz smiled.

The two embraced again — and there was nothing funny in the action. It is a singular thing that the sight of two men kissing is conducive either to laughter or to tears. There is no medium emotion.

"My dear friend — my very dear friend," said the count, "God be with you always. We may meet again — or we may not."

Steinmetz walked down the Nevski Prospekt on the left-hand pavement — no one walks on the other — and the sleigh followed him. He turned into a large, brilliantly lighted café, and loosened his coat.

"Give me beer," he said to the waiter; "a very large quantity of it."

The man smiled obsequiously as he set the foaming mug before him.

"Is it that his Excellency is cold?" he enquired.

"No, it isn't," answered Steinmetz. "Quite the contrary."

He drank the beer, and holding out his hand in the shadow of the table, he noticed that it trembled only a little.

"That is better," he murmured. "But I must sit here a while longer. I suppose I was upset. That is what they call it — upset! I have never been like that before. Those lamps in the Prospekt! Gott! how they jumped up and down!"

He pressed his hand over his eyes as if to shut out the brightness of the room — the glaring gas and brilliant decorations — the shining bottles and the many tables which would not keep still.

"Here," he said to the man, "give me more beer."

Presently he rose, and, getting rather clumsily into his sleigh, drove back at the usual breakneck pace to the palace at the upper end of the English Quay.

He sent an ambiguous message to Paul, saying that he had returned and was dressing for dinner. This ceremony he went through slowly, as one dazed by a great fall or a heavy fatigue. His servant, a quick, silent man, noticed the strangeness of his manner, and like a wise servant only betrayed the result of his observation by a readier service, a quicker hand, a quieter motion.

As Steinmetz went to the drawing room he glanced at his watch. It was twenty minutes past seven. He still had ten minutes to spare before dinner.

He opened the drawing room door. Etta was sitting by the fire, alone. She glanced back over her shoulder in a quick, hunted way which had only become apparent to Steinmetz since her arrival at Petersburg.

"Good-evening," she said.

"Good-evening, madame," he answered.

He closed the door carefully behind him.

Chapter XX

AN OFFER OF FRIENDSHIP

*E*tta did not move when Steinmetz approached, except, indeed, to push one foot farther out toward the warmth of the wood fire. She certainly was very neatly shod. Steinmetz was one of her few failures. She had never got any nearer to the man. Despite his gray hair and bulky person she argued that he was still a man, and therefore an easy victim to flattery — open to the influence of beauty.

"I wonder why," she said, looking into the fire, "you hate me."

Steinmetz looked down at her with his grim smile. The mise en scène was perfect, from the thoughtful droop of the head to the innocent display of slipper.

"I wonder why you think that of me," he replied.

"One cannot help perceiving that which is obvious."

"While that which is purposely made obvious serves to conceal that which may exist behind it," replied the stout man.

Etta paused to reflect over this. Was Steinmetz going to make love to her? She was not an inexperienced girl, and knew that there was nothing impossible or even improbable in the thought. She wondered what Karl Steinmetz must have been like when he was a young man. He had a deft way even now of planting a double entendre when he took the trouble. How could she know that his manner was always easiest, his attitude always politest, toward the women whom he despised. In his way this man was a philosopher. He had a theory that an exaggerated politeness is an insult to a woman's intellect.

"You think I do not care," said the Princess Howard Alexis.

"You think I do not admire you," replied Steinmetz imperturbably.

She looked up at him.

"Do you not give me every reason to think so?" she returned, with a toss of the head.

She was one of those women — and there are not a few — who would quarrel with you if you do not admire them.

"Not intentionally, princess. I am, as you know, a German of no very subtle comprehension. My position in your household appears to me to be a little above the servants, although the prince is kind enough to make a friend of me and his friends are so good as to do the same. I do not complain. Far from it. I am well paid. I am interested in my work. I am more or less my own master. I am very fond of Paul. You — are kind and forbearing. I do my best — in a clumsy way, no doubt — to spare you my heavy society. But of course I do not presume to form an opinion upon your — upon you."

"But I want you to form an opinion," she said petulantly.

"Then you must know that I could only form one which would be pleasing to you."

"I know nothing of the sort," replied Etta. "Of course I know that all that you say about position and work is mere irony. Paul thinks there is no one in the world like you."

Steinmetz glanced sharply down at her. He had never considered the possibility that she might love Paul. Was this, after all, jealousy? He had attributed it to vanity.

"And I have no doubt he is right," she went on. Suddenly she gave a little laugh. "Don't you understand?" she said. "I want to be friends."

She did not look at him, but sat with pouting lips holding out her hand.

Karl Steinmetz had been up to the elbows, as it were, in the diplomacy of an unscrupulous, grasping age ever since his college days. He had been behind the scenes in more than one European crisis, and that which goes on behind the scenes is not always edifying or conducive to a squeamishness of touch. He was not the man to be mawkishly afraid of soiling his fingers. But the small white hand rather disconcerted him.

He took it, however, in his great, warm, soft grasp, held it for a moment, and relinquished it.

"I don't want you to address all your conversation to Maggie, and to ignore me. Do you think Maggie so very pretty?"

There was a twist beneath the gray mustache as he answered, "Is that all the friendship you desire? Does it extend no farther than a passing wish to be first in petty rivalries of daily existence? I am afraid, my dear princess, that my friendship is a heavier matter — a clumsier thing than that."

"A big thing not easily moved," she suggested, looking up with her dauntless smile.

He shrugged his great shoulders.

"It may be — who knows? I hope it is," he answered.

"The worst of those big things is that they are sometimes in the way," said Etta reflectively, without looking at him.

"And yet the life that is only a conglomeration of trifles is a poor life to look back upon."

"Meaning mine?" she asked.

"Your life has not been trifling," he said gravely.

She looked up at him, and then for some moments kept silence while she idly opened and shut her fan. There was in the immediate vicinity of Karl Steinmetz a sort of atmosphere of sympathy which had the effect of compelling confidence. Even Etta was affected by it. During the silence recorded she was quelling a sudden desire to say things to this man which she had never said to any. She only succeeded in part.

"Do you ever feel an unaccountable sensation of dread," she asked, with a weary little laugh; "a sort of foreboding with nothing definite to forebode?"

"Unaccountable — no," replied Steinmetz. "But then I am a German — and stout, which may make a difference. I have no nerves."

He looked into the fire through his benevolent gold-rimmed spectacles.

"Is it nerves — or is it Petersburg?" she asked abruptly. "I think it is Petersburg. I hate Petersburg."

"Why Petersburg more than Moscow or Nijni or — Tver?"

She drew in a long, slow breath, looking him up and down the while from the corners of her eyes.

"I do not know," she replied collectedly; "I think it is damp. These houses are built on reclaimed land, I believe. This was all marsh, was it not?"

He did not answer her question, and somehow she seemed to expect no reply. He stood blinking down into the fire while she watched him furtively from the corners of her eyes, her lips parched and open, her face quite white.

A few moments before she had protested that she desired his friendship. She knew now that she could not brave his enmity. And the one word "Tver" had done it all! The mere mention of a town, obscure and squalid, on the upper waters of the mighty Volga in Mid-Russia!

During those few moments she suddenly came face to face with her position. What had she to offer this man? She looked him up and down — stout, placid, and impenetrable. Here was no common adventurer seeking place — no coxcomb seeking ladies' favors — no pauper to be bought with gold. She had no means of ascertaining how much he knew, how much he suspected. She had to deal with a man who held the best cards and would not play them. She could never hope to find out whether his knowledge and his suspicions were his alone or had been imparted to others. In her walk through life she had jostled mostly villains; and a villain is no very dangerous foe, for he fights on slippery ground. Except Paul she had never had to do with a man who was quite honest, upright, and fearless; and she had fallen into the common error of thinking that all such are necessarily simple, unsuspicious, and a little stupid.

She breathed hard, living through years of anxiety in a few moments of time, and she could only realize that she was helpless, bound hand and foot in this man's power.

It was he who spoke first. In the smaller crises of life it is usually the woman who takes this privilege upon herself; but the larger situations need a man's steadier grasp.

"My dear lady," he said, "if you are content to take my friendship as it is, it is yours. But I warn you it is no showy drawing room article. There will be no compliments, no pretty speeches, no little gifts of flowers, and such trumpery amenities. It will all be very solid and middle-aged, like myself."

"You think," returned the lady, "that I am fit for nothing better than pretty speeches and compliments and floral offerings?"

She broke off with a forced little laugh, and awaited his verdict with defiant eyes upraised. He returned the gaze through his placid spectacles; her beauty, in its setting of brilliant dress and furniture, soft lights, flowers, and a thousand feminine surroundings, failed to dazzle him.

"I do," he said quietly.

"And yet you offer me your friendship?"

He bowed in acquiescence.

"Why?" she asked.

"For Paul's sake, my dear lady."

She shrugged her shoulders and turned away from him.

"Of course," she said, "it is quite easy to be rude. As it happens, it is precisely for Paul's sake that I took the trouble of speaking to you on this matter. I do not wish him to be troubled with such small domestic affairs; and therefore, if we are to live under the same roof, I shall deem it a favor if you will, at all events, conceal your disapproval of me."

He bowed gravely and kept silence. Etta sat with a little patch of color on either cheek, looking into the fire until the door was opened and Maggie came in.

Steinmetz went toward her with his grave smile, while Etta hid a face which had grown haggard.

Maggie glanced from one to the other with frank interest. The relationship between these two had rather puzzled her of late.

"Well," said Steinmetz, "and what of St. Petersburg?"

"I am not disappointed," replied Maggie. "It is all I expected and more. I am not blasée like Etta. Everything interests me."

"We were discussing Petersburg when you came in," said Steinmetz, drawing forward a chair. "The princess does not like it. She complains of — nerves."

"Nerves!" exclaimed Maggie, turning to her cousin. "I did not suspect you of having them."

Etta smiled, a little wearily.

"One never knows," she answered, forcing herself to be light, "what one may come to in old age. I saw a gray hair this morning. I am nearly thirty-three, you know. When glamour goes, nerves come."

"Well, I suppose they do — especially in Russia, perhaps. There is a glamour about Russia, and I mean to cultivate it rather than nerves. There is a glamour about everything — the broad streets, the Neva, the snow, and the cold. Especially the people. It is always especially the people, is it not?"

"It is the people, my dear young lady, that lend interest to the world."

"Paul took me out in a sleigh this morning," went on Maggie, in her cheerful voice that knew no harm. "I liked everything — the policemen in their little boxes at the street corners, the officers in their fur coats, the cabmen, everybody. There is something so mysterious about them all. One can easily make up stories about everybody one meets in Petersburg. It is so easy to think that they are not what they seem. Paul, Etta, even you, Herr Steinmetz, may not be what you seem."

"Yes, that is so," answered Steinmetz, with a laugh.

"You may be a Nihilist," pursued Maggie. "You may have bombs concealed up your sleeves; you may exchange mysterious passwords with people in the streets; you may be much less innocent than you appear."

"All that may be so," he admitted.

"You may have a revolver in the pocket of your dress-coat," went on Maggie, pointing to the voluminous garment with her fan.

His hand went to the pocket in question, and produced exactly what she had suggested. He held out his hand with a small silver-mounted revolver lying in the palm of it.

"Even that," he said, "may be so."

Maggie looked at it with a sudden curiosity, her bright eyes grave.

"Loaded?" she asked.

"Yes."

"Then I will not examine it. How curious! I wonder how near to the mark I may have been in other ways."

"I wonder," said Steinmetz, looking at Etta. "And now tell us something about the princess. What do you suspect her of?"

At this moment Paul came into the room, distinguished-looking and grave.

"Miss Delafield," pursued Steinmetz, turning to the newcomer, "is telling us her suspicions about ourselves. I am already as good as condemned to Siberia. She is now about to sit in judgment on the princess."

Maggie laughed.

"Herr Steinmetz has pleaded guilty to the worst accusation," she said. "On the other counts I leave him to his own conscience."

"Anything but that," urged Steinmetz.

Paul came forward, and Maggie rather obviously avoided looking at him.

"Tell us of Paul's crimes first," said Etta, rather hurriedly. She glanced at the clock, whither Karl Steinmetz's eyes had also traveled.

"Oh, Paul," said Maggie, rather indifferently. Indeed, it seemed as if her lightness of heart had suddenly failed her. "Well, perhaps he is deeply involved in schemes for the resurrection of the Polish kingdom, or something of that sort."

"That sounds tame," put in Steinmetz. "I think you would construct a better romance respecting the princess. In books it is always the beautiful princesses who are most deeply dyed in crime."

Maggie opened her fan and closed it again.

"Well," she said, tapping on the arm of her chair with it; "I give Etta a mysterious past. She is the sort of person who would laugh and dance at a ball with the knowledge that there was a mine beneath the floor."

"I do not think I am," said Etta, with a shudder. She rose rather hurriedly, and crossed the room with a great rustle of silks.

"Stop her!" she whispered, as she passed Steinmetz.

Chapter XXI

A SUSPECTED HOUSE

*T*he Countess Lanovitch and Catrina were sitting together in the too-luxurious drawing room that overlooked the English Quay and the Neva. The double windows were rigorously closed, while the inner panes were covered with a thick rime. The sun was just setting over the marshes that border the upper waters of the Gulf of Finland, and lit up the snow-clad city with a rosy glow which penetrated to the room where the two women sat.

Catrina was restless, moving from chair to chair, from

fireplace to window, with a lack of repose which would certainly have touched the nerves of a less lethargic person than the countess.

"My dear child!" that lady was exclaiming with lackadaisical horror, "we cannot go to Thors yet. The thought is too horrible. You never think of my health. Besides, the gloom of the everlasting snow is too painful. It makes me think of your poor mistaken father, who is probably shoveling it in Siberia. Here, at all events, one can avoid the window — one need not look at it."

"The policy of shutting one's eyes is a mistake," said Catrina.

She had risen, and was standing by the window, her stunted form being framed, as it were, in a rosy glow of pink.

The countess heaved a little sigh and gazed idly at the fire. She did not understand Catrina. She was afraid of her. There was something rugged and dogged which the girl had inherited from her father — that Slavonic love of pain for its own sake — which makes Russian patriots and thinkers strange, incomprehensible beings.

"I question it, Catrina," said the elder lady; "but perhaps it is a matter of health. Dr. Stantovitch told me, quite between ourselves, that if I had given way to my grief at the time of the trial he would not have held himself responsible for the consequences."

"Dr. Stantovitch," said Catrina, "is a humbug."

"My dear child!" exclaimed the countess, "he attends all the noble ladies of Petersburg."

"Precisely," answered Catrina.

She was woman enough to enter into futile arguments with her mother, and man enough to despise herself for doing it.

"Why do you want to go back to Thors so soon?" murmured the elder lady, with a little sigh of despair. She knew she was playing a losing game very badly. She was mentally shuddering at the recollection of former sleigh-journeying from Tver to Thors.

"Because I am sure father would like us to be there this hard winter."

"But your father is in Siberia," put in the countess, which remark was ignored.

"Because if we do not go before the snow begins to melt we shall have to do the journey in carriages over bad roads, which is sure to knock you up. Because our place is at Thors, and no one wants us here. I hate Petersburg. It is no use living here unless one is rich and beautiful and popular. We are none of those things, so we are better at Thors."

"But we have many nice friends here, dear. You will see, this afternoon. I expect quite a reception. By the way, I hope Kupfer has sent the little cakes. Your father used to be so fond of them. I wonder if we could send him a box to Siberia. He would enjoy them, poor man! He might give some to the prison people, and thus obtain a little alleviation. Yes; the Comte de Chauxville said he would come on my first reception-day, and, of course, Paul and his wife must return my call. They will come today. I am anxious to see her. They say she is beautiful and dresses well."

Catrina's broad white teeth gleamed for a moment in the flickering firelight, as she clenched them over her lower lip.

"And therefore Paul's happiness in life is assured," she said, in a hard voice.

"Of course. What more could he want?" murmured the countess, in blissful ignorance of any irony.

Catrina looked at her mother with a gleam of utter contempt in her eyes. That is one of the privileges of a great love, whether it bring happiness or misery — the contempt for all who have never known it.

While they remained thus the sound of sleigh-bells on the quiet English Quay made itself heard through the double windows. There was a clang of many tones, and the horses pulled up with a jerk. The color left Catrina's face quite suddenly, as if wiped away, leaving her ghastly. She was going to see Paul and his wife.

Presently the door opened, and Etta came into the room with the indomitable assurance which characterized her movements and earned for her a host of feminine enemies.

"Mme. la Comtesse," she said, with her most gracious smile, taking the limp hand offered to her by the Countess Lanovitch.

Catrina stood in the embrasure of the window, hating her.

Paul followed on his wife's heels, scarcely concealing his

boredom. He was not a society man. Catrina came forward and exchanged a formal bow with Etta, who took in her plainness and the faults of her dress at one contemptuous glance. She smiled with the perfect pity of a good figure for no figure at all. Paul was shaking hands with the countess. When he took Catrina's hand her fingers were icy, and twitched nervously within his grasp.

The countess was already babbling to Etta in French. The Princess Howard Alexis always began by informing Paul's friends that she knew no Russian. For a moment Paul and Catrina were left, as it were, alone. When the countess was once fairly roused from her chronic lethargy her voice usually acquired a metallic ring which dominated any other conversation that might be going on in the room.

"I wish you happiness," said Catrina, and no one heard her but Paul. She did not raise her eyes to his, but looked vaguely at his collar. Her voice was short and rather breathless, as if she had just emerged from deep water.

"Thank you," answered Paul simply.

He turned and somewhat naturally looked at his wife. Catrina's thoughts followed his. A man is at a disadvantage in the presence of the woman who loves him. She usually sees through him — a marked difference between masculine and feminine love. Catrina looked up sharply and caught his eyes resting on Etta.

"He does not love her — he does not love her!" was the thought that instantly leaped into her brain.

And if she had said it to him he would have contradicted her flatly and honestly, and in vain.

"Yes," the countess was saying with lazy volubility; "Paul is one of our oldest friends. We are neighbors in the country, you know. He has always been in and out of our house like one of the family. My poor husband was very fond of him."

"Is your husband dead, then?" asked Etta in a low voice, with a strange haste.

"No; he is only in Siberia. You have perhaps heard of his misfortune — Count Stépan Lanovitch."

Etta nodded her head with the deepest sympathy.

"I feel for you, countess," she said. "And yet you are so brave — and mademoiselle," she said, turning to Catrina. "I hope we shall see more of each other in Tver."

Catrina bowed jerkily and made no reply. Etta glanced at her sharply. Perhaps she saw more than Catrina knew.

"I suppose," she said to the countess, with that inclusive manner which spreads the conversation out, "that Paul and Mlle. de Lanovitch were playmates?"

The reply lay with either of the ladies, but Catrina turned away.

"Yes," answered the countess; "but Catrina is only twenty-four — ten years younger than Paul."

"Indeed!" with a faint, cutting surprise.

Indeed Etta looked younger than Catrina. On a l'âge de son coeur, and if the heart be worn it transmits its weariness to the face, where such signs are ascribed to years. So the little stab was justified by Catrina's appearance.

While the party assembled were thus exchanging social amenities, a past master in such commerce joined them in the person of Claude de Chauxville.

He smiled his mechanical, heartless smile upon them all, but when he bowed over Etta's hand his face was grave. He expressed no surprise at seeing Paul and Etta, though his manner betokened that emotion. There was no sign of this meeting having been a prearranged matter, brought about by himself through the easy and innocent instrumentality of the countess.

"And you are going to Tver, no doubt?" he said almost at once to Etta.

"Yes," answered that lady, with a momentary hunted look in her eyes. It is strange how an obscure geographical name may force its way into our lives, never to be forgotten. Queen Mary of England struck a note of the human octave when she protested that the word "Calais" was graven on her heart. It seemed to Etta that "Tver" was written large wheresoever she turned, for the conscience looks through a glass and sees whatever may be written thereon overspreading every prospect.

"The prince," continued De Chauxville, turning to Paul, "is a great sportsman, I am told — a mighty hunter. I wonder why Englishmen always want to kill something."

Paul smiled, without making an immediate answer. He was

not the man to be led into the danger of repartee by such as De Chauxville.

"We have a few bears left," he said.

"You are fortunate," protested De Chauxville. "I shot one when I was younger. I was immensely afraid, and so was the bear. I have a great desire to try again."

Etta glanced at Paul, who returned De Chauxville's bland gaze with all the imperturbability of a prince.

The countess's cackling voice broke in at this juncture, as perhaps De Chauxville had intended it to do.

"Then why not come and shoot ours?" she said. "We have quite a number of them in the forests at Thors."

"Ah, Mme. la Comtesse," he answered, with outspread, deprecatory hands, "but that would be taking too great an advantage of your hospitality and your well-known kindness."

He turned to Catrina, who received him with a half-concealed frown. The countess bridled and looked at her daughter with obvious maternal meaning, as one who was saying, "There — you bungled your prince, but I have procured you a baron."

"The abuse of hospitality is the last refuge of the needy," continued De Chauxville oracularly. "But my temptation is strong; shall I yield to it, mademoiselle?"

Catrina smiled unwillingly.

"I would rather leave it to your own conscience," she said. "But I fail to see the danger you anticipate."

"Then I accept, madame," said De Chauxville, with the engaging frankness which ever had a false ring in it.

If the whole affair had been prearranged in Claude de Chauxville's mind, it certainly succeeded more fully than is usually the case with human schemes. If, on the other hand, this invitation was the result of chance, Fortune had favored Claude de Chauxville beyond his deserts.

The little scene had played itself out before the eyes of Paul, who did not want it; of Etta, who desired it; and of Catrina, who did not exactly know what she wanted, with the precision of a stage-play carefully rehearsed.

Claude de Chauxville had unscrupulously made use of feminine vanity with all the skill that was his. A little glance toward Etta, as he accepted the invitation, conveyed to her the fact that she was the object of his clever little plot; that it was in order to be near her that he had forced the Countess Lanovitch to invite him to Thors; and Etta, with all her shrewdness, was promptly hoodwinked. Vanity is a handicap assigned to clever women by Fate, who handicaps us all without appeal. De Chauxville saw by a little flicker of the eyelids that he had not missed his mark. He had hit Etta where his knowledge of her told him she was unusually vulnerable. He had made one ally. The countess he looked upon with a wise contempt. She was easier game than Etta. Catrina he understood well enough. Her rugged simplicity had betrayed her secret to him before he had been five minutes in the room. Paul he despised as a man lacking finesse and esprit — a truly French form of contempt. For Frenchmen have yet to learn that such qualities have remarkably little to do with love.

Claude de Chauxville was one of those men — alas! too many — who owe their success in life almost entirely to some feminine influence or another. Whenever he came into direct opposition to men it was his instinct to retire from the field. Behind Paul's back he despised him; before his face he cringed.

"Then, perhaps," he said, when the princess was engaged in the usual farewells with the countess, and Paul was moving toward the door — "then, perhaps, prince, we may meet again before the spring — if the countess intends her invitation to be taken seriously."

"Yes," answered Paul; "I often shoot at Thors."

"If you do not happen to come over, perhaps I may be allowed to call and pay my respects — or is the distance too great?"

"You can do it in an hour and a half with a quick horse, if the snow is good," answered Paul.

"Then I may make it au revoir?" enquired De Chauxville, holding out a frank hand.

"Au revoir," said Paul, "if you wish it."

And he turned to say good-bye to Catrina.

As De Chauxville had arrived later than the other visitors, it was quite natural that he should remain after they had left, and it may be safely presumed that he took good care to pin the Countess Lanovitch down to her rash invitation.

"Why is that man coming to Tver?" said Paul, rather gruffly, when Etta and he were settled beneath the furs of the sleigh. "We do not want him there."

"I expect," replied Etta rather petulantly, "that we shall be so horribly dull that even M. de Chauxville will be a welcome alleviation."

Paul said nothing. He gave a little sign to the driver, and the horses leaped forward with a musical clash of their silver bells.

Chapter XXII

THE SPIDER AND THE FLY

*I*t is to be feared that there is a lamentable lack of local color in the present narrative. Having safely arrived at Petersburg, we have nothing to tell of that romantic city — no hints at deep-laid plots, no prison, nor tales of jail-birds — tales with salt on them, bien entendu — the usual grain. We have hardly mentioned the Nevski Prospekt, which street by ancient right must needs figure in all Russian romance. We have instead been prating of drawing rooms and mere interiors of houses, which today are the same all the world over. A Japanese fan is but a Japanese fan, whether it hang on the wall of a Canadian drawing room or the matting of an Indian bunga-low. An Afghan carpet is the same on any floor. It is the foot that treads the carpet which makes one to differ from another.

Whether it be in Petersburg or Pekin, it still must be the human being that lends the interest to the still life around it. A truce, therefore, to picturesque description — sour grapes to the present pen — of church and fort and river, with which the living persons of whom we tell have little or nothing to do.

Maggie was alone in the great drawing room of the house at the end of the English Quay — alone and grave. Some people, be it noted, are gravest when alone, and they are wise, for the world has too much gravity for us to go about it with a long face, making matters worse. Let each of us be the center of his own gravity. Maggie Delafield had, perhaps, that spark in the brain for which we have but an ugly word. We call it "pluck." And by it we are enabled to win a losing game — and, harder still, to lose a losing game — without much noise or plaint.

Whatever this girl's joys or sorrows may have been — and pray you, madam, remember that no man ever knows his neighbor's heart! — she succeeded as well as any in concealing both. There are some women who tell one just enough about themselves to prove that they can understand and sympathize. Maggie was of these; but she told no more.

She was alone when Paul came into the room. It was a large room, with more than one fireplace. Maggie was reading, and she did not look round. Paul stopped — warming himself by the fire nearest to the door. He was the sort of man to come into a room without any remark.

Maggie looked up for a moment, glancing at the wood fire. She seemed to know for certain that it was Paul.

"Have you been out?" she asked.

"Yes — calling."

He came toward her, standing beside her with his hands clasped behind his back, looking into the fire.

"Socially," he said, with a quiet humor, "I am not a success."

Her book dropped upon her knees, her two hands crossed upon its pages. She stared at the glowing logs as if his thoughts were written there.

"I do not want to give way," he went on, "to a habit of morbid introspection, but socially I am a horrid failure."

There was a little smile on the girl's face, not caused by his grave humor. It would appear that she was smiling at something beyond that — something only visible to her own mental vision.

"Perhaps you do not try," she suggested practically.

"Oh, yes, I do. I try in several languages. I have no small-talk."

"You see," she said gravely, "you are a large man."

"Does that make any difference?" he asked simply.

She turned and looked at him as he towered by her side — looked at him with a queer smile.

"Yes," she answered, "I think so."

For some moments they remained thus without speaking — in a peaceful silence. Although the room was very large, it was peaceful. What is it, by the way, that brings peace to the atmosphere of a room, of a whole house sometimes? It can only be something in the individuality of some person in it. We talk glibly of the comfort of being settled — the peacefulness, the restfulness of it. Some people, it would appear, are always settled — of settled convictions, settled mind, settled purpose. Paul Howard Alexis was perhaps such a person.

At all events, the girl sitting in the low chair by his side seemed to be under some such influence, seemed to have escaped the unrest which is said to live in palaces.

When she spoke it was with a quiet voice, as one having plenty of time and leisure.

"Where have you been?" she asked practically. Maggie was always practical.

"To the Lanovitches', where we met the Baron de Chauxville."

"Ah!"

"Why — ah?"

"Because I dislike the Baron de Chauxville," answered Maggie in her decisive way.

"I am glad of that — because I hate him!" said Paul. "Have you any reason for your dislike?"

Miss Delafield had a reason, but it was not one that she could mention to Paul. So she gracefully skirted the question.

"He has the same effect upon me as snails," she explained airily.

Then, as if to salve her conscience, she gave the reason, but disguised, so that he did not recognize it.

"I have seen more of M. de Chauxville than you have," she said gravely. "He is one of those men of whom women do see more. When men are present he loses confidence, like a cur when a thoroughbred terrier is about. He dislikes you. I should take care to give M. de Chauxville a wide berth if I were you, Paul."

She had risen, after glancing at the clock. She turned down the page of her book, and looking up suddenly, met his eyes, for a moment only.

"We are not likely to drop into a close friendship," said Paul. "But — he is coming to Thors, twenty miles from Osterno."

There was a momentary look of anxiety in the girl's eyes, which she turned away to hide.

"I am sorry for that," she said. "Does Herr Steinmetz know it?"

"Not yet."

Maggie paused for a moment. She was tracing with the tip of her finger a pattern stamped on the binding of the book. It would seem that she had something more to say. Then suddenly she went away without saying it.

In the meantime Claude de Chauxville had gently led the Countess Lanovitch to invite him to stay to dinner. He accepted the invitation with becoming reluctance, and returned to the Hotel de Berlin, where he was staying, in order to dress. He was fully alive to the expediency of striking while the iron is hot — more especially where women are concerned. Moreover, his knowledge of the countess led him to fear that she would soon tire of his society. This lady had a lamentable facility for getting to the bottom of her friends' powers of entertainment within a few days. It was De Chauxville's intention to make secure his invitation to Thors, and then to absent himself from the countess.

At dinner he made himself vastly agreeable, recounting many anecdotes fresh from Paris, which duly amused the Countess Lanovitch, and somewhat shocked Catrina, who was not advanced or inclined to advance.

After dinner the guest asked Mlle. Catrina to play. He

opened the grand piano in the inner drawing room with such gallantry and effusion that the sanguine countess, post-prandially somnolescent in her luxurious chair, began re-hearsing different modes of mentioning her son-in-law, the baron.

"Yes," she muttered to herself, "and Catrina is plain — terribly plain."

Thereupon she fell asleep.

De Chauxville had a good memory, and was, moreover, a good and capable liar. So Catrina did not find out that he knew nothing whatever of music. He watched the plain face as the music rose and fell, himself impervious to its transcen-dent tones. With practiced cunning he waited until Catrina was almost intoxicated with music — an intoxication to which all great musicians are liable.

"Ah!" he said. "I envy you your power. With music like that one can almost imagine that life is what one would wish it to be."

She did not answer, but she wandered off into another air — a slumber song.

"The Schlummerlied," said De Chauxville softly. "It al-most has the power to send a sorrow to sleep."

This time she answered him — possibly because he had not looked at her.

"Such never sleep," she said.

"Do you know that, too?" he asked, not in a tone that wanted reply.

She made no answer.

"I am sorry," he went on. "For me it is different, I am a man. I have man's work to do. I can occupy myself with ambition. At all events, I have a man's privilege of nursing revenge."

He saw her eyes light up, her breast heave with a sudden sigh. Something like a smile wavered for a moment beneath his waxed mustache.

Catrina's fingers, supple and strong, struck in great chords the air of a gloomy march from the half-forgotten muse of some monastic composer. While she played, Claude de Chauxville proceeded with his delicate touch to play on the hidden chords of an untamed heart.

"A man's privilege," he repeated musingly.

"Need it be such?" she asked.

For the first time his eyes met hers.

"Not necessarily," he answered, and her eyes dropped before his narrow gaze.

He sat back in his chair, content for the moment with the progress he had made. He glanced at the countess. He was too experienced a man to be tricked. The countess was really asleep. Her cap was on one side, her mouth open. A woman who is pretending to sleep usually does so in becoming attitudes.

De Chauxville did not speak again for some minutes. He sat back in his chair, leaning his forehead on his hand, while he peeped through his slim fingers. He could almost read the girl's thoughts as she put them into music.

"She does not hate him yet," he was reflecting. "But she needs only to see him with Etta a few times and she will come to it."

The girl played on, throwing all the pain in her passionate, untamed heart into the music. She knew nothing of the world; for half of its temptations, its wiles, its wickednesses were closed to her by the plain face that God had given her. For beautiful women see the worst side of human nature — they usually deal with the worst of men. Catrina was an easy tool in the hands of such as Claude de Chauxville; for he had dealt with women and that which is evil in women all his life, and the only mistakes he ever made were those characteristic errors of omission attaching to a persistent ignorance of the innate good in human nature. It is this same innate good that upsets the calculations of most villains.

Absorbed as she was in her great grief, Catrina was in no mood to seek for motives — to split a moral straw. She only knew that this man seemed to understand her as no one had ever understood her. She was content with the knowledge that he took the trouble to express and to show a sympathy of which those around her had not suspected her to be in need.

The moment had been propitious, and Claude de Chauxville, with true Gallic insight, had seized it. Her heart was sore and lonely — almost breaking — and she was without the worldly wisdom which tells us that such hearts must, at all costs, be hidden from the world. She was without religious teaching — quite without that higher moral teaching which is independent of creed and conformity, which is only learnt at a good mother's knee. Catrina had not had a good mother. She had had the countess — a weak-minded, self-indulgent, French-novel-reading woman. Heaven protect our children from such mothers!

In the solitude of her life Catrina Lanovitch had conceived a great love — a passion such as a few only are capable of attaining, be it for weal or woe. She had seen this love ignored — walked under foot by its object with a grave deliberation which took her breath away when she thought of it. It was all in all to her; to him it was nothing. Her philosophy was simple. She could not sit still and endure. At this time it seemed unbearable. She must turn and rend some one. She did not know whom. But some one must suffer. It was in this that Claude de Chauxville proposed to assist her.

"It is preposterous that people should make others suffer and go unpunished," he said, intent on his noble purpose.

Catrina's eyelids flickered, but she made no answer. The soreness of her heart had not taken the form of a definite revenge as yet. Her love for Paul was still love, but it was perilously near to hatred. She had not reached the point of wishing definitely that he should suffer, but the sight of Etta — beautiful, self-confident, carelessly possessive in respect to Paul — had brought her within measurable distance of it.

"The arrogance of those who have all that they desire is insupportable," the Frenchman went on in his favorite, non-committing, epigrammatic way.

Catrina — a second Eve — glanced at him, and her silence gave him permission to go on.

"Some men have a different code of honor for women, who are helpless."

Catrina knew vaguely that unless a woman is beloved by the object of her displeasure, she cannot easily make him suffer.

She clenched her teeth over her lower lip. As she played, a new light was dawning in her eyes. The music was a marvel, but no one in the room heard it.

"I would be pitiless to all such men," said De Chauxville.

"They deserve no pity, for they have shown none. The man who deceives a woman is worthy of —"

He never finished the sentence. Her deep, passionate eyes met his. Her hands came down with one final crash on the chords. She rose and crossed the room.

"Mother," she said, "shall I ring for tea?"

When the countess awoke, De Chauxville was turning over some sheets of music at the piano.

Chapter XXIII

A WINTER SCENE

*B*etween Petersburg and the sea there are several favorite islands more or less assigned to the foreigners residing in the Russian capital. Here the English live, and in summer the familiar cries of the tennis-lawn may be heard, while in winter snow-shoeing, skating, and tobogganing hold merry sway.

It was here, namely, on the island of Christeffsky, that a great ice fête was held on the day preceding the departure of the Howard Alexis household for Tver. The fête was given by one of the foreign ambassadors — a gentleman whose wife was accredited to the first place in Petersburg society. It was absolutely necessary, Steinmetz averred, for the whole Howard Alexis party to put in an appearance.

The fête was supposed to begin at four in the afternoon, and by five o'clock all St. Petersburg — all, c'est à dire, worthy of mention in that aristocratic city — had arrived. One may be sure Claude de Chauxville arrived early, in beautiful furs with a pair of silver-plated skates under his arm. He was an influential member of the Cercle des Patineurs in Paris. Steinmetz arrived soon after, to look on, as he told his many friends. He was, he averred, too stout to skate and too heavy for the little iron sleds on the ice-hills.

"No, no!" he said, "there is nothing left for me but to watch. I shall watch De Chauxville," he added, turning to that graceful skater with a grim smile. De Chauxville nodded and laughed.

"You have been doing that anytime this twenty years, mon ami," he said, as he stood upright on his skates and described an easy little figure on the outside edge backward.

"And have always found you on slippery ground."

"And never a fall," said De Chauxville over his shoulder, as he shot away across the brilliantly lighted pond.

It was quite dark. A young moon was rising over the city, throwing out in dark relief against the sky a hundred steeples and domes. The long, thin spire of the Fortress Church — the tomb of the Romanoffs — shot up into the heavens like a dagger. Near at hand, a thousand electric lights and colored lanterns, cunningly swung on the branches of the pines, made a veritable fairyland. The ceaseless song of the skates, on ice as hard as iron, mingled with the strains of a band playing in a kiosk with open windows. From the ice-hills came the swishing scream of the iron runners down the terrific slope. The Russians are a people of great emotions. There is a candor in their recognition of the needs of the senses which does not obtain in our self-conscious nature. These strangely constituted people of the North — a budding nation, a nation which shall some day overrun the world — are easily intoxicated. And there is a deliberation about their methods of seeking this enjoyment which appears at times almost brutal. There is nothing more characteristic than the ice-hill.

Imagine a slope as steep as a roof, paved with solid blocks of ice, which are subsequently frozen together by flooding with water; imagine a sledge with steel runners polished like a knife; imagine a thousand lights on either side of this glittering path, and you have some idea of an ice-hill. It is certainly the strongest form of excitement imaginable — next, perhaps, to whale-fishing.

There is no question of breathing, once the sledge has been started by the attendant. The sensation is somewhat suggestive of a fall from a balloon, and yet one goes to the top again, as surely as the drunkard will return to his bottle. Fox-hunting is child's play to it, and yet grave men have prayed that they might die in pink.

Steinmetz was standing at the foot of the ice-hill when an arm was slipped within his.

"Will you take me down?" asked Maggie Delafield.

He turned and smiled at her — fresh and blooming in her furs.

"No, my dear young lady. But thank you for suggesting it."

"Is it very dangerous?"

"Very. But I think you ought to try it. It is a revelation. It is an epoch in your life. When I was a younger man I used to sneak away to an ice-hill where I was not known, and spend hours of the keenest enjoyment. Where is Paul?"

"He has just gone over there with Etta."

"She refuses to go?"

"Yes," answered Maggie.

Steinmetz looked down at his companion with his smile of quiet resignation.

"You tell me you are afraid of mice," he said.

"I hate mice," she replied. "Yes — I suppose I am afraid of them."

"The princess is not afraid of *rats* — she is afraid of very little, the princess — and yet she will not go on the ice-hill. What strange creatures, mademoiselle! Come, let us look for Paul. He is the only man who may be trusted to take you down."

They found Paul and Etta together in one of the brilliantly lighted kiosks where refreshments were being served, all hot and steaming, by fur-clad servants. It was a singular scene. If a coffee cup was left for a few moments on the table by the watchful servitors, the spoon froze to the saucer. The refreshments — bread and butter, dainty sandwiches of caviare, of pâté de foie gras, of a thousand delicatessen from Berlin and Petersburg — were kept from freezing on hot-water dishes. The whole scene was typical of life in the northern capital, where wealth wages a successful fight against climate. Open fires burned brilliantly in iron tripods within the doorway of the tent, and at intervals in the gardens. In a large hall a string band consoled those whose years or lungs would not permit of the more vigorous outdoor entertainments.

Steinmetz made known to Paul Maggie's desire to risk her life on the ice-hills, and gallantly proposed to take care of the princess until his return.

"Then," said Etta gaily, "you must skate. It is much too cold to stand about. They are going to dance a cotillon."

"If it is your command, princess, I obey with alacrity."

Etta spoke rapidly, looking round her all the while with the bright enjoyment which overspreads the faces of some women at almost any form of entertainment, provided there be music, brilliant lights, and a crowd of people. One cannot help wondering a little what the minds of such fair ladies must consist of, to be thrown off their balance by such outward influences. Etta's eyes gleamed with excitement. She was beautifully dressed in furs, which adornment she was tall and stately enough to carry to full advantage. She held her graceful head with regal hauteur, every inch a princess. She was enjoying her keenest pleasure — a social triumph. No whisper escaped her, no glance, no nudge of admiring or envious notice. On Steinmetz's arm she passed out of the tent; the touch of her hand on his sleeve reminded him of a thoroughbred horse stepping on to turf, so full of life, of electric thrill, of excitement was it. But then, Karl Steinmetz was a cynic. No one else could have thought of comparing Etta's self-complaisant humor to that of a horse in a racing paddock.

They procured skates and glided off hand in hand, equally proficient, equally practiced, maybe on this same lake; for both had learned to skate in Russia.

They talked only of the present, of the brilliancy of the fête, of the music, of the thousand lights. Etta was quite incapable of thinking or talking of any other subject at that moment.

Steinmetz distinguished Claude de Chauxville easily enough, and avoided him with some success for a short time. But De Chauxville soon caught sight of them.

"Here is M. de Chauxville," said Etta, with a pleased ring in her voice. "Leave me with him. I expect you are tired."

"I am not tired, but I am obedient," replied Steinmetz, as the Frenchman came up with his fur cap in his hand, bowing gracefully. Claude de Chauxville usually overdid things. There is something honest in a clumsy bow which had no place in his courtly obeisance.

Although Steinmetz continued to skate in a leisurely way, he also held to his original intention of looking on. He saw Paul and Maggie come back to the edge of the lake, accompanied by an English lady of some importance in Russia, with whom Maggie presently went away to the concert-room.

Steinmetz glided up to Paul, who was lighting a cigarette at the edge of the pond, where an attendant stood by an open wood fire with cigarettes and hot beverages.

"Get a pair of skates," said the German. "This ice is marvelous — colossa-a-a-l."

He amused himself with describing figures, like a huge grave-minded boy, until Paul joined him.

"Where is Etta?" asked the prince at once.

"Over there with De Chauxville."

Paul said nothing for a few moments. They skated side by side round the lake. It was too cold to stand still even for a minute.

"I told you," remarked Paul at length, "that that fellow is coming to Thors."

"I wish he would go to the devil," said Steinmetz.

"No doubt he will in time," answered Paul carelessly.

"Yes; but not soon enough. I assure you, Paul, I do not like it. We are just in that position that the least breath of suspicion will get us into endless trouble. The authorities know that Stépan Lanovitch has escaped. At any moment the Charity League scandal may be resuscitated. We do not want fellows like De Chauxville prowling about. I know the man. He is a d———d scoundrel who would sell his immortal soul if he could get a bid for it. What is he coming to Thors for? He is not a sportsman; why, he would be afraid of a cock pheasant, though he would be plucky enough among the hens. You don't imagine he is in love with Catrina, do you?"

"No," said Paul sharply, "I don't."

Steinmetz raised his bushy eyebrows. Etta and De Chauxville skated past them at that moment, laughing gaily.

"I have been thinking about it," went on Steinmetz, "and I have come to the conclusion that our friend hates you personally. He has a grudge against you of some sort. Of course he hates me — cela va sans dire. He has come to Russia to watch us. That I am convinced of. He has come here bent on mischief. It may be that he is hard up and is to be bought. He is always to be bought, ce bon De Chauxville, at a price. We shall see."

Steinmetz paused and glanced at Paul. He could not tell him more. He could not tell him that his wife had sold the Charity League papers to those who wanted them. He could not tell him all that he knew of Etta's past. None of these things could Karl Steinmetz, in the philosophy that was his, tell to the person whom they most concerned. And who are we that we may hold him wrong? The question of telling and withholding is not to be dismissed in a few words. But it seems very certain that there is too much telling, too much speaking out, and too little holding in, in these days of much publicity. There is a school of speakers-out, and would to Heaven they would learn to hold their tongues. There is a school for calling a spade by no other name, and they have still to learn that the world is by no means interested in their clatter of shovels.

The Psalmist knew much of which he did not write, and the young men of the modern school of poesy and fiction know no more, but they lack the good taste of the singer of old. That is all.

Karl Steinmetz was a man who formed his opinion on the best basis — namely, experience, and that had taught him that a bold reticence does less harm to one's neighbor than a weak volubility.

Paul was an easy subject for such treatment. His own method inclined to err on the side of reticence. He gave few confidences and asked none, as is the habit of Englishmen.

"Well," he said, "I do not suppose he will stay long at Thors, and I know that he will not stay at all at Osterno. Besides, what harm can he actually do to us? He cannot well go about making enquiries. To begin with, he knows no Russian."

"I doubt that," put in Steinmetz.

"And, even if he does, he cannot come poking about in Osterno. Catrina will give him no information. Maggie hates him. You and I know him. There is only the countess."

"Who will tell him all she knows! She would render that service to a drosky driver."

Paul shrugged his shoulders.

There was no mention of Etta. They stood side by side, both thinking of her, both looking at her, as she skated with De Chauxville. There lay the danger, and they both knew it. But she was the wife of one of them and their lips were necessarily sealed.

"And it will be permitted," Claude de Chauxville happened to be saying at that moment, "that I call and pay my respects to an exiled princess?"

"There will be difficulties," answered Etta, in that tone which makes it necessary to protest that difficulties are nothing under some circumstances — the which De Chauxville duly protested with much fervor.

"You think that twenty miles of snow would deter me," he said.

"Well, they might."

"They might if — well —"

He left the sentence unfinished — the last resource of the sneak and the coward who wishes to reserve to himself the letter of the denial in the spirit of the meanest lie.

Chapter XXIV

HOME

A tearing, howling wind from the north — from the boundless snow-clad plains of Russia that lie between the Neva and the Yellow Sea; a gray sky washed over as with a huge brush dipped in dirty whitening; and the plains of Tver a spotless, dazzling level of snow.

The snow was falling softly and steadily, falling, as it never falls in England, in little more than fine powder, with a temperature forty degrees below freezing-point. A drift — constant, restless, never altering — sped over the level plain like the dust on a high-road before a steady wind. This white scud — a flying scud of frozen water — was singularly like the scud that is blown from the crest of the waves by a cyclone in the China Seas. Any object that broke the wind — a stunted pine, a broken tree-trunk, a Government road-post — had at its leeward side a high, narrow snow-drift tailing off to the dead level of the plain. Where the wind dropped the snow rose at once. But these objects were few and far between. The deadly monotony of the scene — the trackless level, the preposterous dimensions of the plain, the sense of distance that is conveyed only by the steppe and the great desert of Gobi when the snow lies on it — all these tell the same grim truth to all who look on them: the old truth that man is but a small thing and his life but as the flower of the grass.

Across the plain of Tver, before the north wind, a single

sleigh was tearing as fast as horse could lay hoof to ground
— a sleigh driven by Paul Howard Alexis, and the track of it
was as a line drawn from point to point across a map.

A striking feature of the winter of Northern Russia is the
glorious uncertainty of its snowfalls. At Tver the weather-wise
had said:

"The snow has not all fallen yet. More is coming. It is
yellow in the sky, although March is nearly gone."

The landlord of the hotel (a good enough resting-place
facing the broad Volga) had urged upon M. le Prince the
advisability of waiting, as is the way of landlords all the world
over. But Etta had shown a strange restlessness, a petulant
desire to hurry forward at all risks. She hated Tver; the hotel
was uncomfortable, there was an unhealthy smell about the
place.

Paul acceded readily enough to her wishes. He rather liked
Tver. In a way he was proud of this busy town — a center of
Russian civilization. He would have liked Etta to be favorably
impressed with it, as any prejudice would naturally reflect
upon Osterno, 140 miles across the steppe. But with a characteristic silent patience he made the necessary preparations
for an immediate start.

The night express from St. Petersburg had deposited them
on the platform in the early morning. Steinmetz had preceded
them. Closed sleighs from Osterno were awaiting them. A
luxurious breakfast was prepared at the hotel. Relays of horses
were posted along the road. The journey to Osterno had been
carefully planned and arranged by Steinmetz — a king among
organizers. The sleigh drive across the steppe was to be accomplished in ten hours.

The snow had begun to fall as they clattered across the
floating bridge of Tver. It had fallen ever since, and the
afternoon lowered gloomily. In America such visitations are
called "blizzards"; here in Russia it is merely "the snow." The
freezing wind is taken as a matter of course.

At a distance of one hundred miles from Tver, the driver
of the sleigh containing Etta, Maggie, and Paul had suddenly
rolled off his perch. His hands were frostbitten; a piteous blue
face peered out at his master through ice-laden eyebrows,
mustache, and beard. In a moment Maggie was out in the

snow beside the two men, while Etta hastily closed the door.

"He is all right," said Paul; "it is only the cold. Pour some brandy into his mouth while I hold the ice aside. *Don't* take off your gloves. The flask will stick to your fingers."

Maggie obeyed with her usual breezy readiness, turning to nod reassurance to Etta, who, truth to tell, had pulled up the rime-covered windows, shutting out the whole scene.

"He must come inside," said Maggie. "We are nice and warm with all the hot-water cans."

Paul looked rather dubiously toward the sleigh.

"You can carry him, I suppose?" said the girl cheerfully. "He is not very big — he is all fur coat."

Etta looked rather disgusted, but made no objection, while Paul lifted the frozen man into the seat he had just vacated.

"When you are cold I will drive," cried Maggie, as Paul shut the door. "I should love it."

Thus it came about that a single sleigh was speeding across the plain of Tver.

Paul, with the composure that comes of a large experience, gathered the reins in his two hands, driving with both and with extended arms, after the manner of Russian yemschiks. For a man must accommodate himself to circumstance, and fingerless gloves are not conducive to a finished style of handling the ribbons.

This driver knew that the next station was twenty miles off; that at any moment the horses might break down or plunge into a drift. He knew that in the event of such emergencies it would be singularly easy for four people to die of cold within a few miles of help. But he had faced such possibilities a hundred times before in this vast country, where the standard price of a human life is no great sum. He was not, therefore, dismayed, but rather took delight in battling with the elements, as all strong men should, and most of them, thank Heaven, do.

Moreover he battled successfully, and before the moon was well up drew rein outside the village of Osterno, to accede at last to the oft-repeated prayer of the driver that he might return to his task.

"It is not meet," the man had gruffly said, whenever a short halt was made to change horses, "that a great prince should drive a yemschik."

"It is meet," answered Paul simply, "for one man to help another."

Then this man of deeds and not of words clambered into the sleigh and drew up the windows, hiding his head as he drove through his own village, where every man was dependent for life and being on his charity.

They were silent, for the ladies were tired and cold.

"We shall soon be there," said Paul reassuringly. But he did not lower the windows and look out, as any man might have wished to do on returning to the place of his birth.

Maggie sat back, wrapped in her furs. She was meditating over the events of the day, and more particularly over a certain skill, a quickness of touch, a deft handling of stricken men which she had noted far out on the snowy steppe a few hours earlier. Paul was a different man when he had to deal with pain and sickness; he was quicker, brighter, full of confidence in himself. For the great sympathy was his — that love of the neighbor which is thrown like a mantle over the shoulders of some men, making them different from their fellows, securing to them that love of great and small which, perchance, follows some when they are dead to that place where a human testimony may not be all in vain.

At the castle all was in readiness for the prince and princess, their departure from Tver having been telegraphed. On the threshold of the great house, before she had entered the magnificent hall, Etta's eyes brightened, her fatigue vanished. She played her part before the crowd of bowing servants with that forgetfulness of mere bodily fatigue which is expected of princesses and other great ladies. She swept up the broad staircase, leaning on Paul's arm, with a carriage, a presence, a dazzling wealth of beauty, which did not fail to impress the onlookers. Whatever Etta may have failed to bring to Paul Howard Alexis as a wife, she made him a matchless princess.

He led her straight through the drawing room to the suite of rooms which were hers. These consisted of an anteroom, a small drawing room, and her private apartments beyond.

Paul stopped in the drawing room, looking round with a simple satisfaction in all that had been done by his orders for Etta's comfort.

"These," he said, "are your rooms."

He was no adept at turning a neat phrase — at reeling off a pretty honeymoon welcome. Perhaps he expected her to express delight, to come to him, possibly, and kiss him, as some women would have done.

She looked round critically.

"Yes," she said, "they are very nice."

She crossed the room and drew aside the curtain that covered the double-latticed windows. The room was so warm that there was no rime on the panes. She gave a little shudder, and he went to her side, putting his strong, quiet arm around her.

Below them, stretching away beneath the brilliant moonlight, lay the country that was his inheritance, an estate as large as a large English county. Immediately beneath them, at the foot of the great rock upon which the castle was built, nestled the village of Osterno — straggling, squalid.

"Oh!" she said dully, "this is Siberia; this is terrible!"

It had never presented itself to him in that light, the wonderful stretch of country over which they were looking.

"It is not so bad," he said, "in the daylight."

And that was all; for he had no persuasive tongue.

"That is the village," he went on, after a little pause. "Those are the people who look to us to help them in their fight against terrible odds. I hoped — that you would be interested in them."

She looked down curiously at the little wooden huts, half-buried in the snow; the smoking chimneys; the twinkling, curtainless windows.

"What do you expect me to do?" she asked in a queer voice.

He looked at her in a sort of wonderment. Perhaps it seemed to him that a woman should have no need to ask such a question.

"It is a long story," he said; "I will tell you about it another time. You are tired now, after your journey."

His arm slipped from her waist. They stood side by side. And both were conscious of a feeling of difference. They were not the same as they had been in London. The atmosphere of Russia seemed to have had some subtle effect upon them.

Etta turned and sat slowly down on a low chair before the

fire. She had thrown her furs aside, and they lay in a luxurious heap on the floor. The maids, hearing that the prince and princess were together, waited silently in the next room behind the closed door.

"I think I had better hear it now," said Etta.

"But you are tired," protested her husband. "You had better rest until dinner-time."

"No; I am not tired."

He came toward her and stood with one elbow on the mantelpiece, looking down at her — a quiet, strong man, who had already forgotten his feat of endurance of a few hours earlier.

"These people," he said, "would die of starvation and cold and sickness if we did not help them. It is simply impossible for them in the few months that they can work the land to cultivate it so as to yield anymore than their taxes. They are overtaxed, and no one cares. The army must be kept up and a huge Civil Service, and no one cares what happens to the peasants. Some day the peasants *must* turn, but not yet. It is a question for all Russian land-owners to face, and nobody faces it. If anyone tries to improve the condition of his peasants — they were happier a thousand times as serfs — the bureaucrats of Petersburg mark him down and he is forced to leave the country. The whole fabric of this Government is rotten, but everyone, except the peasants, would suffer by its fall, and therefore it stands."

Etta was staring into the fire. It was impossible to say whether she heard with comprehension or not. Paul went on:

"There is nothing left, therefore, but to go and do good by stealth. I studied medicine with that view. Steinmetz has scraped and economized the working of the estate for the same purpose. The Government will not allow us to have a doctor; they prevent us from organizing relief and education on anything like an adequate scale. They do it all by underhand means. They have not the pluck to oppose us openly! For years we have been doing what we can. We have almost eradicated cholera. They do not die of starvation now. And they are learning — very slowly, but still they are learning. We — I — thought you might be interested in your people; you might want to help."

She gave a short little nod. There was a suggestion of suspense in her whole being and attitude, as if she were waiting to hear something which she knew could not be avoided.

"A few years ago," he went on, "a gigantic scheme was set on foot. I told you a little about it — the Charity League."

Her lips moved, but no sound came from them, so she nodded a second time. A tiny carriage-clock on the mantelpiece struck seven, and she looked up in a startled way, as if the sound had frightened her. The castle was quite still. Silence seemed to brood over the old walls.

"That fell through," he went on, "as I told you. It was betrayed. Stépan Lanovitch was banished. He has escaped, however; Steinmetz has seen him. He succeeded in destroying some of the papers before the place was searched after the robbery — one paper in particular. If he had not destroyed that, I should have been banished. I was one of the leaders of the Charity League. Steinmetz and I got the thing up. It would have been for the happiness of millions of peasants if it had not been betrayed. In time — we shall find out who did it."

He paused. He did not say what he would do when he had found out.

Etta was staring into the fire. Her lips were dry. She hardly seemed to be breathing.

"It is possible," he went on in his strong, quiet, inexorable voice, "that Stépan Lanovitch knows now."

Etta did not move. She was staring into the fire — staring — staring.

Then she slowly fainted, rolling from the low chair to the fur hearthrug.

Paul picked her up like a child and carried her to the bedroom, where the maids were waiting to dress her.

"Here," he said, "your mistress has fainted from the fatigue of the journey."

And, with his practiced medical knowledge, he himself tended her.

Chapter XXV
OSTERNO

"Always gay; always gay!" laughed Steinmetz, rubbing his broad hands together and looking down into the face of Maggie, who was busy at the breakfast-table.

"Yes," answered the girl, glancing toward Paul, leaning against the window reading his letters. "Yes, always gay. Why not?"

Karl Steinmetz saw the glance. It was one of the little daily incidents that one sees and half forgets. He only half forgot it.

"Why not, indeed?" he answered. "And you will be glad to hear that Ivanovitch is as ready as yourself this morning to treat the matter as a joke. He is none the worse for his freezing, and all the better for his experience. You have added another friend, my dear young lady, to a list which is, doubtless, a very long one."

"He is a nice man," answered Maggie. "How is it," she asked, after a little pause, "that there are more men in the lower classes whom one can call nice than among their betters?"

Paul paused between two letters, hearing the question. He looked up as if interested in the answer, but did not join in the conversation.

"Because dealing with animals and with nature is more conducive to niceness than too much trafficking with human beings," replied Steinmetz promptly.

"I suppose that is it," said Maggie, lifting the teapot lid and looking in. "At all events, it is the sort of answer one might expect from you. You are always hard on human nature."

"I take it as I find it," replied Steinmetz, with a laugh, "but I do not worry about it like some people. Now, Paul would like to alter the course of the world."

As he spoke he half turned toward Paul, as if suggesting that he should give an opinion, and this little action had the effect of putting a stop to the conversation. Maggie had plenty to say to Steinmetz, but toward Paul her mental attitude was different. She was probably unaware of this little fact.

"There," she said, after a pause, "I have obeyed Etta's instructions. She does not want us to begin, I suppose?"

"No," replied Paul. "She will be down in a minute."

"I hope the princess is not overtired," said Steinmetz, with a certain formal politeness which seemed to accompany any mention of Etta's name.

"Not at all, thank you," replied Etta herself, coming into the room at that moment. She looked fresh and self-confident. "On the contrary, I am full of energy and eagerness to explore the castle. One naturally takes an interest in one's baronial halls."

With this she walked slowly across to the window. She stood there looking out, and everyone in the room was watching. On looking for the first time on the same view, a few moments earlier, Maggie had uttered a little cry of surprise, and had then remained silent. Etta looked out of the window and said nothing. It was a most singular out-look — weird, uncouth, prehistoric, as some parts of the earth still are. The castle was built on the edge of a perpendicular cliff. On this side it was impregnable. Any object dropped from the breakfast-room window would fall a clear two hundred feet to the brawling Oster River. The rock was black, and shining like the topmost crags of an Alpine mountain where snow and ice have polished the bare stone. Beyond and across the river lay the boundless steppe — a sheet of virgin snow.

Etta stood looking over this to the far horizon, where the

white snow and the gray sky softly merged into one. Her first remark was characteristic, as first and last remarks usually are.

"And as far as you can see is yours?" she asked.

"Yes," answered Paul simply, with that calm which only comes with hereditary possession.

The observation attracted Steinmetz's attention. He went to another window, and looked across the waste critically.

"Four times as far as we can see is his," he said.

Etta looked out slowly and comprehensively, absorbing it all like a long, sweet drink. There was no hereditary calmness in her sense of possession.

"And where is Thors?" she asked.

Paul stretched out his arm, pointing with a lean, steady finger:

"It lies out there," he answered.

Another of the little incidents that are only half forgotten. Some of the persons assembled in that room remembered the pointing finger long afterward.

"It makes one feel very small," said Etta, turning to the breakfast-table — "at no time a pleasant sensation. Do you know," she said, after a little pause, "I think it probable that I shall become very fond of Osterno, but I wish it was nearer to civilization."

Paul looked pleased. Steinmetz had a queer expression on his face. Maggie murmured something about one's surroundings making but little difference to one's happiness, and the subject was wisely shelved.

After breakfast Steinmetz withdrew.

"Now," said Paul, "shall I show you the old place, you and Maggie?"

Etta signified her readiness, but Maggie said that she had letters to write, that Etta could show her the castle another time, when the men were out shooting, perhaps.

"But," said Etta, "I shall do it horribly badly. They are not my ancestors, you know. I shall attach the stories to the wrong people, and locate the ghost in the wrong room. You will be wise to take Paul's guidance."

"No, thank you," replied Maggie, quite firmly and frankly. "I feel inclined to write; and the feeling is rare, so I must take advantage of it."

The girl looked at her cousin with something in her honest blue eyes that almost amounted to wonder. Etta was always surprising her. There was a whole gamut of feeling, an octave of callow, half-formed girlish instincts, of which Etta seemed to be deprived. If she had ever had them, no trace was left of their whilom presence. At first Maggie had flatly refused to come to Russia. When Paul pressed her to do so, she accepted with a sort of wonder. There was something which she did not understand.

The same instinct made her refuse now to accompany Paul and Etta over their new home. Again Etta pressed her, show-ing her lack of some feeling which Maggie indefinitely knew she ought to have had. This time Paul made no sign. He added no word to Etta's persuasions, but stood gravely looking at his wife.

When the door had closed behind them, Maggie stood for some minutes by the window looking out over the snow-clad plain, the rugged, broken rocks beneath her.

Then she turned to the writing-table. She resolutely took pen and paper, but the least thing seemed to distract her attention — the coronet on the note-paper cost her five minutes of far-off reflection. She took up the pen again, and wrote "Dear Mother."

The room grew darker. Maggie looked up. The snow had begun again. It was driving past the window with a silent, purposeful monotony. The girl drew the writing-case toward her. She examined the pen critically and dipped it into the ink. But she added nothing to the two words already written.

The castle of Osterno is almost unique in the particular that one roof covers the ancient and the modern buildings. The vast reception-rooms, worthy of the name of state-rooms, adjoin the small stone-built apartments of the fortress which Paul's ancestors held against the Tartars. This grimmer side of the building Paul reserved to the last for reasons of his own, and Etta's manifest delight in the grandeur of the more modern apartments fully rewarded him. Here, again, that side of her character manifested itself which has already been shown. She was dazzled and exhilarated by the splendor of it all, and the immediate effect was a feeling of affection toward the man to whom this belonged; who was in act, if not in word, laying it at her feet.

When they passed from the lofty rooms to the dimmer passages of the old castle Etta's spirits visibly dropped, her interest slackened. He told her of tragedies enacted in by-gone times — such ancient tales of violent death and broken hearts as attach themselves to gray stone walls and dungeon keeps. She only half listened, for her mind was busy with the splendors they had left behind, with the purposes to which such splendors could be turned. And the sum total of her thoughts was gratified vanity.

Her bright presence awakened the gloom of ages within the dimly lit historic rooms. Her laugh sounded strangely light and frivolous and shallow in the silence of the ages which had brooded within these walls since the days of Tamerlane. It was perhaps the greatest tragedy of the Alexis family, this beautiful tragedy that walked by the side of Paul.

"I am glad your grandfather brought French architects here and built the modern side," she said. "These rooms are, of course, very interesting, but gloomy — horribly gloomy, Paul. There is a smell of ghosts and dullness."

"All the same, I like these rooms," answered Paul. "Steinmetz and I used to live entirely on this side of the house. This is the smoking-room. We shot those bears, and all the deer. That is a wolf's head. He killed a keeper before I finished him off."

Etta looked at her husband with a curious little smile. She sometimes felt proud of him, despite the ever present knowledge that, intellectually speaking, she was his superior. There was something strong and simple and manly in a sort of mediaeval way that pleased her in this big husband of hers.

"And how did you finish him off?" she asked.

"I choked him. That bear knocked me down, but Steinmetz shot him. We were four days out in the open after that elk. This is a lynx — a queer face — rather like De Chauxville; the dogs killed him."

"But why do you not paper the room," asked Etta, with a shiver, "instead of this gloomy paneling? It is so mysterious and creepy. Quite suggestive of secret passages."

"There are no secret passages," answered Paul. "But there is a room behind here. This is the door. I will show it to you presently. I have things in there I want to show you. I keep all my medicines and appliances in there. It is our secret surgery and office. In that room the Charity League was organized."

Etta turned away suddenly and went to the narrow window, where she sat on a low window-seat, looking down into the snow-clad depths.

"I did not know you were a doctor," she said.

"I doctor the peasants," replied Paul, "in a rough-and-ready way. I took my degree on purpose. But, of course, they do not know that it is I; they think I am a doctor from Moscow. I put on an old coat, and wear a scarf, so that they cannot see my face. I only go to them at night. It would never do for the Government to know that we attempt to do good to the peasants. We have to keep it a secret even from the people themselves. And they hate us. They groan and hoot when we drive through the village. But they never attempt to do us any harm; they are too much afraid of us."

When Etta rose and came toward him her face was colorless.

"Let me see this room," she said.

He opened the door and followed her into the apartment, which has already been described. Here he told further somewhat bald details of the work he had attempted to do. It is to be feared that he made neither an interesting nor a romantic story of it. There were too many details — too much statistic, and no thrilling realism whatever. The experiences of a youthful curate in Bethnal Green would have made high tragedy beside the tale that this man told his wife of the land upon which God has assuredly laid His curse — Aceldama, the field of blood.

Etta listened, and despite herself she became interested. She was sitting in a chair usually occupied by Steinmetz. There was a faint aroma of tobacco smoke. The atmosphere of the room was manly and energetic.

Paul showed her his simple stores of medicine — the old coat saturated with disinfectants which had become the recognized outward sign of the Moscow doctor.

"And do other people, other noblemen, try to do this sort of thing too?" asked Etta at length.

"Catrina Lanovitch does," replied Paul.

"What? The girl with the hair?"

"Yes," answered Paul. He had never noticed Catrina's hair. Etta's appraising eye had seen more in one second than Paul had perceived in twenty years.

"Yes," he answered. "But, of course, she is handicapped."

"By her appearance?"

"No; by her circumstances. Her name is sufficient to handicap her every moment in this country. But she does a great deal. She — she found me out, confound her!"

Etta had risen; she was looking curiously at the cupboard where Paul's infected clothes were hanging. He had forbidden her to go near it. She turned and looked at him.

"Found you out! How?" she asked, with a queer smile.

"Saw through my disguise."

"Yes — she would do that!" said Etta aloud to herself.

"What is this door?" she asked, after a pause.

"It leads to an inner room," replied Paul, "where Steinmetz usually works."

He passed in front of her and opened the door. As he was doing so Etta went on in the train of her thoughts:

"So Catrina knows?"

"Yes."

"And no one else?"

Paul made no answer; for he had passed on into the smaller room, where Steinmetz was seated at a writing-table.

"Except, of course, Herr Steinmetz?" Etta went on interrogatively.

"Madame," said the German, looking up with his pleasant smile, "I know *everything.*"

And he went on writing.

Chapter XXVI
BLOODHOUNDS

*T*he table d'hôte of the Hôtel de Moscou at Tver had just begun. The soup had been removed; the diners were engaged in igniting their first cigarette at the candles placed between each pair of them for that purpose. By nature the modern Russian is a dignified and somewhat reserved gentleman. By circumstance he has been schooled into a state of guarded unsociability. If there is a seat at a public table conveniently removed from those occupied by earlier arrivals the new-comer invariably takes it. In Russia one converses – as in Scotland one jokes – with difficulty.

A Russian table d'hôte is therefore anything but hilarious in its tendency. A certain number of grave-faced gentlemen and a few broad-jowled ladies are visibly constrained by the force of circumstance to dine at the same table and hour, et voilà tout. There is no pretence that anymore sociable and neighborly motive has brought them together. Indeed, they each suspect the other of being a German, or a Nihilist, or, worse still, a Government servant. They therefore sit as far apart as possible, and smoke cigarettes between and during the courses with that self-centered absorption which would be rude, if it were not entirely satisfactory, to the average Briton. The ladies, of course, have the same easy method of showing a desire for silence and reflection in a country where nurses carrying infants usually smoke in the streets, and where a dainty confectioner's assistant places her cigarette between her lips in order to leave her hands free for the service of her customers.

The table d'hôte of the Hôtel de Moscou at Tver was no exception to the general rule. In Russia, by the way, there are no exceptions to general rules. The personal habits of the native of Cronstadt differ in no way from those of the Czar's subject living in Petropavlovsk, eight thousand miles away.

Around the long table of the host were seated, at respectable intervals, a dozen or more gentlemen, who gazed stolidly at each other from time to time, while the host himself smiled broadly upon them all from that end of the room where the lift and the smell of cooking exercise their calling — the one to spoil the appetite, the other to pander to it when spoilt.

Of these dozen gentlemen we have only to deal with one — a man of broad, high forehead, of colorless eyes, of a masklike face, who consumed what was put before him with as little noise as possible. Known in Paris as "Ce bon Vassili," this traveler. But in Paris one does not always use the word *bon* in its English sense of "good."

M. Vassili was evidently desirous of attracting as little attention as circumstances would allow. He was obviously doing his best to look like one who traveled in the interest of braid or buttons. Moreover, when Claude de Chauxville entered the table d'hôte room, he concealed whatever surprise he may have felt behind a cloud of cigarette smoke. Through the same blue haze he met the Frenchman's eye, a moment later, without the faintest twinkle of recognition.

These two worthies went through the weird courses provided by a cook professing a knowledge of French *cuisine* without taking any compromising notice of each other. When the meal was over Vassili inscribed the number of his bedroom in large figures on the label of his bottle of St. Emilion — after the manner of wise commercial-travelers in continental hotels. He subsequently turned the bottle round so that Claude de Chauxville could scarcely fail to read the number, and with a vague and general bow he left the room.

In his apartment the genial Vassili threw more wood into the stove, drew forward the two regulation armchairs, and lighted all the candles provided. He then rang the bell and ordered liqueurs. There was evidently something in the nature of an entertainment about to take place in apartment No. 44 of the Hôtel de Moscou.

Before long a discreet knock announced the arrival of the expected visitor.

"Entrez!" cried Vassili; and De Chauxville stood before him, with a smile which in French is called crâne.

"A pleasure," said Vassili, behind his wooden face, "that I did not anticipate in Tver."

"And consequently one that carries its own mitigation. An unanticipated pleasure, mon ami, is always inopportune. I make no doubt that you were sorry to see me."

"On the contrary. Will you sit?"

"I can hardly believe," went on De Chauxville, taking the proffered chair, "that my appearance was opportune – on the principle, ha! ha! that a flower growing out of place is a weed. Gentlemen of the – eh – Home Office prefer, I know, to travel quietly!" He spread out his expressive hands as if smoothing the path of M. Vassili through this stony world. "Incognito," he added guilelessly.

"One does not publish one's name from the housetops," replied the Russian, with a glimmer of pride in his eyes, "especially if it happen to be not quite obscure; but between friends, my dear baron – between friends."

"Yes. Then what are you doing in Tver?" enquired De Chauxville, with engaging frankness.

"Ah, that is a long story. But I will tell you – never fear – I will tell you on the usual terms."

"Viz?" enquired the Frenchman, lighting a cigarette.

Vassili accepted the match with a bow, and did likewise. He blew a guileless cloud of smoke toward the dingy ceiling.

"Exchange, my dear baron, exchange."

"Oh, certainly," replied De Chauxville, who knew that Vassili was in all probability fully informed as to his movements past and prospective. "I am going to visit some old friends in this Government – the Lanovitches, at Thors."

"Ah!"

"You know them?"

Vassili raised his shoulders and made a little gesture with his cigarette, as much as to say, "Why ask?"

De Chauxville looked at his companion keenly. He was wondering whether this man knew that he — Claude de Chauxville — loved Etta Howard Alexis, and consequently hated her husband. He was wondering how much or how little this impenetrable individual knew and suspected.

"I have always said," observed Vassili suddenly, "that for unmitigated impertinence give me a diplomatist."

"Ah! And what would you desire that I should, for the same commodity, give you now?"

"A woman."

There was a short silence in the room while these two birds of a feather reflected.

Suddenly Vassili tapped himself on the chest with his forefinger.

"It was I," he said, "who crushed that very dangerous movement — the Charity League."

"I know it."

"A movement, my dear baron, to educate the moujik, if you please. To feed him and clothe him, and teach him — to be discontented with his lot. To raise him up and make a man of him. Pah! He is a beast. Let him be treated as such. Let him work. If he will not work, let him starve and die."

"The man who cannot contribute toward the support of those above him in life is superfluous," said De Chauxville glibly.

"Precisely. Now, my dear baron, listen to me!" The genial Vassili leaned forward and tapped with one finger on the knee of De Chauxville, as if knocking at the door of his attention.

"I am all ears, mon bon monsieur," replied the Frenchman, rather coldly. He had just been reflecting that, after all, he did not want any favor from Vassili for the moment, and the manner of the latter was verging on the familiar.

"The woman — who — sold — me — the Charity League papers dined at my house in Paris — a fortnight ago," said Vassili, with a staccato tap on his companion's knee by way of emphasis to each word.

"Then, my friend, I cannot — congratulate — you — on the society — in — which you move," replied De Chauxville, mimicking his manner.

"Bah! She was a princess!"

"A princess?"

"Yes, of your acquaintance, M. le Baron! And she came to my house with her — eh — husband — the Prince Paul Howard Alexis."

This was news indeed. De Chauxville leaned back and passed his slim white hand across his brow with a slow pressure, as if wiping some writing from a slate — as if his forehead bore the writing of his thoughts and he was wiping it away. And the thoughts he thus concealed — who can count them? For thoughts are the quickest and the longest and the saddest things of this life. The first thought was that if he had known this three months earlier he could have made Etta marry him. And that thought had a thousand branches. With Etta for his wife he might have been a different man. One can never tell what the effect of an acquired desire may be. One can only judge by analogy, and it would seem that it is a frustrated desire that makes the majority of villains.

But the news coming, thus too late, only served an evil purpose. For in that flash of thought Claude de Chauxville saw Paul's secrets given to him; Paul's wealth meted out to him; Paul in exile; Paul dead in Siberia, where death comes easily; Paul's widow Claude de Chauxville's wife. He wiped all the thoughts away, and showed to Vassili a face that was as composed and impertinent as usual.

"You said 'her — eh — husband,'" he observed. "Why? Why did you add that little 'eh,' my friend?"

Vassili rose and walked to the door that led through into his bedroom from the salon in which they were sitting. It was possible to enter the bedroom from another door and over-hear any conversation that might be passing in the sitting room. The investigation was apparently satisfactory, for the Russian came back. But he did not sit down. Instead, he stood leaning against the tall china stove.

"Needless to tell you," he observed, "the antecedents of the — princess."

"Quite needless."

"Married seven years ago to Charles Sydney Bamborough," promptly giving the unnecessary information which was not wanted.

De Chauxville nodded.

"Where is Sydney Bamborough?" asked Vassili, with his masklike smile.

"Dead," replied the other quietly.

"Prove it."

De Chauxville looked up sharply. The cigarette dropped from his fingers to the floor. His face was yellow and drawn, with a singular tremble of the lips, which were twisted to one side.

"Good God!" he whispered hoarsely.

There was only one thought in his mind — a sudden wild desire to rise up and stand by Etta against the whole world. Verily we cannot tell what love may make of us, whither it may lead us. We only know that it never leaves us as it found us.

Then, leaning quietly against the stove, Vassili stated his case.

"Rather more than a year ago," he said, "I received an offer of the papers connected with a great scheme in this country. After certain enquiries had been made I accepted the offer. I paid a fabulous price for the papers. They were brought to me by a lady wearing a thick veil — a lady I had never seen before. I asked no questions, and paid her the money. It subsequently transpired that the papers had been stolen, as you perhaps know, from the house of Count Stépan Lanovitch — the house to which you happen to be going — at Thors. Well, that is all ancient history. It is to be supposed that the papers were stolen by Sydney Bamborough, who brought them here — probably to this hotel, where his wife was staying. He handed her the papers, and she conveyed them to me in Paris. But before she reached Petersburg they would have been missed by Stépan Lanovitch, who would naturally suspect the man who had been staying in his house, Bamborough — a man with a doubtful reputation in the diplomatic world, a professed doer of dirty jobs. Foreseeing this, and knowing that the League was a big thing, with a few violent members on its books, Sydney Bamborough did not attempt to leave Russia by the western route. He probably decided to go through Nijni, down the Volga, across the Caspian, and so on to Persia and India. You follow me?"

"Perfectly!" answered De Chauxville coldly.

"I have been here a week," went on the Russian spy, "making enquiries. I have worked the whole affair out, link by link, till the evening when the husband and wife parted. She went west with the papers. Where did he go?"

De Chauxville picked up the cigarette, looked at it curiously, as at a relic — the relic of the moment of strongest emotion through which he had ever passed — and threw it into the ash-tray. He did not speak, and after a moment Vassili went on, stating his case with lawyerlike clearness.

"A body was found on the steppe," he said; "the body of a middle-aged man dressed as a small commercial traveler would dress. He had a little money in his pocket, but nothing to identify him. He was buried here in Tver by the police, who received their information by an anonymous post-card posted in Tver. The person who had found the body did not want to be implicated in any enquiry. Now, who found the body? Who was the dead man? Mrs. Sydney Bamborough has assumed that the dead man was her husband; on the strength of that assumption she has become a princess. A frail foundation upon which to build up her fortunes, eh?"

"How did she know that the body had been found?" asked De Chauxville, perceiving the weak point in his companion's chain of argument.

"It was reported shortly in the local newspapers," replied Vassili, "and repeated in one or two continental journals, as the police were of opinion that the man was a foreigner. Anyone watching the newspapers would see it — otherwise the incident might pass unobserved."

"And you think," said De Chauxville, suppressing his excitement with an effort, "that the lady has risked everything upon a supposition?"

"Knowing the lady, I do."

De Chauxville's dull eyes gleamed for a moment with an unwonted light. All the civilization of the ages will not eradicate the primary instincts of men — and one of these, in good and bad alike, is to protect women. The Frenchman bit the end of his cigarette, and angrily wiped the tobacco from his lips.

"She may have information of which you are ignorant," he suggested.

"Precisely. It is that particular point which gives me trouble at the present moment. It is that that I wish to discover."

De Chauxville looked up coolly. He saw his advantage.

"Hence your sudden flow of communicativeness?" he said.

Vassili nodded.

"You cannot find out for yourself, so you seek my help?" went on the Frenchman.

Again the Russian nodded his head.

"And your price?" said De Chauxville, drawing in his feet and leaning forward, apparently to study the pattern of the carpet. The action concealed his face. He was saving Etta, and he was ashamed of himself.

"When you have the information you may name your own price," said the Russian coldly.

There was a long silence. Before speaking De Chauxville turned and took a glass of liqueur from the table. His hand was not quite steady. He raised the glass quickly and emptied it. Then he rose and looked at his watch. The silence was a compact.

"When the lady dined with you in Paris, did she recognize you?" he asked.

"Yes; but she did not know that I recognized her."

For the moment they both overlooked Steinmetz.

De Chauxville stood reflecting.

"And your theory," he said, "respecting Sydney Bamborough — what is it?"

"If he got away to Nijni and the Volga, it is probable that he is in Eastern Siberia or in Persia at this moment. He has not had time to get right across Asia yet."

De Chauxville moved toward the door. With his fingers on the handle he paused again.

"I leave early tomorrow morning," he said.

Vassili nodded, or rather he bowed, in his grand way.

Then De Chauxville went out of the room. They did not shake hands. There is sometimes shame among thieves.

Chapter XXVII

IN THE WEB

"What I propose is that Catrina takes you for a drive, my dear baron, with her two ponies."

The countess had taken very good care to refrain from making this proposal to Catrina alone. She was one of those mothers who rule their daughters by springing surprises upon them in a carefully selected company where the daughter is not free to reply.

De Chauxville bowed with outspread hands.

"If it will not bore mademoiselle," he replied.

The countess looked at her daughter with an unctuous smile, as if to urge her on to make the most of this opportunity. It was one of the countess's chief troubles that she could not by hook or crook involve Catrina in any sort of a love intrigue. She was the sort of mother who would have preferred to hear scandal about her daughter to hearing nothing.

"If it will not freeze monsieur," replied Catrina, with uncompromising honesty.

De Chauxville laughed in his frank way.

"I am not afraid of coldness — of the atmosphere, mademoiselle," he replied. "I am most anxious to see your beautiful country. It was quite dark during the last hour of my journey last night, and I had snow-sleepiness. I saw nothing."

"You will see nothing but snow," said Catrina.

"Which is like the reserve of a young girl," added the

Frenchman. "It keeps warm that which is beneath it."

"You need not be afraid with Catrina," chimed in the countess, nodding and becking in a manner that clearly showed her assumption to herself of some vague compliment. "She drives beautifully. She is not nervous in that way. I have never seen anyone drive like her."

"I have no doubt," said De Chauxville, "that mademoiselle's hands are firm, despite their diminutiveness."

The countess was charmed — and showed it. She frowned at Catrina, who remained grave and looked at the clock.

"When would you like to go?" she asked De Chauxville, with that complete absence of affectation which the Russian, of all women of the world, alone have mastered in their conversation with men.

"Am I not at your service — now and always?" responded the gallant baron.

"I hope not," replied Catrina quietly. "There are occasions when I have no use for you. Shall we say eleven o'clock?"

"With pleasure. Then I will go and write my letters now," said the baron, quitting the room.

"A charming man!" ejaculated the countess, before the door was well closed.

"A fool!" corrected Catrina.

"I do not think you can say that, dear," sighed the countess, more in sorrow than in anger.

"A clever one," answered Catrina. "There is a difference. The clever ones are the worst."

The countess shrugged her shoulders hopelessly, and Catrina left the room. She went upstairs to her own little den, where the piano stood. It was the only room in the house that was not too warm, for here the window was occasionally opened — a proceeding which the countess considered scarcely short of criminal.

Catrina began to play, feverishly, nervously, with all the weird force of her nature. She was like a very sick person seeking a desperate remedy — racing against time. It was her habit to take her breaking heart thus to the great masters, to interpret their thoughts in their music, welding their melodies to the needs of her own sorrow. She only had half an hour. Of late music had failed her a little. It had not given her the comfort she had usually extracted from solitude and the piano. She was in a dangerous humor. She was afraid of trusting herself to De Chauxville. The time fled, and her humor did not change. She was still playing when the door opened, and the countess stood before her flushed and angry, either or both being the effect of stairs upon emotion.

"Catrina!" the elder lady exclaimed. "The sleigh is at the door, and the count is waiting. I cannot tell what you are thinking of. It is not everybody who would be so attentive to you. Just look at your hair. Why can't you dress like other girls?"

"Because I am not made like other girls," replied Catrina — and who knows what bitterness of reproach there was in such an answer from daughter to mother?

"Hush, child," replied the countess, whose anger usually took the form of personal abuse. "You are as the good God made you."

"Then the good God must have made me in the dark," cried Catrina, flinging out of the room.

"She will be down directly," said the Countess Lanovitch to De Chauxville, whom she found smoking a cigarette in the hall. "She naturally — he! he! — wishes to make a careful toilet."

De Chauxville bowed gravely, without committing himself to any observation, and offered her a cigarette, which she accepted. Having achieved his purpose, he did not now propose to convey the impression that he admired Catrina.

In a few moments the girl appeared, drawing on her fur gloves. Before the door was opened the countess discreetly retired to the enervating warmth of her own apartments.

Catrina gathered up the reins and gave a little cry, at which the ponies leaped forward, and in a whirl of driven snow the sleigh glided off between the pines.

At first there was no opportunity of conversation, for the ponies were fresh and troublesome. The road over which they were passing had not been beaten down by the passage of previous sleighs, so that the powdery snow rose up like dust, and filled the eyes and mouth.

"It will be better presently," gasped Catrina, wrestling with her fractious little Tartar thoroughbreds, "when we get out on to the high-road."

De Chauxville sat quite still. If he felt any misgiving as to her power of mastering her team he kept it to himself. There was a subtle difference in his manner toward Catrina when they were alone together, a suggestion of camaraderie, of a common interest and a common desire, of which she was conscious without being able to put definite meaning to it.

It annoyed and alarmed her. While giving her full attention to the management of the sleigh, she was beginning to dread the first words of this man, who was merely wielding a cheap power acquired in the shady course of his career. There is nothing so disarming as the assumed air of intimate knowledge of one's private thoughts and actions. De Chauxville assumed this air with a skill against which Catrina's dogged strength of character was incapable of battling. His manner conveyed the impression that he knew more of Catrina's inward thoughts than any other living being, and she was simple enough to be frightened into the conclusion that she had betrayed herself to him. There is no simpler method of discovering a secret than to ignore its existence.

It is possible that De Chauxville became aware of Catrina's sidelong glances of anxiety in his direction. He may have divined that silence was more effective than speech.

He sat looking straight in front of him, as if too deeply absorbed in his own thoughts to take even a passing interest in the scenery.

"Why did you come here?" asked Catrina suddenly.

De Chauxville seemed to awake from a revery. He turned and looked at her in assumed surprise. They were on the high-road now, where the snow was beaten down, so conversation was easy.

"But — to see you, mademoiselle."

"I am not *that* sort of girl," answered Catrina coldly. "I want the truth."

De Chauxville gave a short laugh and looked at her.

"Prophets and kings have sought the truth, mademoiselle, and have not found it," he said lightly.

Catrina made no answer to this. Her ponies required considerable attention. Also, there are some minds like large banking houses — not dealing in small change. That which passes in or out of such minds has its own standard of importance. Such people are not of much use in these days, when we like to touch things lightly, adorning a tale but pointing no moral.

"I would ask you to believe that your society was one incentive to make me accept the countess's kind hospitality," the Frenchman observed after a pause.

"And?"

De Chauxville looked at her. He had not met many women of solid intellect.

"And?" repeated Catrina.

"I have others, of course."

Catrina gave a little nod and waited.

"I wish to be near Alexis," added De Chauxville.

Catrina was staring straight in front of her. Her face had acquired a habit of hardening at the mention of Paul's name. It was stonelike now, and set. Perhaps she might have forgiven him if he had loved her once, if only for a little while. She might have forgiven him, if only for the remembrance of that little while. But Paul had always been a man of set purpose, and such men are cruel. Even for her sake, even for the sake of his own vanity, he had never pretended to love Catrina. He had never mistaken gratified vanity for dawning love, as millions of men do. Or perhaps he was without vanity. Some few men are so constructed.

"Do you love him so?" asked Catrina, with a grim smile distorting her strong face.

"As much as you, mademoiselle," replied De Chauxville.

Catrina started. She was not sure that she hated Paul. Toward Etta, there was no mistake in her feeling, and this was so strong that, like an electric current, there was enough of it to pass through the wife and reach the husband.

Passion, like character, does not grow in crowded places. In great cities men are all more or less alike. It is only in solitary abodes that strong natures grow up in their own way. Catrina had grown to womanhood in one of the solitary places of the earth. She had no facile axiom, no powerful precedent, to guide her every step through life. The woman who was in daily contact with her was immeasurably beneath her in mental power, in force of character, in those possibilities of love or hatred which go to make a strong life for good or for evil. By the side of her daughter the Countess Lanovitch was as the willow, swayed by every wind, in the neighborhood of the oak, crooked and still and strong.

"In Petersburg you pledged yourself to help me," said De Chauxville. And although she knew that in the letter this was false, she did not contradict him. "I came here to claim fulfillment of your promise."

The hard blue eyes beneath the fur cap stared straight in front of them. Catrina seemed to be driving like one asleep, for she noted nothing by the roadside. So far as eye could reach over the snow-clad plain, through the silent pines, these two were alone in a white, dead world of their own. Catrina never drove with bells. There was no sound beyond the high-pitched drone of the steel runners over the powdery snow. They were alone; unseen, unheard save of that Ear that listens in the waste places of the world.

"What do you want me to do?" she asked.

"Oh, not very much!" answered De Chauxville — a cautious man, who knew a woman's humor. Catrina driving a pair of ponies in the clear, sharp air of Central Russia, and Catrina playing the piano in the enervating, flower-scented atmosphere of a drawing room, were two different women. De Chauxville was not the man to mistake the one for the other.

"Not very much, mademoiselle," he answered. "I should like Mme. la Comtesse to invite the whole Osterno party to dine, and sleep, perhaps, if one may suggest it."

Catrina wanted this too. She wanted to torture herself with the sight of Etta, beautiful, self-confident, carelessly cognizant of Paul's love. She wanted to see Paul look at his wife with the open admiration which she had set down as something else than love — something immeasurably beneath love as Catrina understood that passion. Her soul, brooding under a weight of misery, was ready to welcome any change, should it only mean a greater misery.

"I can manage that," she said, "if they will come. It was a prearranged matter that there should be a bear-hunt in our forests."

"That will do," answered De Chauxville reflectively; "in a few days, perhaps, if it suits the countess."

Catrina made no reply. After a pause she spoke again, in her strange, jerky way.

"What will you gain by it?" she asked.

De Chauxville shrugged his shoulders.

"Who knows?" he answered. "There are many things I want to know; many questions which can be answered only by one's own observation. I want to see them together. Are they happy?"

Catrina's face hardened.

"If there is a God in heaven, and he hears our prayers, they ought not to be," she replied curtly.

"She looked happy enough in Petersburg," said the Frenchman, who never told the truth for its own sake. Whenever he thought that Catrina's hatred needed stimulation he mentioned Etta's name.

"There are other questions in my mind," he went on, "some of which you can answer, mademoiselle, if you care to."

Catrina's face expressed no great willingness to oblige.

"The Charity League," said De Chauxville, looking at her keenly; "I have always had a feeling of curiosity respecting it. Was, for instance, our friend the Prince Pavlo implicated in that unfortunate affair?"

Catrina flushed suddenly. She did not take her eyes from the ponies. She was conscious of the unwonted color in her cheeks, which was slowly dying away beneath her companion's relentless gaze.

"You need not trouble to reply, mademoiselle," said De Chauxville, with his dark smile; "I am answered."

Catrina pulled the ponies up with a jerk, and proceeded to turn their willing heads toward home. She was alarmed and disturbed. Nothing seemed to be safe from the curiosity of this man, no secret secure, no prevarication of the slightest avail.

"There are other questions in my mind," said De Chauxville quietly, "but not now. Mademoiselle is no doubt tired."

He leaned back, and when at length he spoke it was to give utterance to the trite commonplace of which he made a conversational study.

Chapter *XXVIII*

IN THE CASTLE OF THORS

A week later Catrina, watching from the window of her own small room, saw Paul lift Etta from the sleigh, and the sight made her clench her hands until the knuckles shone like polished ivory.

She turned and looked at herself in the mirror. No one knew how she had tried one dress after another since luncheon, alone in her two rooms, having sent her maid down stairs. No one knew the bitterness in this girl's heart as she contemplated her own reflection.

She went slowly down stairs to the long, dimly lighted drawing room. As she entered she heard her mother's cackling voice.

"Yes, princess," the countess was saying, "it is a quaint old house; little more than a fortified farm, I know. But my husband's family were always strange. They seem always to have ignored the little comforts and elegancies of life."

"It is most interesting," answered Etta's voice, and Catrina stepped forward into the light.

Formal greetings were exchanged, and Catrina saw Etta look anxiously toward the door through which she had just come. She thought that she was looking for her husband. But it was Claude de Chauxville for whose appearance Etta was waiting.

Paul and Steinmetz entered at the same moment by another door, and Catrina, who was talking to Maggie in English, suddenly stopped.

"Ah, Catrina," said Paul, "we have broken new ground for you. There was no track from here to Osterno through the forest. I made one this afternoon, so you have no excuse for remaining away, now."

"Thank you," answered Catrina, withdrawing her cold hand hurriedly from his friendly grasp.

"Miss Delafield," went on Paul, "admires our country as much as you do."

"I was just telling mademoiselle," said Maggie, speaking French with an honest English accent.

Paul nodded, and left them together.

"Yes," the countess was saying at the other end of the gloomy room; "yes, we are greatly attached to Thors: Catrina, perhaps, more than I. I have some happy associations, and many sorrowful ones. But then — mon Dieu! — how isolated we are!"

"It is rather far from — anywhere," acceded Etta, who was not attending, although she appeared to be interested.

"Far! Princess, I often wonder how Paris and Thors can be in the same world! Before our — our troubles we used to live in Paris a portion of the year. At least I did, while my poor husband traveled about. He had a hobby, you know, poor man! Humanity was his hobby. I have always found that men who seek to do good to their fellows are never thanked. Have you noticed that? The human race is not grateful en gros. There is a little gratitude in the individual, but none in the race."

"None," answered Etta absently.

"It was so with the Charity League," went on the countess volubly. She paused and looked round with her feeble eyes.

"We are all friends," she went on; "so it is safe to mention the Charity League, is it not?"

"No," answered Steinmetz from the fireplace; "no, madame. There is only one friend to whom you may safely mention that."

"Ah! Bad example!" exclaimed the countess playfully. "You are there! I did not see you enter. And who is that friend?"

"The fair lady who looks at you from your mirror," replied

Steinmetz, with a face of stone.

The countess laughed and shook her cap to one side.

"Well," she said, "I can do no harm in talking of such things, as I know nothing of them. My poor husband — my poor mistaken Stépan — placed no confidence in his wife. And now he is in Siberia. I believe he works in a bootmaker's shop. I pity the people who wear the boots; but perhaps he only puts in the laces. You hear, Paul? He placed no confidence in his wife, and now he is in Siberia. Let that be a warning to you — eh, princess? I hope he tells you everything."

"Put not your trust in princesses," said Steinmetz from the hearthrug, where he was still warming his hands, for he had driven Maggie over. "It says so in the Bible."

"Princes, profane one!" exclaimed the countess with a laugh — "princes, not princesses!"

"It may be so. I bow to your superior literary attainments," replied Steinmetz, looking casually and significantly at a pile of yellow-backed foreign novels on a side-table.

"No," the countess went on, addressing her conversation to Etta; "no, my husband — figure to yourself, princess — told me nothing. I never knew that he was implicated in this great scheme. I do not know now who else was concerned in it. It was all so sudden, so unexpected, so terrible. It appears that he kept the papers in this very house — in that room through there. It was his study —"

"My dear countess, silence!" interrupted Steinmetz at this moment, breaking into the conversation in his masterful way and enabling Etta to get away. Catrina, at the other end of the room, was listening, hard-eyed, breathless. It was the sight of Catrina's face that made Steinmetz go forward. He had not been looking at Catrina, but at Etta, who was perfect in her composure and steady self-control.

"Do you want to enter the boot trade also?" asked Steinmetz cheerfully, in a lowered voice.

"Heaven forbid!" cried the countess.

"Then let us talk of safer things."

The short twilight was already brooding over the land. The room, lighted only by small square windows, grew darker and darker until Catrina rang for lamps.

"I hate a dark room," she said shortly to Maggie.

When De Chauxville came in, a few minutes later, Catrina was at the piano. The room was brilliantly lighted, and on the table gleamed and glittered the silver tea-things. The intermediate meal had been disposed of, but the samovar had been left alight, as is the habit at Russian afternoon teas.

Catrina looked up when the Frenchman entered, but did not cease playing.

"There is no need for introductions, I think," said the countess.

"We all know M. de Chauxville," replied Paul quietly, and the two men exchanged a glance.

De Chauxville shook hands with the newcomers, and, while the countess prepared tea for him, launched into a long description of the preparations for the bear-hunt of the following day. He addressed his remarks exclusively to Paul, as between enthusiasts and fellow-sportsmen. Gradually Paul thawed a little, and made one or two suggestions which betrayed a deep knowledge and a dawning interest.

"We shall only be three rifles," said De Chauxville, "Steinmetz, you, and I; and I must ask you to bear in mind the fact that I am no shot — a mere amateur, my dear prince. The countess has been good enough to leave the whole matter in my hands. I have seen the keepers, and I have arranged that they come tonight at eleven o'clock to see us and to report progress. They know of three bears, and are attempting to ring them."

The Frenchman was really full of information and enthusiasm. There were many details upon which he required Paul's advice, and the two men talked together with less constraint than they had hitherto done. De Chauxville had picked up a vast deal of technical matter, and handled his little knowledge with a skill which bade fair to deprive it of its proverbial danger. He presently left Steinmetz and the prince engaged in a controversy with the countess as to a meeting place at the luncheon-hour.

Maggie and Catrina were at the piano. Etta was looking at a book of photographs.

"A charming house, princess," said De Chauxville, in a voice that all could hear while the music happened to be soft. But Catrina's music was more remarkable for strength than for softness.

"Charming," replied Etta.

The music rose into a swelling burst of harmonious chords.

"I must see you, princess," said De Chauxville.

Etta glanced across the room toward her husband and Steinmetz.

"Alone," added the Frenchman coolly.

Etta turned a page of the album and looked critically into a photograph.

"Must!" she said, with a little frown.

"Must!" repeated De Chauxville.

"A word I do not care about," said Etta, with raised eyebrows.

The music was soft again.

"It is ten years since I held a rifle," said De Chauxville. "Ah, madame, you do not know the excitement. I pity ladies, for they have no sport — no big game."

"Personally, monsieur," answered Etta, with a bright laugh, "I do not grudge you your big game. Suppose you miss the bear, or whatever it may be?"

"Then," said De Chauxville, with a brave shrug of the shoulders, "it is the turn of the bear. The excitement is his — the laugh is with him."

Catrina's foot was upon the loud pedal again.

"Nevertheless, madame," said De Chauxville, "I make so bold as to use the word. You perhaps know me well enough to be aware that I am rarely bold unless my ground is sure."

"I should not boast of it," answered Etta; "there is nothing to be proud of. It is easy enough to be bold if you are certain of victory."

"When defeat would be intolerable, even a certain victory requires care! And I cannot afford to lose."

"Lose what?" enquired Etta.

De Chauxville looked at her, but he did not answer. The music was soft again.

"I suppose that at Osterno you set no value upon a bearskin," he said after a pause.

"We have many," admitted Etta. "But I love fur, or trophies of any description. Paul has killed a great deal."

"Ah!"

"Yes," answered Etta, and the music rose again. "I should like to know," she went on, "upon what assumption you make use of a word which does not often — annoy me."

"I have a good memory, madame. Besides," he paused, looking round the room, "there are associations within these walls which stimulate the memory."

"What do you mean?" asked Etta, in a hard voice. The hand holding the album suddenly shook like a leaf in the wind.

De Chauxville had stood upright, his hand at his mustache, after the manner of a man whose small-talk is exhausted. It would appear that he was wondering how he could gracefully get away from the princess to pay his devoirs elsewhere.

"I cannot tell you now," he answered; "Catrina is watching us across the piano. You must beware, madame, of those cold blue eyes."

He moved away, going toward the piano, where Maggie was standing behind Catrina's chair. He was like a woman, inasmuch as he could not keep away from his failures.

"Are you advanced, Miss Delafield?" he asked, with his deferential little bow. "Are you modern?"

"I am neither; I have no desire for even the cheapest form of notoriety. Why do you ask?" replied Maggie.

"I was merely wondering whether we were to count you among our rifles tomorrow. One never knows what ladies will do next; not ladies — I apologize — women. I suppose it is those who are not by birth ladies who aspire to the proud name of women. The modern Woman — with a capital W — is not a lady — n'est ce pas?"

"She does not mind your abuse, monsieur," laughed Maggie. "So long as you do not ignore her, she is happy. But you may set your mind at rest as regards tomorrow. I have never let off a gun in my life, and I am sensible enough not to begin on bears."

De Chauxville made a suitable reply, and remained by the piano talking to the two young ladies until Etta rose and came toward them. He then crossed to the other side of the room and engaged Paul in the discussion of further plans for the morrow.

It was soon time to dress for dinner, and Etta was forced

to forego the opportunity she sought to exchange a word alone with De Chauxville. That astute gentleman carefully avoided allowing her this opportunity. He knew the value of a little suspense.

During dinner and afterward, when at length the gentlemen came to the drawing room, the conversation was of a sporting tendency. Bears, bear-hunting, and bear stories held supreme sway. More than once De Chauxville returned to this subject. Twice he avoided Etta.

In some ways this man was courageous. He delayed giving Etta her opportunity until there was a question of retiring to bed in view of the early start required by the next day's arrangements. It had been finally settled that the three younger ladies should drive over to a woodman's cottage at the far end of the forest, where luncheon was to be served. While this item of the program was arranged De Chauxville looked straight at Etta across the table.

At length she had the chance afforded to her, deliberately, by De Chauxville.

"What did you mean?" she asked at once.

"I have received information which, had I known it three months ago, would have made a difference in your life."

"What difference?"

"I should have been your husband, instead of that thick-headed giant."

Etta laughed, but her lips were for the moment colorless.

"When am I to see you alone?"

Etta shrugged her shoulders. She had plenty of spirit.

"Please do not be dramatic or mysterious; I am tired. Good-night."

She rose and concealed a simulated yawn.

De Chauxville looked at her with his sinister smile, and Etta suddenly saw the resemblance which Paul had noted between this man and the grinning mask of the lynx in the smoking-room at Osterno.

"When?" repeated he.

Etta shrugged her shoulders.

"I wish to speak to you about the Charity League," said De Chauxville.

Etta's eyes dilated. She made a step or two away from him,

but she came back.

"I shall not go to the luncheon tomorrow, if you care to leave the hunt early."

De Chauxville bowed.

Chapter XXIX

ANGLO-RUSSIAN

*A*t bedtime Catrina went to Maggie's room with her to see that she had all that she could desire. A wood fire was burning brightly in the open French stove; the room was lighted by lamps. It was warm and cheery. A second door led to the little music-room which Catrina had made her own, and beyond was her bedroom.

Maggie had assured her hostess that she had everything that she could wish, and that she did not desire the services of Catrina's maid. But the Russian girl still lingered. She was slow to make friends — not shy, but diffident and suspicious. Her friendship once secured was a thing worth possessing. She was inclined to bestow it upon this quiet, self-contained English girl. In such matters the length of an acquaintance goes for nothing. A long acquaintanceship does not necessarily mean friendship — one being the result of circumstance, the other of selection.

"The princess knows Russian?" said Catrina suddenly.

She was standing near the dressing-table, where she had been absently attending to the candles. She wheeled round and looked at Maggie, who was hospitably sitting on a low chair near the fire. She was sorry for the loneliness of this girl's life. She did not want her to go away just yet. There was another chair by the fire, inviting Catrina to indulge in those maiden confidences which attach themselves to slippers and hair-brushings.

Maggie looked up with a smile which slowly ebbed away. Catrina's remark was of the nature of a defiance. Her half-diffident rôle of hostess was suddenly laid aside.

"No; she does not," answered the English girl.

Catrina came forward, standing over Maggie, looking down at her with eyes full of antagonism.

"Excuse me. I saw her understand a remark I made to one of the servants. She was not careful. I saw it distinctly."

"I think you must be mistaken," answered Maggie quietly. "She has been in Russia before for a few weeks; but she did not learn the language. She told me so herself. Why should she pretend not to know Russian, if she does?"

Catrina made no answer. She sat heavily down in the vacant chair. Her attitudes were uncouth and strong — a perpetual source of tribulation to the countess. She sat with her elbow on her knee, staring into the fire.

"I did not mean to hate her; I did not want to," she said. "If it had been you, I should not have hated you."

Maggie's clear eyes wavered for a moment. A faint color rose to her face. She leaned back so that the firelight did not reach her. There was a silence, during which Maggie unclasped a bracelet with a little snap of the spring. Catrina did not hear the sound. She heard nothing. She did not appear to be aware of her surroundings. Maggie unclasped another bracelet noisily. She was probably regretting her former kindness of manner. Catrina had come too near.

"Are you not judging rather hastily?" suggested Maggie, in a measured voice which heightened the contrast between the two. "I find it takes some time to discover whether one likes or dislikes new acquaintances."

"Yes; but you English are so cold and deliberate. You do not know what it is to hate — or to care."

"Perhaps we do," said Maggie; "but we say less about it."

Catrina turned and looked at her with a queer smile.

"Less!" she laughed. "Nothing — you say nothing. Paul is

the same. I have seen. I know. You have said nothing since you came to Thors. You have talked and laughed; you have given opinions; you have spoken of many things, but you have said nothing. You are the same as Paul — one never knows. I know nothing about you. But I like you. You are her cousin?"

"Yes."

"And I hate her!"

Maggie laughed. She was quite steady and loyal.

"When you get to know her you will change, perhaps," she said.

"Perhaps I know her now better than you do!"

Maggie laughed in her cheery, practical way.

"That seems hardly likely, considering that I have known her since we were children."

Catrina shrugged her shoulders in an honest if somewhat mannerless refusal to discuss the side issue. She returned to the main question with characteristic stubbornness.

"I shall always hate her," she said. "I am sorry she is your cousin. I shall always regret that, and I shall always hate her. There is something wrong about her — something none of you know except Karl Steinmetz. He knows everything — Herr Steinmetz."

"He knows a great deal," admitted Maggie.

"Yes; and that is why he is sad. Is it not so?"

Catrina sat staring into the fire, her strange, earnest eyes almost fierce in their concentration.

"Did she pretend that she loved him at first?" she asked suddenly.

Receiving no answer, she looked up and fixed her searching gaze on the face of her companion. Maggie was looking straight in front of her in the direction of the fire, but not with eyes focused to see anything so near at hand. She bore the scrutiny without flinching. As soon as Catrina's eyes were averted the masklike stillness of her features relaxed.

"She does not take that trouble now," added the Russian girl, in reply to her own question. "Did you see her tonight when we were at the piano? M. de Chauxville was talking to her. They were keeping two conversations going at the same time. I could see by their faces. They said different things when the music was loud. I hate her. She is not true to Paul. M. de Chauxville knows something about her. They have something in common which is not known to Paul or to any of us! Why do you not speak? Why do you sit staring into the fire with your lips so close together?"

"Because I do not think that we shall gain anything by discussing Paul and his wife. It is no business of ours."

Catrina laughed — a lamentable, mirthless laugh.

"That is because she is your cousin; and he — he is nothing to you. You do not care whether he is happy or not!"

Catrina had turned upon her companion fiercely. Maggie swung round in her chair to pick up her bracelets, which had slipped from her knees to the floor.

"You exaggerate things," she said quietly. "I see no reason to suppose that Paul is unhappy. It is because you have taken this unreasoning dislike to her."

She took a long time to collect three bracelets. Then she rose and placed them on the dressing-table.

"Do you want me to go?" asked Catrina, in her blunt way.

"No," answered Maggie, civilly enough; but she extracted a couple of hair-pins rather obviously.

Catrina heeded the voice and not the action.

"You English are all alike," she said. "You hold one at arm's length. I suppose there is some one in England for whom you care — who is out of all this — away from all the troubles of Russia. This has nothing to do with your life. It is only a passing incident — a few weeks to be forgotten when you go back. I wonder what he is like — the man in England. You need not tell me. I am not curious in that way. I am not asking you to tell me. I am just wondering. For I know there is some one. I knew it when I first saw you. You are so quiet, and settled, and self-contained — like a person who has played a game and knows for certain that it is lost or won, and does not want to play again. Your hair is very pretty; you are very pretty, you quiet English girl. I wonder what you think about behind your steady eyes."

"I?" said Maggie, with a little laugh. "Oh — I think about my dresses, and the new fashions, and parties, and all the things that girls do think of."

Catrina shook her head. She looked stubborn and unconvinced. Then suddenly she changed the conversation.

"Do you like M. de Chauxville?" she asked.

"No."

"Does Paul like him?"

"I don't know."

Catrina looked up for a moment only. Then her eyes returned to the contemplation of the burning pine-logs.

"I wonder why you will not talk of Paul," she said, in a voice requiring no answer.

Maggie moved rather uneasily. She had her back turned toward Catrina.

"I am afraid I am rather a dull person," she answered. "I have not much to say about any body."

"And nothing about Paul?" suggested Catrina.

"Nothing. We were talking of M. de Chauxville."

"Yes; I do not understand M. de Chauxville. He seems to me to be the incarnation of insincerity. He poses — even to himself. He is always watching for the effect. I wonder what the effect of himself upon himself may be."

Maggie laughed.

"That is rather complicated," she said. "It requires working out. I think he is deeply impressed with his own astuteness. If he were simpler he would be cleverer."

Catrina was afraid of Claude de Chauxville, and, because this was so, she stared in wonder at the English girl, who dismissed him from the conversation and her thoughts with a few careless words of contempt. Such minds as that of Miss Delafield were quite outside the field of De Chauxville's influence, while that Frenchman had considerable power over highly strung and imaginative natures.

Catrina Lanovitch had begun by tolerating him — had proceeded to make the serious blunder of permitting him to be impertinently familiar, and was now exaggerating in her own mind the hold that he had over her. She did not actually dislike him. So few people had taken the trouble or found the expediency of endeavoring to sympathize with her or understand her nature, that she was unconsciously drawn toward this man whom she now feared.

In exaggerating the power he exercised over herself she somewhat naturally exaggerated also his importance in the world and in the lives of those around him. She had imagined him all-powerful; and the first person to whom she mentioned his name dismissed the subject indifferently. Her own entire sincerity had enabled her to detect the insincerity of her ally. She had purposely made mention of the weak spot which she had discovered, in order that her observation might be corroborated. And this Maggie had failed to do.

With the slightest encouragement, Catrina would have told her companion all that had passed. The sympathy between women is so strong that there is usually only one man who is safe from discussion. In Catrina's case that one man was not Claude de Chauxville. But Maggie Delafield was of different material from this impressionable, impulsive Russian girl. She was essentially British in her capacity for steering a straight personal course through the shoals and quicksands of her neighbors' affairs, as also in the firm grip she held upon her own thoughts. She was by no means prepared to open her mind to the first comer, and in her somewhat slow-going English estimate of such matters Catrina was as yet little more than the first comer.

She changed the subject, and they talked for some time on indifferent topics — such topics as have an interest for girls; and who are we that we may despise them? We jeer very grandly at girls' talk, and promptly return to the discussion of our dogs and pipes and clothing.

But Catrina was not happy under this judicious treatment. She had no one in the world to whom she could impart a thousand doubts and questions — a hundred grievances and one great grief. And it was just this one great grief of which Maggie dreaded the mention. She was quite well aware of its existence — had been aware of it for some time. Karl Steinmetz had thrown out one or two vague hints; everything pointed to it. Maggie could hardly be ignorant of the fact that Catrina had grown to womanhood loving Paul.

A score of times Catrina approached the subject, and with imperturbable steadfastness Maggie held to her determination that Paul was not to be discussed by them. She warded, she evaded, she ignored with a skill which baffled the simple Russian. She had a hundred subterfuges — a hundred skillful turns and twists. Where women learn these matters, Heaven only knows! All our experience of the world, our falls and stumbles on the broken road of life, never teach us some things that are known to the veriest schoolgirl standing on the smoother footpath that women tread.

At last Catrina rose to go. Maggie rose also. Women are relentless where they fight for their own secrets. Maggie morally turned Catrina out of the room. The two girls stood looking at each other for a moment. They had nothing in common. The language in which they understood each other best was the native tongue of neither. Born in different countries, each of a mixed race with no one racial strain in common, neither creed, nor education, nor similarity of thought had aught to draw them together. They looked at each other, and God's hand touched them. They both loved the same man. They did not hate each other.

"Have you everything you want?" asked Catrina.

The question was startling. Catrina's speech was ever abrupt. At first Maggie did not understand.

"Yes, thanks," she answered. "I am very tired. I suppose it is the snow."

"Yes," said Catrina mechanically; "it is the snow."

She went toward the door, and there she paused.

"Does Paul love her?" she asked abruptly.

Maggie made no answer; and, as was her habit, Catrina replied to her own question.

"You know he does not — you know he does not!" she said.

Then she went out, without waiting for an answer, closing the door behind her. The closed door heard the reply.

"It will not matter much," said Maggie, "so long as he never finds it out."

Chapter XXX

WOLF!

*T*he Countess Lanovitch never quitted her own apartments before mid-day. She had acquired a Parisian habit of
being invisible until luncheon-time. The two girls left the
castle of Thors in a sleigh with one attendant at ten o'clock
in order to reach the hut selected for luncheon by mid-day.
Etta did not accompany them. She had a slight headache.

At eleven o'clock Claude de Chauxville returned alone, on
horseback. After the sportsmen had separated, each to gain
his prearranged position in the forest, he had tripped over
his rifle, seriously injuring the delicate sighting mechanism.
He found (he told the servant who opened the door for him)
that he had just time to return for another rifle before the
operation of closing in on the bears was to begin.

"If Madame the Princess," was visible, he went on, would
the servant tell her that M. de Chauxville was waiting in the
library to assure her that there was absolutely no danger to
be anticipated in the day's sport. The princess, it would
appear, was absurdly anxious about the welfare of her husband — an experienced hunter and a dead shot.

Claude de Chauxville then went to the library, where he
waited, booted, spurred, rifle in hand, for Etta.

After a lapse of five minutes or more, the door was opened,
and Etta came leisurely into the room.

"Well?" she enquired indifferently.

De Chauxville bowed. He walked past her and closed the door, which she happened to have left open.

Then he returned and stood by the window, leaning gracefully on his rifle. His attitude, his hunting-suit, his great top-boots, made rather a picturesque object of him.

"Well?" repeated Etta, almost insolently.

"It would have been wiser to have married me," said De Chauxville darkly.

Etta shrugged her shoulders.

"Because I understand you better; I *know* you better than your husband."

Etta turned and glanced at the clock.

"Have you come back from the bear-hunt to tell me this, or to avoid the bears?" she asked.

De Chauxville frowned. A man who has tasted fear does not like a question of his courage.

"I have come to tell you that and other things," he answered.

He looked at her with his sinister smile and a little upward jerk of the head. He extended his open hand, palm upward, with the fingers slightly crooked.

"I hold you, madame," he said — "I hold you in my hand. You are my slave, despite your brave title; my thing, my plaything, despite your servants, and your great houses, and your husband! When I have finished telling you all that I have to tell, you will understand. You will perhaps thank me for being merciful."

Etta laughed defiantly.

"You are afraid of Paul," she cried. "You are afraid of Karl Steinmetz; you will presently be afraid of me."

"I think not," said De Chauxville coolly. The two names just mentioned were certainly not of pleasant import in his ears, but he was not going to let a woman know that. This man had played dangerous cards before now. He was not at all sure of his ground. He did not know what Etta's position was in regard to Steinmetz. Behind the defiant woman there lurked the broad shadow of the man who never defied; who knew many things, but was ignorant of fear.

Unlike Karl Steinmetz, De Chauxville was not a bold player. He liked to be sure of his trick before he threw down his trump card. His method was not above suspicion: he liked to know what cards his adversary held, and one may be sure that he was not above peeping.

"Karl Steinmetz is no friend of yours," he said.

Etta did not answer. She was thinking of the conversation she had had with Steinmetz in Petersburg. She was wondering whether the friendship he had offered — the solid thing as he called it — was not better than the love of this man.

"I have information now," went on De Chauxville, "which would have made you my wife, had I had it sooner."

"I think not," said the lady insolently. She had dealt with such men before. Hers was the beauty that appealed to De Chauxville and such as he. It is not the beautiful women who see the best side of human nature.

"Even now," went on the Frenchman, "now that I know you — I still love you. You are the only woman I shall ever love."

"Indeed!" murmured the lady, quite unmoved.

"Yes; although in a way I despise you — now that I know you."

"Mon Dieu!" exclaimed Etta. "If you have anything to say, please say it. I have no time to probe your mysteries — to discover your parables. You know me well enough, perhaps, to be aware that I am not to be frightened by your cheap charlatanism."

"I know you well enough," retorted De Chauxville hoarsely, "to be aware that it was you who sold the Charity League papers to Vassili in Paris. I know you well enough, madame, to be aware of your present position in regard to your husband. If I say a word in the right quarter you would never leave Russia alive. I have merely to say to Catrina Lanovitch that it was you who banished her father for your own gain. I have merely to hand your name in to certain of the Charity League party, and even your husband could not save you."

He had gradually approached her, and uttered the last words face to face, his eyes close to hers. She held her head up — erect, defiant still.

"So you see, madame," he said, "you belong to me."

She smiled.

"Hand and foot," he added. "But I am soft-hearted."

He shrugged his shoulders and turned away.

"What will you?" he said, looking out of the window. "I love you."

"Nonsense!"

He turned slowly round.

"What?"

"Nonsense!" repeated Etta. "You love power; you are a bully. You love to please your own vanity by thinking that you have me in your power. I am not afraid of you."

De Chauxville leaned gracefully against the window. He still held his rifle.

"Reflect a little," he said, with his cold smile. "It would appear that you do not quite realize the situation. Women rarely realize situations in time. Our friend — your husband — has many of the English idiosyncrasies. He has all the narrow-minded notions of honor which obtain in that country. Added to this, I suspect him of possessing a truly Slavonic fire which he keeps under. 'A smoldering fire —' You know, madame, our French proverb. He is not the man to take a rational and broad-minded view of your little transaction with M. Vassili; more especially, perhaps, as it banished his friend Stépan Lanovitch — the owner of this house, by the way. His reception of the news I have to tell him would be unpleasant — for you."

"What do you want?" interrupted Etta. "Money?"

"I am not a needy adventurer."

"And I am not such a fool, M. de Chauxville, as to allow myself to be dragged into a vulgar intrigue, borrowed from a French novel, to satisfy your vanity."

De Chauxville's dull eyes suddenly flashed.

"I will trouble you to believe, madame," he said, in a low, concentrated voice, "that such a thought never entered my head. A De Chauxville is not a commercial traveler, if you please. No; it may surprise you, but my feeling for you has more good in it than you would seem capable of inspiring. God only knows how it is that a bad woman can inspire a good love."

Etta looked at him in amazement. She did not always understand De Chauxville. No matter for surprise, perhaps;

for he did not always understand himself.

"Then what do you want?" she asked.

"In the meantime, implicit obedience."

"What are you going to use me for?"

"I have ends," replied Claude de Chauxville, who had regained his usual half-mocking composure, "that you will serve. But they will be your ends as well as mine. You will profit by them. I will take very good care that you come to no harm, for you are the ultimate object of all this. At the end of it all I see only — you."

Etta shrugged her shoulders. It is to be presumed that she was absolutely heartless. Many women are. It is when a heartless woman has brains that one hears of her.

"What if I refuse?" asked Etta, keenly aware of the fact that this man was handicapped by his love for her.

"Then I will force you to obedience."

Etta raised her delicate eyebrows insolently.

"Ah!"

"Yes," said De Chauxville, with suppressed anger; "I will force you to obey me."

The princess looked at him with her little mocking smile. She raised one hand to her head with a reflective air, as if a hair-pin were of greater importance than his words. She had dressed herself rather carefully for this interview. She never for a moment overlooked the fact that she was a woman, and beautiful. She did not allow him to forget it either.

Her mood of outraged virtue was now suddenly thrown into the background by a phase of open coquetry. Beneath her eyelids she watched for the effect of her pretty, provoking attitude on the man who loved her. She was on her own territory at this work, playing her own game; and she was more alarmed by De Chauxville's imperturbability than by anything he had said.

"You have a strange way of proving the truth of your own statements."

"What statements?"

She gave a little laugh. Her attitude, her glance, the cunning display of a perfect figure, the laugh, the whole woman, was the incarnation of practiced coquetry. She did not admit, even to herself, that she was afraid of De Chauxville. But she was playing her best cards, in her best manner. She had never known them fail.

Claude de Chauxville was a little white about the lips. His eyelids flickered, but by an effort he controlled himself, and she did not see the light in his eyes for which she looked.

"If you mean," he said coldly, "the statement that I made to you before you were married — namely, that I love you — I am quite content to leave the proof till the future. I know what I am about, madame."

He took his watch from his pocket and consulted it.

"I must go in five minutes," he said. "I have a few instructions to give you, to which I must beg your careful attention."

He looked up, meeting Etta's somewhat sullen gaze with a smile of triumph.

"It is essential," he went on, "that I be invited to Osterno. I do not want to stay there long; indeed, I do not care to. But I must see the place. I dare say you can compass the invitation, madame?"

"It will be difficult."

"And therefore worthy of your endeavor. I have the greatest regard for your diplomatic skill. I leave the matter in your hands, princess."

Etta shrugged her shoulders and looked past him out of the window. De Chauxville was considering her face carefully.

"Another point to be remembered," he went on, "is your husband's daily life at Osterno. The prince is not above suspicion; the authorities are watching him. He is suspected of propagating revolutionary ideas among the peasantry. I should like you to find out as much as you can. Perhaps you know already. Perhaps he has told you, princess. I know that beautiful face! He has told you! Good! Does he take an interest in the peasants?"

Etta did not answer.

"Kindly give me your attention, madame. Does the prince take an interest in the peasants?"

"Yes."

"An active interest?"

"Yes."

"Have you any details?"

"No," answered Etta.

"Then you will watch him, and procure those details."

Etta's face was defiant and pale. De Chauxville never took his eyes from it.

"I have undertaken a few small commissions for an old friend of yours, M. Vassili, whom you obliged once before!" he said; and the defiance faded from her eyes.

"The authorities cannot, in these disturbed times, afford to tolerate princes of an independent turn of mind. Such men are apt to make the peasant think himself more important than he is. I dare say, madame, that you are already tired of Russia. It might perhaps serve your ends if this country was made a little too hot for your husband, eh? I see your proud lips quivering, princess! It is well to keep the lips under control. We, who deal in diplomacy, know where to look for such signs. Yes; I dare say I can get you out of Russia — forever. But you must be obedient. You must reconcile yourself to the knowledge that you have met — your master."

He bowed in his graceful way, spreading out his hands in mock humility. Etta did not answer him. For the moment she could see no outlet to this maze of trouble, and yet she was conscious of not fearing De Chauxville so much as she feared Karl Steinmetz.

"A lenient master," pursued the Frenchman, whose vanity was tickled by the word. "I do not ask much. One thing is to be invited to Osterno, that I may be near you. The other is a humble request for details of your daily life, that I may think of you when absent."

Etta drew in her lips, moistening them as if they had suddenly become parched.

De Chauxville glanced at her and moved toward the door. He paused with his fingers on the handle, and looking back over his shoulder he said:

"Have I made myself quite clear?"

Etta was still looking out of the window with hard, angry eyes. She took no notice of the question.

De Chauxville turned the handle.

"Again let me impress upon you the advisability of implicit obedience," he said, with delicate insolence. "I mentioned the Charity League; but that is not my strongest claim upon your attention. I have another interesting little detail of your life, which I will reserve until another time."

He closed the door behind him, leaving Etta white-lipped.

Chapter *XXXI*

A DANGEROUS EXPERIMENT

A Russian forest in winter is one of nature's places of worship. There are some such places in the world, where nature seems to stand in the presence of the Deity; a sunrise at sea; night on a snow-clad mountain; mid-day in a Russian forest in winter. These places and these times are good for convalescent atheists and such as pose as unbelievers — the cheapest form of notoriety.

Paul had requested Catrina and Maggie to drive as quietly as possible through the forest. The warning was unnecessary, for the stillness of snow is infectious, while the beauty of the scene seemed to command silence. As usual, Catrina drove without bells. The one attendant on his perch behind was a fur-clad statue of servitude and silence. Maggie, leaning back, hidden to the eyes in her sables, had nothing to say to her companion. The way lay through forests of pine — trackless, motionless, virgin. The sun, filtering through the snow-laden branches, cast a subdued golden light upon the ruddy upright trunks of the trees. At times a willow-grouse, white as the snow, light and graceful on the wing, rose from the branch where he had been laughing to his mate with a low, cooing laugh, and fluttered away over the trees.

"A kooropatka," said Catrina, who knew the life of the

forest almost as well as Paul, whose very existence was wrapped up in these things.

Far over the summits of the pines a snipe seemed to be wheeling a sentinel round. He followed them as they sped along, calling out all the while his deep warning note, like that of a lamb crouching beneath a hedge where the wind is not tempered.

Once or twice they heard the dismal howl of a wolf — the most melancholy, the weirdest, the most hopeless of nature's calls. The whole forest seemed to be on the alert — astir and in suspense. The wolf, disturbed in his lair, no doubt heard and understood the cry of the watchful snipe and the sudden silence of the willow-grouse, who loves to sit and laugh when all is safe. A clumsy capercailzie, swinging along over the trees with a great flap and rush of wings, seemed to be intent on his own solitary, majestic business — a very king among the fowls of the air.

Amid the topmost branches of the pines the wind whispered and stirred like a child in sleep; but beneath all was still. Every branch stood motionless beneath its burden of snow. The air was thin, exhilarating, brilliant — like dry champagne. It seemed to send the blood coursing through the veins with a very joy of life.

Catrina noted all these things while cleverly handling her ponies. They spoke to her with a thousand voices. She had roamed in these same forests with Paul, who loved them and understood them as she did.

Maggie, in the midst as it were of a revelation, leaned back and wondered at it all. She, too, was thinking of Paul, the owner of these boundless forests. She understood him better now. This drive had revealed to her a part of his nature which had rather puzzled her — a large, simple, quiet strength which had developed and grown to maturity beneath these trees. We are all part of what we have seen. We all carry with us through life somewhat of the scenes through which we passed in childhood.

Maggie knew now where Paul had learnt the quiet concentration of mind, the absorption in his own affairs, the complete lack of interest in the business of his neighbor which made him different from other men. He had learnt these things at first hand from God's creatures. These forest-dwellers of fur and feather went about their affairs in the same absorbed way, with the same complete faith, the same desire to leave and be left alone. The simplicity of Nature was his. His only craft was forest craft.

"Now you know," said Catrina, when they reached the hut, "why I hate Petersburg."

Maggie nodded. The effect of the forest was still upon her. She did not want to talk.

The woman who received them, the wife of a keeper, had prepared in a rough way for their reception. She had a large fire and bowls of warm milk. The doors and windows had been thrown wide open by Paul's orders. He wanted to spare Maggie too intimate an acquaintance with a Russian interior. The hut was really a shooting-box built by Paul some years earlier, and inhabited by a head-keeper, one learned in the ways of bear and wolf and lynx. The large dwelling-room had been carefully scrubbed. There was a smell of pine-wood and soap. The table, ready spread with a simple luncheon, took up nearly the whole of the room.

While the two girls were warming themselves, a keeper came to the door of the hut and asked to see Catrina. He stood in the little door-way, completely filling it, and explained that he could not come in, as the buckles and straps of his snow-shoes were clogged and frozen. He wore the long Norwegian snow-shoes, and was held to be the quickest runner in the country.

Catrina had a long conversation with the man, who stood hatless, ruddy, and shy.

"It is," she then explained to Maggie, "Paul's own man, who always loads for him and carries his spare gun. He has sent him to tell us that the game has been ringed, and that the beaters will close in on a place called the Schapka Clearing, where there is a woodman's refuge. If we care to put on our snow-shoes, this man will guide us to the clearing and take care of us till the battue is over."

Of course Maggie welcomed the proposal with delight, and after a hasty luncheon the three glided off through the forest as noiselessly as they had come. After a tiring walk of an hour and more they came to the clearing, and were duly concealed in the hut.

No one, the keeper told the ladies, except Paul, knew of their presence in the little wooden house. The arrangements of the beat had been slightly altered at the last moment after the hunters had separated. The keeper lighted a small fire and shyly attended to the ladies, removing their snow-shoes with clumsy fingers. He closed the door, and arranged a branch of larch across the window so that they could stand near it without being seen.

They had not been there long before De Chauxville appeared. He moved quickly across the clearing, skimming over the snow with long, sweeping strides. Two keepers followed him, and after having shown him the rough hiding place prepared for him, silently withdrew to their places. Soon Karl Steinmetz came from another direction, and took up his position rather nearer to the hut, in a thicket of pine and dwarf oak. He was only twenty yards away from the refuge where the girls were concealed.

It was not long before Paul came. He was quite alone, and suddenly appeared at the far end of the clearing, in very truth a mighty hunter, standing nearly seven feet on his snow-shoes. One rifle he carried in his hand, another slung across his back. It was like a silent scene on a stage. The snow-white clearing, with long-drawn tracks across it where the snow-shoes had passed, the still trees, the brilliant sun, and the blue depths of the forest behind; while Paul, like the hero of some grim Arctic saga, a huge fur-clad Northern giant, stood alone in the desolation.

From his attitude it was apparent that he was listening. It was probable that the cries of the birds and the distant howl of a wolf told his practiced ears how near the beaters were. He presently moved across to where De Chauxville was hidden, spoke some words of advice or warning to him, and pointed with his gloved hand in the direction whence the game might be expected to come.

It subsequently transpired that Paul was asking De Chauxville the whereabouts of Steinmetz, who had gained his place of concealment unobserved by either. De Chauxville could give him no information, and Paul went away to his post dissatisfied. Karl Steinmetz must have seen them; he must have divined the subject of their conversation; but he remained hidden and gave no sign.

Paul's post was behind a fallen tree, and the watchers in the hut could see him, while he was completely hidden from any animal that might enter the open clearing from the far end. He turned and looked hard at the hut; but the larch branch across the window effectually prevented him from discovering whether anyone was behind it or not.

Thus they all waited in suspense. A blackcock skimmed across the open space and disappeared unmolested. A wolf — gray, gaunt, sneaking, and lurching in his gait — trotted into the clearing and stood listening with evil lips drawn back. The two girls watched him breathlessly. When he trotted on unmolested, they drew a deep breath as if they had been under water. Paul, with his two rifles laid before him, watched the wolf depart with a smile. The girls could see the smile, and from it learnt somewhat of the man. The keeper beside them gave a little laugh and looked to the hammers of his rifle.

And still there was no sound. It was still, unreal, and like a scene on the stage. The birds, skimming over the tops of the trees from time to time, threw in as it were a note of fear and suspense. There was breathlessness in the air. A couple of hares, like white shadows in their spotless winter coats, shot from covert to covert across the open ground.

Then suddenly the keeper gave a little grunt and held up his hand, listening with parted lips and eager eyes. There was a distinct sound of breaking branches and crackling underwood.

They could see Paul cautiously rise from his knees to a crouching attitude. They followed the direction of his gaze, and before them the monarch of these forests stood in clumsy might. A bear had shambled to the edge of the clearing and was standing upright, growling and grumbling to himself, his great paws waving from side to side, his shaggy head thrust forward with a recurring jerk singularly suggestive of a dandy with an uncomfortable collar. These bears of Northern Russia have not the reputation of being very fierce unless they are aroused from their winter quarters, when their wrath knows no bounds and their courage recognizes no danger. An angry bear is afraid of no living man or beast. Moreover, these kings of the Northern forests are huge beasts, capable of smothering a strong man by falling on him and lying there — a death which has come to more than one daring hunter. The beast's favorite method of dealing with his foe is to claw him to death, or else hug him till his ribs are snapped and crushed into his vitals.

The bear stood poking his head and looking about with little, fiery, bloodshot eyes for something to destroy. His rage was manifest, and in his strength he was a grand sight. The majesty of power and a dauntless courage were his.

It was De Chauxville's shot, and while keeping his eye on the bear, Paul glanced impatiently over his shoulder from time to time, wondering why the Frenchman did not fire. The bear was a huge one, and would probably carry three bullets and still be a dangerous adversary.

The keeper muttered impatiently.

They were watching Paul breathlessly. The bear was approaching him. It would not be safe to defer firing another second.

Suddenly the keeper gave a short exclamation of astonishment and threw up his rifle.

There was another bear behind Paul, shambling toward him, unseen by him. All his attention was riveted on the huge brute forty yards in front of him. It was Claude de Chauxville's task to protect Paul from any flank or rear attack; and Claude de Chauxville was peering over his covert, watching with blanched face the second bear; and lifting no hand, making no sign. The bear was within a few yards of Paul, who was crouching behind the fallen pine and now raising his rifle to his shoulder.

In a flash of comprehension the two girls saw all, through the panes of the closed window. It was still singularly like a scene on the stage. The second bear raised his powerful fore-paws as he approached. One blow would tear open Paul's brain.

A terrific report sent the girls staggering back, for a moment paralyzing thought. The keeper had fired through the window, both barrels almost simultaneously. It was a question how much lead would bring the bear down before he covered the intervening dozen yards. In the confined space of the hut, the report of the heavy double charge was like that of a cannon; moreover, Steinmetz, twenty yards away, had fired at the same moment.

The room was filled with smoke. The two girls were blinded for an instant. Then they saw the keeper tear open the door and disappear. The cold air through the shattered casement was a sudden relief to their lungs, choked with sulfur and the fumes of spent powder.

In a flash they were out of the open door; and there again, with the suddenness of a panorama, they saw another picture — Paul kneeling in the middle of the clearing, taking careful aim at the retreating form of the first bear. They saw the puff of blue smoke rise from his rifle, they heard the sharp report; and the bear rolled over on its face.

Steinmetz and the keeper were walking toward Paul. Claude de Chauxville, standing outside his screen of brushwood, was staring with wide, fear-stricken eyes at the hut which he had thought empty. He did not know that there were three people behind him, watching him. What had they seen? What had they understood?

Catrina and Maggie ran toward Paul. They were on snow-shoes, and made short work of the intervening distance.

Paul had risen to his feet. His face was grave. There was a singular gleam in his eyes, which was not a gleam of mere excitement such as the chase brings into some men's eyes.

Steinmetz looked at him and said nothing. For a moment Paul stood still. He looked round him, noting with experienced glance the lay of the whole incident — the dead form of the bear ten yards behind his late hiding place, one hundred and eighty yards from the hut, one hundred and sixty yards from the spot whence Karl Steinmetz had sent his unerring bullet through the bear's brain. Paul saw it all. He measured the distances. He looked at De Chauxville, standing white-faced at his post, not fifty yards from the carcass of the second bear.

Paul seemed to see no one but De Chauxville. He went straight toward him, and the whole party followed in breathless suspense. Steinmetz was nearest to him, watching with his keen, quiet eyes.

Paul went up to De Chauxville and took the rifle from his

hands. He opened the breech and looked into the barrels. They were clean; the rifle had not been fired off.

He gave a little laugh of contempt, and, throwing the rifle at De Chauxville's feet, turned abruptly away.

It was Catrina who spoke.

"If you had killed him," she said, "I would have killed you!"

Steinmetz picked up the rifle, closed the breech, and handed it to De Chauxville with a queer smile.

Chapter XXXII

A CLOUD

*W*hen the Osterno party reached home that same evening the starosta was waiting to see Steinmetz. His news was such that Steinmetz sent for Paul, and the three men went together to the little room beyond the smoking-room in the old part of the castle.

"Well?" said Paul, with the unconscious hauteur which made him a prince to these people.

The starosta spread out his hands.

"Your Excellency," he answered, "I am afraid."

"Of what?"

The starosta shrugged his narrow shoulders in cringing deprecation.

"Excellency, I do not know. There is something in the village — something in the whole country. I know not what it is. It is a feeling — one cannot see it, one cannot define it; but it is there, like the gleam of water at the bottom of a deep well. The moujiks are getting dangerous. They will not speak to me. I am suspected. I am watched."

His shifty eyes, like black beads, flitted from side to side as he spoke. He was like a weasel at bay. It was the face of a man who went in bodily fear.

"I will go with you down to the village now," said Paul. "Is there any excuse — any illness?"

"Ah, Excellency," replied the chief, "there is always that excuse."

Paul looked at the clock.

"I will go now," he said. He began his simple preparations at once.

"There is dinner to be thought of," suggested Steinmetz, with a resigned smile. "It is half-past seven."

"Dinner can wait," replied Paul in English. "You might tell the ladies that I have gone out, and will dine alone when I come back."

Steinmetz shrugged his broad shoulders.

"I think you are a fool," he said, "to go alone. If they discover your identity they will tear you to pieces."

"I am not afraid of them," replied Paul, with his head in the medicine cupboard, "anymore than I am afraid of a horse. They are like horses; they do not know their own strength."

"With this difference," added Steinmetz, "that the moujik will one day make the discovery. He is beginning to make it now. The starosta is quite right, Paul. There is something in the air. It is about time that you took the ladies away from here and left me to manage it alone."

"That time will never come again," answered Paul. "I am not going to leave you alone again."

He was pushing his arms into the sleeves of the old brown coat reaching to his heels, a garment which commanded as much love and respect in Osterno as ever would an angel's wing.

Steinmetz opened the drawer of his bureau and laid a revolver on the table.

"At all events," he said, "you may as well have the where-withal to make a fight of it, if the worst comes to the worst."

"As you like," answered Paul, slipping the fire-arm into his pocket.

The starosta moved away a pace or two. He was essentially a man of peace.

Half an hour later it became known in the village that the Moscow doctor was in the house of one Ivan Krass, where he was prepared to see all patients who were now suffering from infectious complaints. The door of this cottage was soon besieged by the sick and the idle, while the starosta stood in the door-way and kept order.

Within, in the one dwelling-room of the cottage, were assembled as picturesque and as unsavory a group as the most enthusiastic modern "slummer" could desire to see.

Paul, standing by the table with two paraffin lamps placed behind him, saw each suppliant in turn, and all the while he kept up a running conversation with the more intelligent, some of whom lingered on to talk and watch.

"Ah, John the son of John," he would say, "what is the matter with you? It is not often I see you. I thought you were clean and thrifty."

To which John the son of John replied that the winter had been hard and fuel scarce, that his wife was dead and his children stricken with influenza.

"But you have had relief; our good friend the starosta —"

"Does what he can," grumbled John, "but he dare not do much. The bárins will not let him. The nobles want all the money for themselves. The Emperor is living in his palace, where there are fountains of wine. We pay for that with our taxes. You see my hand — I cannot work; but I must pay the taxes, or else we shall be turned out into the street."

Paul, while attending to the wounded hand — an old story of an old wound neglected, and a constitution with all the natural healing power drained out of it by hunger and want and vodka — Paul, ever watchful, glanced round and saw sullen, lowering faces, eager eyes, hungry, cruel lips.

"But the winter is over now. You are mistaken about the nobles. They do what they can. The Emperor pays for the relief that you have had all these months. It is foolish to talk as you do."

"I only tell the truth," replied the man, wincing as Paul deliberately cut away the dead flesh. "We know now why it is that we are all so poor."

"Why?" asked Paul, pouring some lotion over a wad of lint and speaking indifferently.

"Because the nobles —" began the man, and some one nudged him from behind, urging him to silence.

"You need not be afraid of me," said Paul. "I tell no tales, and I take no money."

"Then why do you come?" asked a voice in the background. "Some one pays you; who is it?"

"Ah, Tula," said Paul, without looking up. "You are there, are you? The great Tula. There is a hardworking, sober man, my little fathers, who never beats his wife, and never drinks, and never borrows money. A useful neighbor! What is the matter with you, Tula? You have been too sparing with the vodka, no doubt. I must order you a glass every hour."

There was a little laugh. But Paul, who knew these people, was quite alive to the difference of feeling toward himself. They still accepted his care, his help, his medicine; but they were beginning to doubt him.

"There is your own prince," he went on fearlessly to the man whose hand he was binding up. "He will help you when there is real distress."

An ominous silence greeted this observation.

Paul raised his head and looked round. In the dim light of the two smoky lamps he saw a ring of wild faces. Men with shaggy beards and hair all entangled and unkempt, with fierce eyes and lowering glances; women with faces that unsexed them. There were despair and desperation and utter reckless-ness in the air, in the attitude, in the hearts of these people. And Paul had worked among them for years. The sight would have been heart-breaking had Paul Howard Alexis been the sort of man to admit the possibility of a broken heart. All that he had done had been frustrated by the wall of heartless bureaucracy against which he had pitched his single strength. There was no visible progress. These were not the faces of men and women moving up the social scale by the aid of education and the deeper self-respect that follows it. Some of them were young, although they hardly looked it. They were young in years, but old in life and misery. Some of them he knew to be educated. He had paid for the education himself. He had risked his own personal freedom to procure it for them, and misery had killed the seed.

He looked on this stony ground, and his stout heart was torn with pity. It is easy to be patient in social economy when that vague jumble of impossible ideas is calmly discussed across the dinner-table. But the result seems hopelessly distant when the mass of the poor and wretched stand before one in the flesh.

Paul knew that this little room was only a specimen of the whole of Russia. Each of these poor peasants represented a million — equally hopeless, equally powerless to contend with an impossible taxation.

He could not give them money, because the tax-collector had them all under his thumb and would exact the last kopeck. The question was far above his single-handed reach, and he did not dare to meet it openly and seek the assistance of the few fellow-nobles who faced the position without fear.

He could not see in the brutal faces before him one spark of intelligence, one little gleam of independence and self-respect which could be attributed to his endeavor; which the most sanguine construction could take as resulting from his time and money given to a hopeless cause.

"Well," he said. "Have you nothing to tell me of your prince?"

"You know him," answered the man who had spoken from the safe background. "We need not tell you."

"Yes," answered Paul; "I know him."

He would not defend himself.

"There," he went on, addressing the man whose hand was now bandaged. "You will do. Keep clean and sober, and it will heal. Get drunk and go dirty, and you will die. Do you understand, Ivan Ivanovitch?"

The man grunted sullenly, and moved away to give place to a woman with a baby in her arms.

Paul glanced into her face. He had known her a few years earlier a happy child playing at her mother's cottage door.

She drew back the shawl that covered her child, with a faint, far-off gleam of pride in her eyes. There was something horribly pathetic in the whole picture. The child-mother, her rough, unlovely face lighted for a moment with that gleam from Paradise which men never know; the huge man bending over her, and between them the wizened, disease-stricken little waif of humanity.

"When he was born he was a very fine child," said the mother.

Paul glanced at her. She was quite serious. She was looking at him with a strange pride on her face. Paul nodded and drew aside the shawl. The baby was staring at him with wise, grave eyes, as if it could have told him a thing or two if it had only been gifted with the necessary speech. Paul knew that look. It meant starvation.

"What is it?" asked the child-mother. "It is only some little illness, is it not?"

"Yes; it is only a little illness."

He did not add that no great illness is required to kill a small child. He was already writing something in his pocket-book. He tore the leaf out and gave it to her.

"This," he said, "is for you – yourself, you understand? Take that each day to the starosta and he will give you what I have written down. If you do not eat all that he gives you and drink what there is in the bottle as he directs you, the baby will die – you understand? You must give nothing away; nothing even to your husband."

The next patient was the man whose voice had been heard from the safe retreat of the background. His dominant malady was obvious. A shaky hand, an unsteady eye, and a bloated countenance spoke for themselves. But he had other diseases more or less developed.

"So you have no good to tell of your prince," said Paul, looking into the man's face.

"Our prince, Excellency! He is not our prince. His forefathers seized this land; that is all."

"Ah! Who has been telling you that?"

"No one," grumbled the man. "We know it; that is all."

"But you were his father's serfs, before the freedom. Let me see your tongue. Yes; you have been drinking – all the winter. Ah! is not that so, little father? Your parents were serfs before the freedom."

"Freedom!" growled the man. "A pretty freedom! We were better off before."

"Yes; but the world interfered with serfdom, because it got

its necessary touch of sentiment. There is no sentiment in starvation."

The man did not understand. He grunted acquiescence nevertheless. The true son of the people is always ready to grunt acquiescence to all that sounds like abuse.

"And what is this prince like? Have you seen him?" went on Paul.

"No; I have not seen him. If I saw him I would kick his head to pieces."

"Ah, just open your mouth a little wider. Yes; you have a nasty throat there. You have had diphtheria. So you would kick his head to pieces. Why?"

"He is a tchinovnik — a government spy. He lives on the taxes. But it will not be for long. There is a time coming —"

"Ah! What sort of a time? Now, you must take this to the starosta. He will give you a bottle. It is not to drink. It is to wash your throat with. Remember that, and do not give it to your wife by way of a tonic as you did last time. So there are changes coming, are there?"

"There is a change coming for the prince — for all the princes," replied the man in the usual taproom jargon. "For the Emperor too. The poor man has had enough of it. God made the world for the poor man as well as for the rich. Riches should be equally divided. They are going to be. The country is going to be governed by a Mir. There will be no taxes. The Mir makes no taxes. It is the tchinovniks who make the taxes and live on them."

"Ah, you are very eloquent, little father. If you talk like this in the kabak no wonder you have a bad throat. There, I can do no more for you. You must wash more and drink less. You might try a little work perhaps; it stimulates the appetite. And with a throat like that I should not talk so much if I were you. Next!"

The next comer was afflicted with a wound that would not heal — a common trouble in cold countries.

While attending to this sickening sore Paul continued his conversation with the last patient.

"You must tell me," he said, "when these changes are about to come. I should like to be there to see. It will be interesting."

The man laughed mysteriously.

"So the government is to be by a Mir, is it?" went on Paul.

"Yes; the poor man is to have a say in it."

"That will be interesting. But at the Mir everyone talks at once and no one listens; is it not so?"

The man made no reply.

"Is the change coming soon?" asked Paul coolly.

But there was no reply. Some one had seized the loquacious orator of the kabak, and he was at that moment being quietly hustled out of the room.

After this there was a sullen silence, which Paul could not charm away, charm he never so wisely.

When his patients had at last ebbed away he lighted a cigarette and walked thoughtfully back to the castle. There was danger in the air, and this was one of those men upon whom danger acts as a pleasant stimulant.

Chapter XXXIII
THE NET IS DRAWN

During the days following Paul's visit to the village the ladies did not see much male society. Paul and Steinmetz usually left the castle immediately after breakfast and did not return till nightfall.

"Is there anything wrong?" Maggie asked Steinmetz on the evening of the second day.

Steinmetz had just come into the vast drawing room dressed for dinner — stout, placid, and very clean-looking. They were alone in the room.

"Nothing, my dear young lady — yet," he answered, coming forward and rubbing his broad palms slowly together.

Maggie was reading an English newspaper. She turned its pages without pausing to notice the black and sticky obliterations effected by the postal authorities before delivery. It was no new thing to her now to come upon the press censor's handiwork in the columns of such periodicals and newspapers as Paul received from England.

"Because," she said, "if there is you need not be afraid of telling me."

"To have that fear would be to offer you an insult," replied Steinmetz. "Paul and I are investigating matters, that is all. The plain truth, my dear young lady, is that we do not know ourselves what is in the wind. We only know there is something. You are a horsewoman — you know the feeling of a restive horse. One knows that he is only waiting for an excuse to shy or to kick or to rear. One feels it thrilling in him. Paul and I have that feeling in regard to the peasants. We are going the round of the outlying villages, steadily and carefully. We are seeking for the fly on the horse's body — you understand?"

"Yes, I understand."

She gave a little nod. She had not lost color, but there was an anxious look in her eyes.

"Some people would have sent to Tver for the soldiers," Steinmetz went on. "But Paul is not that sort of man. He will not do it yet. You remember our conversation at the Charity Ball in London?"

"Yes."

"I did not want you to come then. I am sorry you have come now."

Maggie laid aside the newspaper with a little laugh.

"But, Herr Steinmetz," she said, "I am not afraid. Please remember that. I have absolute faith in you — and in Paul."

Steinmetz accepted this statement with his grave smile.

"There is only one thing I would recommend," he said, "and that is a perfect discretion. Speak of this to no one, especially to no servants. You remember your own mutiny in India. Gott! what wonderful people you English are — men and women alike! You remember how the ladies kept up and brazened it out before the servants. You must do the same. I think I hear the rustle of the princess's dress. Yes! And there is no news in the papers, you say?"

"None," replied Maggie.

It may not have been entirely by chance that Claude de Chauxville drove over to Osterno to pay his respects the next day, and expressed himself desolated at hearing that the prince had gone out with Herr Steinmetz in a sleigh to a distant corner of the estate.

"My horses must rest," said the Frenchman, calmly taking off his fur gloves. "Perhaps the princess will see me."

A few minutes later he was shown into the morning-room.

"Did I see Mlle. Delafield on snow-shoes in the forest as I came along?" De Chauxville asked the servant in perfect Russian before the man left the room.

"Doubtless, Excellency. She went out on her snow-shoes half an hour ago."

"That is all right," said the Frenchman to himself when the door was closed.

He went to the fire and warmed his slim white fingers. There was an evil smile lurking beneath his mustache.

When Etta opened the door a minute later he bowed low, without speaking. There was a suggestion of triumph in his attitude.

"Well?" said the princess, without acknowledging his salutation.

De Chauxville raised his eyebrows with the resigned surprise of a man to whom no feminine humor is new. He brought forward a chair.

"Will you sit?" he said, with exaggerated courtesy. "I have much to say to you. Besides, we have all the time. Your husband and his German friend are miles away. I passed Miss Delafield in the forest. She is not quite at home on her snow-shoes yet. She cannot be back for at least half an hour."

Etta bit her lip as she looked at the chair. She sat slowly down and drew in the folds of her rich dress.

"I have the good fortune to find you alone."

"So you have informed me," she replied coldly.

De Chauxville leaned against the mantelpiece and looked down at her thoughtfully.

"At the bear-hunt the other day," he said, "I had the

misfortune to — well, to fall out with the prince. We were not quite at one on a question of etiquette. He thought that I ought to have fired. I did not fire; I was not ready. It appears that the prince considered himself to be in danger. He was nervous — flurried."

"You are not always artistic in your untruths," interrupted Etta. "I know nothing of the incident to which you refer, but in lying you should always endeavor to be consistent. I am sure Paul was not nervous — or flurried."

De Chauxville smiled imperturbably. His end was gained. Etta obviously knew nothing of his attempt to murder Paul at the bear-hunt.

"It was nothing," he went on; "we did not come to words. But we have never been much in sympathy; the coldness is intensified, that is all. So I took the opportunity of calling when I knew he was away."

"How did you know he was away?"

"Ah, madame, I know more than I am credited with."

Etta gave a little laugh and shrugged her shoulders.

"You do not care for Osterno?" suggested De Chauxville.

"I hate it!"

"Precisely. And I am here to help you to get away from Russia once for all. Ah! you may shake your head. Some day, perhaps, I shall succeed in convincing you that I have only your interests at heart. I am here, princess, to make a little arrangement with you — a final arrangement, I hope."

He paused, looking at her with a sudden gleam in his eyes.

"Not the last of all," he added in a different tone. "That will make you my wife."

Etta allowed this statement to pass unchallenged. Her courage and energy were not exhausted. She was learning to nurse her forces.

"Your husband," went on De Chauxville, after he had sufficiently enjoyed the savor of his own words, "is a brave man. To frighten him it is necessary to resort to strong measures. The last and the strongest measure in the diplomat's scale is the People. The People, madame, will take no denial. It is a game I have played before — a dangerous game, but I am not afraid."

"You need not trouble to be theatrical with me," put in

Etta scornfully. She was sitting with a patch of color in either cheek. At times this man had the power of moving her, and she was afraid of allowing him to exercise it. She knew her own weakness — her inordinate vanity; for vanity is the weakness of strong women. She was ever open to flattery, and Claude de Chauxville flattered her in every word he spoke; for by act and speech he made it manifest that she was the motive power of his existence.

"A man who plays for a high stake," went on the Frenchman, in a quieter voice, "must be content to throw his all on the table time after time. A week tonight — Thursday, the 5th of April — I will throw down my all on the turn of a card. For the People are like that. It is rouge or noir — one never knows. We only know that there is no third color, no compromise."

Etta was listening now with ill-disguised interest. At last he had given her something definite — a date.

"On Thursday," he went on, "the peasants will make a demonstration. You know as well as I do — as well as Prince Pavlo does, despite his imperturbable face — that the whole country is a volcano which may break forth at any moment. But the control is strong, and therefore there is never a large eruption — a grumble here, a gleam of fire there, a sullen heat everywhere! But it is held in check by the impossibility of communication. It seems strange, but Russia stands because she has no penny postage. The great crash will come, not by force of arms, but by ways of peace. The signal will be a postal system, the standard of the revolution will be a postage-stamp. All over this country there are millions waiting and burning to rise up and crush despotism, but they are held in check by the simple fact that they are far apart and they cannot write to each other. When, at last, they are brought together, there will be no fight at all, because they will overwhelm their enemies. That time, madame, has not come yet. We are only at the stage of tentative underground rumblings. But a little eruption is enough to wipe out one man if he be standing on the spot."

"Go on," said Etta quietly — too quietly, De Chauxville might have thought, had he been calmer.

"I want you," he went on, "to assist me. We shall be ready

on Thursday. I shall not appear in the matter at all; I have strong colleagues at my back. Starvation and misery, properly handled, are strong incentives."

"And how do you propose to handle them?" asked Etta in the same quiet voice.

"The peasants will make a demonstration. The rest we must leave to — well, to the course of fortune. I have no doubt that our astute friend Karl Steinmetz will manage to hold them in check. But whatever the end of the demonstration, the outcome will be the impossibility of a longer residence in this country for the Prince Pavlo Alexis. A regiment of soldiers could hardly make it possible."

"I do not understand," said Etta, "what you describe as a demonstration — is it a rising?"

De Chauxville nodded, with a grin.

"In force, to take what they want by force?" asked the princess.

De Chauxville spread out his hands in his graceful Gallic way.

"That depends."

"And what do you wish me to do?" asked Etta, with the same concentrated quiet.

"In the first place, to believe that no harm will come to you, either directly or indirectly. They would not dare to touch the prince; they will content themselves with breaking a few windows."

"What do you want me to do?" repeated Etta.

De Chauxville paused.

"Merely," he answered lightly, "to leave open a door — a side door. I understand that there is a door in the old portion of the castle leading up by a flight of stairs to the smoking-room, and thence to the new part of the building."

Etta did not answer. De Chauxville glanced at his watch and walked to the window, where he stood looking out. He was too refined a person to whistle, but his attitude was suggestive of that mode of killing time.

"This door I wish you to unbar yourself before dinner on Thursday evening," he said, turning round and slowly coming toward her.

"And I refuse to do it," said Etta.

"Ah!"

Etta sprung to her feet and faced him — a beautiful woman, a very queen of anger. Her blazing eyes were on a level with his.

"Yes," she cried, with clenched fists, standing her full height till she seemed to look down into his mean, foxlike face. "Yes; I refuse to betray my husband —"

"Stop! He is not your husband!"

Slowly the anger faded out of her eyes; her clenched fists relaxed. Her fingers were scraping nervously at the silk of her dress, like the fingers of a child seeking support. She seemed to lose several inches of her majestic stature.

"What do you mean?" she whispered. "What do you mean?"

"Sydney Bamborough is your husband," said the Frenchman, without taking his dull eyes from her face.

"He is dead!" she hissed.

"Prove it!"

He walked past her and leaned against the mantelpiece in the pose of easy familiarity which he had maintained during the first portion of their interview.

"Prove it, madame!" he said again.

"He died at Tver," she said; but there was no conviction in her voice. With her title and position to hold to, she could face the world. Without these, what was she?

"A local newspaper reports that the body of a man was discovered on the plains of Tver and duly buried in the pauper cemetery," said De Chauxville indifferently. "Your husband — Sydney Bamborough, I mean — was, for reasons which need not be gone into here, in the neighborhood of Tver at the time. A police officer, who has since been transferred to Odessa, was of the opinion that the dead man was a foreigner. There are about twelve thousand foreigners in Tver — operatives in the manufactories. Your husband — Sydney Bamborough, bien entendu — left Tver to proceed eastward and cross Siberia to China in order to avoid the emissaries of the Charity League, who were looking out for him at the western frontier. He will be due at one of the treaty ports in China in about a month. Upon the supposition that the body discovered on the plains of Tver was that of your husband, you took the opportunity of becoming a princess. It was enterprising. I admire your spirit. But it was dangerous. I, madame, can suppress Sydney Bamborough when he turns up. I have two arrows in my quiver for him; one is the Charity League, the other the Russian Government, who want him. Your husband — I beg your pardon, the prince — would perhaps take a different view of the case. It is a pretty story. I will tell it to him unless I have your implicit obedience."

Etta stood dry-lipped before him. She tried to speak, but no words came from her lips.

De Chauxville looked at her with a quiet smile of triumph, and she knew that he loved her. There is no defining love, nor telling when it merges into hatred.

"Thursday evening, before dinner," said De Chauxville.

And he left her standing on the hearthrug, her lips moving and framing no words.

Chapter XXXIV

AN APPEAL

"Have you spoken to the princess?" asked Steinmetz, without taking the cigar from his lips.

They were driving home through the forest that surrounded Osterno as the sea surrounds an island. They were alone in the sleigh. That which they had been doing had required no servant. Paul was driving, and consequently the three horses were going as hard as they could. The snow flew past their faces like the foam over the gunwale of a boat that is thrashing into a ten-knot breeze. Yet it was not all snow. There were flecks of foam from the horses' mouths mingled with it.

"Yes," answered Paul. His face was set and hard, his eyes stern. This trouble with the peasants was affecting him more keenly than he suspected. It was changing the man's face — drawing lines about his lips, streaking his forehead with the marks of care. His position can hardly be realized by an Englishman unless it be compared to that of the captain of a great sinking ship full of human souls who have been placed under his care.

"And what did she say?" asked Steinmetz.

"That she would not leave unless we all went with her."

Steinmetz drew the furs closer up round him.

"Yes," he said, glancing at his companion's face, and seeing little but the eyes, by reason of the sable collar of his coat, which met the fur of his cap; "yes, and why not?"

"I cannot leave them," answered Paul. "I cannot go away now that there is trouble among them. What it is, goodness only knows! They would never have got like this by themselves. Somebody has been at them, and I don't think it is the Nihilists. It is worse than that. Some devil has been stirring them up, and they know no better. He is still at it. They are getting worse day by day, and I cannot catch him. If I do, by God! Steinmetz, I'll twist his neck."

Steinmetz smiled grimly.

"Yes," he answered, "you are capable of it. For me, I am getting tired of the moujik. He is an inveterate, incurable fool. If he is going to be a dangerous fool as well, I should almost be inclined to let him go to the devil in his own way."

"I dare say; but you are not in my position."

"No; that is true, Pavlo. They were not my father's serfs. Generations of my ancestors have not saved generations of their ancestors from starvation. My fathers before me have not toiled and slaved and legislated for them. I have not learnt medicine that I might doctor them. I have not risked my health and life in their sties, where pigs would refuse to live. I have not given my whole heart and soul to their welfare, to receive no thanks, but only hatred. No, it is different for me. I owe them nothing, mein lieber; that is the difference."

"If I agree to make a bolt for Petersburg tomorrow will you come?" retorted Paul.

"No," answered the stout man.

"I thought not. Your cynicism is only a matter of words, Steinmetz, and not of deeds. There is no question of either of us leaving Osterno. We must stay and fight it right out here."

"That is so," answered Steinmetz, with the Teutonic stolidity of manner which sometimes came over him. "But the ladies — what of them?"

Paul did not answer. They were passing over the rise of a heavy drift. It was necessary to keep the horses up to their work, to prevent the runners of the sleigh sinking into the snow. With voice and whip Paul encouraged them. He was kind to animals, but never spared them — a strong man, who gave freely of his strength and expected an equal generosity.

"This is no place for Miss Delafield," added Steinmetz, looking straight in front of him.

"I know that!" answered Paul sharply. "I wish to God she was not here!" he added in a lower tone, and the words were lost beneath the frozen mustache.

Steinmetz made no answer. They drove on through the gathering gloom. The sky was of a yellow gray, and the earth reflected the dismal hue of it. Presently it began to snow, driving in a fine haze from the north. The two men lapsed into silence. Steinmetz, buried in his furs like a great, cumbrous bear, appeared to be half asleep. They had had a long and wearisome day. The horses had covered their forty miles and more from village to village, where the two men had only gathered discouragement and foreboding. Some of the starostas were sullen; others openly scared. None of them were glad to see Steinmetz. Paul had never dared to betray his identity. With the gendarmes — the tchinovniks — they had not deemed it wise to hold communication.

"Stop!" cried Steinmetz suddenly, and Paul pulled the horses on to their haunches.

"I thought you were asleep," he said.

There was no one in sight. They were driving along the new road now, the high-way Paul had constructed from Osterno to Tver. The road itself was, of course, indistinguishable, but the telegraph posts marked its course.

Steinmetz tumbled heavily out of his furs and went toward the nearest telegraph post.

"Where is the wire?" he shouted.

Paul followed him in the sleigh. Together they peered up into the darkness and the falling snow. The posts were there, but the wire was gone. A whole length of it had been removed. They were cut off from civilization by one hundred and forty miles of untrodden snow.

Steinmetz clambered back into the sleigh and drew up the fur apron. He gave a strange little laugh that had a ring of boyish excitement in it. This man had not always been stout and placid. He too had had his day, and those who knew him said that it had been a stirring one.

"That settles one question," he said.

"Which question?" asked Paul.

He was driving as hard as the horses could lay hoof to ground, taken with a sudden misgiving and a great desire to reach Osterno before dark.

"The question of the ladies," replied Steinmetz. "It is too late for them to go now."

The village, nestling beneath the grim protection of Osterno, was deserted and forlorn. All the doors were closed, the meager curtains drawn. It was very cold. There was a sense of relief in this great frost; for when Nature puts forth her strength men are usually cowed thereby.

At the castle all seemed to be in order. The groom, in his great sheepskin coat, was waiting in the doorway. The servants threw open the vast doors, and stood respectfully in the warm, brilliantly lighted hall while their master passed in.

"Where is the princess?" Steinmetz asked his valet, while he was removing the evidences of a long day in the open air.

"In her drawing room, Excellency."

"Then go and ask her if she will give me a cup of tea in a few minutes."

And the man, a timorous German, went.

A few minutes later Steinmetz, presenting himself at the door of the little drawing room attached to Etta's suite of rooms, found the princess in a matchless tea-gown waiting beside a table laden with silver tea appliances. A dainty

samovar, a tiny teapot, a spirit-lamp and the rest, all in the
wonderful silver-work of the Slavonski Bazaar in Moscow.

"You see," she said with a smile, for she always smiled on
men, "I have obeyed your orders."

Steinmetz bowed gravely. He was one of the few men who
could see that smile and be strong. He closed the door
carefully behind him. No mention was made of the fact that
his message had implied, and she had understood, that he
wished to see her alone. Etta was rather pale. There was an
anxious look in her eyes — behind the smile, as it were. She
was afraid of this man. She looked at the flame of the
samovar, busying herself among the tea-things with pretty
curving fingers and rustling sleeves. But the tea was never
made.

"I begin to think," said Steinmetz, coming to the point in
his bluff way, "that you are a sort of beautiful Jonah, a
graceful stormy petrel, a fair Wandering Jewess. There is
always trouble where you go."

She glanced at his broad face, and read nothing there.

"Go on," she said. "What have I been doing now? How
you do hate me, Herr Steinmetz!"

"Perhaps it is safer than loving you," he answered, with his
grim humor.

"I suppose," she said, with a quaint little air of resignation
which was very disarming, "that you have come here to scold
me — you do not want any tea?"

"No; I do not want any tea."

She turned the wick of the spirit-lamp, and the peaceful
music of the samovar was still. In her clever eyes there was a
little air of sidelong indecision. She could not make up her
mind how to take him. Her chiefest method was so old as to
be biblical. Yet she could not take him with her eyelids. She
had tried.

"You are horribly grave," she said.

"The situation," he replied, "is horribly grave."

Etta looked up at him as he stood before her, and the
lamp-light, falling on the perfect oval of her face, showed it
to be white and drawn.

"Princess," said the man, "there are in the lives of some of
us times when we cease to be men and women, and become

mere human beings. There are times, I mean, when the thousand influences of sex die at one blow of fate. This is such a time. We must forget that you are a beautiful woman; I verily believe that there is none more beautiful in the world. I once knew one whom I admired more, but that was not because she was more beautiful. That, however, is my own story, and this" — he paused and looked round the little room, furnished, decorated for her comfort — "this is your story. We must forget that I am a man, and therefore subject to the influence of your beauty."

She sat looking up into his strong, grave face, and during all that followed she never moved.

"I know you," he said, "to be courageous, and must ask you to believe that I exaggerate nothing in what I am about to tell you. I tell it to you instead of leaving Paul to do so because I know his complete fearlessness, and his blind faith in a people who are unworthy of it. He does not realize the gravity of the situation. They are his own people. A sailor never believes that his own ship is unseaworthy."

"Go on!" said Etta, for he had paused.

"This country," he continued, "is unsettled. The people of the estate are on the brink of a revolt. You know what the Russian peasant is. It will be no Parisian émeute, half noise, half laughter. We cannot hope to hold this old place against them. We cannot get away from it. We cannot send for help because we have no one to send. Princess, this is no time for half-confidences. I know — for I know these people better even than Paul knows them — I am convinced that this is not the outcome of their own brains. They are being urged on by some one. There is some one at their backs. This is no revolt of the peasants, organized by the peasants. Princess, you must tell me all you know!"

"I — I," she stammered, "I know nothing!"

And then suddenly she burst into tears, and buried her face in a tiny, useless handkerchief. It was so unlike her and so sudden that Steinmetz was startled.

He laid his great hand soothingly on her shoulder.

"I know," he said quietly, "I know more than you think. I am no saint, princess, myself. I too have had my difficulties. I have had my temptations, and I have not always resisted.

God knows it is difficult for men to do always the right thing. It is a thousand times more difficult for women. When we spoke together in Petersburg, and I offered you my poor friendship, I was not acting in the dark. I knew as much then as I do now. Princess, I knew about the Charity League papers. I knew more than any except Stépan Lanovitch, and it was he who told me."

He was stroking her shoulder with the soothing movements that one uses toward a child in distress. His great hand, broad and thick, had a certain sense of quiet comfort and strength in it. Etta ceased sobbing, and sat with bowed head, looking through her tears into the gay wood fire. It is probable that she failed to realize the great charity of the man who was speaking to her. For the capacity for evil merges at some point or other into incapability for comprehending good.

"Is that all he knows?" she was wondering.

The suggestion that Sydney Bamborough was not dead had risen up to eclipse all other fear in her mind. In some part her thought reached him.

"I know so much," he said, "that it is safest to tell me more. I offered you my friendship because I think that no woman could carry through your difficulties unaided. Princess, the admiration of Claude de Chauxville may be pleasant, but I venture to think that my friendship is essential."

Etta raised her head a little. She was within an ace of handing over to Karl Steinmetz the rod of power held over her by the Frenchman. There was something in Steinmetz that appealed to her and softened her, something that reached a tender part of her heart through the coating of vanity, through the hardness of worldly experience.

"I have known De Chauxville twenty-five years," he went on, and Etta deferred her confession. "We have never been good friends, I admit. I am no saint, princess, but De Chauxville is a villain. Some day you may discover, when it is too late, that it would have been for Paul's happiness, for your happiness, for everyone's good to have nothing more to do with Claude de Chauxville, I want to save you that discovery. Will you act upon my advice? Will you make a stand now? Will you come to me and tell me all that De Chauxville knows about you that he could ever use against you? Will you give yourself into my hands — give me your battle to fight? You cannot do it alone. Only believe in my friendship, princess. That is all I ask."

Etta shook her head.

"I think not," she answered, in a voice too light, too superficial, too hopelessly shallow for the depth of the moment. She was thinking only of Sydney Bamborough, and of that dread secret. She fought with what arms she wielded best — the lightest, the quickest, the most baffling.

"As you will," said Steinmetz.

Chapter XXXV

ON THE EDGE OF THE STORM

A Russian village kabak, with a smoking lamp, of which the chimney is broken. The greasy curtains drawn across the small windows exclude the faintest possibility of a draught. The moujik does not like a draught; in fact, he hates the fresh air of heaven. Air that has been breathed three or four times over is the air for him; it is warmer. The atmosphere of this particular inn is not unlike that of every other inn in the White Empire, inasmuch as it is heavily seasoned with the scent of cabbage soup. The odor of this nourishing compound is only exceeded in unpleasantness by the taste of the same. Added to this warm smell there is the smoke of a score of the very cheapest cigarettes. The Russian peasant smokes his cigarette now. It is the first step, and it does not cost him much. It is the dawn of progress — the thin end of the wedge which will broaden out into anarchy. The poor man who smokes a cigarette is sure to pass on to socialistic opinions and troubles in the marketplace. Witness the cigarette-smoking countries. Moreover, this same poor man is not a pleasant companion. He smokes a poor cigarette.

There is also the smell of vodka, which bottled curse is standing in tumblers all down the long table. The news has spread in Osterno that vodka is to be had for the asking at the kabak, where there is a meeting. Needless to say, the meeting is a large one. Foolishness and thirst are often found in the same head — a cranium which, by the way, is exceptionally liable to be turned by knowledge or drink.

If the drink at the kabak of Osterno was dangerous, the knowledge was no less so.

"I tell you, little fathers," an orator was shouting, "that the day of the capitalist has gone. The rich men — the princes, the nobles, the great merchants, the monopolists, the tchinovniks — tremble. They know that the poor man is awakening at last from his long lethargy. What have we done in Germany? What have we done in America? What have we done in England and France?"

Whereupon he banged an unwashed fist upon the table with such emphasis that more than one of the audience clutched his glass of vodka in alarm, lest a drop of the precious liquor should be wasted.

No one seemed to know what had been done in Germany, in America, in England, or in France. The people's orator is a man of many questions and much fist-banging. The moujiks of Osterno gazed at him beneath their shaggy brows. Half of them did not understand him. They were as yet uneducated to a comprehension of the street orator's periods. A few of the more intelligent waited for him to answer his own questions, which he failed to do. A vague and ominous question carries as much weight with some people as a statement, and has the signal advantage of being less incriminating.

The speaker — a neckless, broad-shouldered ruffian of the type known in England as "unemployed" — looked round with triumphant head well thrown back. From his attitude it was obvious that he had been the salvation of the countries named, and had now come to Russia to do the same for her.

He spoke with the throaty accent of the Pole. It was quite evident that his speech was a written one — probably a printed harangue issued to him and his compeers for circulation throughout the country. He delivered many of the longer words with a certain unctuous roll of the tongue, and an emphasis indicating the fact that he did not know their meaning.

"From afar," he went on, "we have long been watching you. We have noted your difficulties and your hardships, your sickness, your starvation. 'These men of Tver,' we have said, 'are brave and true and steadfast. We will tell them of liberty.' So I have come to you, and I am glad to see you. Alexander Alexandrovitch, pass the bottle down the table. You see, little fathers, I have not come begging for your money. No; keep your kopecks in your pocket. We do not want your money. We are no tchinovniks. We prove it by giving you vodka to keep your throats wet and your ears open. Fill up your glasses — fill up your glasses!"

The little fathers of Osterno understood this part of the harangue perfectly, and acted upon it.

The orator scratched his head reflectively. There was a certain businesslike mouthing of his periods, showing that he had learnt all this by heart. He did not press all his points home in the manner of one speaking from his own brain.

"I see before me," he went on, without an overplus of sequence, "men worthy to take their place among the rulers of the world — eh — er — rulers of the world, little fathers."

He paused and drank half a tumbler of vodka. His last statement was so obviously inapplicable — what he actually did see was so very far removed from what he said he saw — that he decided to relinquish the point.

"I drink," he cried, "to Liberty and Equality!"

Some of the little fathers also drank, to assuage an hereditary thirst.

"And now," continued the orator, "let us get to business. I think we understand each other?"

He looked round with an engaging smile upon faces brutal enough to suit his purpose, but quite devoid of intelligence. There was not much understanding there.

"The poor man has one only way of making himself felt

— force. We have worked for generations, we have toiled in silence, and we have gathered strength. The time has now come for us to put forth our strength. The time has gone by for merely asking for what we want. We asked, and they heard us not. We will now go and take!"

A few who had heard this speech or something like it before shouted their applause at this moment. Before the noise had subsided the door opened, and two or three men pushed their way into the already overcrowded room.

"Come in, come in!" cried the orator; "the more the better. You are all welcome. All we require, then, little fathers, is organization. There are nine hundred souls in Osterno; are you going to bow down before one man? All men are equal — moujik and bárin, krestyanin and prince. Why do you not go up to the castle that frowns down upon the village, and tell the man there that you are starving, that he must feed you, that you are not going to work from dawn till eve while he sits on his velvet couch and smokes his gold-tipped cigarettes. Why do you not go and tell him that you are not going to starve and die while he eats caviare and peaches from gold plates and dishes?"

A resounding bang of the fist finished this fine oration, and again the questions were unanswered.

"They are all the same, these aristocrats," the man thundered on. "Your prince is as the others, I make no doubt. Indeed, I know; for I have been told by our good friend Abramitch here. A clever man our friend Abramitch, and when you get your liberty — when you get your Mir — you must keep him in mind. Your prince, then — this Howard Alexis — treats you like the dirt beneath his feet. Is it not so? He will not listen to your cry of hunger. He will not give you a few crumbs of food from his gold dishes. He will not give you a few kopecks of the millions of rubles that he possesses. And where did he get those rubles? Ah! where did he get them — eh? Tell me that!"

Again the interrogative unwashed fist. As the orator's wild and frenzied eye traveled round the room it lighted on a form near the door — a man standing a head and shoulders above anyone in the room, a man enveloped in an old brown coat, with a woolen shawl round his throat, hiding half his face.

"Who is that?" cried the orator, with an unsteady, pointing finger. "He is no moujik. Is that a tchinovnik, little fathers? Has he come here to our meeting to spy upon us?"

"You may ask them who I am," replied the giant. "They know; they will tell you. It is not the first time that I tell them they are fools. I tell them again now. They are fools and worse to listen to such windbags as you."

"Who is it?" cried the paid agitator. "Who is this man?"

His eyes were red with anger and with vodka; his voice was unsteady. His outstretched hand shook.

"It is the Moscow doctor," said a man beside him — "the Moscow doctor."

"Then I say he is no doctor!" shouted the orator. "He is a spy — a Government spy, a tchinovnik! He has heard all we have said. He has seen you all. Brothers, that man must not leave this room alive. If he does, you are lost men!"

Some few of the more violent spirits rose and pressed tumultuously toward the door. The agitator shouted and screamed, urging them on, taking good care to remain in the safe background himself. Every man in the room rose to his feet. They were full of vodka and fury and ignorance. Spirit and tall talk, taken on an empty stomach, are dangerous stimulants.

Paul stood with his back to the door and never moved.

"Sit down, fools!" he cried. "Sit down! Listen to me. You dare not touch me; you know that."

It seemed that he was right, for they stopped with staring, stupid eyes and idle hands.

"Will you listen to me, whom you have known for years, or to this talker from the town? Choose now. I am tired of you. I have been patient with you for years. You are sheep; are you fools also, to be dazzled by the words of an idle talker who promises all and gives nothing?"

There was a sullen silence. Paul had lost his power over them, and he knew it. He was quite cool and watchful. He knew that he was in danger. These men were wild and ignorant. They were mad with drink and the brave words of the agitator.

"Choose now!" he shouted, feeling for the handle of the door behind his back.

They made no sign, but watched the faces of their leaders.

"If I go now," said Paul, "I never come again!"

He opened the door. The men whom he had nursed and clothed and fed, whose lives he had saved again and again, stood sullen and silent.

Paul passed slowly out and closed the door behind him. Without it was dark and still. There would be a moon presently, and in the meantime it was preparing to freeze harder than ever.

Paul walked slowly up the village street, while two men emerged separately from the darkness of by-lanes and followed him. He did not heed them. He was not aware that the thermometer stood somewhere below zero. He did not even trouble to draw on his fur gloves.

He felt like a man whose own dogs have turned against him. The place that these peasants had occupied in his heart had been precisely that vacancy which is filled by dogs and horses in the hearts of many men. There was in his feeling for them that knowledge of a complete dependence by which young children draw and hold a mother's love.

Paul Howard Alexis was not a man to analyze his thoughts. Your strong man is usually ignorant of the existence of his own feelings. He is never conscious of them. Paul walked slowly through the village of Osterno, and realized, in his uncompromising honesty, that of the nine hundred men who lived therein there were not three upon whom he could rely. He had upheld his peasants for years against the cynic truths of Karl Steinmetz. He had resolutely refused to admit even to himself that they were as devoid of gratitude as they were of wisdom. And this was the end of all!

One of the men following him hurried on and caught him up.

"Excellency," he gasped, breathless with his haste, "you must not come here alone any longer. I am afraid of them — I have no control."

Paul paused, and suited his pace to the shorter legs of his companion.

"Starosta!" he said. "Is that you?"

"Yes, Excellency. I saw you go into the kabak, so I waited outside and watched. I did not dare to go inside. They will

not allow me there. They are afraid that I should give information."

"How long have these meetings been going on?"

"The last three nights, Excellency, in Osterno; but it is the
same all over the estate."

"Only on the estate?"

"Yes, Excellency."

"Are you sure of that?"

"Yes, Excellency."

Paul walked on in silence for some paces. The third man
followed them without catching them up.

"I do not understand, Excellency," said the starosta anxiously. "It is not the Nihilists."

"No; it is not the Nihilists."

"And they do not want money, Excellency; that seems
strange."

"Very!" admitted Paul ironically.

"And they give vodka."

This seemed to be the chief stumbling-block in the starosta's road to a solution of the mystery.

"Find out for me," said Paul, after a pause, "who this man
is, where he comes from, and how much he is paid to open
his mouth. We will pay him more to shut it. Find out as much
as you can, and let me know tomorrow."

"I will try, Excellency; but I have little hope of succeeding.
They distrust me. They send the children to my shop for what
they want, and the little ones have evidently been told not to
chatter. The moujiks avoid me when they meet me. What can
I do?"

"You can show them that you are not afraid of them,"
answered Paul. "That goes a long way with the moujik."

They walked on together through the lane of cottages,
where furtive forms lurked in door-ways and behind curtains.
And Paul had only one word of advice to give, upon which
he harped continually: "Be thou very courageous — be thou
very courageous." Nothing new, for so it was written in the
oldest book of all. The starosta was a timorous man, needing
such strong support as his master gave him from time to time.

At the great gates of the park they paused, and Paul gave
the mayor of Osterno a few last words of advice. While they

were standing there the other man who had been following joined them.

"Is that you, Steinmetz?" asked Paul, his hand thrust with suspicious speed into his jacket pocket.

"Yes."

"What are you doing here?"

"Watching you," answered Karl Steinmetz, in his mild way. "It is no longer safe for either of us to go about alone. It was mere foolery your going to that kabak."

Chapter XXXVI
À TROIS

Of all the rooms in the great castle Etta liked the morn-ing-room best. Persons of a troubled mind usually love to look upon a wide prospect. The mind, no doubt, fears the unseen approach of detection or danger, and transmits this dread to the eye, which likes to command a wide view all around.

The great drawing room was only used after dinner. Until that time the ladies spent the day either in their own boudoirs or in the morning-room looking over the cliff. Here, while the cold weather lasted, Etta had tea served, and thither the gentlemen usually repaired at the hour set apart for the homely meal. They had come regularly the last few evenings. Paul and Steinmetz had suddenly given up their long drives to distant parts of the estate.

Here the whole party was assembled on the Sunday afternoon following Paul's visit to the village kabak, and to them came an unexpected guest. The door was thrown open, and Claude de Chauxville, pale, but self-possessed and quiet, came into the room. The perfect ease of his manner bespoke a practiced familiarity with the position difficult. His last parting with Paul and Steinmetz had been, to say the least of it, strained. Maggie, he knew, disliked and distrusted him. Etta hated and feared him.

He was in riding costume — a short fur jacket, fur gloves, a cap in his hand, and a silver-mounted crop. A fine figure of a man — smart, well turned out, well-groomed — a gentleman.

"Prince," he said frankly, "I have come to throw myself upon your generosity. Will you lend me a horse? I was riding in the forest when my horse fell over a root and lamed himself. I found I was only three miles from Osterno, so I came. My misfortune must be my excuse for this — intrusion."

Paul performed graciously enough that which charity and politeness demanded of him. There are plenty of people who trade unscrupulously upon these demands, but it is probable that they mostly have their reward. Love and friendship are stronger than charity and politeness, and those who trade upon the latter are rarely accorded the former.

So Paul ignored the probability that De Chauxville had lamed his horse on purpose, and offered him refreshment while his saddle was being transferred to the back of a fresh mount. Farther than that he did not go. He did not consider himself called upon to offer a night's hospitality to the man who had attempted to murder him a week before.

With engaging frankness De Chauxville accepted everything. It is an art soon acquired and soon abused. There is something honest in an ungracious acceptance of favors. Steinmetz suggested that perhaps M. de Chauxville had lunched sparsely, and the Frenchman admitted that such was the case, but that he loved afternoon tea above all meals.

"It is so innocent and simple — I know. I have the same feeling myself," concurred Steinmetz courteously.

"Do you ride about the country much alone?" asked Paul, while the servants were setting before this uninvited guest a few more substantial delicacies.

"Ah, no, prince! This is my first attempt, and if it had not procured me this pleasure I should say that it will be my last."

"It is easy to lose yourself," said Paul; "besides" — and the two friends watched the Frenchman's face closely — "besides, the country is disturbed at present."

De Chauxville was helping himself daintily to pâté de foie gras.

"Ah, indeed! Is that so?" he answered. "But they would not hurt me — a stranger in the land."

"And an orphan, too, I have no doubt," added Steinmetz, with a laugh. "But would the moujik pause to enquire, my very dear De Chauxville?"

"At all events, I should not pause to answer," replied the Frenchman, in the same, light tone. "I should evacuate. Ah, mademoiselle," he went on, addressing Maggie, "they have been attempting to frighten you, I suspect, with their stories of disturbed peasantry. It is to keep up the lurid local color. They must have their romance, these Russians."

And so the ball was kept rolling. There was never any lack of conversation when Steinmetz and De Chauxville were together, nor was the talk without sub-flavor of acidity. At length the center of attention himself diverted that attention. He inaugurated an argument over the best cross-country route from Osterno to Thors, which sent Steinmetz out of the room for a map. During the absence of the watchful German he admired the view from the window, and this strategetic movement enabled him to say to Etta aside:

"I must see you before I leave the house; it is absolutely necessary."

Not long after the return of Steinmetz and the final decision respecting the road to Thors, Etta left the room, and a few minutes later the servant announced that the baron's horse was at the door.

De Chauxville took his leave at once, with many assurances of lasting gratitude.

"Kindly," he added, "make my adieux to the princess; I will not trouble her."

Quite by accident he met Etta at the head of the state staircase, and expressed such admiration for the castle that she opened the door of the large drawing room and took him to see that apartment.

"What I arranged for Thursday is for the day after tomorrow – Tuesday," said De Chauxville, as soon as they were alone. "We cannot keep them back any longer. You understand – the side door to be opened at seven o'clock. Ah! who is this?"

They both turned. Steinmetz was standing behind them, but he could not have heard De Chauxville's words. He closed the door carefully, and came forward with his grim smile.

"À nous trois!" he said, and the subsequent conversation was in the language in which these three understood each other best.

De Chauxville bit his lip and waited. It was a moment of the tensest suspense.

"À nous trois!" repeated Steinmetz. "De Chauxville, you love an epigram. The man who overestimates the foolishness of others is himself the biggest fool concerned. A lame horse – the prince's generosity – making your adieux. Mon Dieu! you should know me better than that after all these years. No, you need not look at the door. No one will interrupt us. I have seen to that."

His attitude and manner indicated a complete mastery of the situation, but whether this assumption was justified by fact or was a mere trick it was impossible to say. There was in the man something strong and good and calm – a manner never acquired by one who has anything to conceal. His dignity was perfect. One forgot his stoutness, his heavy breathing, his ungainly size. He was essentially manly, and a presence to be feared. The strength of his will made itself felt.

He turned to the princess with the grave courtesy that always marked his attitude toward her.

"Madame," he said, "I fully recognize your cleverness in raising yourself to the position you now occupy. But I would remind you that that position carries with it certain obligations. It is hardly dignified for a princess to engage herself in a vulgar love intrigue in her own house."

"It is not a vulgar love intrigue!" cried Etta, with blazing eyes. "I will not allow you to say that! Where is your boasted friendship? Is this a sample of it?"

Karl Steinmetz bowed gravely, with outspread hands.

"Madame, that friendship is at your service, now as always."

De Chauxville gave a scornful little laugh. He was biting the end of his mustache as he watched Etta's face. For a moment the woman stood — not the first woman to stand thus — between two fears. Then she turned to Steinmetz. The victory was his — the greatest he had ever torn from the grasp of Claude de Chauxville.

"You know," she said, "that this man has me in his power."

"You alone. But not both of us together," answered Steinmetz.

De Chauxville looked uneasy. He gave a careless little laugh.

"My good Steinmetz, you allow your imagination to run away with you. You interfere in what does not concern you."

"My very dear De Chauxville, I think not. At all events, I am going to continue to interfere."

Etta looked from one to the other. She had at the first impulse gone over to Steinmetz. She was now meditating drawing back. If De Chauxville kept cool all might yet be well — the dread secret of the probability of Sydney Bamborough being alive might still be withheld from Steinmetz. For the moment it would appear that she was about to occupy the ignominious position of the bone of contention. If these two men were going to use her as a mere excuse to settle a lifelong quarrel of many issues, it was probable that there would not be much left of her character by the time that they had finished.

She had to decide quickly. She decided to assume the role of peacemaker.

"M. de Chauxville was on the point of going," she said. "Let him go."

"M. de Chauxville is not going until I have finished with him, madame. This may be the last time we meet. I hope it is."

De Chauxville looked uneasy. His was a ready wit, and fear was the only feeling that paralyzed it. Etta looked at him. Was his wit going to desert him now when he most needed it? He had ridden boldly into the lion's den. Such a proceeding requires a certain courage, but a higher form of intrepidity is required to face the lion standing before the exit.

De Chauxville looked at Steinmetz with shifty eyes. He was very like the mask of the lynx in the smoking-room, even to the self-conscious, deprecatory smile on the countenance of the forest sneak.

"Keep your temper," he said; "do not let us quarrel in the presence of a lady."

"No; we will keep the quarrel till afterward."

Steinmetz turned to Etta.

"Princess," he said, "will you now, in my presence, forbid this man to come to this or any other house of yours? Will you forbid him to address himself either by speech or letter to you again?"

"You know I cannot do that," replied Etta.

"Why not?"

Etta made no answer.

"Because," replied De Chauxville for her, "the princess is too wise to make an enemy of me. In that respect she is wiser than you. She knows that I could send you and your prince to Siberia."

Steinmetz laughed.

"Nonsense!" he said. "Princess," he went on, "if you think that the fact of De Chauxville numbering among his friends a few obscure police spies gives him the right to persecute you, you are mistaken. Our friend is very clever, but he can do no harm with the little that he knows of the Charity League."

Etta remained silent. The silence made Steinmetz frown.

"Princess," he said gravely, "you were indignant just now because I made so bold as to put the most natural construction upon the circumstances in which I found you. It was a prearranged meeting between De Chauxville and yourself. If the meeting was not the outcome of an intrigue such as I mentioned, nor the result of this man's hold over you on account of the Charity League, what was it? I beg of you to answer."

Etta made no reply. Instead, she raised her eyes and looked at De Chauxville.

"Without going into affairs which do not concern you,"

said the Frenchman, answering for her, "I think you will recognize that the secret of the Charity League was quite sufficient excuse for me to request a few minutes alone with the princess."

Of this Steinmetz took no notice. He was standing in front of Etta, between De Chauxville and the door. His broad, deeply lined face was flushed with the excitement of the moment. His great mournful eyes, yellow and drawn with much reading and the hardships of a rigorous climate, were fixed anxiously on her face.

Etta was not looking at him. Her eyes were turned toward the window, but they did not see with comprehension. She was stony and stubborn.

"Princess," said Steinmetz, "answer me before it is too late. Has De Chauxville any other hold over you?"

Etta nodded, and the little action brought a sudden gleam to the Frenchman's eyes.

"If," said Steinmetz, looking from one to the other, "if you two have been deceiving Paul I will have no mercy, I warn you of that."

Etta turned on him.

"Can you not believe me?" she cried. "I have practiced no deception in common with M. de Chauxville."

"The Charity League is quite enough for you, my friend," put in the Frenchman hurriedly.

"You know no more of the Charity League than you did before — than the whole world knew before — except this lady's share in the disposal of the papers," said Steinmetz.

"And this lady's share in the disposal of the papers will not be welcome news to the prince," answered De Chauxville.

"Welcome or unwelcome, he shall be told of it tonight."

Etta looked round sharply, her lips apart and trembling.

"By whom?" asked De Chauxville.

"By me," replied Steinmetz.

There was a momentary pause. De Chauxville and Etta exchanged a glance. Etta felt that she was lost. This Frenchman was not one to spare either man or woman from any motive of charity or chivalry.

"Even if that is so," he said, "the princess is not relieved from the embarrassment of her situation."

"No?"

"No, my astute friend. There is a little matter connected with Sydney Bamborough which has come to my knowledge."

Etta moved, but she said nothing. The sound of her breathing was startlingly loud.

"Ah! Sydney Bamborough," said Steinmetz slowly. "What about him?"

"He is not dead; that is all."

Karl Steinmetz passed his broad hand down over his face, covering his mouth for a second.

"But he died. He was found on the steppe, and buried at Tver."

"So the story runs," said De Chauxville, with easy sarcasm. "But who found him on the steppe? Who buried him at Tver?"

"I did, my friend."

The next second Steinmetz staggered back a step or two as Etta fell heavily into his arms. But he never took his eyes off De Chauxville.

Chapter XXXVII

À DEUX

Steinmetz laid Etta on a sofa. She was already recovering consciousness. He rang the bell twice, and all the while he kept his eye on De Chauxville. A quick touch on Etta's wrist and breast showed that this man knew something of women and of those short-lived fainting fits that belong to strong emotions.

The maid soon came.

"The princess requires your attention," said Steinmetz, still watching De Chauxville, who was looking at Etta and neglecting his opportunities.

Steinmetz went up to him and took him by the arm.

"Come with me," he said.

The Frenchman could have taken advantage of the presence of the servant to effect a retreat, but he did not dare to do so. It was essential that he should obtain a few words with Etta. To effect this, he was ready even to face an interview with Steinmetz. In his heart he was cursing that liability to inconvenient fainting fits that make all women unreliable in a moment of need.

He preceded Steinmetz out of the room, forgetting even to resent the large, warm grasp on his arm. They went through the long, dimly lit passage to the old part of the castle, where Steinmetz had his rooms.

"And now," said Steinmetz, when they were alone with closed doors, "and now, De Chauxville, let us understand each other."

De Chauxville shrugged his shoulders. He was not thinking of Steinmetz yet. He was still thinking of Etta and how he could get speech with her. With the assurance which had carried him through many a difficulty before this, the Frenchman looked round him, taking in the details of the room. They were in the apartment beyond the large smoking room — the anteroom, as it were, to the little chamber where Paul kept his medicine-chest, his disguise, all the compromising details of his work among the peasants. The broad writing-table in the middle of the room stood between the two men.

"Do you imagine yourself in love with the princess?" asked Steinmetz suddenly, with characteristic bluntness.

"If you like," returned the other.

"If I thought that it was that," said the German, looking at him thoughtfully, "I would throw you out of the window. If it is anything else, I will only throw you down stairs."

De Chauxville bit his thumb-nail anxiously. He frowned across the table into Steinmetz's face. In all their intercourse he had never heard that tone of voice; he had never seen quite that look on the heavy face. Was Steinmetz aroused at last? Steinmetz aroused was an unknown quantity to Claude de Chauxville.

"I have known you now for twenty-five years," went on Karl Steinmetz, "and I cannot say that I know any good of you. But let that pass; it is not, I suppose, my business. The world is as the good God made it. I can do nothing toward bettering it. I have always known you to be a scoundrel — a fact to be deplored — and that is all. But so soon as your villainy affects my own life, then, my friend, a more active recognition of it is necessary."

"Indeed!" sneered the Frenchman.

"Your villainy has touched Paul's life, and at that point it touches mine," continued Karl Steinmetz, with slow anger. "You followed us to Petersburg — thence you dogged us to the Government of Tver. You twisted that foolish woman, the Countess Lanovitch, round your finger, and obtained from her an invitation to Thors. All this in order to be near one of us. Ach! I have been watching you. Is it only after twenty-five years that I at last convince you that I am not such a fool as you are pleased to consider me?"

"You have not convinced me yet," put in De Chauxville, with his easy laugh.

"No, but I shall do so before I have finished with you. Now, you have not come here for nothing. It is to be near one of us. It is not Miss Delafield; she knows you. Some women — good women — have an instinct given to them by God for a defense against such men — such things as you. Is it I?"

He touched his broad chest with his two hands, and stood defying his life-long foe.

"Is it me that you follow? If so, I am here. Let us have done with it now."

De Chauxville laughed. There was an uneasy look in his eyes. He did not quite understand Steinmetz. He made no answer. But he turned and looked at the window. It is possible that he suddenly remembered the threat concerning it.

"Is it Paul?" continued Steinmetz. "I think not. I think you are afraid of Paul. Remains the princess. Unless you can convince me to the contrary, I must conclude that you are trying to get a helpless woman into your power."

"You always were a champion of helpless ladies," sneered De Chauxville.

"Ah! You remember that, do you? I also — I remember it. It is long ago, and I have forgiven you; but I have not forgotten. What you were then you will be now. Your record is against you."

Steinmetz was standing with his back to what appeared to be the only exit from the room. There were two other doors concealed in the oaken panels, but De Chauxville did not know that. He could not take his eyes from the broad face of his companion, upon which there were singular blotches of color.

"I am waiting," said the German, "for you to explain your conduct."

"Indeed!" replied De Chauxville. "Then, my friend, you will have to continue waiting. I fail to recognize your right to make enquiry into my movements. I am not responsible to any man for my actions, least of all to you. The man who manages his neighbor's affairs mismanages his own. I would recommend you to mind your own business. Kindly let me pass."

De Chauxville's words were brave enough, but his lips were unsteady. A weak mouth is apt to betray its possessor at inconvenient moments. He waved Steinmetz aside, but he made no movement toward the door. He kept the table between him and his companion.

Steinmetz was getting calmer. There was an uncanny hush about him.

"Then I am to conclude," he said, "that you came to Russia in order to persecute a helpless woman. Her innocence or her guilt is, for the moment, beside the question. Neither is any business of yours. Both, on the contrary, are my affair. Innocent or guilty, the Princess Howard Alexis must from this moment be freed from your persecution."

De Chauxville shrugged his shoulders. He tapped on the floor impatiently with the toe of his neat riding-boot.

"Allons!" he said. "Let me pass!"

"Your story of Sydney Bamborough," went on Steinmetz coldly, "was a good one wherewith to frighten a panic-stricken woman. But you brought it to the wrong person when you brought it to me. Do you suppose that I would have allowed the marriage to take place unless I knew that Bamborough was dead?"

"You may be telling the truth about that incident or you may not," said De Chauxville. "But my knowledge of the betrayal of the Charity League is sufficient for my purpose."

"Yes," admitted Steinmetz grimly, "you have information there with possibilities of mischief in it. But I shall discount most of it by telling Prince Pavlo tonight all that I know, and I know more than you do. Also, I intend to seal your lips before you leave this room."

De Chauxville stared at him with a dropping lip. He gulped down something in his throat. His hand was stealing round under the fur jacket to a pocket at the back of his trousers.

"Let me out!" he hissed.

There was a gleam of bright metal in the sunlight that poured in through the window. De Chauxville raised his arm sharply, and at the same instant Steinmetz threw a book in his face. A loud report, and the room was full of smoke.

Steinmetz placed one hand on the table and, despite his weight, vaulted it cleanly. This man had taken his degree at Heidelberg, and the Germans are the finest gymnasts in the world. Moreover, muscle, once made, remains till death. It was his only chance, for the Frenchman had dodged the novel, but it spoiled his aim. Steinmetz vaulted right on to him, and De Chauxville staggered back.

In a moment Steinmetz had him by the collar; his face was gray, his heavy eyes ablaze. If anything will rouse a man, it is being fired at point-blank at a range of four yards with a .280 revolver.

"Ach!" gasped the German; "you would shoot me, would you?"

He wrenched the pistol from De Chauxville's fingers and threw it into the corner of the room. Then he shook the man like a garment.

"First," he cried, "you would kill Paul, and now you try to shoot me! Good God! what are you? You are no man. Do you know what I am going to do with you? I am going to thrash you like a dog!"

He dragged him to the fireplace. Above the mantelpiece a stick-rack was affixed to the wall, and here were sticks and riding-whips. Steinmetz selected a heavy whip. His eyes were shot with blood; his mouth worked beneath his mustache.

"So," he said, "I am going to settle with you at last."

De Chauxville kicked and struggled, but he could not get free. He only succeeded in half choking himself.

"You are going to swear," said Steinmetz, "never to approach the princess again — never to divulge what you know of her past life."

The Frenchman was almost blue in the face. His eyes were wild with terror.

And Karl Steinmetz thrashed him.

It did not last long. No word was spoken. The silence was only broken by their shuffling feet, by the startling report of each blow, by De Chauxville's repeated gasps of pain.

The fur jacket was torn in several places. The white shirt appeared here and there. In one place it was stained with red.

At last Steinmetz threw him huddled into one corner of the room. The chattering face, the wild eyes that looked up at him, were terrible to see.

"When you have promised to keep the secret you may go," said Steinmetz. "You must swear it."

De Chauxville's lips moved, but no sound came from them. Steinmetz poured some water into a tumbler and gave it to him.

"It had to come to this," he said, "sooner or later. Paul would have killed you; that is the only difference. Do you swear by God in heaven above you that you will keep the princess's secret?"

"I swear it," answered De Chauxville hoarsely.

Steinmetz was holding on to the back of a high chair with both hands, breathing heavily. His face was still livid. That which had been white in his eyes was quite red.

De Chauxville was crawling toward the revolver in the corner of the room, but he was almost fainting. It was a question whether he would last long enough to reach the fire-arm. There was a bright patch of red in either liver-colored cheek; his lips were working convulsively. And Steinmetz saw him in time. He seized him by the collar of his coat and dragged him back. He placed his foot on the little pistol and faced De Chauxville with glaring eyes. De Chauxville rose to his feet, and for a moment the two men looked into each other's souls. The Frenchman's face was twisted with pain. No word was said.

Such was the last reckoning between Karl Steinmetz and the Baron Claude de Chauxville.

The Frenchman went slowly toward the door. He faltered and looked round for a chair. He sat heavily down with a little exclamation of pain and exhaustion, and felt for his pocket-handkerchief. The scented cambric diffused a faint, dainty odor of violets. He sat forward with his two hands on his knees, swaying a little from side to side. Presently he raised his handkerchief to his face. There were tears in his eyes.

Thus the two men waited until De Chauxville had recovered himself sufficiently to take his departure. The air was full of naked human passions. It was rather a gruesome scene.

At last the Frenchman stood slowly up, and with characteristic thought of appearances fingered his torn coat.

"Have you a cloak?" asked Steinmetz.

"No."

The German went to a cupboard in the wall and selected a long riding-cloak, which he handed to the Frenchman without a word.

Thus Claude de Chauxville walked to the door in a cloak which had figured at many a Charity League meeting. Assuredly the irony of Fate is a keener thing than any poor humor we have at our command. When evil is punished in this present life there is no staying of the hand.

Steinmetz followed De Chauxville through the long passage they had traversed a few minutes earlier and down the broad staircase. The servants were waiting at the door with the horse put at the Frenchman's disposal by Paul.

De Chauxville mounted slowly, heavily, with twitching lips. His face was set and cold now. The pain was getting bearable, the wounded vanity was bleeding inwardly. In his dull eyes there was a gleam of hatred and malice. It was the face of a man rejoicing inwardly over a deep and certain vengeance.

"It is well!" he was muttering between his clenched teeth

as he rode away, while Steinmetz watched him from the doorstep. "It is well! Now I will not spare you."

He rode down the hill and through the village, with the light of the setting sun shining on a face where pain and deadly rage were fighting for the mastery.

Chapter XXXVIII

A TALE THAT IS TOLD

Karl Steinmetz walked slowly upstairs to his own room. The evening sun, shining through the small, deeply embrasured windows, fell on a face at no time joyous, now tired and worn. He sat down at his broad writing-table, and looked round the room with a little blink of the eyelids.

"I am getting too old for this sort of thing," he said.

His gaze lighted on the heavy riding-whip thrown on the ground near the door where he had released Claude de Chauxville, after the terrible punishment meted out to that foe with heavy Teutonic hand. Steinmetz rose, and picking up the whip with the grunt of a stout man stooping, replaced it carefully in the rack over the mantelpiece.

He stood looking out of the window for a few moments.

"It will have to be done," he said resolutely, and rang the bell.

"My compliments to the prince," he said to his servant, who appeared instantly, "and will he come to me here."

When Paul came into the room a few minutes later Steinmetz was standing by the fire. He turned and looked gravely at the prince.

"I have just kicked De Chauxville out of the house," he said.

The color left Paul's face quite suddenly.

"Why?" he asked, with hard eyes. He had begun to distrust Etta, and there is nothing so hard to stop as the growth of distrust.

Steinmetz did not answer at once.

"Was it not *my* privilege?" asked Paul, with a grim smile. There are some smiles more terrible than any frown.

"No," answered Steinmetz, "I think not. It is not as bad as that. But it is bad enough, mein lieber! — it is bad enough! I horsewhipped him first for myself. Gott! how pleasant that was! And then I kicked him out for you."

"Why?" repeated Paul, with a white face.

"It is a long story," answered Steinmetz, without looking at him. "He knows too much."

"About whom?"

"About all of us."

Paul walked away to the window. He stood looking out, his hands thrust into the side-pockets of his jacket, his broad back turned uncompromisingly upon his companion.

"Tell me the story," he said. "You need not hurry over it. You need not trouble to — spare me. Only let it be quite complete — once for all."

Steinmetz winced. He knew the expression of the face that was looking out of the window.

"This man has hated me all his life," he said. "It began as such things usually do between men — about a woman. It was years ago. I got the better of him, and the good God got the better of me. She died, and De Chauxville forgot her. I — have not forgotten her. But I have tried to do so. It is a slow process, and I have made very little progress; but all that is my affair and beside the question. I merely mention it to show you that De Chauxville had a grudge against me —"

"This is no time for mistaken charity," interrupted Paul. "Do not try to screen any body. I shall see through it."

There was a little pause. Never had that silent room been so noiseless.

"In after-life," Steinmetz went on, "it was our fate to be at

variance several times. Our mutual dislike has had no opportunity of diminishing. It seems that, before you married, De
Chauxville was pleased to consider himself in love with Mrs.
Sydney Bamborough. Whether he had any right to think
himself ill-used, I do not know. Such matters are usually
known to two persons only, and imperfectly by them. It
would appear that the wound to his vanity was serious. It
developed into a thirst for revenge. He looked about for some
means to do you harm. He communicated with your enemies,
and allied himself to such men as Vassili of Paris. He followed
us to Petersburg, and then he had a stroke of good fortune.
He found out — who betrayed the Charity League!"

Paul turned slowly round. In his eyes there burned a dull,
hungering fire. Men have seen such a look in the eyes of a
beast of prey, driven, famished, cornered at last, and at last
face to face with its foe.

"Ah! He knows that!" he said slowly.

"Yes, God help us! he knows that."

"And who was it?"

Steinmetz moved uneasily from one foot to the other.

"It was a woman," he said.

"A woman?"

"A woman — you know," said Steinmetz slowly.

"Good God! Catrina?"

"No, not Catrina."

"Then who?" cried Paul hoarsely. His hands fell heavily on
the table.

"Your wife!"

Paul knew before the words were spoken.

He turned again, and stood looking out of the window
with his hands thrust into his pockets. He stood there for
whole minutes in an awful stillness. The clock on the mantelpiece, a little traveling timepiece, ticked in a hurried way
as if anxious to get on. Down beneath them, somewhere in
the courtyards of the great castle, a dog — a deep-voiced
wolf-hound — was baying persistently and nervously, listening for the echo of its own voice amid the pines of the desert
forest.

Steinmetz watched Paul's motionless back with a sort of
fascination. He moved uneasily, as if to break a spell of silence

almost unbearable in its intensity. He went to the table and sat down. From mere habit he took up a quill pen. He looked at the point of it and at the inkstand. But he had nothing to write. There was nothing to say.

He laid the pen aside, and sat leaning his broad head upon the palm of his hand, his two elbows on the table. Paul never moved. Steinmetz waited. His own life had been no great success. He had had much to bear, and he had borne it. He was wondering heavily whether any of it had been as bad as what Paul was bearing now while he looked out of the window with his hands in his pockets, saying nothing.

At length Paul moved. He turned, and, coming toward the table, laid his hand on Steinmetz's broad shoulder.

"Are you sure of it?" he asked, in a voice that did not sound like his own at all — a hollow voice like that of an old man.

"Quite; I have it from Stépan Lanovitch — from the princess herself."

They remained thus for a moment. Then Paul withdrew his hand and walked slowly to the window.

"Tell me," he said, "how she did it."

Steinmetz was playing with the quill pen again. It is singular how at great moments we perform trivial acts, think trivial thoughts. He dipped the pen in the ink, and made a pattern on the blotting-pad with dots.

"It was an organized plan between husband and wife," he said. "Bamborough turned up at Thors and asked for a night's lodging, on the strength of a very small acquaintance. He stole the papers from Stépan's study and took them to Tver, where his wife was waiting for them. She took them on to Paris and sold them to Vassili. Bamborough began his journey eastward, knowing presumably that he could not escape by the western frontier, but lost his way on the steppe. You remember the man whom we picked up between here and Tver, with his face all cut to pieces? — he had been dragged by the stirrup. That was Sydney Bamborough. The good God had hit back quickly."

"How long have you known this?" asked Paul, in a queer voice.

"I saw it suddenly in the princess's face, one day in Petersburg — a sort of revelation. I read it there, and she saw me reading. I should have liked to keep it from you, for your sake as well as for hers. Our daily life is made possible only by the fact that we know so little of our neighbors. There are many things of which we are better ignorant right up to the end. This might have been one of them. But De Chauxville found it out, and it is better that I should tell you than he."

Paul did not look around. The wolf-hound was still barking at its own echo — a favorite pastime of those who make a great local stir in the world.

"Of course," said Paul, after a long pause, "I have been a great fool. I know that. But —"

He turned and looked at Steinmetz with haggard eyes.

"But I would rather go on being a fool than suspect anyone of a deception like this."

Steinmetz was still making patterns on the blotting-pad.

"It is difficult for us men," he said slowly, "to look at these things from a woman's point of view. They hold a different sense of honor from ours — especially if they are beautiful. And the fault is ours — especially toward the beautiful ones. There may have been temptations of which we are ignorant."

Paul was still looking at him. Steinmetz looked up slowly, and saw that he had grown ten years older in the last few minutes. He did not look at him for more than a second, because the sight of Paul's face hurt him. But he saw in that moment that Paul did not understand. This strong man, hard in his youthful strength of limb and purpose, would be just, but nothing more. And between man and man it is not always justice that is required. Between man and woman justice rarely meets the difficulty.

"Comprendre c'est pardonner," quoted Steinmetz vaguely.

He hesitated to interfere between Paul and his wife. Axioms are made for crucial moments. A man's life has been steered by a proverb before this. Some, who have no religion, steer by them all the voyage.

Paul walked slowly to the chair he usually occupied, opposite to Steinmetz, at the writing-table. He walked and sat down as if he had traveled a long distance.

"What is to be done?" asked Steinmetz.

"I do not know. I do not think that it matters much. What do you recommend?"

"There is so much to be done," answered Steinmetz, "that it is difficult to know what to do first. We must not forget that De Chauxville is furious. He will do all the harm of which he is capable at once. We must not forget that the country is in a state of smoldering revolt, and that we have two women, two English ladies, entrusted to our care."

Paul moved uneasily in his chair. His companion had struck the right note. This large man was happiest when he was tiring himself out.

"Yes; but about Etta?" he said.

And the sound of his voice made Steinmetz wince. There is nothing so heartrending as the sight of dumb suffering.

"You must see her," answered he reflectively. "You must see her, of course. She may be able to explain."

He looked across the table beneath his shaggy gray eyebrows. Paul did not at that moment look a likely subject for explanations — even the explanations of a beautiful woman. But there was one human quantity which in all his experience Karl Steinmetz had never successfully gauged — namely, the extent of a woman's power over the man who loves, or at one time has loved her.

"She cannot explain away Stépan Lanovitch's ruined life. She can hardly explain away a thousand deaths from unnatural causes every winter, in this province alone."

This was what Steinmetz dreaded — justice.

"Give her the opportunity," he said.

Paul was looking out of the window. His singularly firm mouth was still and quiet — not a mouth for explanations.

"I will, if you like," he said.

"I do like, Paul. I beg of you to do it. And remember that — she is not a man."

This, like other appeals of the same nature, fell on stony ground. Paul simply did not understand it. In all the years of his work among the peasants it is possible that some well-spring of conventional charity had been dried up — scorched in the glare of burning injustice. He was not at this moment in a mood to consider the only excuse that Steinmetz seemed to be able to urge.

The sun had set long ago. The short twilight lay over the snow-covered land with a chill hopelessness. Steinmetz looked at his watch. They had been together an hour — one of those hours that count as years in a life time. He had to peer into the face of the watch in order to see the hands. The room was almost dark, and no servant ever came to it, unless summoned.

Paul was looking down at his companion, as if waiting to hear the time. At great moments we are suddenly brought face to face with the limits of human nature. It is at such moments that we find that we are not gods, but only men. We can only feel to a certain extent, only suffer up to a certain point.

"We must dress for dinner," said Steinmetz. "Afterward — well, afterward we shall see."

"Yes," answered Paul. And he did not go.

The two men stood looking at each other for a moment. They had passed through much together — danger, excitement, and now they were dabbling in sorrow. It would appear that this same sorrow runs like a river across the road of our life. Some of us find the ford and plash through the shallows — shallow ourselves — while others flounder into deep water. These are they who look right on to the greater events, and fail to note the trivial details of each little step. Paul was wading through the deep water, and this good friend of his was not inclined to stand upon the bank. It is while passing through this river that Fortune sends some of us a friend, who is ever afterward different from all others.

Paul stood looking down at the broad, heavy face of the man who loved him like a father. It was not easy for him to speak. He seemed to be making an effort.

"I do not want you to think," he said at last, "that it is as bad as it might have been. It might have been worse — much worse — had I not made a mistake in regard to my own feelings when I married her. I will try and do the right thing by her. Only at present there does not seem to be much left, except you."

Steinmetz looked up with his quaintly resigned smile.

"Ah, yes," he said, "I am there always."

Chapter XXXIX

HUSBAND AND WIFE

*K*arl Steinmetz had shown the depth of his knowledge of men and women when he commented on that power of facing danger with an unruffled countenance which he was pleased to attribute to English ladies above all women. During the evening he had full opportunity of verifying his own observations.

Etta came down to dinner smiling and imperturbable. On the threshold of the drawing room she exchanged a glance with Karl Steinmetz; and that was all. At dinner it was Maggie and Paul who were silent. Etta talked to Steinmetz — brightly, gaily, with a certain courage of a very high order; for she was desperate, and she did not show it.

At last the evening came to an end. Maggie had sung two songs. Steinmetz had performed on the piano with a marvelous touch. All had played their parts with the brazen faces which Steinmetz, in his knowledge of many nations, assigned to the Anglo-Saxon race before others.

At last Etta rose to go to bed, with a little sharp sigh of great suspense. It was coming.

She went up to her room, bidding Maggie good-night in the passage. In a mechanical way she allowed the deft-handed maid to array her in a dressing gown — soft, silken, a dainty triumph in its way. Then, almost impatiently, she sent the maid away when her hair was only half released. She would brush it herself. She was tired. No, she wanted nothing more.

She sat down by the fire, brush in hand. She could hardly breathe. It was coming.

She heard Paul come to his dressing-room. She heard his deep, quiet voice reply to some question of his valet's. Then the word "Good-night" in the same quiet voice. The valet had gone. There was only the door now between her and — what? Her fingers were at the throat of her dressing gown. The soft lace seemed to choke her.

Then Paul knocked at the door. It was coming. She opened her lips, but at first could make no sound.

"Come in!" she said at length hoarsely.

She wondered whether he would kill her. She wondered whether she was in love with her husband. She had begun wondering that lately; she was wondering it when he came in. He had changed his dress-coat for a silk-faced jacket, in which he was in the habit of working with Steinmetz in the quiet room after the household had gone to bed.

She looked up. She dropped the brush, and ran toward him with a great rustle of her flowing silks.

"Oh, Paul, what is it?" she cried.

She stopped short, not daring to touch him, before his cold, set face.

"Have you seen anyone?" she whispered.

"Only De Chauxville," he answered, "this afternoon."

"Indeed, Paul," she protested hastily, "it was nothing. A message from Catrina Lanovitch. It was only the usual visit of an acquaintance. It would have been very strange if he had not called. Do you think I could care for a man like that?"

"I never did think so until now," returned Paul steadily. "Your excuses accuse you. You may care for him. I do not know; I — do — not — care."

She turned slowly and went back to her chair.

Mechanically she took up the brush, and shook back her beautiful hair.

"You mean you do not care for me," she said. "Oh, Paul! be careful."

Paul stood looking at her. He was not a subtle-minded man at all. He was not one of those who take it upon themselves to say that they understand women — using the word in an offensively general sense, as if women were situated midway between the human and the animal races. He was old-fashioned enough to look upon women as higher and purer than men, while equally capable of thought and self-control. He had, it must be remembered, no great taste for fictional literature. He had not read the voluminous lucubrations of the modern woman writer. He had not assisted at the nauseating spectacle of a woman morally turning herself inside out in three volumes and an interview.

No, this man respected women still; and he paid them an honor which, thank Heaven, most of them still deserve. He treated them as men in the sense that he considered them to be under the same code of right and wrong, of good and evil.

He did not understand what Etta meant when she told him to be careful. He did not know that the modern social code is like the Spanish grammar — there are so many exceptions that the rules are hardly worth noting. And one of our most notorious modern exceptions is the married woman who is pleased to hold herself excused because outsiders tell her that her husband does not understand her.

"I do not think," said Paul judicially, "that you can have cared very much whether I loved you or not. When you married me you knew that I was the promoter of the Charity League; I almost told you. I told you so much that, with your knowledge, you must have been aware of the fact that I was heavily interested in the undertaking which you betrayed. You married me without certain proof of your husband's death, such was your indecent haste to call yourself a princess. And now I find, on your own confession, that you have a clandestine understanding with a man who tried to murder me only a week ago. Is it not rather absurd to talk of caring?"

He stood looking down at her, cold and terrible in the white heat of his suppressed Northern anger.

The little clock on the mantelpiece, in a terrible hurry, ticked with all its might. Time was speeding. Every moment was against her. And she could think of nothing to say simply because those things that she would have said to others would carry no weight with this man.

Etta was leaning forward in the luxurious chair, staring with haggard eyes into the fire. The flames leaped up and gleamed on her pale face, in her deep eyes.

"I suppose," she said, without looking at him, "that you will not believe me when I tell you that I hate the man. I knew nothing of what you refer to as happening last week; his attempt to murder you, I mean. You are a prince, and all-powerful in your own province. Can you not throw him into prison and keep him there? Such things are done in Russia. He is more dangerous than you think. Please do it — please —"

Paul looked at her with hard, unresponsive eyes. Lives depended on his answer.

"I did not come here to discuss Claude de Chauxville," he said, "but you, and our future."

Etta drew herself up as one under the lash, and waited with set teeth.

"I propose," he said, in a final voice which made it no proposition at all, "that you go home to England at once with — your cousin. This country is not safe for you. The house in London will be at your disposal. I will make a suitable settlement on you, sufficient to live in accordance with your title and position. I must ask you to remember that the name you bear has hitherto been an unsullied one. We have been proud of our princesses — up to now. In case of any trouble reaching you from outside sources connected with this country, I should like you to remember that you are under my protection and that of Steinmetz. Either of us will be glad at any time to consider any appeal for assistance that you may think fit to make. You will always be the Princess Howard Alexis."

Etta gave a sudden laugh.

"Oh, yes," she said, and her face was strangely red, "I shall still be the Princess Alexis."

"With sufficient money to keep up the position," he went on, with the cruel irony of a slow-spoken man.

A queer, twisted smile passed across Etta's face — the smile of one who is in agony and will not shriek.

"There are certain stipulations which I must make in self-defense," went on Paul. "I must ask you to cease all communication of whatever nature with the Baron de Chauxville. I am not jealous of him — now. I do not know why."

He paused, as if wondering what the meaning of this might be. Etta knew it. The knowledge was part of her punishment.

"But," continued her husband. "I am not going to sacrifice the name my mother bore to the vanity of a French coxcomb. You will be kind enough to avoid all society where it is likely that you should meet him. If you disregard my desires in this matter, I shall be compelled to take means to enforce them."

"What means?"

"I shall reduce your allowance."

Their eyes met, and perhaps that was the bitterest moment in Etta's life. Dead things are better put out of sight at once. Etta felt that Paul's dead love would grin at her in every sovereign of the allowance which was to be hers. She would never get away from it; she could never shake off its memory.

"Am I to live alone?" asked Etta, suddenly finding her voice.

"That is as you like," answered Paul, perhaps purposely misunderstanding her. "You are at liberty to have any friend or companion you wish. Perhaps — your cousin."

"Maggie?"

"Yes," answered Paul. For the first time since he had entered the room his eyes were averted from Etta's face.

"She would not live with me," said the princess curtly.

Paul seemed to be reflecting. When he next spoke it was in a kinder voice.

"You need not tell the circumstances which have given rise to this arrangement."

Etta shrugged her shoulders.

"That," went on Paul, "rests entirely with yourself. You may be sure that I will tell no one. I am not likely to discuss it with anyone whomsoever."

Etta's stony eyes softened for a moment. She seemed to be alternating between hatred of this man and love of him — a dangerous state for any woman. It is possible that, if he had held his hand out to her, she would have been at his feet in a wild, incoherent passion of self-hatred and abasement. Such moments as these turn our lives and determine them. Paul knew nothing of the issue hanging on this moment, on the passing softness of her eyes. He knew nothing of the danger in which this woman stood, of the temptation with which she was wrestling. He went on in his blindness, went on being only just.

"If," he said, "you have any further questions to ask, I shall always be at your service. For the next few days I shall be busy. The peasants are in a state of discontent verging on rebellion. We cannot at present arrange for your journey to Tver, but as soon as it is possible I will tell you."

He looked at the clock, and made an imperceptible movement toward the door.

Etta glanced up sharply. She did not seem to be breathing.

"Is that all?" she asked, in a dull voice.

There was a long silence, tense and throbbing, the great silence of the steppe.

"I think so," answered Paul at length. "I have tried to be just."

"Then justice is very cruel."

"Not so cruel as the woman who for a few pounds sells the happiness of thousands of human beings. Steinmetz advised me to speak to you. He suggested the possibility of circumstances of which we are ignorant. He said that you might be able to explain."

Silence.

"Can you explain?"

Silence. Etta sat looking into the fire. The little clock hurried on. At length Etta drew a deep breath.

"You are the sort of man," she said, "who does not understand temptation. You are strong. The devil leaves the strong in peace. You have found virtue easy because you have never wanted money. Your position has always been assured. Your name alone is a password through the world. Your sort are always hard on women who — who — What have I done, after all?"

Some instinct bade her rise to her feet and stand before him — tall, beautiful, passionate, a woman in a thousand, a fit mate for such as he. Her beautiful hair in burnished glory round her face gleamed in the firelight. Her white fingers clenched, her arms thrown back, her breast panting beneath the lace, her proud face looking defiance into his — no one but a prince could have braved this princess.

"What have I done?" she cried a second time. "I have only

fought for myself, and if I have won, so much the greater credit. I am your wife. I have done nothing the law can touch. Thousands of women moving in our circle are not half so good as I am. I swear before God I am —"

"Hush!" he said, with upraised hand. "I never doubted that."

"I will do anything you wish," she went on, and in her humility she was very dangerous. "I deceived you, I know. But I sold the Charity League before I knew that you — that you thought of me. When I married you I didn't love you. I admit that. But Paul — oh, Paul, if you were not so good you would understand."

Perhaps he did understand; for there was that in her eyes that made her meaning clear.

He was silent; standing before her in his great strength, his marvelous and cruel self-restraint.

"You will not forgive me?"

For a moment she leaned forward, peering into his face. He seemed to be reflecting.

"Yes," he said at length, "I forgive you. But if I cared for you, forgiveness would be impossible."

He went slowly toward the door. Etta looked round the room with drawn eyes; their room — the room he had fitted up for his bride with the lavishness of a great wealth and a great love.

He paused, with his hand on the door.

"And," she said, with fiery cheeks, "does your forgiveness date from tonight?"

"Yes!"

He opened the door.

"Good-night!" he said, and went out.

Chapter XL
STÉPAN RETURNS

At daybreak the next morning Karl Steinmetz was awakened by the familiar cry of the wolf beneath his window. He rose and dressed hastily. The eastern sky was faintly pink; a rosy twilight moved among the pines. He went down stairs and opened the little door at the back of the castle.

It was, of course, the starosta, shivering and bleached in the chilly dawn.

"They have watched my cottage, Excellency, all night. It was only now that I could get away. There are two strange sleighs outside Domensky's hut. There are marks of many sleighs that have been and gone. Excellency, it is unsafe for anyone to venture outside the castle today. You must send to Tver for the soldiers."

"The prince refuses to do that."

"But why, Excellency? We shall be killed!"

"You do not know the effect of platoon firing on a closely packed mob, starost. The prince does," replied Steinmetz, with his grim smile.

They spoke together in hushed voices for half an hour, while the daylight crept up the eastern sky. Then the starosta stole away among the still larches, like the wolf whose cry he imitated so perfectly.

Steinmetz closed the door and went upstairs to his own room, his face grave and thoughtful, his tread heavy with the weight of anxiety.

The day passed as such days do. Etta was not the woman to plead a conventional headache and remain hidden. She came down to breakfast, and during that meal was boldly conversational.

"She has spirit," reflected Karl Steinmetz behind his quiet gray eyes. He admired her for it, and helped her. He threw back the ball of conversation with imperturbable good humor.

They were completely shut in. No news from the outer world penetrated to the little party besieged within their own stone walls. Maggie, fearless and innocent, announced her intention of snow-shoeing, but was dissuaded therefrom by Steinmetz with covert warnings.

During the morning each was occupied in individual affairs. At luncheon time they met again. Etta was now almost defiant. She was on her mettle. She was so near to loving Paul that a hatred of him welled up within her breast whenever he repelled her advances with uncompromising reticence.

They did not know — perhaps she hardly knew herself — that the opening of the side-door depended upon her humor.

In the afternoon Etta and Maggie sat, as was their wont, in the morning-room looking out over the cliff. Of late their intercourse had been slightly strained. They had never had much in common, although circumstances had thrown their lives together. It is one of the ills to which women are heir that they have frequently to pass their whole lives in the society of persons with whom they have no real sympathy. Both these women were conscious of the little rift within the lute, but such rifts are better treated with silence. That which comes to interfere with a woman's friendship will not often bear discussion.

At dusk Steinmetz went out. He had an appointment with the starosta.

Paul was sitting in his own room, making a pretence of work, about five o'clock, when Steinmetz came hurriedly to him.

"A new development," he said shortly. "Come to my room."

Paul rose and followed him through the double doorway

built in the thickness of the wall.

Steinmetz's large room was lighted only by a lamp standing on the table. All the light was thrown on the desk by a large green shade, leaving the rest of the room in a semi-darkness.

At the far end of the room a man was standing in an expectant attitude. There was something furtive about this intruder, and at the same time familiar to Paul, who peered at him through the gloom.

Then the man came hurriedly forward.

"Ah, Pavlo, Pavlo!" he said in a deep, hollow voice. "I could not expect you to know me."

He threw his arms around him, and embraced him after the simple manner of Russia. Then he held him at arm's length.

"Stépan!" said Paul. "No, I did not know you."

Stépan Lanovitch was still holding him at arm's length, examining him with the large faint blue eyes which so often go with an exaggerated philanthropy.

"Old," he muttered, "old! Ah, my poor Pavlo! I heard in Kiew — you know how we outlaws hear such things — that you were in trouble, so I came to you."

Steinmetz in the background raised his patient eyebrows.

"There are two men in the world," went on the voluble Lanovitch, "who can manage the moujiks of Tver — you and I; so I came. I will help you, Pavlo; I will stand by you. Together we can assuredly quell this revolt."

Paul nodded, and allowed himself to be embraced a second time. He had long known Stépan Lanovitch of Thors as one of the many who go about the world doing good with their eyes shut. For the moment he had absolutely no use for this well-meaning blunderer.

"I am afraid," he said, "that it has got beyond control. We cannot stamp it out now except by force, and I would rather not do that. Our only hope is that it may burn itself out. The talkers must get hoarse in time."

Lanovitch shook his head.

"They have been talking since the days of Ananias," he said, "and they are not hoarse yet. I fear, Pavlo, there will never be peace in the world until the talkers are hoarse."

"How did you get here?" asked Paul, who was always

businesslike.

"I brought a pack on my back and sold cotton. I made myself known to the starosta, and he communicated with good Karl here."

"Did you learn anything in the village?" asked Paul.

"No; they suspected me. They would not talk. But I understand them, Pavlo, these poor simple fools. A pebble in the stream would turn the current of their convictions. Tell them who is the Moscow doctor. It is your only chance."

Steinmetz grunted acquiescence and walked wearily to the window. This was only an old and futile argument of his own.

"And make it impossible for me to live another day among them," said Paul. "Do you think St. Petersburg would countenance a prince who works among his moujiks?"

Stépan Lanovitch's pale blue eyes looked troubled. Steinmetz shrugged his shoulders.

"They have brought it on themselves," he said.

"As much as a lamb brings the knife upon itself by growing up," replied Paul.

Lanovitch shook his white head with a tolerant little smile. He loved these poor helpless peasants with a love as large as and a thousand times less practical than Paul's.

In the meantime Paul was thinking in his clear, direct way. It was this man's habit in life and in thought to walk straight past the side issues.

"It is like you, Stépan," he said at length, "to come to us at this time. We feel it, and we recognize the generosity of it, for Steinmetz and I know the danger you are running in coming back to this country. But we cannot let you do it — No, do not protest. It is quite out of the question. We might quell the revolt; no doubt we should — the two of us together. But what would happen afterward? You would be sent back to Siberia, and I should probably follow you for harboring an escaped convict."

The face of the impulsive philanthropist dropped pathetically. He had come to his friend's assistance on the spur of the moment. He was destined, as some men are, to plunge about the world seeking to do good. And it has been decreed that good must be done by stealth and after deliberation only. He who does good on the spur of the moment usually sows a seed of dissension in the trench of time.

"Also," went on Paul, with that deliberate grasp of the situation which never failed to astonish the ready-witted Steinmetz; "also, you have other calls upon your energy. You have other work to do."

Lanovitch's broad face lightened up; his benevolent brow beamed. His capacity for work had brought him to the shoemaker's last in Tomsk. It is a vice that grows with indulgence.

"It has pleased the Authorities," went on Paul, who was shy of religious turns of phrase, "to give us all our own troubles. Mine — such as they are, Stépan — must be managed by myself. Yours can be faced by no one but you. You have come at the right moment. You do not quite realize what your coming means to Catrina."

"Catrina! Ah!"

The weak blue eyes looked into the strong face and read nothing there.

"I doubt," said Paul, "whether it is right for you to continue sacrificing Catrina for the sake of the little good that you are able to do. You are hampered in your good work to such an extent that the result is very small, while the pain you give is very great."

"But is that so, Pavlo? Is my child unhappy?"

"I fear so," replied Paul gravely, with his baffling self-restraint. "She has not much in common with her mother, you understand."

"Ah, yes!"

"It is you to whom she is attached. Sometimes it is so with children and parents. One cannot tell why."

Steinmetz looked as if he could supply information upon the subject: but he remained silent, standing, as it were, in an acquiescent attitude.

"You have fought your fight," said Paul. "A good fight, too. You have struck your blow for the country. You have sown your seed, but the harvest is not yet. Now it is time to think of your own safety, of the happiness of your own child."

Stépan Lanovitch turned away and sat heavily down. He leaned his two arms on the table, and his chin upon his clenched hands.

"Why not leave the country now; at all events for a few years?" went on Paul, and when a man who is accustomed to command stoops to persuade, it is strong persuasion that he wields. "You can take Catrina with you. You will be assuring her happiness, which, at all events, is something tangible – a present harvest! I will drive over to Thors now and bring her back. You can leave tonight and go to America."

Stépan Lanovitch raised his head and looked hard into Paul's face.

"You wish it?"

"I think," answered Paul steadily, "that it is for Catrina's happiness."

Then Lanovitch rose up and took Paul's hand in his work-stained grip.

"Go, my son! It will be a great happiness to me. I will wait here," he said.

Paul went straight to the door. He was a man with a capacity for prompt action, which seemed to rise to demand. Steinmetz followed him out into the passage and took him by the arm.

"You cannot do it," he said.

"Yes, I can," replied Paul. "I can find my way through the forest. No one will venture to follow me there in the dark."

Steinmetz hesitated, shrugged his shoulders, and went back into the room.

The ladies at Thors were dressed for dinner – were, indeed, awaiting the announcement of that meal – when Paul broke in upon their solitude. He did not pause to lay aside his furs, but went into the long, low room, withdrawing his seal gloves painfully, for it was freezing as it only can freeze in March.

The countess assailed him with many questions, more or less sensible, which he endured patiently until the servant had left the room. Catrina, with flushed cheeks, stood looking at him, but said nothing.

Paul withdrew his gloves and submitted to the countess' futile tugs at his fur coat. Then Catrina spoke.

"The Baron de Chauxville has left us," she said, without knowing exactly why.

For the moment Paul had forgotten Claude de Chauxville's existence.

"I have news for you," he said; and he gently pushed the chattering countess aside. "Stépan Lanovitch is at Osterno. He arrived tonight."

"Ah, they have set him free, poor man! Does he wear chains on his ankles — is his hair long? My poor Stépan! Ah, but what a stupid man!"

The countess collapsed into a soft chair. She chose a soft one, obviously. It has to be recorded here that she did not receive the news with unmitigated joy.

"When he was in Siberia," she gasped, "one knew at all events where he was; and now, mon Dieu! what an anxiety!"

"I have come over to see whether you will join him tonight and go with him to America," said Paul, looking at her.

"To — America — tonight! My dear Paul, are you mad? One cannot do such things as that. America! that is across the sea."

"Yes," answered Paul.

"And I am such a bad sailor. Now, if it had been Paris —"

"But it cannot be," interrupted Paul. "Will you join your father tonight?" he added, turning to Catrina.

The girl was looking at him with something in her eyes that he did not care to meet.

"And go to America?" she asked, in a lifeless voice.

Paul nodded.

Catrina turned suddenly away from him and walked to the fire, where she stood with her back toward him — a small, uncouth figure in black and green, the lamplight gleaming on her wonderful hair. She turned suddenly again, and, coming back, stood looking into his face.

"I will go," she said. "You think it best?"

"Yes," he answered; "I think it best."

She drew a sharp breath and was about to speak when the countess interrupted her.

"What!" she cried. "You are going away tonight like this, without any luggage! And pray what is to become of me?"

"You can join them in America," said Paul, in his quietest tone. "Or you can live in Paris, at last."

Chapter XLI

DUTY

*I*t was not now a very cold night. There were fleecy clouds thrown like puffs of smoke against the western sky. The moon, on the wane, — a small crescent lying on its back, — was lowering toward the horizon. The thermometer had risen since sunset, as it often does in March. There was a suggestion of spring in the air. It seemed that at last the long winter was drawing to a close; that the iron grip of frost was relaxing.

Paul went out and inspected the harness by the light of a stable lantern held in the mittened hand of a yemschick. He had reasons of his own for absenting himself while Catrina bade her mother farewell. He was rather afraid of these women.

The harness inspected, he began reckoning how many hours of moonlight might still be vouchsafed to him. The stableman, seeing the direction of his gaze, began to talk of the weather and the possibilities of snow in the near future. They conversed in low voices together.

Presently the door opened and Catrina came quickly out, followed by a servant carrying a small hand-bag.

Paul could not see Catrina's face. She was veiled and furred to the eyelids. Without a word the girl took her seat in the sleigh, and the servant prepared the bear-skin rugs. Paul gathered up the reins and took his place beside her. A few moments were required to draw up the rugs and fasten them with straps; then Paul gave the word and the horses leaped forward.

As they sped down the avenue Catrina turned and looked her last on Thors.

Before long Paul wheeled into the trackless forest. He had come very carefully, steering chiefly by the moon and stars, with occasional assistance from a bend of the winding river. At times he had taken to the ice, following the course of the stream for a few miles. No snow had fallen; it would be easy to return on his own track. Through this part of the forest no road was cut.

For nearly half an hour they drove in silence. Only the whistle of the iron-bound runners on the powdery snow, the creak of the warming leather on the horses, the regular breathing of the team, broke the stillness of the forest. Paul hoped against hope that Catrina was asleep. She sat by his side, her arm touching his sleeve, her weight thrown against him at such times as the sleigh bumped over a fallen tree or some inequality of the ground.

He could not help wondering what thoughts there were behind her silence. Steinmetz's good-natured banter had come back to his memory, during the last few days, in a new light.

"Paul," said the woman at his side quite suddenly, breaking the silence of the great forest where they had grown to life and sorrow almost side by side.

"Yes."

"I want to know how this all came about. It is not my father's doing. There is something quick, and practical, and wise which suggests you and Herr Steinmetz. I suspect that you have done this — you and he — for our happiness."

"No," answered Paul; "it was mere accident. Your father heard of our trouble in Kiew. You know him — always impulsive and reckless. He never thinks of the danger. He came to help us."

Catrina smiled wanly.

"But it *is* for our happiness, is it not, Paul? You know that it is — that is why you have done it. I have not had time yet to realize what I am doing, all that is going to happen. But if it is your doing, I think I shall be content to abide by the result."

"It is not my doing," replied Paul, who did not like her wistful tone. "It is the outcome of circumstances. Circumstances have been ruling us all lately. We seem to have no time to consider, but only to do that which seems best for the moment."

"And it is best that I should go to America with my father?" Her voice was composed and quiet. In the dim light he could not see her white lips; indeed, he never looked.

"It seems so to me, undoubtedly," he said. "In doing this, so far as we can see at present, it seems certain that you are saving your father from Siberia. You know what he is; he never thinks of his own safety. He ought never to have come here tonight. If he remains in Russia, it is an absolute certainty that he will sooner or later be rearrested. He is one of those good people who require saving from themselves."

Catrina nodded. At times duty is the kedge-anchor of happiness. The girl was dimly aware that she was holding to this. She was simple and unsophisticated enough to consider Paul's opinion infallible. At the great cross-roads of life we are apt to ask the way of any body who happens to be near. Catrina might perhaps have made a worse choice of counsel, for Paul was honest.

"As you put it," she said, "it is clearly my duty. There is a sort of consolation in that, however painful it may be at the time. I suppose it is consolatory to look back and think that at all events one did one's duty."

"I don't know," answered Paul simply; "I suppose so."

Looking back was not included in his method of life, which was rather characterized by a large faith and a forward pressure. Whenever there was question of considering life as an abstract, he drew within his shell with a manlike shyness. He had no generalities ready for each emergency.

"Would father have gone alone?" she asked, with a very human thrill of hope in her voice.

"No," answered Paul steadily, "I think not. But you can ask him."

They had never been so distant as they were at this moment — so cold, such mere acquaintances. And they had played together in one nursery.

"Of course, if that is the case," said the girl, "my duty is quite clear."

"It required some persuasion to make him consent to go, even with you," said Paul.

A rough piece of going — for there was no road — debarred further conversation at this time. The sleigh rolled and bumped over one fallen tree after another. Paul, with his feet stretched out, wedged firmly into the sleigh, encouraged the tired horses with rein and voice. Catrina was compelled to steady herself with both hands on the bar of the apron; for the apron of a Russian sleigh is a heavy piece of leather stretched on a wooden bar.

"Then you think my duty is quite clear?" repeated the girl at length.

Paul did not answer at once.

"I am sure of it," he said.

And there the question ended. Catrina Lanovitch, who had never been ruled by those about her, shaped her whole life unquestioningly upon an opinion.

They did not speak for some time, and then it was the girl who broke the silence.

"I have a confession to make and a favor to ask," she said bluntly.

Paul's attitude denoted attention, but he said nothing.

"It is about the Baron de Chauxville," she said.

"Ah!"

"I am a coward," she went on. "I did not know it before. It is rather humiliating. I have been trying for some weeks to tell you something, but I am horribly afraid of it. I am afraid you will despise me. I have been a fool — worse, perhaps. I never knew that Claude de Chauxville was the sort of person he is. I allowed him to find out things about me which he never should have known — my own private affairs, I mean. Then I became frightened, and he tried to make use of me. I think he makes use of everybody. *You* know what he is."

"Yes," answered Paul, "I know."

"He hates you," she went on. "I do not want to make mischief, but I suppose he wanted to marry the princess. His vanity was wounded because she preferred you, and he wanted to be avenged upon you. Wounds to the vanity never heal. I do not know how he did it, Paul, but he made me help him in his schemes. I could have prevented you from going to the bear hunt, for I suspected him then. I could have prevented my mother from inviting him to Thors. I could have put a thousand difficulties in his way, but I did not. I helped him. I told him about the people and who were the worst — who had been influenced by the Nihilists and who would not work. I allowed him to stay on here and carry out his plan. All this trouble among the peasants is his handiwork. He has organized a regular rising against you. He is horribly clever. He left us yesterday, but I am convinced that he is in the neighborhood still."

She stopped and reflected. There was something wanting in the story, which she could not supply. It was a motive. A half-confession is almost an impossibility. When we speak of ourselves it must be all or nothing — preferably, nothing.

"I do not know why I did it," she said. "It was a sort of period I went through. I cannot explain."

He did not ask her to do so. They were singularly like brother and sister in their mental attitude. They had driven through twenty miles of forest which belonged to one or other of them. Each was touched by the intangible, inexplicable dignity that belongs to the possession of great lands — to the inheritance of a great name.

"That is the confession," she said.

He gave a little laugh.

"If none of us had worse than that upon our consciences," he answered, "there would be little harm in the world, De Chauxville's schemes have only hurried on a crisis which was foreordained. The progress of humanity cannot be stayed. They have tried to stay it in this country. They will go on trying until the crash comes. What is the favor you have to ask?"

"You must leave Osterno," she urged earnestly; "it is unsafe to delay even a few hours. M. de Chauxville said there would be no danger. I believed him then, but I do not now. Besides, I know the peasants. They are hard to rouse, but once excited they are uncontrollable. They are afraid of nothing. You must get away tonight."

Paul made no answer.

She turned slowly in her seat and looked into his face by the light of the waning moon.

"Do you mean that you will not go?"

He met her glance with his grave, slow smile.

"There is no question of going," he answered. "You must know that."

She did not attempt to persuade. Perhaps there was something in his voice which she as a Russian understood — a ring of that which we call pig-headedness in others.

"It must be splendid to be a man," she said suddenly, in a ringing voice. "One feeling in me made me ask you the favor, while another was a sense of gladness at your certain refusal. I wish I was a man. I envy you. You do not know how I envy you, Paul."

Paul gave a quiet laugh — such a laugh as one hears in the trenches after the low hum of a passing ball.

"If it is danger you want, you will have more than I in the next week," he answered. "Steinmetz and I knew that you were the only woman in Russia who could get your father safely out of the country. That is why I came for you."

The girl did not answer at once. They were driving on the road again now, and the sleigh was running smoothly.

"I suppose," she said reflectively at length, "that the secret of the enormous influence you exercise over all who come in contact with you is that you drag the best out of everyone — the best that is in them."

Paul did not answer.

"What is that light?" she asked suddenly, laying her hand on the thick fur of his sleeve. She was not nervous, but very watchful. "There — straight in front."

"It is the sleigh," replied Paul, "with your father and Steinmetz. I arranged that they should meet us at the cross-roads. You must be at the Volga before daylight. Send the horses on to Tver. I have given you Minna and The Warrior; they can do the journey with one hour's rest, but you must drive them."

Catrina had swayed forward against the bar of the apron in a strange way, for the road was quite smooth. She placed her gloved hands on the bar and held herself upright with a peculiar effort.

"What?" said Paul. For she had made an inarticulate sound.

"Nothing," she answered. Then, after a pause, "I did not know that we were to go so soon. That was all."

Chapter XLII

THE STORM BURSTS

*T*he large drawing room was brilliantly lighted. Another weary day had dragged to its close. It was the Tuesday evening – the last Tuesday in March five years ago. The starosta had not been near the castle all day. Steinmetz and Paul had never lost sight of the ladies since breakfast time. They had not ventured out of doors. There was in the atmosphere a sense of foreboding – the stillness of a crisis. Etta had been defiant and silent – a dangerous humor – all day. Maggie had watched Paul's face with steadfast, quiet eyes full of courage, but she knew now that there was danger.

The conversation at breakfast and luncheon had been maintained by Steinmetz – always collected and a little humorous. It was now dinner time. The whole castle was brilliantly lighted, as if for a great assembly of guests. During the last week a fuller state – a greater ceremony – had been observed by Paul's orders, and Steinmetz had thought more than once of that historical event which appealed to his admiration most – the Indian Mutiny.

Maggie was in the drawing room alone. She was leaning one hand and arm on the mantelpiece, looking thoughtfully into the fire. The rustle of silk made her turn her head. It was

Etta, beautifully dressed, with a white face and eyes dull with suspense.

"I think it is warmer tonight," said Maggie, urged by a sudden necessity of speech, hampered by a sudden chill at the heart.

"Yes," answered Etta. And she shivered.

For a moment there was a little silence and Etta looked at the clock. It was ten minutes to seven.

A high wind was blowing, the first of the equinoctial gales heralding the spring. The sound of the wind in the great chimney was like the moaning of high rigging at sea.

The door opened and Steinmetz came in. Etta's face hardened, her lips closed with a snap. Steinmetz looked at her and at Maggie. For once he seemed to have no pleasantry ready for use. He walked toward a table where some books and newspapers lay in pleasant profusion. He was standing there when Paul came into the room. The prince glanced at Maggie. He saw where his wife stood, but he did not look at her.

Steinmetz was writing something on half a sheet of notepaper, in pencil. He pushed it across the table toward Paul, who drew it nearer to him.

"Are you armed?" were the written words.

Paul crushed the paper in the hollow of his hand and threw it into the fire, where it burned away. He also glanced at the clock. It was five minutes to seven.

Suddenly the door was thrown open and a manservant rushed in — pale, confused, terror-stricken. He was a giant footman in the gorgeous livery of the Alexis.

"Excellency," he stammered in Russian, "the castle is surrounded — they will kill us — they will burn us out —"

He stopped abashed before Paul's pointing finger and stony face.

"Leave the room!" said Paul. "You forget yourself."

Through the open door-way to which Paul pointed peered the ashen faces of other servants huddled together like sheep.

"Leave the room!" repeated Paul, and the man obeyed him, walking to the door unsteadily with quivering chin. On the threshold he paused. Paul stood pointing to the door. He had a poise of the head — some sudden awakening of the blood that had coursed in the veins of hereditary potentates. Maggie looked at him; she had never known him like this. She had known the man, she had never encountered the prince.

The big clock over the castle boomed out the hour, and at the same instant there arose a roar like the voice of the surf on a Malabar shore. There was a crashing of glass almost in the room itself. Already Steinmetz was drawing the curtains closer over the windows in order to prevent the light from filtering through the interstices of the closed shutters.

"Only stones," he said to Paul, with his grim smile; "it might have been bullets."

As if in corroboration of his suggestion the sharp ring of more than one fire-arm rang out above the dull roar of many voices.

Steinmetz crossed the room to where Etta was standing, white-lipped, by the fire. Her clenched hand was gripping Maggie's wrist. She was half hidden behind her cousin. Maggie was looking at Paul. Etta was obviously conscious of Steinmetz's gaze and approach.

"I asked you before to tell me all you knew," he said. "You refused. Will you do it now?"

Etta met his glance for a moment, shrugged her shoulders, and turned her back on him. Paul was standing in the open door-way with his back turned toward them — alone. The palace had never looked so vast as it did at that moment — brilliantly lighted, gorgeous, empty.

Through the hail of blows on the stout doors, the rattle of stones at the windows, the prince could hear yells of execration and the wild laughter that is bred of destruction. He turned and entered the room. His face was gray and terrible.

"They have no chance," he said, "of effecting an entrance by force; the lower windows are barred. They have no ladders, Steinmetz and I have seen to that. We have been expecting this for some days."

He turned toward Steinmetz as if seeking confirmation. The din was increasing. When the German spoke he had to shout.

"We can beat them back if we like. We can shoot them down from the windows. But" — he paused, shrugged his shoulders, and laughed — "what will you! This prince will not shoot his father's serfs."

"We must leave you," went on Paul. "We must beware of treachery. Whatever happens, we shall not leave the house. If the worst comes, we make our last stand in this room. Whatever happens, stay here till we come."

He left the room, followed by Steinmetz. There were only three doors in the impregnable stone walls; the great entrance, a side door for use in times of deep snow, and the small concealed entrance by which the starosta was in the habit of reaching his masters.

For a moment the two men stood at the head of the stairs listening to the wild commotion. They were turning to descend the state stairs when a piercing shriek, immediately drowned by a yell of triumph, broke the silence of the interior of the castle. There was a momentary stillness, followed by another shriek.

"They are in!" said Steinmetz. "The side door."

And the two men looked at each other with wide eyes full of knowledge.

As they ran to the foot of the broad staircase the tramp of scuffling feet, the roar of angry voices, came through the passages from the back of curtained doorways. The servants' quarters seemed to be pandemonium. The sounds approached.

"Half-way up!" said Paul, and they ran half-way up the broad staircase side by side. There they stood and waited.

In a moment the baize doors were burst open, and a scuffling mass of men and women poured into the hall — a very sewer of humanity.

A yell of execration signalized their recognition of the prince.

"They are mad!" said Steinmetz, as the crowd surged forward toward the stairs with waving arms and the dull gleam of steel; with wild faces turned upward, wild mouths bellowing hatred and murder.

"It is a chance — it may stop them!" said Steinmetz.

His arm was outstretched steadily. A loud report, a little puff of smoke shooting upward to the gilded ceiling, and for one brief moment the crowd stood still, watching one of their ringleaders, who was turning and twisting on his side half a dozen steps from the bottom.

The man writhed in silence with his hand to his breast, and the crowd stood aghast. He held up his hand and gazed at it with a queer stupefaction. The blood dripped from his fingers. Then his chin went up as if some one was gripping the back of his neck. He turned over slowly and rolled to the bottom of the stairs.

Then Paul raised his voice.

"Listen to me!" he said.

But he got no farther, for some one shot at him from the background, over the frantic heads of the others, and missed him. The bullet lodged in the wall at the head of the stairs, in the jamb of the gorgeous door-way. It is there today.

There was a yell of hatred, and an ugly charge toward the stairs; but the sight of the two revolvers held them there — motionless for a few moments. Those in front pushed back, while the shouters in the safe background urged them forward by word and gesture.

Two men holding a hundred in check! But one of the two was a prince, which makes all the difference, and will continue to make that difference, despite halfpenny journalism, until the end of the world.

"What do you want?" cried Paul.

"Oh, I will wait!" he shouted, in the next pause. "There is plenty of time — when you are tired of shouting."

Several of them proceeded to tell him what they wanted. An old story, too stale for repetition here. Paul recognized in the din of many voices the tinkling arguments of the professional agitator all the world over — the cry of "Equality! Equality!" when men are obviously created unequal.

"Look out!" said Paul; "I believe they are going to make a rush."

All the while the foremost men were edging toward the stairs, while the densely packed throng at the back were struggling among themselves. In the passages behind, some were yelling and screaming with a wild intonation which Steinmetz recognized. He had been through the Commune.

"Those fellows at the back have been killing some one," he said; "I can tell by their voices. They are drunk with the sight of blood."

Some new orator gained the ears of the rabble at this

moment, and the ill-kempt heads swayed from side to side.

"It is useless," he cried, "telling him what you want. He will not give it you. Go and take it! Go and take it, little fathers; that is the only way!"

Steinmetz raised his hand and peered down into the crowd, looking for the man of eloquence, and the voice was hushed.

At this moment, however, the yelling increased, and through the door-way leading to the servants' quarters came a stream of men — bloodstained, ragged, torn. They were waving arms and implements above their heads.

"Down with the aristocrats! kill them — kill them!" they were shrieking.

A little volley of fire-arms further excited them. But vodka is not a good thing to shoot upon, and Paul stood untouched, waiting, as he had said, until they were tired of shouting.

"Now," yelled Steinmetz to him in English, "we must go. We can make a stand at the head of the stairs, then the door-way, then —" He shrugged his shoulders. "Then — the end," he added, as they moved up the stairs step by step, backward. "My very good friend," he went on, "at the door we must begin to shoot them down. It is our only chance. It is, moreover, our duty toward the ladies."

"There is one alternative," answered Paul.

"The Moscow Doctor?"

"Yes."

"They may turn," said Paul; "they are just in that humor."

The newcomers were the most dangerous. They were forcing their way to the front. There was no doubt that, as soon as they could penetrate the densely packed mob, they would charge up the stairs, even in face of a heavy fire. The reek of vodka was borne up in the heated atmosphere, mingled with the nauseating odor of filthy clothing.

"Go," said Steinmetz, "and put on your doctor's clothes. I can keep them back for a few minutes."

There was no time to be lost. Paul slipped away, leaving Steinmetz alone at the summit of the state stairway, standing grimly, revolver in hand.

In the drawing room Paul found Maggie, alone.

"Where is Etta?" he asked.

"She left the room some time ago."

"But I told her to stay," said Paul.

To this Maggie made no answer. She was looking at him with an anxious scrutiny.

"Did they shoot at you?" she asked.

"Yes; but not straight," he answered, with a little laugh, as he hurried on.

In a few moments he was back in the drawing room, a different man, in the rough, stained clothes of the Moscow Doctor. The din on the stairs was louder. Steinmetz was almost in the door-way. He was shooting economically, picking his men.

With an effort Paul dragged one or two heavy pieces of furniture across the room, in the form of a rough barricade. He pointed to the hearthrug where Maggie was to stand.

"Ready!" he shouted to Steinmetz. "Come!"

The German ran in, and Paul closed the barricade.

The rabble poured in at the open door, screaming and shouting. Bloodstained, ragged, wild with the madness of murder, they crowded to the barricade. There they stopped, gazing stupidly at Paul.

"The Moscow Doctor — the Moscow Doctor!" passed from lip to lip. It was the women who shouted it the loudest. Like the wind through a forest it swept out of the room and down the stairs. Those crowding up pushed on and uttered the words as they came. The room was packed with them.

"Yes!" shouted Steinmetz, at the top of his great voice, "and the prince!"

He knew the note to strike, and struck with a sure hand. The barricade was torn aside, and the people swept forward, falling on their knees, groveling at Paul's feet, kissing the hem of his garment, seizing his strong hands in theirs.

It was a mighty harvest. That which is sown in the people's hearts bears a thousandfold at last.

"Get them out of the place — open the big doors," said Paul to Steinmetz. He stood cold and grave among them.

Some of them were already sneaking toward the door — the ringleaders, the talkers from the towns — mindful of their own necks in this change of feeling.

Steinmetz hustled them out, bidding them take their dead with them. Some of the servants reappeared, peeping, white-faced, behind curtains. When the last villager had crossed the threshold, these ran forward to close and bar the great doors.

"No," said Paul, from the head of the stairs, "leave them open."

So the great doors stood defiantly open. The lights of the state staircase flared out over the village as the peasants crept crest-fallen to their cottages. They glanced up shamefacedly, but they had no word to say.

Steinmetz, in the drawing room, looked at Paul with his resigned semi-humorous shrug of the shoulders.

"Touch-and-go, mein lieber!" he said.

"Yes; an end of Russia for us," answered the prince.

He moved toward the door leading through to the old castle.

"I am going to look for Etta," he said.

"And I," said Steinmetz, going to the other entrance, "am going to see who opened the side door."

Chapter XLIII

BEHIND THE VEIL

"Will you come with me?" said Paul to Maggie. "I will send the servants to put this room to rights."

Maggie followed him out of the room, and together they went through the passages, calling Etta and looking for her. There was an air of gloom and chilliness in the rooms of the old castle. The outline of the great stones, dimly discernible through the wall-paper, was singularly suggestive of a fortress thinly disguised.

"I suppose," said Paul, "that Etta lost her nerve."

"Yes," answered Maggie doubtfully; "I think it was that."

Paul went on. He carried a lamp in one steady hand.

"We shall probably find her in one of these rooms," he said. "It is so easy to lose one's self among the passages and staircases."

They passed on through the great smoking-room, with its hunting trophies. The lynx, with its face of Claude de Chauxville, grinned at them darkly from its pedestal.

Half-way down the stairs leading to the side door they met Steinmetz coming hastily up. His face was white and drawn with horror.

"You must not go down here," he said, in a husky voice, barring the passage with his arm.

"Why not?"

"Go up again!" said Steinmetz breathlessly. "You must not go down here."

Paul laid his hand on the broad arm stretched across the stairway. For a moment it almost appeared to be a physical struggle, then Steinmetz stepped aside.

"I beg of you," he said, "not to go down."

And Paul went on, followed by Steinmetz, and behind them, Maggie. At the foot of the stairs a broader passage led to the side door, and from this other passages opened into the servants' quarters, and communicated through the kitchens with the modern building.

It was evident that the door leading to the grassy slope at the back of the castle was open, for a cold wind blew up the stairs and made the lamps flicker.

At the end of the passage Paul stopped.

Steinmetz was a little behind him, holding Maggie back.

The two lamps lighted up the passage and showed the white form of the Princess Etta lying huddled up against the wall. The face was hidden, but there was no mistaking the beautiful dress and hair. It could only be Etta. Paul stooped down and looked at her, but he did not touch her. He went a few paces forward and closed the door. Beyond Etta a black form lay across the passage, all trodden underfoot and disheveled. Paul held the lamp down, and through the mud and blood Claude de Chauxville's clear-cut features were outlined.

Death is always unmistakable, though it be shown by nothing more than a heap of muddy clothes.

Claude de Chauxville was lying across the passage. He had been trodden underfoot by the stream of maddened peasants who had entered by this door which had been opened for them, whom Steinmetz had checked at the foot of the stairs by shooting their ringleader.

De Chauxville's scalp was torn away by a blow, probably given with a spade or some blunt instrument. His hand, all muddy and bloodstained, still held a revolver.

The other hand was stretched out toward Etta, who lay across his feet, crouching against the wall. Death had found and left her in an attitude of fear, shielding her bowed head from a blow with her upraised hands. Her loosened hair fell in a long wave of gold down to the bloodstained hand outstretched toward her. She was kneeling in De Chauxville's blood, which stained the stone floor of the passage.

Paul leaned forward and laid his fingers on the bare arm, just below a bracelet which gleamed in the lamplight. She was quite dead. He held a lamp close to her. There was no mark or scratch upon her arm or shoulder. The blow which had torn her hair down had killed her without any disfigurement. The silken skirt of her dress, which lay across the passage, was trampled and stained by the tread of a hundred feet.

Then Paul went to Claude de Chauxville. He stooped down and slipped his skilled fingers inside the torn and mud-stained clothing. Here also was death.

Paul stood upright and looked at them as they lay, silent, motionless, with their tale untold. Maggie and Steinmetz stood watching him. He went to the door, which was of solid oak four inches thick, and examined the fastenings. There had been no damage done to bolt, or lock, or hinge. The door had been opened from the inside. He looked slowly round, measuring the distances.

"What is the meaning of it?" he said at length to Steinmetz, in a dull voice. Maggie winced at the sound of it.

Steinmetz did not answer at once, but hesitated — after the manner of a man weighing words which will never be forgotten by their hearers.

"It seems to me," he said, with a slow, wise charity, the best of its kind, "quite clear that De Chauxville died in trying to save her — the rest must be only guesswork."

Maggie had come forward and was standing beside him.

"And in guessing let us be charitable — is it not so?" he said, turning to her, with a twist of his humorous lips.

"I suppose," he went on, after a little pause, "that Claude de Chauxville has been at the bottom of all our trouble. All his life he has been one of the stormy petrels of diplomacy. Wherever he has gone trouble has followed later. By some means he obtained sufficient mastery over the princess to compel her to obey his orders. The means he employed were threats. He had it in his power to make mischief, and in such affairs a woman is so helpless that we may well forgive that which she may do in a moment of panic. I imagine that he frightened the poor lady into obedience to his command that she should open this door. Before dinner, when we were all in the drawing room, I noted a little mark of dust on the white silk skirt of her dress. At the time I thought only that her maid had been careless. Perhaps you noticed it, mademoiselle? Ladies note such things."

He turned to Maggie, who nodded her head.

"That," he went on, "was the dust of these old passages. She had been down here. She had opened this door."

He spread out his hands in deprecation. In his quaint Germanic way he held one hand out over the two motionless forms in mute prayer that they might be forgiven.

"We all have our faults," he said. "Who are we to judge each other? If we understood all, we might pardon. The two strongest human motives are ambition and fear. She was ruled by both. I myself have seen her under the influence of sudden panic. I have noted the working of her great ambition. She was probably deceived at every turn by that man, who was a scoundrel. He is dead, and death is understood to wipe out all debts. If I were a better man than I am, I might speak well of him. But — ach Gott! that man was a scoundrel! I think the good God will judge between them and forgive that poor woman. She must have repented of her action when she heard the clatter of the rioters all round the castle. I am sure she did that. I am sure she came down here to shut the door, and found Claude de Chauxville here. They were probably talking together when the poor mad fools who killed them came round to this side of the castle and found them. They recognized her as the princess. They probably mistook him for the prince. It is what men call a series of coincidences. I wonder what God calls it?"

He broke off, and, stooping down, he drew the lapel of the Frenchman's cloak gently over the marred face.

"And let us remember," he said, "that he tried to save her. Some lives are so. At the very end a little reparation is made. In life he was her evil genius. When he died they trampled him underfoot in order to reach her. Mademoiselle, will you come?"

He took Maggie by the arm and led her gently away. She was shaking all over, but his hand was steady and wholly kind.

He led her up the narrow stairs to her own room. In the little boudoir the fire was burning brightly; the lamps were lighted, just as the maid had left them at the first alarm.

Maggie sat down, and quite suddenly she burst into tears.

Steinmetz did not leave her. He stood beside her, gently stroking her shoulder with his stout fingers. He said nothing, but the gray mustache only half concealed his lips, which were twisted with a little smile full of tenderness and sympathy.

Maggie was the first to speak.

"I am all right now," she said. "Please do not wait any longer, and do not think me a very weak-minded person. Poor Etta!"

Steinmetz moved away toward the door.

"Yes," he said; "poor Etta! It is often those who get on in the world who need the world's pity most."

At the door he stopped.

"Tomorrow," he said, "I will take you home to England. Is that agreeable to you, mademoiselle?"

She smiled at him sadly through her tears.

"Yes, I should like that," she said. "This country is horrible. You are very kind to me."

Steinmetz went down stairs and found Paul at the door talking to a young officer, who slowly dismounted and lounged into the hall, conscious of his brilliant uniform —

of his own physical capacity to show off any uniform to full advantage.

He was a lieutenant in a Cossack regiment, and as he bowed to Steinmetz, whom Paul introduced, he swung off his high astrakhan cap with a flourish, showing a fair boyish face.

"Yes," he continued to Paul in English; "the general sent me over with a sotnia of men, and pretty hungry you will find them. We have covered the whole distance since daybreak. A report reached the old gentleman that the whole countryside was about to rise against you."

"Who spread the report?" asked Steinmetz.

"I believe it originated down at the wharfs. It has been traced to an old man and his daughter, — a sort of peddler, I think, who took a passage down the river, — but where they heard the rumor I don't know."

Paul and Steinmetz carefully avoided looking at each other. They knew that Catrina and Stépan Lanovitch had sent back assistance.

"Of course," said Paul, "I am very glad to see you, but I am equally glad to inform you that you are not wanted. Steinmetz will tell you all about it, and when you are ready for dinner it will be ready for you. I will give instructions that the men be cared for."

"Thanks. The funny thing is that I am instructed, with your approval, to put the place under martial law and take charge."

"That will not be necessary, thanks," answered Paul, going out of the open door to speak to the wild-looking Cossacks sent for his protection.

In Russia, as in other countries where life is cheaply held, the death formalities are small. It is only in England, where we are so careful for the individual and so careless of the type, that we have to pay for dying, and leave a mass of red-tape formalities for our friends.

While the young officer was changing his uniform for the evening finery which his servant's forethought had provided, Paul and Steinmetz hurriedly arranged what story of the evening should be given to the world. Knowing the country as they did, they were enabled to tell a true tale, which was yet devoid of that small personal interest that gossips love.

And all the world ever knew was that the Princess Howard Alexis was killed by the revolted peasants while attempting to escape by a side door, and that the Baron Claude de Chauxville, who was staying in the neighborhood, met his death in attempting to save her from the fury of the mob.

On the recommendation of Karl Steinmetz, Paul placed the castle and village under martial law, and there and then gave the command to the young Cossack officer, pending further instructions from his general, commanding at Tver.

The officer dined with Steinmetz, and under the careful treatment of that diplomatist inaugurated a reign of military autocracy, which varied pleasingly between strict discipline and boyish neglect.

Before the master of the situation had slept off the effect of his hundred-mile ride and a heavy dinner, the next morning Steinmetz and Maggie were ready to start on their journey to England.

The breakfast was served in the room abutting on the cliff in the dim light of a misty morning.

The lamps were alight on the table, and Paul was waiting when Maggie came down cloaked for her journey. Steinmetz had breakfasted.

They said good-morning, and managed to talk of ordinary things until Maggie was supplied with coffee and toast and a somewhat heavy, manly helping of a breakfast-dish. Then came a silence.

Paul broke it at length with an effort, standing, as it were, on the edge of the forbidden topic.

"Steinmetz will take you all the way," he said, "and then come back to me. You can safely trust yourself to his care."

"Yes," answered the girl, looking at the food set before her with a helpless stare. "It is not that. Can I safely trust Etta's memory to your judgment? You are very stern, Paul. I think you might easily misjudge her. Men do not always understand a woman's temptations."

Paul had not sat down. He walked away to the window, and stood there looking out into the gloomy mists.

"It is not because she was my cousin," said Maggie from the table; "it is because she was a woman leaving her memory to be judged by two men who are both — hard."

Paul neither looked round nor answered.

"When a woman has to form her own life, and renders it a prominent one, she usually makes a huge mistake of it," said the girl.

She waited a moment, and then she pleaded once more, hastily, for she heard a step approaching.

"If you only understood everything you might think differently — it is because you cannot understand."

Then Paul turned round slowly.

"No," he said, "I cannot understand it, and I do not think that I ever shall."

And Steinmetz came into the room.

In a few minutes the sleigh bearing Steinmetz and Maggie disappeared into the gloom, closely followed by a couple of Cossacks acting as guard and carrying dispatches.

So Etta Sydney Bamborough — the Princess Howard Alexis — came back after all to her husband, lying in a nameless grave in the churchyard by the Volga at Tver. Within the white walls — beneath the shadow of the great spangled cupola — they await the Verdict, almost side by side.

Chapter XLIV
KISMET

Between Brandon in Suffolk and Thetford in Norfolk runs a quiet river, the Little Ouse, where few boats break the stillness of the water. On either bank stand whispering beech trees, and so low is the music of the leaves that the message of Ely's distant bells floats through them on a quiet evening as far as Brandon and beyond it.

Three years after Etta's death, in the glow of an April sunset, a Canadian canoe was making its stealthy way up the river. The paddle crept in and out so gently, so lazily and peacefully, that the dabchicks and other waterfowl did not cease their chatter of nests and other April matters as the canoe glided by.

So quiet, indeed, was its progress that Karl Steinmetz — suddenly white-headed, as strong old men are apt to find themselves — did not heed its approach. He was sitting on the bank with a gun, a little rifle, lying on the grass beside him. He was half-asleep in the enjoyment of a large Havana cigar. The rays of the setting sun, peeping through the lower branches, made him blink lazily like a large, good-natured cat.

He turned his head slowly, with a hunter's consciousness of the approach of some one, and contemplated the canoe with a sense of placid satisfaction.

The small craft was passing in the shadow of a great tree — stealing over the dark, unruffled depth. A girl dressed in white, with a large diaphanous white hat and a general air of brisk English daintiness, was paddling slowly and with no great skill.

"A picture," said Steinmetz to himself with Teutonic deliberation. "Gott im Himmel! what a pretty picture to make an old man young!"

Then his gray eyes opened suddenly and he rose to his feet.

"Coloss-a-al!" he muttered. He dragged from his head a lamentable old straw hat and swept a courteous bow.

"Mademoiselle," he said, "ah, what happiness! After three years!"

Maggie stopped and looked at him with troubled eyes; all the color slowly left her face.

"What are you doing here?" she asked. And there was something like fear in her voice.

"No harm, mademoiselle, but good. I have come down from big game to vermin. I have here a saloon rifle. I wait till a water-rat comes, and then I shoot him."

The canoe had drifted closer to the land, the paddle trailing in the water.

"You are looking at my white hairs," he went on, in a sudden need of conversation. "Please bring your boat a little nearer."

The paddle twisted lazily in the water like a fish's tail.

"Hold tight," he said, reaching down.

With a little laugh he lifted the canoe and its occupant far up on to the bank.

"Despite my white hairs," he said, with a tap of both hands on his broad chest.

"I attach no importance to them," she answered, taking his proffered hand and stepping over the light bulwark. "I have gray ones myself. I am getting old too."

"How old?" he asked, looking down at her with his old bluntness.

"Twenty-eight."

"Ah, they are summers," he said; "mine have turned to winters. Will you sit here where I was sitting? See, I will spread this rug for your white dress."

Maggie paused, looking through the trees toward the sinking sun. The light fell on her face and showed one or two lines which had not been there before. It showed a patient tenderness in the steady eyes which had always been there — which Catrina had noticed in the stormy days that were past.

"I cannot stay long," she replied. "I am with the Faneaux at Brandon for a few days. They dine at seven."

"Ah! her ladyship is a good friend of mine. You remember her charity ball in town, when it was settled that you should come to Osterno. A strange world, mademoiselle — a very strange world, so small, and yet so large and bare for some of us!"

Maggie looked at him. Then she sat down.

"Tell me," she said, "all that has happened since then."

"I went back," answered Steinmetz, "and we were duly exiled from Russia. It was sure to come. We were too dangerous. Altogether too quixotic for an autocracy. For myself I did not mind, but it hurt Paul."

There was a little pause, while the water lapped and whispered at their feet.

"I heard," said Maggie at length, in a measured voice, "that he had gone abroad for big game."

"Yes — to India."

"He did not go to America?" enquired Maggie indifferently. She was idly throwing fragments of wood into the river.

"No," answered Steinmetz, looking straight in front of him. "No, he did not go to America."

"And you?"

"I — oh, I stayed at home. I have taken a house. It is behind the trees. You cannot see it. I live at peace with all men and pay my bills every week. Sometimes Paul comes and stays with me. Sometimes I go and stay with him in London or in Scotland. I smoke and shoot water-rats, and watch the younger generation making the same mistakes that we made in our time. You have heard that my country is in order again? They have remembered me. For my sins they have made me a count. Bon Dieu! I do not mind. They may make me a prince, if it pleases them."

He was watching her face beneath his grim old eyebrows.

"These details bore you," he said.

"No."

"When Paul and I are together we talk of a new heaven and a new Russia. But it will not come in our time. We are only the sowers, and the harvest is not yet. But I tell Paul that he has not sown wild oats, nor sour grapes, nor thistles."

He paused, and the expression of his face changed to one of semi-humorous gravity.

"Mademoiselle," he went on, "it has been my lot to love the prince like a son. It has been my lot to stand helplessly by while he passed through many troubles. Perhaps the good God gave him all his troubles at first. Do you think so?"

Maggie was looking straight in front of her across the quiet river.

"Perhaps so," she said.

Steinmetz also stared in front of him during a little silence. The common thoughts of two minds may well be drawn together by the contemplation of a common object. Then he turned toward her.

"It will be a happiness for him to see you," he said quietly.

Maggie ceased breaking small branches and throwing them into the river. She ceased all movement, and scarcely seemed to breathe.

"What do you mean?" she asked.

"He is staying with me here."

Maggie glanced toward the canoe. She drew a short, sharp breath, but she did not move.

"Mademoiselle," said Steinmetz earnestly, "I am an old man, and in my time I have dabbled pretty deeply in trouble. But taking it all around, even my life has had its compensations. And I have seen lives which, taken as a mere mortal existence, without looking to the hereafter at all, have been quite worth the living. There is much happiness in life to make up for the rest. But that happiness must be firmly held. It is so easily slipped through the fingers. A little irresolution — a little want of moral courage — a little want of self-confidence — a little pride, and it is lost. You follow me?"

Maggie nodded. There was a great tenderness in her eyes — such a tenderness as, resting on men, may bring them nearer to the angels.

Steinmetz laid his large hand over hers.

"Mademoiselle," he went on, "I believe that the good God sent you along this lonely river in your boat. Paul leaves me tomorrow. His arrangements are to go to India and shoot tigers. He will sail in a week. There are things of which we never speak together — there is one name that is never mentioned. Since Osterno you have avoided meeting him. God knows I am not asking for him anything that he would be afraid to ask for himself. But he also has his pride. He will not force himself in where he thinks his presence unwelcome."

Steinmetz rose somewhat ponderously and stood looking down at her. He did not, however, succeed in meeting her eyes.

"Mademoiselle," he said, "I beg of you most humbly — most respectfully — to come through the garden with me toward the house, so that Paul may at least know that you are here."

He moved away and stood for a moment with his back turned to her, looking toward the house. The crisp rustle of her dress came to him as she rose to her feet.

Without looking round, he walked slowly on. The path

through the trees was narrow, two could not walk abreast. After a few yards Steinmetz emerged on to a large, sloping lawn with flower beds, and a long, low house above it. On the covered terrace a man sat writing at a table. He was surrounded by papers, and the pen in his large, firm hand moved rapidly over the sheet before him.

"We still administer the estate," said Steinmetz, in a low voice. "From our exile we still sow our seed."

They approached over the mossy turf, and presently Paul looked up — a strong face, stern and self-contained; the face of a man who would always have a purpose in life, who would never be petty in thought or deed.

For a moment he did not seem to recognize them. Then he rose, and the pen fell on the flags of the terrace.

"It is mademoiselle!" said Steinmetz, and no other word was spoken.

Maggie walked on in a sort of unconsciousness. She only knew that they were all acting an inevitable part, written for them in the great libretto of life. She never noticed that Steinmetz had left her side, that she was walking across the lawn alone.

Paul came to meet her, and took her hand in silence. There was so much to say that words seemed suddenly valueless; there was so little to say that they were unnecessary.

For that which these two had to tell each other cannot be told in minutes, nor yet in years; it cannot even be told in a lifetime, for it is endless, and it runs through eternity.

THE END

www.ingramcontent.com/pod-product-compliance
Lightning Source LLC
Chambersburg PA
CBHW060425030726
47495CB00003B/744